Day's Dying Glory

CROWVUS

First Published in 2017
Crowvus, 53 Argyle Square, Wick, KW1 5AJ

ISBN 978-0-9957860-0-4

For comments and questions about "Day's Dying Glory"
contact the author directly at daysdyingglory@gmail.com

www.crowvus.com

for Daddy,

CHRISTMAS 2014

I hope that you read
and enjoy
this!

With lots and lots of love,
x X x

CHAPTER ONE
Thursday 20ᵗʰ March 1806

Petrovia Lodge was all that could be expected of a country house for a family of a not inconsiderable income. It had a single tower that stretched three storeys high where the rest of the heavy stone stood at only two floors. It had a large canopied porch and a modernised orangery on the south facing wall. Ludicrous though its existence was, as the tall hills stopped much of the summer sun, Mrs Tenterchilt had begged her husband to build one for the development to her three daughters' gardening and painting skills as, however useless it was as an orangery, the view was exquisite. It was the only house to be seen in the valley, although the nearest neighbours were in fact only at a distance of two miles if one skirted around the hill to its furthest side. A healthy stream ran with alarming speed through the valley's centre and there were stunted and overhanging trees that followed it as it rushed through. At times, the hills themselves would become alive with the sounds of the river as it charged off into realms unknown.

Major Tenterchilt had come by ownership of Petrovia Lodge in the strangest of manners. He had encountered a man at a gambling table in London who, when relieved of his handheld money, raised the stakes by throwing in the deeds to his lodge in Scotland. For what else has a retired man of money to do with his income but gamble? Major Tenterchilt, who was by all accounts a larger than life character, promised his own estate outside London in return, a foolish gesture perhaps but he knew he possessed the best hand the game could offer. Being a man of honour, Mr Kildare was forced to sign over the deeds and for some years the lodge remained uninhabited and unvisited. Major Tenterchilt's luck, however, was drawing to an end and, when next he placed his estate as ante, he was forced to acknowledge defeat to a Mr Bryn-Portland. There were whispers around the table that a clever cheat and a quick hand had played on such a momentous loss of judgement on Major Tenterchilt's side. Yet, as only gentlemen were present, it was concluded that the correct course of conduct had been followed and Major Tenterchilt had to return to his wife and tell her to pack her belongings and ready the children for their departure to Scotland.

If Mrs Tenterchilt was at all unhappy with her new surroundings, she never allowed it to show. Indeed, she did all she could to prepare and settle her three daughters and encourage them to understand that, whilst Papa had lost the four hundred acre estate in a game of cards, he had also gained a remote corner of the Scottish countryside in just the same way. Her only moral from this, which she instilled with great vigour, was that gambling was intrinsically wrong and she would not permit Major Tenterchilt to waste any further time, money, nor estate in such frivolous madness. Robbed of his recreational hobby, Major Tenterchilt began carving and building things from the trees by the stream which he would fell, leaving them to grow back quicker and bushier than before.

In truth, building the orangery was the least he could do for a wife who had stood by him through his mindless gambling. On his considerable military pension he arranged for his three daughters to be privately tutored by a various array of governesses and teachers. None seemed to last and it was no secret to any of the persons living in the lodge that this was the fault of the eldest daughter, Arabella.

Arabella was the impressionable age of twelve when her father's misplaced bet sent them north of the border, but in those twelve years she had been far from idle, learning secrets of beauty that would both ensnare any man and cause envy amongst any of her own sex. To her, Scotland was stifling, with few boys of an age to make suitors, and those she did see were fleeting visitors or seasonal travellers who used the river to water their animals. Mrs Tenterchilt would not allow the word gypsy to be used and always welcomed them into the kitchen, ensuring beforehand that someone was present to be certain nothing was stolen and everything was cleaned after they had touched it. Arabella adored and revelled in such a task and, whenever the young men would come requesting water from the kitchen pump, they always left smiling and with an image of Arabella's lips planted firmly on their cheek. Shameless though she seemed, her heart was good and, filled with romantic ideas, she sought only to share that good heart.

Ten years of life at Petrovia Lodge had driven Arabella to distraction. She had grown up in the certainty of holding the elevated claim of London society, albeit on the periphery. Now she was lucky to see more than a handful of people and her mother would never permit a match with those she did see. The only other soul Arabella encountered was Hamish, beautifully named to the surrounding landscape.

Hamish, or Mish as the girls came to know him, was caught by Major Tenterchilt poaching on Lodge land. He had been the son of a local family, but both his parents had died and he had been forced from his home under the regime of clearance that seemed so rampant throughout the Highlands and which gave the haunting and enchanting emptiness to the glen in which the lodge was situated. If Mish was repentant for his crime, he never showed any sign of it, even as Major Tenterchilt caught and beat him for it. Hamish was to be charged with the offence the moment Major Tenterchilt could find an official, but somehow, as fate so often does, the course of this doomed boy turned. Whilst he sat on the kitchen floor, tied by one of Major Tenterchilt's famous knots on the evening of his capture, Arabella emerged from the neighbouring hall. Her bare feet were like gentle strokes upon the earth as she entered and it was all the young Scotsman could do to sit and watch her. As a young lady, now sixteen, Arabella seemed perfect to him.

She had entered with no notion of the boy even being there, for Major Tenterchilt spoke only rarely to her and never of such things that he considered business. She was carrying a small candle that was burned almost to extinction and she hummed a little tune as if she believed it would help keep her warm, for she shivered uncontrollably. The late hour of her venture was the reason she had come herself, for they did employ two maids in the running of the house, Anne and Penny, but Arabella did not wish to wake them.

'There are words.'

Arabella spun to face the intruder in her house and to her thoughts. The fragile candle flew from her slender grasp and dropped to the stone floor in a shower of molten wax. She did not scream for, as the eldest in a family all of the fairer sex, she had learnt the position of bravery. Instead, upon recognising that the young man before her was securely tethered and that her finest linen nightshirt was hemmed with foul smelling wax, she simply sobbed with disappointment and annoyance.

'Don't weep,' Hamish pleaded, trying to pull at the rope that had him tethered like an animal.

'Why are you in our kitchen?' Arabella implored. 'You cannot be the first course in tomorrow's meal.'

'Why not?' he asked, spellbound by this image in white, which seemed to him purer than the moonlight that caught it.

Arabella ceased her crying and knelt down before Hamish. 'There is not nearly enough meat on you.' Her critical gaze took in all his looks, from the long straggled hair on his head, which was so fair it seemed white, to his tattered, hole-ridden boots. His whole body seemed as weary and unkempt as the extremes and the only feature to endear the native to her was his open smile. She placed her hand on his boots and looked straight into his eyes.

'What were you telling me?'

'There are words,' Hamish paused, feeling at once that the touch of her hand made him giddy and dried his throat. 'To the song that you were humming.'

'I heard it when Papa took us to a concert in Edinburgh.'

Hamish stared hard at her, his eyes sharp in their watery nature. For a time he simply beheld her, feeling confused between intoxicated fascination and nauseous distaste at her embodiment of all he deplored in the world. For the first time in her sixteen years, Arabella felt uncomfortable under the gaze of a man. He was openly staring at her in a manner so judgemental that she removed her hand and recoiled from him. She was preparing to rise to her feet and walk away when the curious boy began singing:

> *English bribes were all in vain*
> *And ever purer we may be*
> *Silver cannot buy the heart*
> *That only beats for thine and thee*

'I trust you do not mean that,' Arabella whispered, more concerned than affronted. 'Is that why Papa has you tied up here? He has killed men for less, and with just cause.'

'You are his daughter?'

'Yes. And you his prisoner.'

'Yes, indeed, but for nothing so noble as the king's cause. He caught me hunting on his land. Your land.'

'Poaching,' she corrected him. 'My father has a right and duty to uphold the law on our land.'

'Have I less right to eat?'

Despite his clear lack of manners and education, there was a quality to this prisoner that made him intriguing and Arabella, in her honest simplicity, felt unsure that her father had done the right thing. She shifted to sit beside him against the wall and tilted her head to one side so that her brown hair draped down.

'What is your name?'

'Hamish.' He did not turn to face her as she regarded him once again, feeling the calculating weight of her eyes enough of a burden.

'Well, I shall do what I can to dissuade my father from prosecuting you, though in return I am certain he will expect something.'

'That is how the English work.'

'It is how life works, and you would do well to remember that there are rules to it.'

'What is your name, mistress?'

'Arabella Tenterchilt. And now I must leave you, for I came down only for some water and discovered far more than I would have thought to.'

'Then let this be farewell, Arabella Tenterchilt. I am in no doubt that I shall be removed before you arise from sleep to speak words of defence on my sorry behalf.'

Whatever tone in which Hamish had delivered this brief, though regretfully grateful, speech seemed to connect to the guilt and pity of Arabella's young heart for, when the next person entered the kitchen an hour before the dawn, it was to find Arabella asleep with her head on Hamish's shoulder and his on the girl's head. Poor Anne, who found them, rushed immediately to Arabella's side and shook her awake.

'Miss? If your father should find you like this his anger will be against you as much as the boy.'

And so, whilst Anne hid the event and spared the daughter from scandal, Arabella and her mother persuaded Major Tenterchilt that Hamish could be their labourer and Mrs Tenterchilt decided on their need of an orangery. Hamish never spoke of that evening, nor did Arabella, although from that incident onwards Anne took it upon herself to protect the young mistress' interests, seeing her heart was perhaps too open and embracing.

And so Hamish became a brother to the three daughters and, despite their initial encounter, even Major Tenterchilt grew affectionate towards him. As six years passed, Hamish became stronger and his assistance throughout their little estate created boats, carts, and the tiny garden house that they loved almost as much as they had come to love the Lodge. Whatever closeness had been shared between Arabella and Hamish seemed to have passed and been forgotten.

Imogen was particularly fond of her new brother. Despite her social positioning and birth, all she truly wanted was to teach children; to have little charges who, in her mind, would hang on her every word. In truth, as Arabella believed in romance, Imogen believed in anything. She wished to absorb all the knowledge she could inherit and was frequently disappointed as tutor after tutor was removed, in some cases forcibly when Major Tenterchilt found Arabella smiling adoringly across at them. Imogen simply wanted to learn and to pass that learning on to someone else. In this respect she was the noblest of the three sisters. Hamish was invaluable to her, speaking of such gallantry and chivalry that had been performed by his ancestors, and recalling the Highland lifestyle as it had been in his grandfather's day before the butchery and slaughter of Cumberland as he wantonly devastated the Highland culture and people.

Of course, Major Tenterchilt would never tolerate such rebellious conversing, so Imogen and Hamish would meet in secret in the new orangery, watching the stars and discussing the history of the land they sat upon. Imogen was forming a fragile connection to the land she was in, her idealised thinking giving rise to the idea that she might be able to teach people in the knowledge of their hardships and suffering. In return, Hamish was allowed to unburden his heavy thoughts regarding his own history and justify his being in such an English household in the firm knowledge that he was educating them regarding the truth of the country they had invaded.

The third and final sister could scarcely be explained or described as the least. Catherine, although to her mother's despair she always introduced herself as Cat, caused poor Mrs Tenterchilt to shake with disappointment. The same year that Hamish arrived at Petrovia Lodge, the mother had declared that her daughter was no longer her concern and handed over her upbringing to Major Tenterchilt. This suited Catherine beautifully for, whilst Arabella dreamt of being a courtly lady and Imogen of sharing her knowledge, all Catherine wished to do was join the army. So for six years, from the age of twelve, Catherine believed she could truly follow in her father's footsteps and fight. She trained in fencing whenever a willing adversary would consent and for this she began to grow fond of Hamish, for he was often the only opponent capable of matching her in strength and manner. On occasions Mrs Tenterchilt would watch them from her glass panelled orangery and all colour would drain from her face.

'Penny,' she would call, and her maid would be at her side in an instant. 'See what creature I have created, neither man in body nor woman in heart. Whatever is to become of my poor, confused Catherine?'

'She will find her feet in society, ma'am, and one day she will be a gentleman's wife. You see if it is not so.'

Penny was as loyal to Mrs Tenterchilt as a servant could be. She would comfort, coax and ease her whenever possible and was always on hand to assist her in any way that was asked of her. She and Anne were half-sisters and it was no secret that Anne had held her position in the family's keeping only as a result of the loyal efforts on Penny's part, yet these two ladies were as much a part of the family as any other person in the Lodge.

It was a dull, overcast day, unnaturally still with no hope of the wind dispersing the cloud. March made a dismal month so far into the mountains and, being truly English in their outlook, this was the precise topic of conversation that was shared at the supper table that evening.

'I do not believe I have seen the sun in nearly forty days, Mama,' Arabella grumbled. 'How I miss London in this merry month of March.'

'I do not believe you have kept count,' Catherine muttered under her breath, laughing in a raucous manner after the words had been spoken.

'Catherine,' Imogen hissed, more dismayed by her manly guffaw than the snide remark concerning their eldest sister.

'Some of us were not born to soil our hands with sweat and manual work,' Arabella retorted.

'Arabella,' Imogen gasped. 'You should not use words like sweat, it is so undignified, and most certainly never at the table.'

Catherine rose to her feet. Now at the age of eighteen, she towered over her older sisters and it was a certainty none could deny that, woman or not, she truly would be enough to intimidate any army. Gracing only her father with any acknowledgement, Catherine turned to the door and was approaching it when Major Tenterchilt spoke.

'My dear, my dears, I think we will host a dinner party.'

'A dinner party?' Arabella gasped with excitement beyond any she had known in the ten years they had been in Scotland.

'Indeed, if your mother is willing.'

'Willing?' Mrs Tenterchilt whispered, almost choking on the word. 'My dear Major Tenterchilt, may I not remind you that we have but two maids and Mish. There is no hope that we can entertain as once we did in London.'

'But my dear, how are our daughters to marry? They never see a man.'

'I do not understand why we should marry, Papa,' Catherine responded.

'No, no, my dears, I am quite decided. In fact the invitations are already spreading across the country as we sit here speaking.'

'Oh Papa,' Arabella rushed to her father and embraced him earnestly.

Imogen, in her own reserved way, shared Arabella's ecstasy. She quietly thanked her father and mother and dropped the slightest of curtseys to Hamish, before leaving the room. Arabella followed close behind, dancing her way out of the room and seizing Catherine to be her partner. With a smile, Hamish watched the three girls leave.

'I will do what I can, Mrs Tenterchilt. I shall have the Lodge as modestly tasteful as any garish London home.'

'It will be shameful, Mish, but I thank you for your concern.'

Hamish bowed his head and left the dining room. Six years of living with the Tenterchilts had not prepared him for this sudden attack of priggish snobbery that appeared to have gripped Mrs Tenterchilt. And yet he could not hide the smile that crossed his features at their comedic nature concerning other people. Being allowed to share their table was a comparatively new experience, not dating more than two years, for Catherine had pleaded on his behalf that, if she, as a daughter half disowned, should dine there, then Hamish as a son, in part adopted, had the same right.

'If I were to go in to the army someday, Mish, I should enter as a captain,' she had informed him with all seriousness. 'And I should have you as my lieutenant.'

'I will not join the army, Cat,' he had replied whilst he continued to sharpen the sword her father had bestowed upon her. 'And nor will you. You're a woman. You cannot kill people.'

'What is it about your brutish sex that makes you believe that women are so innocent? One day, I shall join the army. I know I shall. Poor Papa has no son to follow him into the life and I mean to ensure that his legacy will continue.'

'The way to do that is not by running away to join the army. It is by marrying and having a family and children to whom you can tell the great adventures of their grandfather. His legacy will last far longer that way.'

Catherine had not answered him but purposefully walked away, leaving Hamish sharpening the sword.

Hamish walked through the orangery and out into the dull day. What change this place had endured. That his people, his family, had been driven away to make way for the intrusive building of the Lodge, which seemed as misplaced as the Tenterchilts. Now, with the prospect of bringing a company of such extreme outsiders to find a husband for each daughter, he felt it his duty to speak out, his duty to his family's memory and the land that had fed and protected him for his first sixteen years.

Whatever anxious words gave rise to the tense and raised voices of Major and Mrs Teneterchilt were not clear to him as he stood staring down the valley to the river. It escaped him why anyone would choose to go dancing in city halls or dining from fashionable porcelain when such a view was here without the need for hard work or strutting posturing.

When the house was finally asleep that evening and the gloaming light had flushed through and drained out the colour from the valley, Imogen silently stepped down the stairs and out to the orangery. She noiselessly closed the door behind her and tiptoed over to Hamish, who had his back turned and was staring through the glass as though he could see something in the night. Occasionally the clouds passed for fleeting moments and a bolt of lightning would streak through the valley as the crescent moon caught its reflection in the river. The bare trees allowed the thin light to shine out into the glen for a second before the thick clouds swept over the moon once again.

'Hello?' Imogen whispered after a time, realising that if she did not speak first then Hamish may not notice she was there.

'Sorry,' Hamish replied, making only a little effort to keep his voice down. 'I was thinking.'

'Yes. I am afraid there has been a lot of that from all parties today.'

'It is such a beautiful place.'

'On that we agree.' Imogen moved to stand before him. 'You seem sad, Mish. What has happened to cause you grief?'

Hamish looked down at her, for she stood some eight inches shorter than him, before he shook his head. 'I am a selfish man, Imogen.'

'Nonsense, Mish, I have known only a few people in my life, but you are without a doubt one of the most selfless.'

'You do not understand. When Major Tenterchilt spoke of this party all I could think of was how it would impact upon your family. Trying to marry you all off to one person or another.'

'No, indeed,' Imogen laughed. 'That has never been Papa's intention. He has always been rigidly clear that we are to marry into the army. An officer of some sort, of course. When he had no sons, he was certain that we should all follow his footsteps in some respect.' She drew back one of the wicker chairs and sat down. 'Arabella has her eye on the station of colonel, probably because poor Papa only rose to major before he was wounded, and Arabella is certain to outstrip everyone around her. Sad little Cat seems to think that she may one day be a major like Papa. She will be sorely disappointed when she attempts to enlist.'

'Surely she knows she cannot. I have told her many times.'

'I am rather afraid that nothing will stop her. Papa desperately wanted a son and he has brought Catherine up to be one.'

'And what about yourself?' Hamish asked, sitting down opposite her and trying to look into her face, though it was impossible for she appeared only as a silhouette against the dark night.

'Me?' Imogen asked, laughing delicately and with the refinement she had cultivated over twenty years. 'I shall be content with colonel, private or spinster, for I will not marry without love. I believe that a teacher has no need of a husband, indeed it should be a hindrance to her.'

'The major will not permit you to be a teacher, Imogen, you know it as well as I do.'

'Be that as it may, I have no money, will inherit next to none and have a dowry of pennies. Arabella will be the first and the last of us to marry, mark my words.'

'Then let us make a wager,' Hamish ventured. He could feel a quaint giddiness settling upon his usually calculated mind.

'No, Mish. We do not place bets in this house. Mama strictly forbids it. That is how we came to live here, because Papa lost our estate in a wager.'

'And do you harbour only regret for that move?'

'No, indeed. We should never have met you, or seen this beauty. But I should have had a greater dowry and perhaps be married by now.'

'Is it the case that all women think of is marriage?'

'You might quit this house tomorrow, Mish, to seek and make your fortune. We cannot. All we have is what those men closest to us will bestow upon us.' She sighed and leaned over the table as if to take his hand but stopped herself before the gesture was completed. 'Do not judge me for it, please.'

Having noticed what Imogen had tried to do, Hamish took her hand in his own and offered her a warm smile, though in the darkness she could not have seen. The two remained like that for some time before Imogen recalled her sense of propriety and slid her hands from his grasp and rose to her feet.

'I expect it does not matter, for every young man here will have eyes only for Arabella. Goodnight, Mish.'

Imogen's wish that her adopted brother would decry her final statement was not to be fulfilled and, after waiting a moment in hope, she departed from the orangery to gain some sleep before the night gave way to day. She was unsure that Hamish ever slept, for he was reliably there day or night unless Major Tenterchilt had set him to work. Her room seemed a mile away as she trod silently along the hall. She had taught herself in the daylight which floorboards would creak beneath her and which she could stand upon and now she could successfully meander the maze without granting it a second thought.

The preparations for the dinner took much of the next three weeks, gathering in invitations and preparing the dresses, linen and catering, for which Mrs Tenterchilt categorically stated that her husband would have to employ more help. The arrival of twelve further domestic servants was called upon and the family tailor called up from London to fashion dresses of the newest designs for the ladies of the house. Catherine was initially indignant at this event, although even she could not help admiring herself in the finished product as she stood before the glass. The three weeks of chaos that readied the household were believed to have been enough, although no amount of time could prepare them for the coming events.

The tenth day of April had been set aside for the momentous occasion. All through the day the servants, overseen by Penny, busied to ensure the table was laid with the finest silverware and the most elegant crystal glasses. It had all been brought by Mrs Tenterchilt who, on her departure from London, had announced that Mr Bryn-Portland may have stolen her house by means of the vipers' den but he would not so easily tear her from her prized belongings whilst she still drew breath.

The drawing room had been carefully arranged with the seats in groups of four but with a space great enough to accommodate further conversers to stand. Of the twenty invitations sent out by Major Tenterchilt the returns had been favourable in all cases, save Doctor Fotherby and Major Norton for the former was unable to leave his current work and Major Norton was leading combat in the Indies.

There had been a deep drifting snow storm the previous week and it was the residue of this that took much of the conversation over the first course, before it inevitably turned to the army. The ladies of the house were the only ladies there excepting Mrs Pottinger, wife of the colonel who had served alongside Major Tenterchilt. Mrs Tenterchilt had arranged the seating plan in such a way that Arabella was positioned beside Colonel Pottinger and Mr Jenkyns, Mrs Tenterchilt's cousin, and directly opposite Captain Roger Pottinger, the colonel's son. Imogen was seated beside him, opposite his father and to her left was a Major Bretwood. Catherine had been supposed to sit beside Doctor Fotherby, and was now seated beside an empty chair, although opposite her was Mr Dermot, the family solicitor. It had been a conscious effort to keep her away from the men of the army in the hope that more refined company would encourage a more refined attitude in her.

Throughout the meal Hamish watched on silently. He was dressed in what he considered to be the most ludicrous uniform and forced to display a spectacle of all that he hated of the higher class. Feeling more responsible for the girls than either parent seemed to, he never took his eyes from them and strained to hear each conversation, fearing that some of the men present might take advantage. He felt like an ornament or a prize trophy on a mantelshelf.

'It's the navy that are sounding the drum of recruitment,' Captain Pottinger announced. 'Although they claimed a significant victory off Spain two months since, which could be the beginning of the tide turning in this war.'

'It's nowhere near the end,' one of the officers, Captain Gillard, replied. 'Napoleon has never set foot on a boat for all we know. It's the army that will win the war against him.'

'Ladies,' Mrs Tenterchilt announced, rising to her feet. 'This is not a conversation for our sex. We shall leave the men to discuss such matters with which gentlemen see fit to fill their time.'

Everyone at the table rose as each of the ladies curtseyed and filed out. Imogen took the sleeve of Catherine's dress and pulled her from the room, for it was clear that she had no intention to leave. Mr Dermot also took his leave and followed the women through to the drawing room, and Hamish wished he could do likewise. However, he was forced to recall his position and remained listening to the tales that the men shared as they drank their port and revelled in their times spent in the brotherhood of the army.

'I tell you honestly ladies,' Mr Dermot began as he poured out drinks for them. 'I know nothing of life in the army and I believe I should be very poor in it even if I did.'

'It is very gracious of you to accompany us, Mr Dermot,' Imogen began but was interrupted as Catherine spoke excitedly to Mrs Pottinger.

'I would love to be an officer's wife and follow the army to war.'

'We do not go to the front lines, Miss Catherine.'

'I should.' Catherine continued, ignoring the despairing sighs from her mother and sisters. 'I should creep away and steal a uniform and stand up to Napoleon and his Frog army.'

'Indeed, my dear Miss Catherine, *you* have the bravery to try.'

The room went silent with the stinging tone of Mrs Pottinger's words. She did not seem to notice or care, and to the dismay of all present, continued to relate her meaning to them all.

'When your father was injured,' she went on, looking down at her empty glass thoughtfully and the queer stain of deep red that the port had left there, 'your Mother could not even look at him.'

'Thank you, Mrs Pottinger,' Mrs Tenterchilt whispered, turning whiter than the snow.

'It was only Fotherby's hard work and skill that spared his life. All that blood and death. No place for a woman at all, Miss Catherine.'

'I believe we all understand your meaning, Mrs Pottinger.' Mr Dermot took the glass purposefully from her hand and set it down on the mantelshelf. Imogen excused herself whilst Arabella and Mr Dermot tried to calm Mrs Tenterchilt who swayed slightly as though she expected to faint. Catherine simply laughed.

'I am not at all bothered by the sight of blood, as long as it is Frog blood, which deserves to be spilled.'

'Fighting talk,' Mrs Pottinger replied with an air of approval.

'Enough,' Arabella cried, turning on them. 'You are not ladies at all. If you were you would have the decency to see that you are abusing your host. Mother is on the brink of consciousness and all you wish to do is share chilling and macabre stories.'

Mr Dermot placed his hand gently on her arm. 'Why do you not sit with your mother while I fetch some water and salts.'

Arabella nodded slightly and sat at Mrs Tenterchilt's feet. Catherine and Mrs Pottinger rose as one and walked back to the dining room. Arabella smoothed out the creases of her pale blue dress and laid her head upon her mother's lap. When the men rushed in, driven to the scene of scandal like flies to honey, it was to find Penny and Mr Dermot fussing over Mrs Tenterchilt whilst Arabella sat like a heavenly vision. Hamish, forbidden by rank and position to enquire after the mistress of the house, looked on in a helpless stupor.

'I am quite well,' Mrs Tenterchilt said loudly, ushering her helpers away. 'I fear I must excuse myself for the rest of the evening. Pray, do continue in my absence.' Penny eased Mrs Tenterchilt to her feet and the guests and family looked on in silence as she staggered out of the room. Captain Pottinger walked over to Arabella and offered his hand down to her.

'I am so sorry that my mother seems to have been the cause of this unhappiness.'

'No more than my sister was, I assure you. I have no doubt words will be shared later of a less forgiving nature than we are using now.'

Arabella sat down opposite the fire that crackled in the hearth as Captain Pottinger assisted her into the seat. She smiled up across at him, tilting her head a little to the side in a teasing, playful manner.

'Please, Miss Tenterchilt. Do not do that.'

'What?' Arabella replied, only deepening her gaze and widening her eyes.

'Look at me like that. It is not what you should do.'

'I am embarrassing you,' she whispered, shocked at herself for the first time in twenty-two years. 'I am truly sorry.'

'No, do not apologise.' He stumbled for words but he could not find those which he wished to speak. Instead it was all he could do to sit staring at Arabella as though she were an angel and, indeed, to his eyes she was. However shamelessly she wished to be married, she had the decency to blush under Captain Pottinger's gaze and she lifted her gloved hand to stifle a slight cough.

'Now you embarrass me, sir. I thought myself beyond such things.'

'I am sorry, Miss Tenterchilt, I assure you it was not my intention.' She smiled nervously and looked up as Mr Jenkyns walked over. 'Captain Pottinger, Miss Tenterchilt, I hope I do not interrupt you?'

'No, indeed, cousin,' Arabella began. 'Your entrance arrives at a perfect moment, for the captain and I had paid each other one too many compliments and I believe we were both a little bashful about our conversation.'

'Of that I am pleased to hear,' Mr Jenkyns announced.

'And what is life like in politics?' Arabella asked. She once again tilted her head so that her profile was prominent. Captain Pottinger bowed his own head before looking around the room. The old veterans sat together smoking and guffawing so that their voices filled the air. Catherine and Mrs Pottinger joined the other soldiers who were taking turns to tell a story more shocking than the one before. Only Mr Dermot stood alone, sharing his gaze between the glass in his hand and the three groups of people.

'It is never dull, Miss Tenterchilt,' Mr Jenkyns continued in reply to her question. 'The damnable Irish pose such a threat it is all we can do-'

'Sir,' Captain Pottinger demanded, returning his attention to Mr Jenkyns and Miss Tenterchilt. 'One does not swear in the presence of ladies.'

'My apologies, indeed,' Mr Jenkyns said, taking Arabella's hand and kissing it. 'I felt that when the lady was my family she might forgive such a word.'

'I do indeed forgive it,' Arabella smiled. 'Cat speaks far worse, to shock me I am sure.'

Captain Pottinger spared her a smile and looked back to the room as Major Tenterchilt's voice called out.

'Mr Dermot, you should not be standing there alone with a half-empty glass for company. Have you not yet met my daughters?'

'Indeed I have,' Mr Dermot replied, walking over to the group of merry old gentlemen. 'All three.'

'Hamish,' Major Tenterchilt called and at once Hamish stood forward.

'Fill Dermot's and Bretwood's glasses. Both seem to be short.'

Hamish picked up the decanter and poured more port into the glasses. He walked away and Mr Dermot watched before following him.

'You are a Scot?'

'Indeed, sir.' Hamish looked levelly across and met his gaze.

'Good man.'

'Good man?' he repeated feeling that he was in some way being played as a fool. 'What is good about me simply for being a Scot?'

'My mother was, too. I meant no offence.'

'I am sorry, sir, it was not my place.'

Mr Dermot smiled briefly before walking back towards the old officers but stopped as Hamish whispered,

'Sir, pardon, but do you know where Miss Imogen is?'

'Yes,' Mr Dermot replied and looked upon Hamish with a sudden interest. 'You are more than just a servant, I believe.'

'Not in the company of guests, sir.'

'Wisely answered.' Mr Dermot gave a thin lipped smile. 'She felt unwell at the same time as her mother and excused herself in search of fresh air.'

Hamish bowed his head slightly and immediately left the room. Mr Dermot walked over to the major who was denouncing Hamish's grave dereliction of duty in leaving.

'No, indeed,' Mr Dermot replied calmly. 'I sent him on an errand for my own benefit. How did you come by him?'

'No one uses Scots in their houses,' Colonel Pottinger announced thoughtfully.

'There is a rumour they steal whatever they can get their hands on,' Captain Young announced.

'Indeed?' Mr Dermot asked, with exaggerated innocence. 'My mother was a Scotswoman and a proud lady with it. I have known no one better in my life before or since.'

A stunned silence followed these words and Mr Dermot, noticing that he had left the impact hoped for, departed to discuss matters of war with the younger officers who were by this time fighting for that far greater prize than Britain: a lady's hand. Catherine looked to be enjoying the competition far more than the attention, and as Mr Dermot walked over it was to find that an arm wrestling match was taking place between two of the gentlemen.

Hamish this while had rushed out into the orangery, anxious to find Imogen. The night was deep outside and only shapes could be seen, with no feature or colour within them.

'Miss Imogen?' he hissed, for he neither wanted to alarm his adopted sister nor bring the guests down upon him. There was no reply, but he could see something moving outside across the great front lawn. He hurried out into the night, caring nothing of the wind that whipped into the house. The snow made it difficult to run but, from far beyond the years he had spent with the Tenterchilts, he recalled that he had done this before. He became so engrossed in this memory that he lost his footing, stumbled and would have fallen but a hand took his own.

'Mish?' Imogen whispered. 'Are you well?'

'Those were the words I was to put to you,' Hamish replied. 'Look at you. Your dress is ruined and you will get a chill unless you dry and warm your feet.'

'You sound like Mama,' Imogen laughed.

'With your mother unwell and your father drunk, I rather fear it falls to me to play both parties.'

He offered her his arm which she took graciously and they walked back towards the house. The lights of the drawing room were welcoming and yet as they dragged their feet through the heavy, compact snow it seemed many miles away.

'You have never seen Papa like this, have you?' Imogen laughed. 'To being ten years old I never knew him any other way. This place seemed to calm him, or perhaps it is just the lack of his deplorable army society. Truthfully, Mish, I cannot imagine a worse husband than one who flees his wife to fight for another cause.'

'There are some decent people there, Miss Imogen,' he stopped as she laughed once more.

'Miss Imogen? Please, Mish, you have never called me Miss. Imogen is my name and I would rather you used it.'

'Your cousin, then. He is a politician not an officer, and what of your father's lawyer?'

'I told you before, dear Mish, if I marry it shall be for love. Not money, rank, or even looks. Although I confess intellect is a necessity, for I hope always to have deducted discussions with whoever is in my company.'

'You are quite a rebel, Miss Imogen,' he stated, emphasising her title. 'And whichever man you choose, I can see I will both envy and pity them.'

They laughed in a foolish way as they walked back into the house. Imogen stopped as Penny rushed down the stairs and quickly curtseyed. There was a look of fear on her face and it rooted Imogen to the ground as she looked at the maid.

'What is it, Penny?'

'The Mistress,' Penny stammered. 'Your mother. I think she is quite unwell.'

Imogen took Penny's hand with great force and looked into her frightened eyes. Indeed, she had no reason to distrust the maid for her entire life had been in the service of Mrs Tenterchilt, and now she turned to Hamish feeling the anxiety that was so clear upon the maid's face.

'Go for the doctor, Mish, please.'

'Do not plead with me, Imogen. I shall go with all the speed I can muster.'

'Take Papa's horse, he is much swifter, and with the drunken stupor Papa has created for himself he will not notice or ever know.'

Hamish bowed his head before leaning down and kissing Imogen's cheek, then rushed back outdoors and round to the modest stable that was now full of unfamiliar horses, each as anxious as the people he had just left. He looked through them all until he found Major Tenterchilt's brown gelding, over which he threw a saddle, uncaring of its sidling protests.

Imogen meanwhile stood, uncertain whether she should tell her father or sisters in front of the guests. There was riotous laughter from the drawing room and it echoed throughout the house to her, even though many rooms divided her from it. Nothing could be gained at this early stage by dampening spirits and pulling her father away from his comrades, many of whom he had not seen since he had been forced to move his family to Scotland.

'Take me to her, Penny,' Imogen said firmly.

Mrs Tenterchilt was lying on her bed when they entered. For a time Imogen simply stared around her, for she had never set foot in her parents' room and was amazed by the precious clutter that lay around. The walls were scarcely visible behind portraits and landscapes of the estate where they all knew they belonged. Dresses spilt from two wardrobes and the dressing table was mounded high with crystal jewellery boxes and perfume bottles. At the estate there had been separate rooms for clothes, dressing and sleeping, but here they were all combined into one.

She stirred herself from her thoughts and moved over to her mother's side.

'Mama?' She turned to Penny and asked, 'How long has she been like this?'

'Well,' Penny began, but the poor maid was clearly flustered. She paced what small stretch of floor was clear of furniture and wrung her hands. 'She wished to retire for the night after the embarrassment she felt inflicted with, so I saw her to bed. She was talking to me about Mrs Pottinger and all her history, and it was truly shocking-'

'My mother, Penny,' Imogen interrupted to remind her. 'I am not interested in Mrs Pottinger.'

'Yes. And then she just stopped talking. I had my back turned, for I was trying to put the dress in the wardrobe. So I turned to face her, for she had stopped talking in the middle of a sentence, the middle of a word, perhaps, and she had just fallen back upon her pillow and you find her now as I did then.'

Imogen placed her hand over her mother's face. 'Well, she is still breathing, Penny, so take heart.'

The party downstairs continued despite the exploits and disasters that Penny, Imogen and Hamish experienced. The drawing room became louder and louder until at last Mr Jenkyns tapped the side of his glass to make an announcement and the room fell instantly silent.

'Have no fear gentlemen, ladies, I am not on the verge of making a speech. I feel all evenings of entertainment must surely have some musical diversion, and what should I spy in the corner of the room but a pocket sized pianoforte.' He paused long enough for the gentlemen to raise a cheer. 'And so, gentlemen, my cousin Miss Arabella will now delight you with her playing and singing.'

'Oh, Mr Jenkyns,' Arabella began, ensuring that her voice was both loud enough to hear and disguised as a whisper. 'I never made any promises.'

'You do not have to,' Captain Pottinger whispered.

'No, I will,' Arabella replied taking Mr Jenkyns outstretched arm that he offered her. 'For I have the hush in the room now, it would be a shame to waste it.' She allowed her cousin to guide her over to the piano which he opened for her and she sat down, trying to recall each toiling lesson she had endured to prepare her for this moment.

Mr Dermot sat down in the chair that Arabella had just vacated. There was a queer quality in his eyes that Captain Pottinger misread as rivalry for, when one sinks into the gripping hold of love, one cannot help but see others as potential threats to that happiness. And yet, Captain Pottinger was a true gentleman and so observed such pleasantries as a gentleman should.

'She is quite enchanting, is she not?' Mr Dermot began.

'Yes. Indeed, I have never met a woman with such beauty, eloquence and charm.'

'The entire of her father's worldly goods shall pass to her on the event of the major's death, for he has no son. That will add wealthy to your list of appealing features.'

'For certain, sir, but that is not what a gentleman should consider when courting a lady.' Captain Pottinger turned from the lawyer to face Arabella where she sat at the pianoforte, her graceful fingers caressing and teasing the notes from the instrument. 'She has such a delicate touch,' he whispered, feeling overcome by the enchantment she laid upon him.

'Have you hopes in winning her, Captain?' Mr Dermot asked and the bluntness of his question caused the young man to openly gape at him. 'An impertinent question and very much to the point. I blame the Scot in me.'

'Whatever business is it of yours who seeks Miss Tenterchilt's hand?'

'As I said earlier, she is the major's heir and I am the major's lawyer.'

'Then pardon me, sir,' Captain Pottinger replied offering his hand in the hope that Mr Dermot would take it and accept the apology. 'I believe I mistook your interest in her.'

'I believe you did,' Mr Dermot agreed. He sipped the remnant of the port that was left in the glass and watched with a ferocious shrewdness as the captain turned his lovelorn eyes back to Miss Tenterchilt where she sat, now singing, with her cousin Mr Jenkyns standing at her shoulder. The empty glass that the lawyer now looked into reminded him of Major Tenterchilt's Scottish servant whose disappearance he had covered with the promise of further wine for the revellers. He excused himself from Captain Pottinger's company and walked over to the windows, where the curtains had been drawn but the shutters remained open. Outside, the lights of a carriage filled the drive and he felt his natural spring of curiosity burst within him. Trying to contrive a plan with which he could excuse himself, he was forced to return to the internal side of the curtain as Major Tenterchilt laughed loudly.

'Dear Mr Dermot, my master of the pen. Is my daughter's singing so deplorable that you must seek to escape and hide from it?'

'No, indeed, Major. I only wondered if we had been drinking until dawn, for she recreates with her voice that most magical of symphonies: the dawn chorus.'

It would not have mattered what excuse he gave, for already the old gentlemen were falling about themselves laughing. Arabella rose and looked about the gathered men before rushing from the room.

'A lady's heart and soul are so temperamental,' Captain Young observed, at which point Catherine rose from her seat.

'Perhaps, sir, that is because we feel we are unable to defend them.'

'Wisely answered,' her father chimed. 'Catherine, take your sister's place at the piano.'

'If you wish me to, Papa, but where is the use of a piano in war?'

Catherine walked to the piano and began a sad, mournful piece, during the first chord of which Captain Pottinger excused himself to leave the room. Arabella stood by the doorway, her cheeks streaked and her shoulders shaking.

'Miss Tenterchilt?' he whispered and she jumped, realising that she was no longer alone.

'Forgive me, Captain. I must seem very ungrateful, weeping when you and Mr Jenkyns have been so kind to me this evening.'

'To the contrary,' Captain Pottinger replied. 'I believe the behaviour of old soldiers to be unacceptable for young ladies. If I were not so aggrieved on your behalf, I might cry also.'

'Now you tease me, Captain,' Arabella blushed as she laughed slightly.

'I do, Miss Tenterchilt, but it is worth any berating to see you smile. Might I escort you back inside?'

'No, but please feel free to return yourself. I have a mind to take some air.'

'Then may I accompany you?'

'Thank you, yes.'

The two were about to leave when Hamish appeared at the end of the corridor, walking towards them carrying a light. He cut the most appalling figure, for his uniform was soaked and soiled and there was a desperate eagerness to him that caused him to move with a peculiar sway. Arabella rushed forward and took his arms.

'Mish?' she begged. 'What is it, Mish?'

Before he could drag himself from his confusion, Mr Dermot stepped out of the drawing room and pulled him away from Arabella.

'Speak plainly, man, the lady asked a question. Is it Miss Imogen?'

'No,' Hamish responded, a firmness in his voice as he returned to his senses. 'It is Mrs Tenterchilt. Miss Imogen is with her now, as is Penny-'

'Who is Penny?' Mr Dermot asked.

'Her maid. The doctor is with her, too.'

'Doctor?' Arabella repeated, stepping away from Hamish as though whatever had happened to her mother was in some way his fault. Hamish reached his hand forward to take her arm and watched with envy and hurt as Captain Pottinger comforted her.

'Has he made a diagnosis?' Mr Dermot continued, ignoring the heartrending nature of the events happening before him.

'Yes, he diagnosed Mrs Tenterchilt as suffering from a brain ailment and advised me to fetch Major Tenterchilt at once. Sir, I am no physician, in truth I did not understand him.'

'Good man,' Mr Dermot said, patting Hamish's arm, and despite his confused and dazed state of mind, the young Scotsman once again wondered at the lawyer's choice and timing of those words. 'Go and fetch the major and let this gruesome business be concluded.'

Hamish nodded and marched purposefully into the drawing room. As he entered the room fell silent, but this silence lasted only a moment before drunken laughter filled the room from carpeted floor to beamed ceiling. He walked over to Major Tenterchilt and knelt beside him. Their conversation was drowned out by the merriment until the major rose to his feet quickly and marched out of the room.

'Deuce, man,' Colonel Pottinger exclaimed, addressing Hamish as though he was one of his soldiers. 'What news caused such pallor to the major's face?'

'Speak out, man,' Captain Young added, 'or I shall have you shot where you stand.'

Hamish looked at the drunken men and shook his head. 'My words were for the major, gentlemen, not your good selves.'

'Indignation,' Captain Young spat. 'Insubordination, indeed.' He drew a pistol from his waist.

'Captain Young, do not let drink get the better of you,' Colonel Pottinger advised.

Catherine walked over to Hamish and looked up at him. 'Gentlemen, leave him be. If my father demands secrecy then you, as fellow officers, should respect that.' They all mumbled in agreement and raised what was left in their glasses to their hosts and their regiment. 'Come, Mish, you need to learn how to talk to them, to appeal to their army honour, for that is the only thing that they all share.'

'Cat,' Hamish began. 'Sorry, Miss Catherine.'

'Call me Miss Catherine again, Mish and I will take Captain Young's pistol and shoot you myself.'

'Mrs Tenterchilt, your mother, she is quite unwell, the doctor is with her now and-'

'Mama?'

'Yes.'

'She disowned me, Mish. Should I feel as hurt and scared as I now do after hearing your news? When she tried to denounce me?'

'She is still your mother, Catherine, and no words can break a bond so strong.'

'Should I go to her?'

'No,' Hamish replied with unrivalled certainty. 'You seem to me the only person capable of maintaining any peace in this room. I will stay here with you. It is not right to leave you alone in that room with all the officers.'

Catherine, a loyal daughter in spite of her mother's unrelenting disapproval, reclaimed her seat at the pianoforte and began to sing such songs as the soldiers would know and partake in. As the tall grandfather clock in the hall struck midnight, the drawing room more resembled an officers' mess. They revelled on a night of victory in tuneless, drunken singing.

Those that were able to climb the stairs to the guest rooms were encouraged to do so, whilst some slept on the lounging furniture in the drawing room. Yet for all the current inhabitants of the lodge, when morning came it was with a noticeable difference to the dawn of the day before. Further snow had fallen in the night, which Hamish was already removing from the driveway in the deepest hope that many of their guests would be leaving. Catherine and Major Tenterchilt were already waiting for their guests to gather in the hall before entering the dining room for breakfast. Neither one of them spoke until more people arrived, for neither of them could find any words of comfort to share with the other. The dining room was entered in stunned silence, although in many cases this had more to do with the effects of the alcohol consumed into the small hours of the day. Arabella presented herself a little later, but Imogen did not appear at the table.

When at last the sun was high enough for the soldiers to depart it was with relief, for the merriment of the night before had faded. Captain Pottinger was saddling his horse in preparation for the first leg of his journey, which was to take him as far as Perth, when Arabella tiptoed into the stable. She walked over to him and he did not notice her at first until she cleared her throat. He was startled to such a degree that he stumbled and fell against the side of his horse.

'I trust you will be more vigilant in battle, Captain.' Arabella smiled in a teasing way.

'Have no doubt on that count, Miss Tenterchilt, I have a keen eye.'

'But no doubt a reckless one too, when the enemy surrounds you?'

'I confess that in the past I may have done,' he paused, beholding her with uncertain eyes. She returned his gaze levelly, feeling a warmth grow within her that she could barely suppress. 'But now,' he whispered, 'I shall have something to return for. Miss Tenterchilt?'

Arabella clutched her hands to her stomach feeling that she might faint through excitement and anticipation. 'Yes, Captain Pottinger?'

'Might I see you?'

'Why of course,' she replied feeling a little foolish in her hopes of any great development of romance. 'I stand right before you.'

'Do not jest when I am trying to say words that do not come naturally to me.' He looked down at his hands, pulling his leather riding gloves on and fumbling with them as he fumbled for the words he wished to say. 'I am a man who commands men, who claims their loyalty and respect with a word. Yet here, before you, all my courage melts and those few words I last night dreamt I should tell you, I now cannot find.' He moved a step closer to her and regarded her fragile beauty once more. 'Miss Tenterchilt, I hoped to leave here with a word of comfort from you, a word in affirmation of my hopes that I might see you again, soon, without the need of such a formal party and without the anxiety surrounding your mother. Could you consider me? I know I rank only a captain, but with my father's connections in Horse Guards and through my determined effort to better myself, I hope to be a major soon.' He took her hand and kissed it. 'Do you think you could wait for me?'

Arabella looked at him and pulled back her hand. 'I am through with waiting, Captain. Should I remain a spinster at twenty-five, I am certain to remain a spinster forever. You may find another to satisfy your wants and I should fade away, you might never again consider me.'

'That would be impossible, Miss Tenterchilt.'

'I am not so very struck on majors, having spent my life with one. A captain would be new to me.'

'You would marry me in my captaincy?' Captain Pottinger asked, a flame kindling from the ashes of his heart.

'Is it so improper and unthinkable?' Arabella asked, truly unsure that she was saying the right thing.

'Only that you may consider it so. Might we form an agreement, until such an occasion that I can discuss the matter with your father?'

'Captain Pottinger,' she began, allowing him once again to take her hands and holding his as tightly as he did hers. But whatever else she was to say was lost as Catherine rushed in.

'Here you are,' she announced, not noticing or caring for the events that were unfolding. 'Come, Arabella, it is Mama.' Catherine did not wait to see if she would be following, but ran back to the house. She had no care for her dress, which billowed out as she ran, and thought nothing of the departing soldiers who laughed at the figure she cut.

Imogen had spent the night by her mother's side, listening to her babbling when she tried to talk and her gentle breathing when she slept, and tears had marked her face almost beyond recognition. The doctor, as Major Tenterchilt went to great lengths to state, was not their own doctor who should have attended their party but who, by the cruel twist of fate had remained behind in London to ease the settling of an amputee. It was a decision based on the events of the moment and one that he had chosen poorly, for he may have saved a life at the dinner party. Yet Imogen, as she served the doctor through the night, understood that life was a pattern of such choices and could not in her heart hold Doctor Fotherby's absence against him. She looked down at her mother who lay on the bed. She seemed peaceful as though asleep but there was no breath any more, no spark of life. Major Tenterchilt stood holding his wife's hand and looking down as though he was still drunk and did not believe what his eyes told him. When Catherine and Arabella rushed in, Arabella collapsed on the bed holding her mother's other hand and sobbing down onto it whilst Catherine only stood, surveying the scene around her. She did not weep but had her face set as hard and emotionless as a rock. Imogen thanked the doctor for his efforts and guided him out of the room.

'You have a skill for nursing, I think.' He spoke with the same strong accent as Hamish, and Imogen found some comfort in that.

'I have a skill for weeping, I believe you mean.'

'You have great care, gentleness and attention. A nurse who needs only to be told something once is a valuable tool to any doctor.'

'Thank you, but we failed to save Mama.'

'That is not your fault, Miss Tenterchilt, you have no blame in it.'

Imogen nodded and watched as the doctor clambered into the carriage and was driven down the drive. Hamish walked over to her and sighed.

'I am sorry.'

'Sorry?' Imogen whispered. 'Whatever are you sorry for? You did more for her in life and death than anyone. Oh, Mish, I always knew we could not live forever as we did, but now that the moment has arrived when change is upon us, I scarcely know what to do. Arabella is beside herself with grief, I am afraid Papa might do himself a mischief and Cat seems unable to exhibit any sign of loss or sadness.'

'You must leave the others to grieve as they wish. Besides, I believe Arabella may have a little joy brought out by this gathering.'

'Then all is not lost,' Imogen replied bitterly and picked up the skirt of her dress to run back inside.

Hamish allowed her to leave, making no effort to call her back, realising that his envious and bitter words were cruelly mistimed. The house was plunged into a hateful silence and, with the exceptions of pleasantries, no one spoke to one another until Mrs Tenterchilt had been buried three days later. The cold spell seemed to last long into the spring and even the change in the weather seemed unable to rectify it. All of the family were suppressed by their grief and would hide themselves away to best avoid conversation.

CHAPTER TWO
Saturday 19ᵗʰ April 1806

Nine days after the death of Mrs Tenterchilt, two letters arrived. This in itself was no strange thing, for the major often received post, only that this time one was addressed to Arabella. Hamish felt with a sinking feeling that he knew the contents of it, but dutifully handed it on to the eldest daughter. The other was addressed to the major, and it was this one that was discussed over the dinner table with great solemnity.

'I am going to London,' Major Tenterchilt announced.

'But Papa,' Imogen began as she exchanged a glance with Catherine, 'what will we do without you?'

'I am certain you will find plenty to fill your time and equally certain I will understand none of it. You girls must find something with which to entertain yourselves.'

Imogen sat back as though she had been stung by her father's words and tone, and indeed she had reason to be. Arabella sat silently, staring down at the letter in her hand, while Catherine leaned towards their father and pleaded with him.

'You cannot leave us here, Papa. Why would you even wish to?'

'I must spend some time away from this place. Away from the memories, the guilt. You will be well cared for, and you are to have no concerns over money.'

'Indeed, Papa, for we should be shamefully foolish to attend any form of excursion without a chaperone. What would people think of us?' Imogen sounded frightened as she demanded an answer from him.

'I have made up my mind. I shall not be a prisoner. The only crime I have committed is my love for a dead wife.'

The three girls sat in fearful amazement as their father rose to his feet and walked out of the dining room. Hamish stood silently and felt that his heart would shatter. Half a month ago this had been the happiest family he had imagined, but now in such a short space of time it had crumbled into sorrow and, often, despair. They rose from their seats as if in dreams, although Arabella had a lightness to her step which Hamish felt was occasioned by the letter she still carried in her hand. Imogen and Catherine walked out, too, the older trying to console the younger.

Arabella rushed up to her room and sat down on her bed, placing the letter on her lap. Initially she felt unable to open it and picked it up several times before setting it back down again. All her hopes were enclosed therein. If her father did mean to go to London then she would be unable to leave the lodge and she had attached all of her dreams on the young captain. He was so eloquent and gentle, yet strong and brave and she did not believe another soul even half as chivalrous could exist in the world. At last, after much deliberation, she opened the letter and read it to herself.

'Dearest Miss Tenterchilt,' the letter began. 'I was so sorry to hear of your loss. It is my regret that there is nothing I can do to ease your sorrow. I have reached Edinburgh to the discovery that war on the continent seems to be approaching faster and faster and it is to this end that I must beseech you to forgive me. I can offer you no certainties, nor the security a lady of your standing deserves. Please find it in your heart to forgive me for hoping to have a chance to gain your affections. Yours always, Captain Roger Pottinger.'

She finished reading the letter, unsure whether she wanted to laugh or to weep. How could he call off the engagement so soon, and what possible reason could his job have to do with his choice? Yet surely he loved her, for the letter was so brief and heartfelt in its conviction that there could be no denying it. She rushed over to her dressing table and tore a leaf from her diary and began writing a hurried reply. She did not know to whom she should address it and so sought out her father. He was to be found, as always of late, sitting in his study at an empty desk with a glass of wine in his hand.

'What is it that you want?' he asked without turning around.

'Papa,' Arabella began softly and he turned round.

'Forgive me, my dear, I thought you were that snivelling girl, Penny.'

'I have a letter that needs sending, but I have no address.'

'That will present a few problems for you,' he laughed. 'Who is it for?'

'Captain Pottinger,' she announced lifting her chin obstinately as though she expected to have to argue the fact but her father just smiled.

'I will deliver it when I travel to London.'

'Will that be soon, Papa? Only he may embark to Europe at any time.'

'Tomorrow. Is that quick enough?'

'Perfect,' she replied, thinking only of her father's departure as a means to deliver the letter. She handed it over to him and left the room. She felt curiously invincible, rather like everything around her was only an act and she truly was the star.

The day passed with the members of the family seeing nothing of one another until supper time came and they sat in silence. No words were shared and it was not until Imogen rose to leave that any one of them made a sound.

'I am going tomorrow, my dears. I do not expect to be gone for any great length of time, a few months perhaps, and I will be back before the winter.'

'Meanwhile, we shall sit and sew, Papa,' Catherine retorted. 'Who will teach me my swordsmanship?'

'Sitting and sewing is a better way to find you a husband, my dear.'

'But not to join the army. That is still all I wish to do, more than marry.'

Despite the angry words, each of them kissed their father's cheek before leaving. The night was deep when Imogen finally walked down the stairs and out into the orangery. It was the first time she had come here since her mother's death and it felt queer, as though it had died too, if a room can possibly die. All the nights of hopeful wishing and dreaming she had spent down here, the knowledge she had gained, it all seemed void. Hamish was there, standing staring down at the river with one hand on the glass as though he was reaching for something. He seemed unaware that she had entered and she walked noiselessly up to him, blowing on his neck so that he jumped and spun around to face her. She was surprised to see that tears streaked his face and his eyes were swollen.

'Are you well, Mish?'

'Yes.' His voice was clear and strong, despite his appearance. 'And you, Imogen? Are you well?'

'Thank you, yes.' There was a peculiar quality to his words and tone that agitated her. She sat down at the table and watched thoughtfully as Hamish did the same. Not daring to incur whatever force or feeling was causing his strange behaviour, she sat silently, waiting for him to speak first, but for all the money and promise in the world she could not have guessed the words he was about to speak.

'I am going to join the army, Imogen.'

'What?' she gasped in surprise. 'You are leaving us, and furthermore leaving us for something you deplore and do not believe in?'

'I am so sorry to be departing from you all, but I have my reasons and they are as complex and entangled as you could imagine.' Imogen could only stare at him and he felt compelled to offer a further explanation. 'Imogen, with your father gone it would be wrong for me to remain. How would it appear to people? You have your standing to think of.'

'It would appear that you were our guardian, as our father clearly no longer wishes to be.'

'That is not how people would view this, and I will not bring shame and disrepute to any of you. War is breaking on the continent once more, I intend to go and join it.'

'When will you leave?'

'Tomorrow, with the major.'

'So soon, Mish. Will you write to me?'

'Without failure, Imogen.'

'Had I known before I would have prepared you a gift-'

'You have given me far more than you can imagine, Imogen. You need give me nothing more. Now, I must go and close my eyes, I have a long journey ahead of me.'

Imogen nodded. She watched as Hamish walked from the orangery and tears pulled at her eyes. Certain that there was no one there to bear witness to them, she openly wept and fell asleep there with her head resting on the wicker table.

The following morning found Penny and Anne standing at the door to the lodge and bidding farewell to Major Tenterchilt and Hamish, while the three daughters stood on the driveway. As the coach pulled away from the house and vanished down the drive and along the road beyond the river, all five of the women stared solemnly at nothing. Their thoughts, although very similar to one another, were individually bleak. Eventually Anne walked out with a shawl that she placed about Arabella's shoulders and encouraged her to enter the house. She and Imogen dutifully did so, but Catherine walked away down the lawn towards the river. She was silent in her resolve and ignored the calls and shouts of the others.

For six years her father had been the only parent in her life and now, with the death of the mother who had denounced her, he had disappeared to London. She had been only eight years old when Major Tenterchilt had lost the estate and, in her mind, she had turned London into a magical place. She had not been blessed with perfect looks like Arabella, nor a strong brain like Imogen. All she truly dreamt of was joining the army and fighting the way her father had, and she envisaged London to offer her those opportunities.

CHAPTER THREE
Tuesday 22nd July 1806

Life at Petrovia Lodge drifted on. Arabella found herself looking every day for a letter to be delivered, but her waiting was in vain and, after a month, she despaired that she would ever hear from Captain Pottinger again. She decided that he had resolved to pay no heed to her sentimental letter and embark upon the rest of his life a staunch bachelor. Her diary became her best friend and she closed herself away in her room for countless hours each day.

Catherine, meanwhile, tried to take up needlework, but her stitches were twisted and so untidy that poor Anne soon abandoned any hope of teaching her. As the days went on and the weather turned fairer she was increasingly to be found outdoors. She tended the horses and would disappear for hours at a time riding through the glens. Frequently she returned caked in mud or soaked to the skin, at which time Penny and Anne hurriedly fussed over her.

Imogen had taken only a week to realise that, with her parents' departure, certain rooms of the lodge were never going to be used again and she set to work cataloguing and covering the items in most of the rooms until the only ones left were the girls' bedrooms, the dining room and the kitchen. Any work that they wished to do over the summer months could be done in the orangery and this was where Imogen spent much of her time. Like Arabella, she confided more and more in her journal and buried herself in the books that she had removed from her father's collection before covering them with the same white dustsheets that had turned Petrovia Lodge into a house of white mounds.

May gave way to June, which in turn heralded July. The sun set only in the latest hours of the day and it was on one such evening that Imogen sat in the orangery gazing out at the leafy trees that overhung the river. Something was moving amongst the trees and she rose from her chair, walking to the window to ensure a better view. At once a fully tacked horse came charging towards the house followed by an irate and bedraggled figure. It took Imogen's startled senses a moment to realise that it was Catherine, at which point she dropped her pen and rushed out onto the lawn. The horse paid her no mind but began grazing on the top corner of the lawn. Catherine by contrast walked over to her sister and a stream of words that made little or no sense left her mouth.

'Dratted beast, the river so cold. Of all the places.'

'What are you talking about?'

'He will never make a warhorse.'

'Nor you a warrior,' Imogen chimed. 'You are soaked, come in at once.' She dragged Catherine indoors, ignoring her cries of protest.

'Anne,' Imogen shouted. 'A warm bath before the fire as quickly as you can. Penny, do something about the horse that is chewing up our lawn.'

Imogen helped Catherine out of her sodden clothes while Anne heated some water and set the iron bath before the ready laid fire. Normally no fire would burn in the lodge over the summer months save the one in the kitchen range, but there was always a fire laid ready in each of the grates. Catherine sat down in the tub while Anne set up the screen around her and Imogen picked up Catherine's sodden clothes.

'Where do you go all these times, Cat?' she asked as she looked at the breeches she was holding.

'There is a recruiting sergeant in the town,' came the sleepy reply. 'I was spying on him.'

'Spying? Cat, I love you greatly, but at times I truly understand why Mama despaired of you. Ladies do not spy, they do not wear trousers and under no circumstances do they join the British Army. They never have done since Boadicea and it all ended poorly for her. You would not wish to be Joan of Arc, would you? Only the French allow their women to fight.' Imogen handed the clothes to Anne who took them away to wash. 'I do believe that you cause more work for poor Anne now than when Mama and Papa were still here.'

She got no answer, but expected none. She found Catherine's antics frustrating, for she was of a ripe age to marry and yet wished to be a man. Imogen had resigned herself to a life of spinsterhood, and still clung to her dream of teaching. She walked back to the orangery and closed the doors. The stars were just emerging in the rapidly darkening sky and Imogen felt for a moment a certain giddiness she had not experienced since she was a child. There was a strange sensation that the wind carried to her as she latched the door, of excitement, adventure perhaps. She felt certain that something must have happened, that the world had changed in some way. She picked up her pen and gave an alarmed scream as she stood up to find someone standing at the glass. Within seconds Anne and Arabella rushed in, but by this point Imogen had collapsed on the ground.

'What in heaven's name?' Anne began but stopped as someone tapped on the window. Arabella nervously looked at the man who stood there, holding a horse's reins in one hand.

'It is Master Filman, one of the gypsies,' Anne said flatly and went to open the door.

'I'm so sorry,' he began as soon as the door was open. 'I did not mean to alarm Miss Imogen. I found her horse wandering past. Recognised it at once.'

'Well, we are obliged, Filman. I will get you some pork for your trouble.'

Anne left the orangery and walked into the kitchen to get what was left of the supper.

'A magical woman, your maid,' Filman remarked to Arabella once she had gone. 'She is a dove within the realm of pigeons.'

Arabella was kneeling down and fanning Imogen's face. 'Well, Master Filman, I am certain that she holds you in equally high esteem, for that pork was the best meal we have had in weeks.'

Penny walked over from outdoors and snatched the reins of the horse. 'I will take him, thank you,' she snapped. She did not share her late mistress' kindness towards the gypsies and her temper was already frayed from having to chase the horse through the valley.

Filman handed over the reins as Imogen came to. She blushed terribly as she realised what had happened and explained how she had felt prior to her fright.

'There is an eclipse of the moon,' Filman said sagely. 'It is a time when our hearts speak to our heads instead of the other way around.'

'I am rather afraid I do all my thinking with my heart,' Arabella confessed as she assisted Imogen to her feet once more.

'What careless words to speak before a man,' Anne chided as she walked into the room carrying a covered dish. 'I am certain you can keep the dish, Master Filman, now on your way. I have a house to put to sleep.'

'Thank you, Miss Anne,' Filman replied and excused himself from them, caring not at all for the darkness and seeming almost to enjoy it.

'Miss Anne, indeed,' Anne whispered, blushing as red as the roses on the south facing wall.

The following morning the three sisters breakfasted together and, for the first time in the ten miserable weeks they had endured, they laughed and talked happily. It was as though, in the recounting of their exploits last night, each felt more inclined to share their deeper thoughts and hopes. Arabella disclosed her secret regarding her understanding with Captain Pottinger and both of the other sisters only seemed to share in her excitement and anxiety over her letter and the failure of his to produce any reply. Because of this, all three of them were surprised that when a letter did arrive it was for Imogen, and she instantly felt regretful that it was not instead for her elder sister. Arabella hid her disappointment well and she and Catherine resolved to go riding in the afternoon to the town to see the recruiting sergeant, on the condition that Catherine would dress and behave like a lady.

Imogen did not read her letter immediately but, when they had parted, she went to the orangery and opened it. It was peculiar and laboured penmanship so she knew at once who it was from and read on with excitement.

'Dear Miss Imogen. By the time you receive this letter I will almost certainly have left the country. What chance it is that I should be placed beneath the same Captain Pottinger whose heart Miss Tenterchilt now holds. He is a great leader and I am certain he will do her proud as her husband. At times I see him holding an Irish lace glove that looks all too familiar and every time I think of you all. Indeed, there is not a day that passes when the three of you, more dear to me than sisters, do not occupy my thoughts. It is a cruelty that places you alone and I trust that this letter will find you all in good health of body and spirit. I see Major Tenterchilt only rarely. We are no longer the friends we once were, through my own fault and rash words at his choice of company. Colonel and Mrs Pottinger are ghastly persons and I believe it is their influence that has caused such a change in him. I only hope he does not wait too long to return to you and tell you himself of his foolish ideas. My candle is guttering, dear Imogen, I hold you forever in my thoughts and prayers. Mish.'

Imogen read though the letter again trying to understand it, but she could not follow his references to her father and wondered what had gone so tragically awry as to result in the failure of communication between them. She had imagined with hope and happiness what it would be like to have a written conversation with Hamish but now she felt that she could not possibly return a letter to him after her father's disassociation with him.

She resolved to share the letter with her sisters upon their return, for the unburdening of their thoughts shared over the table at breakfast had given Imogen a new hope that the family may once more come together. They discussed it over supper that night, for it took them that long to return. Arabella was beside herself with excitement and pleasure that Captain Pottinger still held her in such regard, although she still wondered why he had failed to write to her. Catherine seemed to burst with envious excitement that Hamish would be going to war. All of them, however, agreed that they had to uncover the events that had led to the animosity between their father and their adopted brother. To this end they decided to each write a letter, Imogen a reply to Hamish, and Arabella a letter to Captain Pottinger for it occurred to them that, despite their long residence with the man, none of them knew Hamish's surname. Catherine was to write to their father enquiring of his health and skilfully uncovering the truth of what may have happened between him and Hamish.

Having completed their respective letters, each felt that they were doing their part to reconcile Hamish and their father. Napoleon may have been threatening Europe, but here in Petrovia Lodge there was another war being fought and it was one of love and understanding. What could women hope to understand of death through bloody battles? Even Catherine, whose stomach was strong enough for the fight and the ideas, did not know whether she would withstand the actual event of battle.

If life in the lodge had seemed painfully dull for the three Misses Tenterchilt, it was a life that both Hamish and Captain Pottinger longed for. Roger Pottinger had been commissioned into the army in the hope that he would follow in his father's footsteps, and though he desperately wished not to let his parents down, the army would not have been his hope of a career. Initially he had wished to be a tailor but, as the only son of the family, that would never be allowed to happen. Next he begged his father to let him become a merchant, that he might see his own hard work reap a harvest. This was as doomed as the first effort and, by the age of fourteen, he had given up on his hopes and resigned himself to the army. At eighteen he had bought his commission as a lieutenant and by twenty- three he had climbed to the position of captain, more through his ability to inspire men than his ability to fight, for he had been shielded from most conflict until now.

'What are we doing here?' Captain Pottinger asked bleakly. He was sitting on a Spanish hillside with his two lieutenants. They were both of a similar age to him, and looked anxiously at him. 'The French are in Prussia. Why are we here?'

'One could only imagine it is because we are expected to find a back way in to France,' Lieutenant Portland replied. He sighed as he looked up the hill that was like a cliff to his eyes. 'I have a house in Cornwall with cliffs like this in the grounds.'

'It ceases to be grounds when it drops into the sea,' Lieutenant Keith said flatly.

'We had better get them scaled then,' Captain Pottinger said with a new resolve. 'Before we drop into the sea, too.'

He beckoned his men forward and they continued to struggle up the steep shoreline. Hamish brought up the rear of the column. Most of the men who marched there were little more than boys and the clambering seemed to drain all energy from them. At times Hamish had to stand some of them back onto their feet for the shift from boat to land seemed to unsteady them. 'We are to attack here?' Lieutenant Portland whispered as they got to the top. Before them stretched a small force of Spanish, perhaps fifty in total. 'We are outnumbered two to one.'

'But we have the element of surprise,' Lieutenant Keith pointed out.

'Get the men to form ranks just below their line of sight. Then we will storm over en masse and get rid of this frog outpost.' Captain Pottinger watched as the two lieutenants went to execute their orders. There was something about the soldier in the rearguard that seemed a little familiar to him, more so than any of the other and, whenever Captain Pottinger looked at him, he was always unashamedly staring back. When the men were assembled, Captain Pottinger looked along the ranks of them seeing their fearful eyes fixed intently on him.

'Men,' he began in little more than a whisper. 'Beyond this cliff top there are Frenchmen, twice the number that there are of you. You need to shoot two a head, and do not stop shooting until you have killed six each, in fact do not stop while there are any Frenchmen within sight.'

At his signal they rushed over the top of the hill, or tried to, for the incline of the ground was more severe than they had anticipated and five of them were shot dead within the first second of their appearance. Hamish felt sickened, and somewhere in the back of his mind he knew that he had seen all this before, as though he had dreamt of the outcome and was now helpless to resist. He found no difficulty in topping the hill, nor using the weapon that he carried. There was an odd smell, a little like fire, that filled the air and he coughed as he rushed forward. In the smoke that billowed from the gunshots, both British and foreign, he became lost from his other soldiers. He did not stop at the two soldiers, nor the six that Captain Pottinger had ordered him to kill. He kept reloading, crouched in the overgrown vegetation, and shooting everything that moved and which did not wear the red of the king's uniform. Finally he attached his bayonet and rushed forward.

The remainder of the skirmish was short lived and, as the smoke cleared, he realised that they had been victorious in their assault but at such a cost that only eleven men still stood. The carnage on the floor, especially the jerking spasms of men succumbing to death, made him feel nauseous. As Lieutenant Portland walked over to him all Hamish could do was hold his hand up to stop the advance of the man and he stumbled back onto one of the corpses.

'Soldier?' Portland asked sternly.

'Sir?' Hamish automatically responded.

Portland did not reply but offered his hand to Hamish who allowed him to pull him to his feet. Captain Pottinger and Lieutenant Keith were already advancing into the small collection of tents that had been occupied. They emerged moments later with handfuls of papers.

'You did well men, we have succeeded in our mission. Now, home to England.'

'What about the dead, sir?' a young soldier asked.

Standing a short distance away, Captain Pottinger watched Lieutenant Keith oversee the burial of the fallen men. A nauseous feeling gripped him as he saw the corpses of British and French soldiers lying together in the shared grave. He glanced down at the documents in his hand and tried to tell himself that the papers were worth the bloodshed. He could hear his father's voice telling him that these men had died for the mighty war machine that was the British Army but, as he watched the remaining members of his small company covering their dead comrades with earth, he realised that he would never reconcile with his father's beliefs.

The voyage back to England was conducted in silence by Hamish and the other men. An unwelcome memory had festered within Hamish's mind at the horrendous carnage that had been left by their fighting, perhaps only ten minutes in total but so costly in lives. Whatever occupied Captain Pottinger and the other officers was little concern of his and he found himself staring at the timbers above him and dreaming he was back in Scotland.

When at last land was in sight, the company was weary beyond measure and their return to barracks was peppered only slightly with happiness from the letter that awaited there for Captain Pottinger. He gathered it from his desk and smiled slightly to himself.

'Congratulations!' came a cry from the doorway before he had time to open the epistle. It was his father, as he knew it would be. 'Keith tells me that the mission was accomplished successfully. With smooth trips like that you will be promoted in no time, my boy.'

'It was not smooth, Father,' he protested. 'I lost over half of the men.'

'But you got some maps, did you not? Some French maps with artillery units written on them?'

'Yes, I handed them to Keith, who has no doubt delivered them to Horse

Guards by now. Am I due leave yet?'

'Leave? My boy, you are part of the great machine that is war, now. There will be no leave granted to such a highly decorated officer as you.'

'Even so, I wish to request some.'

'Nonsense. I shall see you at dinner. The mess remember, none of this dining with the men nonsense.'

Roger Pottinger watched as his father left the room before opening the letter hurriedly. At once the scent of primrose rushed to him and he smiled to himself before looking down with confusion to a second letter that fell from the envelope. He read the letter in interest.

'Dear Captain Pottinger. From your failure to reply to my last letter I can only imagine that you have rightfully terminated our engagement. I write to you now on behalf of my sisters and myself to beg you to deliver the enclosed letter to our dear friend, Hamish, who I believe finds himself in your company. I trust this letter will find you in the best of health and that you will forgive me for my presumption to ask such a thing of you. Yours in friendship, Arabella Tenterchilt.'

Pottinger rose to his feet and began pacing the floor before proceeding to rummage through the papers on the desk and every draw he could find in his study.

'Damn it!' he shouted in exasperation. 'What letter, Miss Tenterchilt? What letter did you send?'

There was a knock on the door and Portland entered. 'Sir?' he asked in a concerned tone. 'Is everything alright?'

'Hamish,' Pottinger replied quickly. 'Do you know a man amongst the company whose name is Hamish?'

'It is last names here. You know that.'

'Something Scottish, I would imagine.'

'Gordon?'

'Yes, fetch him here this moment.'

Captain Pottinger did not relinquish his search but sought all the more vigorously as Hamish returned. Lieutenant Portland walked over to Captain Pottinger and snatched his wrist.

'Private Hamish Gordon, sir,' he announced loudly before whispering, 'Damn it, Roger, behave like an officer.'

Pottinger calmed himself and nodded. 'Thank you, Lieutenant. I will talk with Private Gordon alone, and do not let even the colonel interrupt us.'

Lieutenant Portland left the room and Hamish stood to attention before his captain.

'At ease, man,' Pottinger said wearily. 'Sit down.'

'Sit down, sir?'

'Yes, you are not here because of the army, you are here because of a mutual friend we share. I knew I had seen you before. It was at the house of Major Tenterchilt on that terrible black day for the family.'

'Yes, sir.'

'Well, Arabella has written and spoke of a letter that I never received.'

'Sir, it is not proper that you talk to me in this way.'

'What happened to that letter?'

'The major was carrying it. I imagine he has it still if you do not.'

Captain Pottinger picked up the second letter and handed it over to Hamish who received it graciously. 'This was enclosed for you. She writes to you a longer letter than to me, I believe.'

'No, sir. This is Miss Imogen's hand, not Miss Tenterchilt's. You need fear no rivals in the claiming of the heart of that young lady.'

'It is good to know that you know them.'

'Like sisters all, and I dearly love them.'

'How lonely I have been in my love of her, thinking that none would understand. I mean to marry her, Private Gordon.'

'I am aware of that, sir, for the lace glove you carry is not a gentleman's garment. I recognised it at once as belonging to Miss Tenterchilt.'

'You are an observant man.'

'I learnt to know them well, Captain Pottinger, and I ask only this of you: Arabella Tenterchilt is the fairest of women, do not let her grow old and frail in her promise to you.'

'Damn it, man, you are right. I shall marry her at once, as soon as I can leave this post, even if only for a week. I will ride all the way up there and all the way back in the blink of an eye.'

'Noble words, sir. For her sake, please do.'

Hamish rose and saluted Captain Pottinger before leaving the room with a mixture of feelings welling within him. He was dismayed at himself as he realised that envy was predominant and that when he arrived back in his quarters he sat for a long while in a foolish stupor. Finally he recalled the letter in his hand and opened it carefully.

'Dearest Hamish,' it began in Imogen's large, flowing script. 'Your letter has left us all amazed for a great number of reasons, not least our confusion and disappointment over your exchange of words with Father. It has been three months since your departure from Petrovia Lodge and in that time, we have heard more from you than from our father. Catherine and Arabella are as mystified as I regarding your letter, although you brought great hope to Arabella concerning the captain, to whom I do believe she has given her heart as well as her glove. I hope you are safely back in England when you receive this, or else safe in any land. We have so much to share with you when you are granted leave, please do not forget us. Your dear friend, Imogen.'

He could find no way to answer such a letter but held it close to him, for it was the embodiment of his dear adopted sisters. He rose from his bunk and walked out of the door, ignoring the other young men who were celebrating their safe return by drinking toasts to their departed comrades. There was nothing to celebrate in his mind. He had joined the army as an escape but all he was escaping to was the realism of slaughter and death.

There was a profound effect on all of the soldiers in his company, only Lieutenant Keith seemed unconcerned by the events. He sat now at a long wooden table with Lieutenant Portland and Captain Pottinger, and many other officers of the regiment.

'I have found a new sergeant major,' Captain Pottinger announced. 'Since the last was killed in Spain.'

'Indeed?' Lieutenant Portland asked. 'Who is that?'

'Fine fellow named Gordon.'

'A Scot?' boomed out his father from the end of the table. 'We should not be promoting Scots before our own.'

'Sir,' Captain Pottinger said softly, trying to maintain his temper. 'He is a good soldier, shown by his return to England. Many of my men did not return.'

'He no doubt hid in the bushes during the attack.'

'Aye, he did, sir,' Lieutenant Keith responded harshly. 'But he killed damn near fifteen frogs from there.'

There was a ripple of amazed chatter around the gathered officers at the reply that a lieutenant had dared to give a colonel, at which point the elder rose to his feet, slamming his clenched fist upon the table as he did so. Each person there knew that Lieutenant Keith had no interest in the promotion of Private Gordon but had, as a fellow Scot, felt the need to defend his own. Colonel Pottinger stood up straight and retorted,

'Were you not a Scot and had some honour, I would demand satisfaction.'

He walked out before any reply could be given and the first sound to shatter the silence was Lieutenant Keith's laugh. All the others joined in a moment later and they continued the rest of the night in revelling and merriment. Captain Pottinger excused himself part way through the evening. He collected his cloak and walked out of the barracks and purposefully through the streets.

Major Tenterchilt was living in London at the house that belonged to Captain Pottinger's parents. He was an official lodger there, paying rent, but benefiting from the Pottingers' extensive social connections. It was a large townhouse with steps leading up to the front door and a basement where the servants prepared food and processed laundry. Captain Pottinger had spent many autumns there as a child, and indeed had not returned to it since being guided into the army. Now it seemed the correct moment, for his honour was at stake with the lady he wished to marry. Walking up to the front door, taking the steps two at a time such was his sense of urgency, he hammered on the door, waiting only a few seconds before hammering again. It was opened by a servant who permitted him entrance to a hall with a wide staircase that was lined with wooden panels showing pictures of birds and animals. But all this opulence was for show. Captain Pottinger knew that the house had been the sole inheritance of his mother and that, had it not passed to her, they should never have afforded it.

'Lord in heaven!' a woman exclaimed as she ran over to him. 'Master Roger, what a fine figure you cut now. Your mother will be so glad you have come.'

'I am not here to see Mrs Pottinger, Bess. I am here to see Major Tenterchilt. Is he in?'

'Yes, of course,' she replied while the man who had opened the door emerged from the drawing room and announced that the major would see him.

Captain Pottinger spared a smile for the maid before sweeping into the room. He was faced with four people and he realised with a sinking feeling that one of them was his father. Colonel Pottinger's eyes narrowed as he looked at him, as though he held him as great a threat as any Frenchman.

'Have you come to beg pardon?' his mother began.

'On the contrary, I have done nothing wrong,' Captain Pottinger replied and looked to the two other people in the room. 'I have come to demand that which by a lady's hand is mine.'

'Harsh words from a brash officer,' Major Tenterchilt replied, rising to his feet. 'What is it you believe I have that is rightfully yours?'

'A letter, deny if you will, was entrusted to you by Miss Tenterchilt on your departure to London. That letter was addressed to me.'

'Good Lord, man,' the major laughed, 'you are absolutely right.'

Captain Pottinger was unsure how to proceed. He had believed that the major had withheld the letter through some sort of design, but he began to realise that the man had simply forgotten all about it.

'Deuce,' the major continued. 'If I could but remember where I laid it. I may have given it to Hamish.'

'But you did not, sir,' Captain Pottinger replied with certainty. 'For I have spoken to Private Gordon regarding the matter.'

'Private Gordon?' Colonel Pottinger exclaimed. 'The Scot you wish to make your sergeant major? Why did you not tell me he was a friend of Major Tenterchilt?'

'Scarcely a friend now, I believe,' the major replied and took the hand of the woman who sat beside him. 'We had heated disagreements.'

'But will he be a suitable sergeant major?' the colonel demanded. His first and foremost concern was always with the army.

'Speaking as a man I would say that he is aggressive in his views, but as a gentleman I must declare that he will excel in whatever position he is given.'

'There, father,' Captain Pottinger retorted. 'Everything will be in order after his promotion. Now, major, the letter if you please.'

'Sir, I humbly beg your forgiveness, for I have no idea where I might have laid it.'

'You place me in a favourable position, Major Tenterchilt, for I came to ask as well as demand from you. Miss Tenterchilt and I wish to be married. I will excuse your dereliction of duty as a son, but certainly not as a captain.'

'What nonsense,' Mrs Pottinger exclaimed. 'You are to marry an heiress.'

'Miss Tenterchilt is an heiress,' Captain Pottinger said firmly. 'Major, do I have your permission?'

The young captain was not entirely sure whether Major Tenterchilt answered favourably owing to his own merit or out of a desire to rebuke Mrs Pottinger for her impertinence in suggesting Arabella was unfit for her son. Yet all that mattered to him was that the major's answer was the one that he wished to hear. He remained in his parents' house long enough to share a celebratory drink with them and then walked back to the barracks, uncaring of the late hour or the rogues who followed and sought him through the city. He had his answer and that was all that mattered to him. He was surrounded by a giddiness and, on his return, sat at his desk and penned his reply.

CHAPTER FOUR
Sunday 7th September 1806

Summer in Petrovia Lodge lacked the exciting comings and goings of London, but it was far from dull. The company of the three sisters had improved immensely and they now spent every moment laughing over things that occurred and celebrating the long summer days. The gypsies had moved on now leaving, as usual, gifts for the family in exchange for the permission to reside on their land. The usual gifts of wooden pegs and finely carved figures of animals were left by the river, but in addition Madame Kerina paid a visit up to the house. It was the eve of their departure and she walked up the lawn, calling out in a strange language and in a loud voice so that the five inhabitants of the lodge rushed out to see what it was. She walked up to Arabella and tied a soft red ribbon about her neck.

'I have seen a child on the lawns of Petrovia Lodge. Do not wear the black of mourning for long, my dear. I hear wedding bells ringing, with laughter but a taste of sorrow.'

'Wedding bells?' Arabella whispered, hardly daring to believe the witch who stood before her, yet desperate to do so.

Madame Kerina did not speak again but hobbled away back to the settlement of caravans. Each of the women looked down at the ribbon around Arabella's neck and, as one, her sisters began congratulating her as though it never occurred to them that the divination may have been incorrect.

September made its appearance in its usual golden way while summer clawed at the earth, doing everything it could to maintain its hold. The fruits of the trees by the river shone as they grew and, where edible, the girls walked down each day to collect them.

'Nothing tastes so good as a freshly picked apple,' Catherine announced as she bit into one.

'We are meant to be taking them back up to the lodge, Cat,' Imogen replied. 'We're already behind with this, and we stand no chance of getting to the top of the trees as Hamish used to.'

'I can get to the top,' Catherine replied fearlessly, gripping the apple she was eating firmly in her teeth and commencing the climbing of the tree.

'You know you should not compare Cat to any man, she has to beat them.' Arabella looked up as Catherine called down.

'A messenger! I think we have a letter!'

The three of them gathered their baskets, which were only half filled with apples, and hurried off. Catherine, who had tucked her skirts in at the waist, arrived first at the lodge but the messenger was still only just coming up the drive. Imogen and Arabella arrived, collapsing in foolish giggles as the carrier approached and handed over the letter.

'Thank you,' they chimed as one. Catherine, who held the letter, looked down at the envelope.

'Guess who it is addressed to,' she said playfully, hiding it behind her back while her sisters pleaded with her to hand it over. 'No, no,' she continued, unable to contain her giddy excitement. 'Guess who it is to and guess who it is from.'

She placed it down on the gravel and sat upon it until both Imogen and Arabella rushed at her and tried to pull her from it. Their merriment ended abruptly as Penny rushed out.

'Miss Catherine, do you know how to wear a dress? I will have to replace all of the stitches if you insist on rolling on the drive.'

Catherine got to her feet and glowered across at the maid. She picked up the letter and handed it to Arabella before wafting her hand at Penny as if she were little more than an annoyance.

'It is from him,' Arabella whispered, holding her stomach which began to turn with nervous excitement.

'Come on, Miss Catherine, Miss Imogen,' Penny said softly, her tone changing entirely with the revelation of this letter's arrival. 'Give Miss Tenterchilt a little privacy.'

Imogen, Catherine and Penny all entered the orangery and stood watching Arabella like three dogs awaiting the return of their master. Arabella, meanwhile, tried to settle her shaking hands to better hold the letter that danced around before her eyes.

'My Dearest Arabella. I cannot apologise enough for my neglect. I never received your letter, which is, to the best of my knowledge, still in your father's close keeping. I can only hope what it might have contained, and trust that my inexperienced heart has guessed correctly. I have seen your father and your dear friend, Private Gordon, who is already in line for his promotion, and I hope soon to be returning with them to Petrovia Lodge. My heart can only dream that you will accept and cast off the black of mourning. Clad yourself in the finest silk, my dear Miss Tenterchilt, for it is my most desperate hope and plea that you shall soon become Mrs Pottinger. Eternally yours, Captain Roger Pottinger.'

Arabella looked down at the letter, trying to find the sentence she had misunderstood, for she could not believe the words before her. She choked on her own ragged, excited breath and turned to the orangery to find three pale faces staring out at her. She could think of nothing but her exorbitant happiness and she danced down the lawn towards the trees at the bottom, and Catherine and Imogen chased after her. Penny had seen enough to know exactly what the letter contained, and returned to the kitchen to share the news with her own sister.

Catherine reached Arabella first and leapt upon her. 'What is it? What did he say?' she chirped as she sat holding onto Arabella's sleeve. Imogen reached the two, quite out of breath.

'Miss Tenterchilt will no longer be my name. I pass the baton on to you, Imogen,' she laughed, and handed Imogen a twig that had fallen from the tree.

'Congratulations,' Catherine and Imogen chimed together and at once Imogen began stringing daisies as a bridal crown for Arabella.

'But there is so much to do,' Imogen began.

'I know,' Arabella agreed happily. 'I hardly know where to begin.'

'I shall carry the title of Miss Tenterchilt proudly,' Imogen said, holding up the twig baton with great reverence as though it really did symbolise something.

'Imogen will never marry,' Catherine said dismissively, 'so I will never get the title.'

There was a chill to Catherine's words that truly struck Imogen. And the worst pain of all was that she could see no way in which it could be proved untrue. She knew she was a gawkish woman and, unless she could meet someone who shared an interest that lay close to her heart, she had no hope of finding a husband.

Imogen was still stinging from these careless words long into the night and she remained awake for quite some time, staring at the ceiling as though she could find the answers to her problems there. Over the next few days she tried to continue without thinking about it, but as she helped prepare Arabella for her wedding, helping Penny brocade the dress and arranging preparations for the meal, she could not escape the cruel truth of Catherine's remark.

Six days after the letter had arrived, the girls were sitting in the orangery, taking in what was left of the late summer sun without sitting outside for there had been a heavy dew.

'I do not care admitting that I am not at all envious of you,' Catherine said, laughing. 'To be married to a man who could at any moment be called to duty.'

'Yes, but Mama always said that she enjoyed the time alone. I suppose the worry is that they will not return.'

'Nonsense. Britain is victorious in every combat, and everyone knows it is the poor privates who are the first to be killed.'

'You do say some odd things, Cat,' Arabella replied. 'I am afraid that is not how combat works. I shall worry for him when he is gone, but it will make me appreciate our time together all the more.'

'Is that coach coming here?' Imogen asked, ignoring what her sisters had been saying. The three of them rose to their feet and peered through the glass and down the drive. 'It must be,' Imogen added. 'I wonder who it could be. You should go, Arabella, in case it is Captain Pottinger. He should not see you in such shabby attire.'

Arabella looked torn between her desire to see her future husband and the sense that Imogen was speaking. Eventually, Catherine realised that her elder sister was not leaving, so she took her sleeve and she and Imogen escorted Arabella from the orangery. They rushed into Arabella's room and looked down on the coach as it pulled in at the house.

Whoever they had expected to see climbing from the carriage they were surprised to find that it was Mr Dermot, their father's lawyer, who was met from the coach by Penny who bobbed a curtsey. The three of them pulled away from the window and Arabella looked despondently at her sisters.

'We should still go and welcome him,' Imogen stated. 'Even though he is not the person we hoped to see.'

'Of course you are right,' Arabella agreed, and Catherine nodded begrudgingly. They walked sullenly down the stairs, although Imogen did her best to hide her feelings behind a welcoming smile. When they reached the bottom of the stairs however, their faces all lit up as one for it was their father who stood there. Imogen rushed forwards and embraced him as Arabella and Catherine followed close behind.

'Oh Papa,' Imogen exclaimed. 'I did not think you would return.'

'Did I not say I would be back in the autumn?'

'But I did not suppose that you would actually manage it.'

'Was it hard to tear yourself from the fabric of London society, Papa?' Arabella asked.

'Not at all. Indeed, I have brought some of the society you speak of up to Petrovia Lodge with me.'

'Yes, we saw Mr Dermot,' Catherine remarked. 'We were spying from the upstairs window in case it was Arabella's future groom.'

'A-ha!' came the reply. 'Then I see some good news has travelled ahead of me.'

'You knew, Papa?' Arabella asked.

'Indeed, yes. He sought me out in London to ask my permission. You have made quite a conquest there, Arabella my dear. Your mother would have been truly delighted.' He kissed each one of them in turn and smiled at them. 'How long it seems since I saw you all, and yet a day has not passed without me thinking of you.'

'You never wrote to us, Papa,' Catherine said, once again with no consideration for the consequences. 'You might have returned at any time.'

'Ah, but I was held in London by something quite special,' he teased.

'Oh, what was it Papa?' Arabella pleaded, for she had never much cared for suspense.

'Come and see for yourselves. It is in the drawing room.'

The three girls entered the drawing room and were politely greeted by Mr Dermot. His eyes seemed to calculate everything and at once all the girls felt that they were being measured against criteria in the lawyer's head. Mr Dermot was a bachelor of some thirty years and had become their father's lawyer only nine years ago, shortly after the Tenterchilt family had been forced to move to Scotland. In the time that he had handled Major Tenterchilt's affairs, since inheriting the job when his father passed away, the major had been extremely comfortable, receiving only as much of his wage as Mr Dermot deemed necessary. It was no secret to anyone that Mrs Tenterchilt had requested Mr Dermot to do this to avoid being moved from the lodge. As a person, Mr Dermot was capable of both frightening and appeasing, a gift in the realms of the law but a formidable barrier in any hope of making him a friend.

'Ladies,' he said graciously, bowing his head. 'I do believe it is not me your father has brought you in here to see.'

'No, no, my dear Mr Dermot, you are quite right,' Major Tenterchilt laughed. 'Come Arabella, Imogen, Cat, there is someone who has been waiting so long to make your acquaintances.'

They filed round neatly to look at the chair by the fire, and this is what they saw: a young woman sat there, perhaps three years older than Arabella, but surely no more. She had perfect curls in a loose bun on the top of her head and looked as though she had stepped straight from a parlour rather than a coach. Everything about her was fair, from her pale yellow hair to her long white fingernails. She was dressed in a pale green and seemed to stand out in the old stone room as being frighteningly new and unexpected. She bowed her head to each of them in turn but made no effort to stand nor to speak.

'Introduce us then, Papa,' Catherine said to her father as though she viewed the prize of this game to be immensely dull.

'Of course,' their father began. 'Forgive me.' Mr Dermot stood to one side, all the while watching the three daughters and gauging their responses. 'Arabella, Imogen, Cat, this is Mrs Tenterchilt, my new wife.'

His words were met with a stunned silence for a moment before Catherine gave a loud laugh. She began laughing so hard that, before they realised, Imogen and Arabella had joined her. The young woman looked shocked, unsure whether she should be affronted or amused.

'Papa,' Catherine said between giggles, 'truthfully, she is scarcely older than Arabella!'

'Wait,' Imogen whispered. 'This is no way to welcome anyone to Petrovia Lodge. I confess,' she began, addressing the newcomer. 'I shall never be able to think of someone so young as a mother, but I do hope you will find friendship here at the lodge for so long as you wish to stay.'

'Thank you, Imogen,' came the reply in a voice that sounded painfully unused to speaking.

Arabella smiled down at her before coaxing her throat to speak. 'Likewise, Mrs Tenterchilt. In the brief while that we share our home, let us be friends.'

'This is madness,' Catherine retorted, feeling the smile drop from her face. 'Papa, how could you marry someone the same age as your daughters?'

'She is not the same age, Catherine, and you will not dictate to me where I may or may not turn my affections.'

It had been a measure of Major Tenterchilt's anger that he had used Catherine's full name, and it was an anger that none of the girls cared to cross. Catherine curtseyed for the benefit of the whole room and walked out to the stables. Arabella, who was clearly as shocked as her sisters, sought a conversation to share with this woman who felt unbearably like an intruder in their lives.

'I am to be married soon,' she blurted out. 'Imogen and Penny are making my dress from the finest muslin. Oh,' she added, 'did you meet Penny?'

'Yes,' came the reply.

'Well you must excuse her. She spent all her life in the service of Mama's family. She will get used to you in time.'

Imogen smiled at Arabella who sat on the chair facing their new mother and they talked together of weddings, dresses and all things feminine. Relief was Imogen's strongest emotion as she walked over to her father. 'I shall go and take the dustsheets from the rooms. It is only right that Mrs Tenterchilt should see our home at its best.'

'My dear Imogen,' Major Tenterchilt replied taking the tops of her arms and looking down into her eyes. 'Where would this family be without your character and insight?'

'I hope I am only being a good daughter, Papa,' she replied, walking away from the drawing room. She went through each of the rooms folding up the great white sheets that she had been so sad to lay over everything only a few months before. She could not understand why she felt sorrowful now to be removing them. The large sheets were so encumbersome that she could only carry two down to the scullery at any one time. Upon returning to remove the remaining sheets from the cluttered library, she was startled to hear a voice behind her.

'I saw the insides of a clock once. I am no engineer but it fascinated me, how it just kept going despite extreme temperature or humidity, the pendulum just kept swinging and the cogs just kept turning, and everyone benefited from it for knowing the time.'

'Pray, do not think me rude, Mr Dermot,' Imogen replied. 'But I do not understand.'

'You are like that clock. You keep going through thick and thin and this family benefits from that. I must speak with you regarding your father's marriage.'

'Sir, I am a woman, I have no grasp upon the law.'

'That is a shame,' Mr Dermot replied. 'I was told that you had a great grasp of everything, and I must admit that I am currently agreeing with that highest of character references.'

'Whoever told you that-'

'Sergeant Major Gordon holds your knowledge in the highest esteem,' Mr Dermot interrupted. 'And I can see by your face that you hold him in a similar position.'

'Hamish?' Imogen whispered, holding her hands to her burning cheeks. 'He's my brother, Mr Dermot, it is his duty to pay me compliments.'

'You make a mistake if you think that, as a Gordon, he believes anything a duty towards the English. He told me that you were the one I should speak to concerning any,' he paused to consider his next word with care. 'Worries that I might have surrounding your father's marriage.'

'And what worries do you have?' Imogen asked, suddenly unsure that she wished to know the answer.

'My worries concern you all,' Mr Dermot announced in a simple tone. 'As you are unaware of it, I shall explain a little of what I know of this match. Miss Hardale, who is your new mother, comes from a well to do family but is the youngest of nine children, I can scarcely imagine the inheritance that lies waiting for her, for her father has promised half to the eldest son and will divide the rest until, as number nine and a woman, only the tiniest share will be hers.'

'I am certain your research is sound, Mr Dermot, but why do you tell me this?'

'She is a woman used to comfortable living, Miss Imogen, and if there is one thing that is certain in all these cases it is that women of her calibre cannot survive living without. The late Mrs Tenterchilt left a substantial amount of money to her husband, and it should remain as your dowries, but she had not reckoned upon her husband being so brief in his mourning. Mr Gordon's concern, my dear Miss Imogen, was that you should have nothing left to inherit, nor even to take with you into married life.'

'Thank you for being so candid, Mr Dermot,' Imogen said thoughtfully, at once unsure that she was grateful for his blunt attitude. 'What else can you tell me about our new mother?'

'Do not suppose her wicked for her desire of money.'

'Even money that belongs to us?'

'Indeed. She is London society and has the empty head to match. All that can fill it, in her eyes, is money.'

'I do not care for money, Mr Dermot, it is more that Mama left it for us. Arabella will be married soon, and I am certain that even the new Mrs Tenterchilt cannot spend money so fast here that she will be without a dowry. For my own part you need have no worries. I do believe it is poor Cat who will suffer.'

'You speak with more truth than you can know, Miss Imogen. The will that Major Tenterchilt penned whilst he was still in the army leaves all his wealth to his son.'

'But he has no son,' Imogen replied, unsure where this conversation was taking her.

'No, he has not,' he agreed. 'But Mrs Tenterchilt is with child.'

'This means nothing,' Imogen whispered, but she felt a chill run through her that proved her wrong even as she spoke the words.

'It could mean you are left without a penny when your father dies.'

'Papa will not die. Besides, I am certain I will have found work by then.

I have not a penny now, either.'

Mr Dermot nodded thoughtfully and walked over to the door. 'You are as sure and steadfast as Sergeant Major Gordon told me you were. My purpose in talking to you was to find out whether you wished me to ask your father to reconsider his will. Can I take it that your answer is to the contrary?'

'Sir, if you and Sergeant Major Gordon conspired to trap me, I do hope I shall escape from your words and webs. But if you truly came here to benefit my sisters and me, I have to tell you, my father's happiness means a great deal to me and I would forego marriage and money for him to maintain that.'

'Well spoken, Miss Imogen.' Mr Dermot did not say anything else to her but walked from the room. Imogen staggered over to the window, feeling that she had fought a duel. The premature evening was closing in and she watched silently, leaning on the sill, until all the colours were washed away and everything became grey.

Imogen still stood there as Anne entered the room carrying a burning candle. 'Miss Imogen?' she asked softly. 'They are all in the dining room, but Penny refuses to serve until you arrive.'

'What do you think of your new mistress, Anne?'

'Well she certainly is not like your Mama was, but she seems sweet enough. She is very beautiful.'

'Thank you, Anne, I shall be through in a moment.' Anne curtseyed and left silently. Imogen had to coax herself to walk out of the room. She could not escape the question that continued to circle in her head concerning Mr Dermot's true motive for coming to the lodge with her father. Surely he had much business in London to consider.

In fact, Mr Dermot had travelled to the lodge for the reason that he had so bluntly declared. He had learnt very early on in his career that the best policy in dealing with the law was to tell the truth, but often in such an outrageous manner that it sowed seeds of doubt within the client's mind. These seeds were now bursting into bloom in Imogen's head. She could not fathom why Mr Dermot and Hamish had combined their efforts to undermine her father's happiness over something as insignificant as a dowry or inheritance. Both men had profited well from her father's generosity, in the least it seemed ungrateful. And she would not believe such a thing of Hamish. She entered the dining room and took her seat between Major Tenterchilt and Catherine. There was a silence in the room for a moment until Penny served the food and at once the table became alive with conversation.

'What do you wish us to call you, Mrs Tenterchilt?' Arabella asked.

'Unless your father has any objections you may call me Alice.'

'Papa?' Imogen asked.

'Alice is her name. I could not coax her to alter both.'

'I am grateful to you, Alice,' Imogen said with great sincerity and glanced fleetingly at Mr Dermot before adding, 'You have made Papa truly happy and that is so very important to us all.'

'Thank you, Imogen,' she replied in a voice as soft and sweet as a lark's song. 'I do truly hope that I can fit in with your way of life here at the lodge. I know I can never fill that space which was left by your dear mother, but I hope to bring as much happiness as I can to the household.'

'Well spoken, my dear,' Major Tenterchilt responded.

The tension in the air seemed to disperse a little although Catherine failed to say a word all dinner. Eventually the conversation turned to war, as it usually did at the major's table.

'Very soon, I believe,' Mr Dermot announced, upon being asked when he expected the war to begin. 'All of us sitting at this table know that it is already happening in secret. Whilst such behaviour is thoroughly expected in my profession, I must admit to a disappointment in the army that they are resorting to such devious extremes of warfare.' There was a playful light in his small, strong eyes as he said this, as though he hoped to ignite some form of debate.

'Mr Dermot,' Major Tenterchilt laughed, feeling like a man who could not be shaken from his good mood. 'I will not rise to any amount of baiting from you. I trust you will have more luck with the fish in the river, for tomorrow we shall engage in a fishing competition and the young ladies may enjoy the end of summer by sharing a picnic with us.'

The major's plans could not be disputed for his mind was made up and, being a man of station, he would see any attempt to alter his plans as insubordination. Catherine seemed pleased by her father's idea of fishing and the following morning appeared with her own line and net, wearing trousers instead of skirts. Major Tenterchilt seemed quite pleased with this while his wife failed to hide her shock and dismay, but Catherine was simply pleased to be her father's son once again and her dreams and hopes of the army were rekindled. She worked hard to ignore everything that Alice said, sharing only pleasantries with the newcomer. Alice did not appear to object to this for she and Arabella discussed plans for the impending marriage whenever possible. Imogen watched all this with hopeful eyes, desperate that Mr Dermot's words might be ill-founded.

The major's planned fishing exploits began at ten o'clock that morning and involved only walking down to the river at the end of the lawn and following it a little further downstream. Penny and Anne accompanied them and laid out the groundsheet blanket for the ladies to sit on and sorted the picnic of sandwiches and cakes into pleasing arrangements on fine plates. Arabella and Alice were talking once more of the wedding and Imogen, without intention, listened in on their conversation.

'I have met your groom, Arabella,' Alice confided. 'He is, indeed, very handsome.'

'You have met him? In what capacity?'

'I was there when he asked your father that he might marry you. He is a very purposeful man. He spoke highly of a confidante, Private Gordon, soon to be his sergeant major, I believe.'

'Hamish, yes. I did not know that they had become such friends.'

'Nor I,' Alice explained. 'It is a concern for Captain Pottinger's parents that he should fall into company with such a man who is not only a Scot, but also a commoner.'

'I have no fear concerning his parents,' Arabella laughed. 'For pomp and arrogance were never more at home with anybody as with them. Hamish is a good man, Alice, and you should not listen to any word said against him. I know I shall not.'

'But he condemned your father's marriage to me, and argued with him as though he had a right to speak so before the major.'

Imogen rose to her feet. 'Alice, I wish to like you and trust you, but you are discussing matters that you cannot hope to understand for you do not know Private Gordon, nor the great respect and love he had for this family and our mother. Be content that you do not speak to or of him, or I fear we may find ourselves with a great disagreement separating us.'

Alice looked on the point of apologising, for truly she did not know that she had said anything that might be seen as wrong. Arabella smiled as her sister walked away, before turning back to Alice.

'It would be wise if our conversation did not stray to Hamish, for he is greatly revered by we three sisters, and clearly not by you. He wrote to inform us that he had experienced a conflict with father, although he is far too much of a gentleman to have told us what the disagreement was. For my part, I am pleased that he and Captain Pottinger have become friends for, beside Papa, there is not another man living who shall ever have my heart.'

'You speak of him so beautifully, Arabella. I hope I might one day inspire such words of praise and affection from Major Tenterchilt.'

'You may wait in vain,' she laughed in reply. 'Men have not the gift of words that we women possess.'

Imogen had left the picnic in the interest of maintaining peace with the new Mrs Tenterchilt and resisting the increasing temptation to lose her patience and temper. She continued walking away from them and down the stream as it circled around the west side of the hill. She had not walked this way often, for it led only to the join of their little stream and the great river that could sometimes be heard from Petrovia Lodge during the spring thaws. This marked the end of their land. She sat here for some time, watching as the competing waters splashed and fought as they plunged into the new, bigger river and then sped away. How long she sat there she did not know but she had removed her shoes and stockings and sat on one of the large flat rocks enjoying the chilling sensation of the water as it rushed past her feet. There was a strong current at the bottom of the river that was only two foot deep at the edges. She sat for some time looking over the flat river valley and beyond to where the hills rapidly rose up once again.

When Mr Dermot appeared at the top of the little bank that led down to the river he could not help but smile as he looked down at her, with her skirts fanned out around her on the large rock. Not wishing to be a Peeping Tom he coughed loudly to make his presence known, but the forceful rush of the river drowned out his efforts. Reluctantly he walked down the bank, cursing himself for wearing such insufficient clothing for this venture. He stepped onto the rock and squatted down behind.

'Miss Imogen?'

Her alarm was apparent, for she screamed so loudly that the hills echoed her cry. She spun around to face her assailant but in her lack of care and concentration the forceful water pulled her legs from beneath her. Her attempt to grab the rock as she slipped proved in vain and she felt the shallow but frighteningly strong river pull her away. Mr Dermot, a city dweller at heart for reasons that his past had instilled into him, was unsure what to do. At great contrariness to his usual measured thinking, he pulled off his coat and jumped down into the river, splashing after Imogen. He caught up with her just before the two rivers met, some ten yards from where they had entered. Grabbing her by her arms, he pulled her out of the river and sought for a way out of the water, but the strong current had carved a small gorge here and he could not carry Imogen up the steep banks. His only alternative was to continue back up the river to where the large flat rock was. He forced his way against the current at a painfully slow speed so that by the time he had covered the ten yards he was so exhausted it took him all his efforts to lift Imogen's unconscious body onto the rock. He remained standing there for a time before he found the energy to clamber from the river himself. He wrapped his dry coat around her and, with a new found burst of energy and determination, he carried her up the steep bank and back to the picnic party.

'Good Lord, man,' Major Tenterchilt began as he rushed over to relieve Mr Dermot of his daughter. 'When I said find her, I did not mean for you to fish her out of the river.' He carried Imogen the rest of the way back to the house, struggling to do so with his wounded leg, but Arabella, Alice and Catherine all aided him whilst Mr Dermot remained where he stood, feeling unbearably weary, too tired even to lower himself to the ground.

When Imogen awoke she found herself in her own room with Catherine sitting beside her on the edge of the bed. She was not paying any notice to Imogen but reading a book and fanning herself with a piece of paper. It was terribly hot in the room and the youngest sister was dressed accordingly, wearing little more than a shift and with her dark brown hair pinned up so as to keep it from her neck. Imogen pushed away the blanket that had been placed over her and Catherine turned to face her.

'How do you feel, Imogen?'

Imogen was unsure how to answer. Indeed, she was unsure how she did feel. Her head was spinning and her heart was pounding so rapidly that she was certain it was the cause of her headache, but she also had an overwhelming sense of energy, as though she could run all the way to Perth and back. There was a curious look in her eyes that puzzled Catherine who asked her question again.

'I feel very much alive,' was the only answer she could find to give.

'You made us all very worried. Even Alice.' Catherine positioned herself on the bed so that she was looking straight at her sister. 'What happened out there?'

'What do you mean?'

'Do not get bashful and coy now, Imogen. I have waited patiently for nearly two days now to hear what happened.'

'Two days?' Imogen echoed, her throbbing head trying to take in what Catherine had just said. 'The last thing I remember was turning round and someone was behind me. I think it might have been Mr Dermot. Then I lost my footing I think and I cannot remember any more.'

'Well, I suppose if that is all you claim to remember, that is all I can expect to hear.'

'What else would you hear, Cat?' Imogen asked, truly concerned.

'How gallant Mr Dermot was and how you had fallen in love with him and I should be the only one of we Tenterchilt girls to remain single.'

'Mr Dermot is a very shrewd and astute man but, in honesty Cat, he frightens me. I never know what his motives are nor when he is telling the truth. I should not have fallen in the river if it had not been for him.'

'Papa sent him to fetch you because it was time to eat. That is not his fault, Imogen. Besides which, you should have been drowned in the river if he had not saved you.' Catherine rose to her feet and passed Imogen the book and paper that she had been holding. 'He left you these,' she said softly. Catherine kissed her sister's forehead and walked out.

Imogen felt dazed, rather like when one stares into the fire for too long. She picked up the book that Catherine had handed her. It was new, not like the tattered leather bound books of their limited library, and she opened it to read the front sheet. It read: 'Ballad and Lyrical Pieces by Walter Scott, Esq.'. Curious to find out why Mr Dermot had given her this she opened the letter and slid over to the candle so that she could read it better, for all the curtains were drawn in her room.

'Miss Imogen,' she read, in a hand that was alarmingly angular and aggressive. 'Forgive me for being unable to remain at Petrovia Lodge to see you return to full health once more. I am left to simply trust in the word of the doctor who has assured your family and myself that you will suffer no permanent damage. For the book I can take no credit, only as a carrier, for Sergeant Major Gordon asked me to deliver it to you, knowing of your love of reading and of the Scottish culture. It brings me no pleasure to relate back to our topic of two days ago, but I was asked by Sergeant Major Gordon to ensure you knew. The new Mrs Tenterchilt is a favourite of Colonel and Mrs Pottinger and, like them, is fiercely opposed to their son, Captain Roger Pottinger, who it is feared may bring disgrace to the family. It is Sergeant Major Gordon's wish, nay plea, that you should ensure Miss Tenterchilt's happiness. I should not ask such a thing, but have seen in you a great strength. I pray for your swift recovery. Your servant.'

Imogen felt overwhelmed and stared at the letter for some time but saw nothing upon it. She was unsure what Hamish and Mr Dermot had schemed concerning Alice, or how many of their words were the truth or the cruellest version of fantasy. And yet, whatever anger and suspicion she felt, she could not shake off the doubt that they may, in fact, be right. She held the book to her and clenched the letter in her fist before correcting herself and slotting it into the drawer beside her bed.

CHAPTER FIVE
Friday 31ˢᵗ October 1806

The following weeks saw the dramatic and rapid decline into the onset of winter, but none of the inhabitants of Petrovia Lodge seemed even to notice. Each day adopted a peculiar pattern. Catherine was always up at dawn and out riding, Arabella and Alice continued to plot and plan the former's wedding. Imogen, now somewhat peripheral in the wedding arrangements, continued to oversee the running of the house while Major Tenterchilt amused himself smoking and reading in the library. They came together at meal times and sat together in the evenings when Imogen would read her new book and Arabella would play piano and Catherine would sit poring over maps as though she were leading an army across them. This steady pattern continued throughout October until, on the last day of the month, Catherine came back from her morning ride earlier than usual and rushed through the house.

'He is on his way, Arabella. Captain Pottinger will be here by dinner.'

The stir that this statement caused throughout the house was immense and everyone rushed to ready themselves or the house for the arrival of the man who was soon to become a part of their family. Arabella was perhaps the calmest. She carefully sorted through her dresses, aided by Anne, and selected a pale yellow one with a white square shawl that threaded through loops on the shoulder. She walked down the stairs like a vision of light, Anne shuffling along after, straightening the small train that followed her. Imogen and Catherine smiled across at the sight of her for she looked unlike they had ever seen her before. She had a radiance that came not from anything that she wore, but from her soul.

Penny was far too experienced as a maid to show any excitement at opening the door to Captain Pottinger, or perhaps she felt a little upset that she would shortly be losing Arabella who was, without any doubt, the daughter who was most like her mother in appearance and mannerisms. She stood back to allow him in and, in the absence of a butler, took his hat and cloak. She vanished down to the drawing room without uttering a word to the poor captain who looked both nervous and excited. When she returned to show Captain Pottinger in to the drawing room, he was uncertain that he wished to follow. Nerves that battle and combat could not shatter fell to pieces at the thought of marriage but it was the promise of his bride that inspired his feet to move forward.

He entered to find everyone seated except for the major, who stood holding his wife's hand in his right and Arabella's in his left. There was silence as Penny closed the door after him and she disappeared back down the hallway. No one in the room was entirely sure what was to be done and the silence prolonged into nervousness until at last Catherine rose from the piano stool and walked over to the poor captain.

'Take a seat, Captain Pottinger, please.'

'Thank you, Miss Catherine,' he replied accepting her offer gratefully. As if this act by the youngest sister awoke them all from their anxious expectation, Imogen recalled her manners and asked,

'Was your journey pleasant, Captain Pottinger?'

'It was wet, Miss Imogen, I confess that the thought of my arrival was the only thing that kept my spirits up.'

'And how you find us!' she laughed. 'All staring at you as though you were a peculiar animal. I am so sorry, Captain Pottinger, we have been shamefully rude.'

'Not at all. I should have spoken at once. Please forgive me, I find myself in a position that I am unfamiliar with.'

'Speak out, dear boy,' the major guffawed. 'You have come here to marry my charming daughter, Arabella.'

'Indeed, sir, that is why I have come.' Captain Pottinger seemed to relax instantly as his eyes met with Arabella's own and he smiled uncontrollably. 'Although I bring other news,' he began, faltering a little. 'News that I believe you should know before you answer my pledge of matrimony.'

'What is it?' Arabella asked, leaning in towards her father as though she needed the extra support.

'Napoleon's forces are sweeping across Europe and an invasion of the continent seems imminent. It is only right that I tell you, for I do not know how long I will be remaining on British soil.'

'Nonsense,' Major Tenterchilt said firmly. 'That simply means you should be married at once.'

Arabella seemed very happy with the answer that her father made on her behalf, for she sat smiling at Captain Pottinger who returned the gesture with relief and adoration. The final preparations were made to allow the marriage to proceed before November ended. Whatever bride or groom thought over those two weeks before they were to be married they shared no concern with anyone and barely talked to each other, bar one occasion when Arabella was alone in the library. Captain Pottinger walked past the door which was slightly open and, upon spying her there, he knocked and entered.

'Captain Pottinger,' Arabella curtseyed slightly and smiled at him.

'May I call you Arabella?'

'It was the name that was given to me,' she replied, her face remaining straight, but her words containing laughter.

'Do not tease me, Miss Tenterchilt,' the captain implored and sighed heavily.

'I am sorry,' she began, lowering the book that she held.

'You find me a poor man, no doubt.'

'To the contrary, I wish only to know that you may be the same happy man I remember meeting in the spring.'

'I am a coward, Miss Tenterchilt,' he said, his voice laboured in regret and shame.

'I shall not hear you say such a thing,' she replied firmly, slamming closed the book in protest. 'I have heard only reports of bravery. Do you say these things in the hope that I might call off our engagement?'

'No,' he said quickly and with an earnestness which pleased Arabella greatly. 'I am afraid I will be a poor husband to you. I am afraid that I will be forced to the continent and made to abandon you so early in our marriage.'

'You need have no fear on that count, Captain Pottinger, for I know you will be well looked after, and that will give me comfort in my concern.'

'I would not have you follow me to battle as my mother followed my father. You are too beautiful to go close to the horrors of war.'

'My dear Captain Pottinger, you need not fear for me, nor should you ever doubt your courage, for so long as I have you I shall be the happiest and luckiest woman alive.'

This secret conversation only three days before the marriage remained in the hearts of the two but the tension that seemed to surround the house was dispelled by it and, though the others knew nothing of its existence, all were grateful for it.

The wedding was a small affair, taking place on the quiet of a midweek morning whilst shops and businesses continued in the little town, uncaring of the union taking place. The sun did not shine, but the rain was held at bay for which the sisters were truly grateful as their dresses would be beyond repair should the ground underfoot become muddy. Major Tenterchilt acted as the witness, whilst the second was the verger, for the major deemed it incorrect for a woman to sign a legal document. Mrs Tenterchilt did not attend, and Imogen could not help the horrible feeling that Mr Dermot may have spoken the truth of her dislike towards Captain Pottinger and, as those seeds of doubt grew, she wondered what lengths she might go to in order to keep the two families apart. Alice had presented the excuse of being unable to travel the short distance as, although never discussed, her pregnancy was now very visible. However, it had not escaped Imogen's notice that, only a week before, Alice had accompanied Arabella to the shop to pick out a veil.

Upon their return to the lodge, Anne and Penny welcomed the new Captain and Mrs Pottinger and, although she knew it should have been strange to her, Arabella felt entirely comfortable with the title. In his officer's uniform both Catherine and Imogen had to agree that the captain was certainly handsome whilst Arabella was radiant in her white dress with pale blue brocade.

'If I felt I should be as beautiful a bride as Arabella,' Catherine remarked to Imogen as they watched the rest of the household walk indoors. 'I should find any man just so I could marry.'

'Cat,' Imogen laughed. 'Now that Arabella will be leaving us for London society, I am certain she will find you a groom as handsome as the captain.'

The following day was met with a taste of sadness as the newlywed couple prepared to depart. Major Tenterchilt was to escort them to Perth in his own carriage before they would be met and escorted by some men of equal rank to the captain to head south to London. Arabella kissed her sisters as they stood together at the front of the house.

'If you should see Hamish whilst you are down there, make sure he remembers us,' Catherine said as she held her sister in a warm embrace. 'I shall miss you terribly. And I know Imogen will, for who now can agree with her when she tells me to behave like a lady?'

'Do not torment and tease her so much, Cat,' Arabella replied. She turned to Imogen and hugged her tightly. 'And you, dear Imogen, have you anyone you wish me to seek out in our bustling capital?'

'I am rather afraid that I know no one there, and those that you know will certainly seek you out, but do remember to make your presence known to Mr Jenkyns, Mama's cousin, when you arrive. It is only polite, although I do believe he will be sorry to find you married.'

'I shall do that, although as a politician I am not sure how much time he will have to receive me. I hear they are employed solely to talk.' She smiled a little before kissing Imogen's forehead. 'Goodbye, Imogen,' she whispered. 'I do not remember our ever being apart. How strange this will be.'

'Do not think of it so. You are married now and have a new family to establish and build. Take care, dear Arabella.'

Arabella climbed into the carriage assisted by her husband. Catherine and Imogen waved as it disappeared down the drive and beyond the river. There was a feeling of loss that grew within each of them as they stood there, leaning against each other and needing the support in both body and soul. Anne walked over to them and took their hands in her own.

'Come inside, you can have a drink of tea with Mrs Tenterchilt.'

'I think that is meant to be a comfort,' Catherine remarked.

'Alice is a lovely soul,' Imogen said, reminding herself that this was the view she ought to hold. 'She will be doubly lost now that Arabella and Papa have gone.'

Alice was sitting by the fire in the library when at last the two sisters found her. She was reading a book earnestly, but she looked up as they entered. Her face was pale and it was clear that she was sad and unwell, for her cheeks were marked with tears. Imogen stepped over to her and took her hand gently.

'Do not be sad, Alice. Papa will be back in under a week, and Catherine and I shall do all we can to make you feel comfortable.' Despite her words and tone Imogen still could not believe that the woman before her, scarcely five years her senior, was her father's new bride.

'I wonder if Arabella will see Hamish when she lives in London,' Catherine mused, ignoring her sister's efforts to console Alice.

'I doubt it, Catherine,' Alice replied, grateful to be able to discuss something else. Imogen stepped back, feeling that her manners and comfort were neither needed nor wanted. 'A lady of society does not cross paths with any soldier unless he be an officer.'

'But he is the favourite of Captain Pottinger. Perhaps he shall be moved through the ranks.'

Imogen did not stay to hear any more of the conversation but excused herself and took the tea Anne had promised her up to her room. Already it was getting dark outside and she lit the fire herself from her candle. She opened the top drawer by her bed and read once more through the letter Mr Dermot had left her two months earlier. She was uncertain whether the letter had been the cause of her annoyance and mistrust towards Alice or whether she should have seen it in time but, whatever the reason, Imogen had found that she could not form any understanding with the woman who she found impossible in all ways. She was a sweet natured soul indeed, yet there was a constant thought in Imogen's mind that, behind her dainty and pleasing demeanour, she might be plotting.

Imogen walked over to her dressing table and took out pen and ink and began writing a letter. It was to Hamish, of course, for at Cat's mention of their adopted brother she had realised with shame that she had not yet thanked him for her book. She spilled rather more of her soul into it than she had meant to, for her mind raced and led her hand to form the words without giving her time for careful choosing. Once it was penned she sealed it immediately and carried it downstairs to Anne who assured her that it would be sent the moment she could find someone to take it.

Subsequently the letter remained at Petrovia Lodge for a further four days and, by the time it arrived in London, December was upon the capital. Napoleon had stormed across Europe and, in his audacity, declared a barricade against the British. The war that had simmered below the surface of European politics began to boil over and, as Captain Pottinger had predicted, conflict was only a moment away. Arabella, who had loved her return to London after so many years' absence, began to feel the strain of the impending war bearing down heavily upon her and, each night upon her husband's return, anxiously asked whether he would be leaving for war. They were living in a small house that belonged to the captain, all that his father would offer for, although Arabella and the captain had visited Colonel and Mrs Pottinger, it was no secret that they did not approve of the match. During these days Arabella missed her sisters with an alarming empty feeling inside her that burnt at times. She could not imagine what it would be like when her beloved Roger was eventually forced to go to war, for she should be absolutely alone. For this reason, two days before Christmas, she sought out her mother's cousin, Mr Jenkyns.

It was a cold afternoon when she arrived at his large house, in the district of Chelsea. Despite the onset of the premature night the house seemed to sparkle white, as though it were built entirely of marble. She was assisted down from the carriage by one of the footmen and walked up to the door where she knocked lightly, afraid to make too much noise, for the district was hushed and so much quieter than her own little corner of the city. Indeed, she had travelled some three miles to reach the house although, for the change in appearance, it may have been thirty. The door was opened by a man wearing a formal red coat with gold brocade and a wig upon his head.

'I have come to see my cousin, Mr Jenkyns,' she said simply.

The footman did not speak but stepped back to allow her in. She entered and tried at once to conceal her amazement for she felt that she had walked into a palace. The entrance hall might have contained half of Petrovia Lodge for, as well as being long and wide, it reached three floors in height. She felt overshadowed and suddenly as though she had no place here. She was relieved of her travelling cloak, bonnet and gloves before a different man, but in the same uniform, walked over and bowed his head to her, clearly stating that she should follow him. Arabella did so meekly and they stepped through a doorway and into a room whose size felt at once more familiar to her. There were two men there, one was her cousin, Mr Jenkyns, the other a stranger.

'Why,' Mr Jenkyns began. 'Unless my eyes do lie to me, it is that greatest of beautiful apparitions, my dear cousin, Arabella.'

'Your eyes and your footman,' the other man laughed before bowing his head slightly, his eyes never leaving Arabella's face except to stray and take in the rest of her form. She began to feel uncomfortable under such scrutiny and, upon seeing this, Mr Jenkyns purposefully cleared his throat, awaking his companion from his entranced gaze.

'My dear Miss Tenterchilt, I did not know you were in Town,' he said, gesturing for her to take a seat.

'Indeed, I live here now, cousin, and I am Miss Tenterchilt no more. I am Mrs Pottinger now.'

'Of course. Then both congratulations and envy do I give to the young captain,' Mr Jenkyns announced. 'He has done the world a great injustice in marrying you.'

'Please, cousin,' Arabella said, blushing under his more than gracious words. 'I cannot let you say such things.'

'Would you permit me to say them, Mrs Pottinger?' the stranger asked.

'Why, no.' She glanced at Mr Jenkyns before looking back. 'You are a stranger to me, it would be quite wrong for you to say such things.'

'Well answered,' he laughed, pointing his finger at her as though he was a teacher and she his pupil. 'Dear Jenkyns, please amend the neglect to this social injunction.'

'My manners fail me,' Mr Jenkyns said quietly, whispering almost like the words were intended for his ears only. 'Mrs Pottinger, this is Mr Harrington, MP.'

'And now that we are acquainted,' Mr Harrington said jovially. 'Allow me to say how disappointed I am to find your title is Mrs.'

'Enough,' Mr Jenkyns said firmly. 'Arabella, excuse us for one moment please.' He walked to the door and looked back then to make sure that Mr Harrington was following him. Arabella watched and listened as they closed the door. Outside in the entrance hall she could hear raised voices that echoed from its immense marble floor to its high flat roof. It was impossible to be sure what they were saying only that they were talking on a topic that seemed to excite and exasperate them both. She used this opportunity to take in her surroundings.

It was a long room with wooden panelling down all four walls, only broken by two doors, the window and the fireplace that had a large and merry blaze occupying it. There was a desk piled high with papers in the corner close to the window and a chair to sit at it, but there was little other furniture in the room, save the four high backed leather armchairs that were placed in a semi-circle around the hearth. There was a magnificent red carpet that ran through the centre of the room with the smallest hint of green and gold flecked through it. Around its edge were polished wooden floorboards, so startlingly different to the entrance hall and yet equally as striking.

Mr Jenkyns entered and walked over to sit down in one of the other armchairs. His feet made a purposeful noise as he stepped and Arabella felt like she was about to take a punishment for something. And yet when he spoke his voice was soft and calming and she listened with grateful ears.

'I apologise for Mr Harrington's behaviour, Mrs Pottinger. He has chosen to leave.'

'Thank you, Mr Jenkyns,' Arabella replied with honest thanks as she realised why the two men had spoken so forcefully in the hall.

'Now, my dear Arabella, how do you find married life?'

'Very pleasing,' she replied. 'Although in truth I know not why I was encouraged to marry a military man, for all I can think of in the long days that he is gone is how soon he will have to leave to go to war.'

'War is imminent, Mrs Pottinger,' Mr Jenkyns replied, sounding strangely proud, and his voice adopted a tone that suggested he felt he was addressing far more people that just herself.

'And that is why I must cherish the moments we have now.'

'Indeed, you must,' he replied in a manner so meek that Arabella was surprised, for he seemed different to the jovial but cutting person he had been at their spring party. 'I am so pleased that you sought me out. As you are in Town and have now made your presence known to me, I will have to invite you and Captain Pottinger to share my Christmas, such as it is.'

'Oh, Mr Jenkyns,' Arabella began, both delighted and embarrassed, for it had not been the purpose of her visit. 'That is not why I called on you.'

'My dear cousin,' Mr Jenkyns said with a laugh. 'If I felt you had come for that purpose you may be assured I should not have invited you. Come, you must tell the dear Colonel and Mrs Pottinger to attend also.'

'Roger's sister, Rose, shall be-'

'Invite her too,' Mr Jenkyns announced and laughed. 'Come, Mrs Pottinger, Christmas will be so much more acceptable with a host of people to share it with. And you may rest assured that our mutual acquaintance, Mr Harrington, shall not be attending.'

They spoke at great length on everything and yet little of note. Arabella informed him of all that had happened since her mother's death; of her father's new wife; of the gypsies; of Mr Dermot saving Imogen from the river and finally of her own quiet wedding to her dearest Captain Pottinger. In return Mr Jenkyns was the perfect host, giving her food and wine, answering any statement left open and showering her and her sisters with more praise than Arabella had ever hoped for. The evening was full and deep when at last Arabella remembered herself and started from her chair.

'I must go,' she said quickly. 'I have surely lost track of time and now the night is complete.'

'You cannot go out alone, Mrs Pottinger.' Mr Jenkyns rose to his feet. 'Come, Arabella, allow me to escort you home. It will be far quicker to take my carriage.'

Arabella looked on the point of arguing before she realised the sense in what he was saying. 'But we must be quick, Mr Jenkyns, I have never been absent on my husband's return before.'

'When you tell him that he is invited to spend Christmas here, I am certain he will forgive your neglect.'

Mr Jenkyns had the groom ready his carriage and assisted Arabella up into it himself before climbing up after her. They talked excitedly of Christmas and the excitements and distractions of Town. Mr Jenkyns promised to take Arabella on a tour of the London parks when the winter gave way to spring and to introduce the family to some of the better circles of society.

'Why would you do all this for me, Mr Jenkyns?' she asked as they stopped outside her modest little house.

'My dear Mrs Pottinger,' he said softly. 'I loved your mother, my cousin, greatly. She was like an elder sister to me. I hope that my love of you will be doing right by her. We are family, Arabella, and that is something to cherish.'

Mr Jenkyns helped her out of the carriage and walked her to the foot of the steps that led up to the front door. She walked up alone and opened it, not looking back once. The narrow hallway was dark, too dark to make out any obstacles that may have been waiting there, but there was a thin sliver of firelight coming from beneath the living room door. She carefully shuffled over to it and opened the door. At once the light and the warmth struck her and she hurriedly and appreciatively removed her hat and cloak. Captain Pottinger was sitting in one of the two armchairs that were in front of the fire, only visible as an arm and hand that held a crystal glass of brandy.

'What are we celebrating, Captain?' Arabella asked putting her outdoor garments on the dark wooden sideboard. She walked over and sat opposite him, but his eyes remained fixed on the fire. 'Roger?' She still received no answer and she began to feel uncomfortable, sensing that it was her initial absence that had resulted in this. 'Where is Chloe?' she continued, rising to her feet and collecting her hat and cloak. 'I could not see anything when I came in. Usually she has a lamp lit at this hour.'

'What hour is it?'

She jumped at the sound of another voice in the room besides her own, for it did not sound like her husband. 'I would imagine it must be seven o'clock.'

'I missed you when I came in. I got so used to being alone before we were married, I never thought on how saddening it is.'

He did not ask where she had been, she realised, but all the same she felt compelled to tell him. 'We have been invited for Christmas to Mr Jenkyns' house in Chelsea. You, me, your sister and your parents.'

'That is very kind of Mr Jenkyns,' Captain Pottinger replied, and with each word he began to sound more and more like himself. 'Especially as he barely knows me or my family.'

'Ah, but you are his family now,' Arabella replied happily. 'Were you terribly angry that I was not here when you returned?'

'Angry?' Captain Pottinger laughed. 'No. Sad and disappointed, but never angry.'

Arabella walked over and kissed his forehead. 'I would rather you were angry. Where is Chloe?'

'She was unwell. I suggested she went to bed.'

'Does she need a doctor?'

'No, she needs to sleep. She is more fatigued than any soldier I ever met and just needed to rest a while.' He rose to his feet and placed the brandy glass on the mantelshelf. 'Let me hang up your hat and cloak.'

'Thank you,' she whispered. 'Has something happened?' she asked quickly. 'Are you protecting me in your silence?'

'It is Christmastide,' he replied kissing her gently. 'The only time in the year when a man may hold his own secrets and counsel.'

The Pottingers spent a merry Christmas in the house and company of Mr Jenkyns who excelled in his role as a host. They spent the day together as Christmas should be spent, in fun and frivolities, and pleasure in the company of others. By contrast, scarcely ten miles away Hamish spent a lonely Christmas. It was not for a lack of people, indeed there were plenty of them around, but they were all like strangers to him. As a naturally self-contained man he had struggled to adapt to his new post as sergeant major, but he had won over the respect of those both above and below him in the ranks. He knew from the letter he now held in his hand that Arabella and his captain had now been married and that the former Miss Tenterchilt was living here in London. He had hoped to have met her, or just have seen her, but he had been disappointed in this.

Christmas at the Tenterchilt household in his own dear Scotland had been a time of unsurpassed gaiety and merriment, for the family had always made it so. Now as he sat at a desk in a tiny room listening to drunken revelry outside in the hall, he picked up a pen and flicked open the inkwell. His letters were peculiar and spiky, having waited so long to learn to write and, as he compared them to Imogen's, he felt a little ashamed.

'My dear Imogen,' he read aloud as he wrote, trying to focus on what he was writing and ignore the noise from outside. 'I am writing to you all on this most reverend day, wishing you to know that you never stray from my thoughts. I have not spoken to Mr Dermot in some time, but am pleased that he delivered the gift for you. Scott appears to be both loved and hated here in the capital, but for the most part I believe the factions are too anxious concerning his next move. One day I hope to be viewed as an individual and not solely as a Scotsman. We have received orders that we will be partaking in war on the continent throughout the next year, although I am hopeful that our pride will not cause us to act rashly. I have seen too many die. Forgive my candid writing, I beg you. I find myself writing to you as I would speak, and discussing all that I have and know. I do sincerely hope that Mr Dermot outlined my concerns for you and was not mysterious and vague as the man so often seems to be. I still have not encountered Mrs Pottinger, although the change in the captain seems great. I wish you all the happiest and most bountiful New Year. Your friend, Hamish.'

As he signed the letter off he looked down at the white bands that were stitched on the sleeve of his coat. One day he hoped that his sacrifice and service to this army would pay off, that he would obtain that which joining the army had promised him, but for now it seemed remote and distant.

Whatever power Hamish possessed with his writings seemed to find their fruit for, as 1807 dawned upon the family, it was met with health and prosperity, and indeed it seemed set to be the greatest year for the Tenterchilt family. Despite a brief skirmish on the continent in January, Napoleon seemed intent on the East and by February Captain Pottinger's company of men had returned to England with barely any losses. The Emperor's invasion of Russia allowed for a brief respite of peace for the company that lasted through much of the first half of the year.

The only thing of note through the long winter in Petrovia Lodge was the arrival of two people, a boy and a girl. As March took hold in the valley it was to the arrival of Doctor Fotherby who had been sent for from London. He was an intriguing gentleman, very tall and terribly thin so that he looked as though he was the one in need of a doctor as opposed to being the doctor himself. He carried the air of a military gentleman, and there was no wonder for he had been an apprentice surgeon at the time Major Tenterchilt had received his debilitating leg wound, and it had been he who had saved the leg from amputation with such newly discussed and promoted care and medication. From that moment fourteen years ago, Major Tenterchilt had trusted no one else within the medical profession, and indeed he believed his first wife would still have been living if Doctor Fotherby had treated her. Catherine and Imogen, however, were unsure if their father truly wished their mother were still alive for he seemed far happier and more content in Alice's company.

So, throughout the month of March, Doctor Fotherby was a guest in the house of the Tenterchilts, having left his London hospital to care for Alice Tenterchilt around the birth. Initially Penny had seemed indignant that a man should be called to assist the midwife but, being a true servant, held her silence.

Imogen and Catherine kept their father company downstairs and unsuccessfully encouraged him to think of other things, while the maids and the midwife tended Alice, and Doctor Fotherby remained by the door to the lying-in room. When, after hours of waiting, there was finally the sound of footsteps on the stairs, the two sisters were as eager as their father to discover the news. Penny entered, scrubbing her hands down the apron she wore and, before the poor maid could say anything, the family demanded updates on the wellbeing of both mother and child.

'All is well. Now,' Penny said at last when she had managed to maintain a calm. 'You may go up.'

Major Tenterchilt hurried up the stairs, followed closely by Imogen and Catherine. Anne was standing by the door and smiled in such a warm and comforting way that the two sisters instantly felt better, whilst their father burst into the room and looked at the scene before him. Alice was lying asleep in the centre of the bed whilst on either side of her were two tightly wrapped bundles that occasionally gurgled and wriggled within their swaddled blankets. Doctor Fotherby shook the major's hand, a genuine smile on his face.

'Congratulations, Major Tenterchilt,' he said with great meaning. 'Mrs Tenterchilt gave birth to twins, a boy and a girl.'

'A son?' he muttered and, despite the happy occasion, Imogen felt her heart sink for a moment as she recalled what Mr Dermot had said to her in the autumn. 'Which is the boy?'

Doctor Fotherby handed him the baby that had been on Alice's right hand side and Imogen glanced across at Catherine but she seemed oblivious to all the threat that the new child presented to their future security. Instead, as Doctor Fotherby handed her new baby sister to her, Imogen saw a side to Catherine she had not known before. She cooed and stroked the cheek of the tiny infant in a manner so unlike her usual approach that Imogen abandoned her worry and saw that these new arrivals could fit in perfectly, and bring out the best in the current members of their family.

Alice was an adoring mother to the children, anxious that everything should be perfect and they should never be alone. Doctor Fotherby remained a further nine days to ensure the safety of mother and children and in that time he regaled the family with tales of his exploits in India, drawing pictures of such creatures as Imogen and Catherine had only heard tell of. Imogen he called 'Eastern Sunrise' and Catherine 'Sleeping Tiger', but when he and the major talked his poetic language vanished and they discussed that topic that occupied men's minds constantly: war. Doctor Fotherby, who had left the army after giving defensive evidence at the court martial of a man who was later shot, was considering entering once again, but unsure that he would be accepted following the manner of his departure.

'Have you thought of the Navy?' Major Tenterchilt asked. 'They are always searching for men and have seen far more active service these last few years.'

'In truth I find London oppressive after the freedom of the army.'

'Freedom in the army?' the major laughed.

'I saw lands that I wish to return to, I have no interest in cities and the choking air that surrounds them.'

'Then what of the East India Company?'

'That, I could foresee.' Doctor Fotherby took a sip of sherry and frowned for a moment. 'Do you ever think back on the army and wish that it still employed you?'

'I did,' Major Tenterchilt confided after a moment. 'But if it had not been for your skill it would be the world and not just the army I would now be absent from. You were too young to leave.'

'Ah,' Doctor Fotherby said loudly as Imogen entered with her new sister. 'Who have you with you today, Eastern Sunrise?'

'The Lady Beatrice,' Imogen announced and walked over to the two of them handing the child to Doctor Fotherby as her father seemed unwilling to take his new daughter. Imogen and Alice shared a concern at how preoccupied Major Tenterchilt was with his son and how uninterested he was in baby Beatrice.

The night before Doctor Fotherby intended to leave she sought him to discuss such issues but she could find no sign of him in the house. She walked down to the kitchen and was startled to find that the back door had been left off the latch. She was on the verge of locking it when she heard giggling laughter from outside. She opened the door and followed both sound and torchlight to the stables. The sight before her eyes was far from anything that she had expected.

Catherine was dressed once again in britches and was holding a long thin sword, which, at this moment was lowered. However she and Doctor Fotherby continued to engage in swordplay up and down the length of the stable corridor. The horses occasionally whinnied or snorted loudly but for the most part they seemed happy of the company. Imogen, wishing to both conclude the unladylike behaviour of her sister and make her presence known, for she did not wish to be seen skulking in the shadows, cleared her throat purposefully. It may have been that the doctor had superior hearing to her sister, or perhaps that Catherine had become used to ignoring such gestures, but Doctor Fotherby lowered the thin blade he carried whilst Catherine continued, striking him on the left forearm. Imogen gasped and rushed forward, while Catherine dropped the sword and clasped the doctor's hand.

'I think that Sleeping Tiger has just awoken,' the doctor laughed and both girls looked at him as though they thought that he was mad.

'You are not hurt?' Imogen asked sharing an anxious glance with Catherine.

Doctor Fotherby rolled up his sleeve and looked down at his arm, which was cut only slightly, although bruising already covered much of it. 'I have suffered worse in the past,' he replied and picked up Catherine's sword by the blade. 'Even the finest soldiers do not practise with freshly sharpened swords.' Catherine looked down at it, slightly disappointed for a moment. 'I know that is your father's sword and I know, too, that he has not used it in many years.'

'But what if you had struck me?' she asked.

'But I did not.'

Catherine took her father's sword from the doctor and walked away, feeling that in some way she had been cheated out of a fair fight. Imogen watched her go and sighed, shaking her head.

'Forgive my sister, Doctor Fotherby,' she said, not turning to face him. 'She is the son my mother never had.'

'But now your father has.'

'Did you know that was why I came to find you?'

'Even a blind man can see where your father's interests lie, and it is not in little Beatrice.'

'I am concerned,' she said turning to face him. His pale face stared back at her with a blank expression. 'What can I do to retain any order of affection in the household?'

'Order of affection?' the doctor repeated as though the very notion was unthinkable. 'You cannot make people love or hate each other. Although at times we all wish we could.'

'But it is not right that Beatrice should be neglected and starved of love because she was born at the same hour as her brother and fate favoured him with the better sex.'

'No,' Doctor Fotherby replied. 'But she will have you and Cat, and Mrs Tenterchilt too. She will not be starved of love, as you say.'

'Of course. You are right, Doctor,' she replied and walked from the stable without a further word. She knew that he was right, that Baby Beatrice would have a very good start in life, but it was not solely the injustice that offended her, it was the manner in which Doctor Fotherby had addressed her.

For his own part, Doctor Fotherby knew far more of the cruelties of love than Imogen had ever encountered. He picked up his sword and stood for some time regarding with pain the past that he had sought to forget and abandon. Seven years ago, on his departure from the army, there had been more at stake than one man's life. There had also been the consideration of the convicted man's daughter and the heart of the young army surgeon who sought to marry her. Doctor Fotherby knew that Sergeant Simmons had been dehydrated and that had caused the momentary madness that had resulted a fit of rage and the striking of an officer. But Sergeant Simmons had been shot for the offence and Doctor Fotherby's family had forbidden him from courting the daughter of a disgraced man. If Miss Simmons had been as heartbroken as the doctor, she showed it in a perplexing manner for, within the year, she had been married to another, whilst Doctor Fotherby resigned his post and began tending the wounded in London.

Doctor Fotherby was gone by the time Imogen and Catherine rose the next morning. If he had shared any words with their father involving the incident last night then the major did not mention it. Life was to return back to its beautiful and steady pace. Winter surrendered to spring and the gardens at Petrovia Lodge, though limited, returned to their summer radiance. Imogen walked out once more to the orangery and sat in the wicker chairs with Beatrice on her knee. She was a large baby and sat comfortably in the crook of Imogen's arm as she read to her the poems of Walter Scott, the book now so well read that the spine was hanging loose. This was of far greater interest to Beatrice who tried to catch it but it was always a little too far from her reach. After concluding her reading of Hellvelyn, Imogen set the book down on the table and picked up Beatrice so that she was facing her.

'That book is from your other brother, Beatrice. He is called Hamish, and I know that he would love you greatly if he should ever meet you.'

Of course Beatrice did not understand her words. A child of only three months in age can understand nothing except a tone, but Imogen enjoyed talking to her, in rather the same way that she enjoyed writing her journal.

'He is a brave soldier now and works with Captain Pottinger, your brother-in-law.' She looked up as Alice entered carrying Josiah, Beatrice's twin.

'I do not believe she shall ever meet her eldest sister,' Alice sighed as she sat opposite Imogen at the table. 'I begged the major to take me to London but he is more than reluctant.'

'We have no house there,' Imogen explained. 'With every visit he is only reminded of his disasters in gambling. Mama would never permit him to even shake dice after that.'

'That seems a little unfair. It is a man's prerogative.'

'In most situations she would have agreed with you, but Papa only came to the estate by way of marrying Mama.'

'I see,' Alice whispered quietly. 'All the same, I miss all my friends in Town terribly and should like to see them.'

'He will relent soon. If you offer him the chance to return and see

Arabella and his good friend the colonel, he will not be able to resist. In truth, however, I do not think that Beatrice and Josiah will be up to the journey.'

'Good heavens,' Alice laughed. 'I cannot take infants into London society. They shall be staying here.'

Imogen forced her lips to smile but she felt terribly disillusioned. In the months passing from the wedding she had assured herself once more that Mr Dermot and Hamish had been incorrect in their judgement of Mrs Tenterchilt, but now she received another blow against her faith in the woman before her.

'It would be a shame if they never met dear Arabella. Or Hamish.'

'Do not talk to her of Private Gordon.'

'He is a sergeant major, now,' Imogen pointed out.

'Whatever rank or post he holds, he is nothing to my children.' Alice sighed heavily. 'He sought in every way possible to divide the major and myself, and has failed on all counts. I shall not have my daughter call any such man her brother.'

Imogen rose to her feet and placed Beatrice down. 'If what you say is indeed the case, then she had better not call me her sister. I shall tell you, Alice, for I see no benefit in trying to save the feelings of one so objectionable as yourself, that Hamish was not the only person who had concerns or objections to your marriage to Papa. I shall make sure that none of my mother's money reaches you, for my mother loved Hamish as a son and embraced an understanding and acceptance of all people. You are solely a society woman, and I think you deserve Petrovia Lodge as little as it deserves you.'

Alice did not answer. Indeed, after such a forceful outburst it was impossible to find the words to say, besides which Imogen had left the orangery before Alice could acknowledge what had just happened.

Imogen, whose active mind never slept, began to understand what Mr Dermot had meant, why Hamish had fallen from favour with her father and, above all, she saw the need to protect her mother's estate or in the least what could be saved of it. To that end as they silently sat around the supper table she began talking.

'Papa,' she said in a voice equally as sweet as Alice's. 'Alice tells me that she greatly misses London, and I know that Arabella misses you. Why do you not go down there and see her?' Alice looked across at her, sensing that her words were driven by something other than good will. 'All Arabella writes of are her trips through parks with Mama's cousin, Mr Jenkyns, and her ghastly in-laws. She and the captain would welcome your company.'

'I could not part Alice from her children,' the major said, unaware of the politics that had fuelled this conversation.

'I will oversee Josiah's and Beatrice's wellbeing. They shall be well cared for.' Imogen smiled across at Alice in what she hoped was a convincing manner. 'Besides, I have spent this afternoon writing letters, and Arabella will be expecting you.'

She had, indeed, spent the afternoon writing letters, however the one to Arabella was only one of them. She had written also to Mr Dermot, asking him whether there was anything that could be done to postpone the inheritance left by the late Mrs Tenterchilt to the major, and she had written to Hamish sharing her burden of confusion and misgivings over her father's choice of wife. To Arabella, she had suggested she meet up with Hamish and share whatever news he had with their father on his next, upcoming, trip to London. She had no intention of allowing every aspect of life to pass her by for, although she had resigned to the idea of being an old maid, the thought of being robbed and left as a poor old maid was beyond her tolerance.

'Then yes,' Major Tenterchilt announced in a pleased manner. 'We will travel down to London in July. That allows us a week to prepare, and a week for your letter to reach Arabella.'

So whilst preparations went underway at Petrovia Lodge, they also began in the capital as Arabella and Captain Pottinger prepared for the long anticipated visit of Major and Mrs Tenterchilt. Upon Imogen's request, although remaining truly ignorant to her younger sister's motive, she asked her husband if they may host Sergeant Major Gordon for a meal.

'It is a little improper and irregular,' Captain Pottinger replied. 'A captain should not hold a social alliance with a man without a commission.'

'But you like Sergeant Major Gordon,' Arabella pleaded. 'Hamish is a dear friend and I cannot bear the thought that he may embark to war without having seen me as your wife. Imogen writes that he both loves and admires you as his leader.'

Captain Pottinger, having a heart altogether too generous for rules and social stigma, smiled across at her. 'Of course he will be invited if that is what you wish. But I beseech you, my love, do not mention this engagement to my parents. I fear it may be the final disregard to rules that the colonel is waiting for. I cannot afford to lose my inheritance.'

'Of course,' Arabella answered with a smile. 'Of course I will not tell them.'

The first day in July, which fell upon a Wednesday, found Hamish standing in the street outside the house that belonged to Captain and Mrs Pottinger. He was wearing his uniform, for beside this he had no suitable clothes, unable to afford the prices of the London tailors and unwilling to attend an invitation without due care and attention to his dress. How many times he walked up the steps only to walk back down them once more, he could not count. Whatever courage for such a dinner drove him forward was constantly beaten by the sense of nervous propriety that made him walk away. Finally the door was opened by Chloe, the maid, who tilted her head to one side and looked levelly across at the man who stood halfway up the steps.

'For twenty minutes now you have paced those steps. I hope you are building yourself an appetite.'

'Twenty minutes?' Hamish asked, his thick heavy accent causing Chloe's eyebrows to arch. 'It has felt like hours.'

Chloe stood back and allowed Hamish to enter. He pulled off his hat and walked into the hallway waiting for the maid to open the door to the living room. When at last she did, he drew in a deep breath and prepared himself with a bittersweet sense of love and duty before stepping in. It had been over a year since Hamish had seen Arabella, since his eyes had rested upon that most heavenly of visions that mortals may view, and in that time he had sought comfort in the knowledge that she was both loved and provided for by a truly chivalrous man. For Imogen had declared truthfully that Sergeant Major Gordon held Captain Pottinger in the highest of regard. But it could not protect him from that moment of envy as his gaze fell upon Arabella and the officer sitting together to welcome him. For seven years, from that first night when Hamish had been a condemned man and Arabella had saved him, he had loved the former Miss Tenterchilt with all that he was. But even that was not enough for such a divine figure.

'Hamish,' Arabella said, leaping to her feet and stepping over to him. 'Tell me you are well.'

'I am well, Mrs Pottinger, and I see that married life suits you remarkably well.'

'That is undoubtedly my blessed choice of husband,' she laughed. She guided Hamish to sit down upon the spare chair that had been brought from the bedroom upstairs to cater for their guest. 'Imogen says that Papa is coming to London shortly. You must see him while he is here.'

'Major Tenterchilt and I have a reconciliation to form before we meet in the company of ladies.' Hamish sat on the edge of the seat and smiled at his hosts. 'I am obliged to find words to say, but in truth I can summon none to mind.'

'Sergeant Major Gordon,' her husband began. 'You are here on a social call, let us not simply discuss weather and idle pleasantries. Mrs Pottinger wishes to be regaled with stories of your valour in our trips abroad, but I pray you, speak nothing of your captain.'

'Valour?' Hamish choked on the word. 'I show no valour in war, only a will and a wish to survive.'

'And so he does,' Captain Pottinger laughed. 'He fights with a drive unlike any other I have known. If fighting and winning was ever in a man's blood then it surely courses your veins, Sergeant Major.'

Hamish bowed his head, feeling that this was a compliment, but all he could see were the faces of those men he had seen fall, and he rubbed his eyes to try and be rid of the image.

'Do we tire you so much?' Arabella asked.

'No,' Hamish said quickly. 'I, too, heard from Imogen recently,' he continued, changing the subject beyond the boundaries of war. The conversation did not revert back to conflict for the evening and they talked and laughed over times at Petrovia Lodge and reminiscing even deeper into history, although Hamish gave away nothing about his life before arriving at the lodge.

Finally, as the night darkened, Hamish rose. 'Thank you for the meal and the company,' he said softly, fastening and straightening the red coat that he wore.

'Will you come and see Papa?' Arabella asked and she took his hand in a desperate pleading.

'How can I refuse you with such a plea?' He looked across at the captain. 'If it is what will make you happy, of course I will do it.'

He picked up his hat and walked from the house in a peculiar daze. He had known of course that it would be different now that Arabella had married but he had convinced himself that she would have changed. To have seen her now and found that the only change that had happened was in favour of her beauty and gentleness, he felt only more lovelorn and helpless than ever. His walk back to the barracks was with several wrong turns and involuntary detours before he finally found his shared room and lay down on the hard bed, ignoring all of the other people in the room. His thoughts were all the company he needed.

CHAPTER SIX
Wednesday 8th July 1807

Whatever the future held in store for Hamish and Captain Pottinger it was certain to involve war for within the fortnight Napoleon had formed an alliance with both Prussia and Russia and suddenly his ludicrous threat of a continental blockade became reality. But before both soldiers lay an obstacle that, at present, seemed to pose a far greater challenge. The arrival of Major and Mrs Tenterchilt in London caused great celebrations amongst their friends. No expense was spared by Colonel Pottinger who, despite a general lack of manners, was still gracious enough to remember that the major had saved his life in the same incident that had caused his premature retirement.

'I wish I was going with you,' Major Tenterchilt expressed at the dining table the first night of their arrival. 'Nothing can beat the adventures of army exploits. You are fortunate, sir, to have your health and that of your son to bear arms in this war. I shall have young Josiah in the army the moment he can fight.'

'But you have a beautiful young wife, now,' Mrs Pottinger remarked. 'She may not wish to see war.'

Captain Pottinger looked at his mother before glancing at Arabella who continued to carry a forced smile. 'How are the two children?' he asked, eager to turn away from the previous subject for the sake of his wife. 'Josiah and Beatrice, is it not?'

'Indeed,' Alice replied, smiling with a sense of pride. 'They were both well when we left Petrovia Lodge, and are in the best of care.'

'Imogen, then,' Arabella laughed. 'No one has ever been better with children than Imogen.'

'Miss Tenterchilt, indeed,' Alice replied. The reluctance to call Imogen by name was noted by all present at the table and there was a silence in the air that no amount of quick thinking from the captain could fill. 'When will you next be at Petrovia, Arabella?' Mrs Tenterchilt continued, seeing that her words had delivered their point succinctly. 'I would love for you to meet your new brother and sister.'

'Indeed, I hope to return and visit when dear Captain Pottinger is free from the promise of war. I must confess that I cannot imagine such a time at present.'

'I pray you will do better at being an officer's wife than your mother,' Mrs Pottinger remarked coolly.

'Enough!' Captain Pottinger said, slamming his fist down on the table and rising to his feet. 'As my wife has far more manners than you, madam, I shall say on her behalf that she is a far greater officer's wife than you will ever be. Come, Arabella,' he said offering his hand down to his wife who took it and stood beside him. 'I do not believe we are welcome here, and in truth I would not spend a minute longer in this house by choice.'

Arabella followed her husband from a room that was both stunned and shamed into silence. It was with mixed emotions that the two of them walked through the London streets, Arabella clinging to the captain's arm. Neither spoke until they had closed their own front door and Arabella began sobbing onto her husband's chest while he held her tightly to him.

'Please find it in your heart to forgive my mother,' he said softly, uncertain whether the words carried a greater weight for his wife or himself. 'She is inexcusable each time she opens her mouth.'

'Was she right?' Arabella asked, looking into Captain Pottinger's eyes. 'Was my mother a bad wife to my father? For he made no attempt to correct her.'

'I did not have the pleasure of meeting your mother except on a few occasions, but I never saw anything to suggest she was anything but loyal to your father.'

Arabella did not make an effort to see her father following this encounter. His stay in London was to be dominated by Colonel and Mrs Pottinger. Arabella made a conscious effort to avoid discussing anything relating to them with her husband, although his sister Rose became one of her truest friends. And she needed her friendship for it was scarcely a week later on the fourteenth day of July, the anniversary of that most terrible day in French history eighteen years earlier, that Captain Roger Pottinger returned with the news that she had long been dreading.

'We are called to war, my dear,' he said softly as they sat together by the empty fireplace. 'Our company is called out to travel to the continent and fight.'

Arabella was silent and studied her hands. She could find no words to express what she felt, the sadness, the fear, the loneliness. She forced her gaze to meet with her husband's, reminding herself that it was far worse for him than it was for her.

'When will you have to leave?' she asked, her voice suddenly hoarse.

'No time at all. We leave on Friday.'

'But today is Tuesday. You will have no time to be made ready.'

'Be that as it may, my dear, Friday we leave.'

She stepped over to sit at his feet, gripping his hands in her own. 'You told me of that post the London Gazette announced, a French master at the Military College. Could you not do that? Great Marlow seems to have so much more appeal than France.'

'I hold a commission, my dear, I cannot sell it on to take a job teaching people to do what I should be doing.'

Arabella nodded and laid her head on his lap, crying silently onto his pale trousers. He stroked her head in a soothing manner and found that he felt happier in the action. A peace grew within him that he had thought would be impossible to ever know.

'I shall ask my sister to visit,' he said at last. 'Rose is as fond of you as she is her own brother.'

'Her company will be most welcome. Indeed, any distraction from my thoughts and worries will be received with thanks. Do you not wish me to accompany you to Europe?'

'We are to take no women.' He swallowed hard before continuing. 'It is a mission of intelligence and one that I cannot foresee will last long enough to make your travelling worth the while.'

'Then you will be back soon?' She looked up at him.

'I hope to be. Before the autumn if luck favours us.'

This news was of great comfort to Arabella and, although she realised that he was uncertain about the nature of the mission, she refused to allow his doubt to cause further fear. Instead she spent their remaining time together being as perfect and as strong as she could, crying only when he was away from the house and filling her thoughts with memories of the happy times they had shared since their marriage in November. When Friday dawned it was to a set face of bravery and Arabella felt the clenching feeling in her stomach that she may be saying farewell forever to her husband.

'I am proud that you are going to war,' she said softly as they stood in the hallway.

'I am not afraid of the war, I am not afraid of fighting. I am afraid of leaving you and knowing that I may never set my eyes upon you this side of death.'

'I know you will,' she replied with certainty, embracing him with a desperate prayer for his safety. 'Hamish will protect you, I know it. Promise me you will protect him.'

'I do swear to always protect your brother.'

Arabella stepped out of the door and watched numbly as the captain's carriage departed. She saw no one else, though the streets were crowded, but stared after the carriage as seconds turned to minutes before Chloe stepped over to her and took her hand.

'Come inside, ma'am,' she said gently. 'I think you need some food.'

'Indeed,' Arabella answered, feeling faint with sorrow. 'I think I do.'

Arabella's assumption that the company travelled to France was a view that was held by many, for it was the French they went to fight. None spared a thought for the city of Stralsund on the southern Baltic coast but, as allies to the Swedes who had been withstanding a French siege for much of the year, Captain Pottinger had been ordered to offer British aid. It was hoped that a small company would be sufficient to carry a message of support, for a substantial fleet of British ships were travelling north to assist against the French.

Pottinger's company was to be landed in Putgarten and make the day long march to the city in as much secrecy as could be managed. Upon their arrival at the town of Rambin, some seven miles from the besieged city, Captain Pottinger was to relay his intelligence to an officer of the Swedish king's army. Upon delivery of the information, the company was to return back to a ship that would remain anchored far enough north to escape sight. It was a simple plan that required only fortune to take their side. His company consisted of forty six men, enough to show a resilient use of firepower, whilst being able to pass with comparative ease as a regiment never could. The sea crossing took almost a week before at last Prussia came into view and, with heavy hearts, Pottinger's company prepared to be taken ashore.

Life in Britain continued, oblivious to the activities of war, save for the heavily weighted reviews of British conquest in the Iberian Peninsula. In Petrovia Lodge all remained ignorant of the departure to Prussia until the arrival of a letter written to Imogen. She had come to recognise the handwriting now, and yearned for each new letter to make an appearance. She missed Hamish terribly, and longed for their late night conversations and lessons, knowing that they would never again come to pass. Now, as Anne brought the letter to her, she, Penny and Catherine all gathered around eagerly to find out what Hamish had written.

'My dear Imogen,' she began reading, shuffling Beatrice so that she was resting on her shoulder. 'I trust this letter finds you and the inhabitants of my beloved Petrovia Lodge well. I was invited to call on Captain and Mrs Pottinger and am called to remark on how well and happy they both looked. We talked at length about you all and the happy times we shared. This letter, however, is-' she stopped and was met by three pairs of eyes staring straight at her.

'What is it?' Catherine asked. 'Is it Papa? Is he taken ill? Or Mish?'

Imogen stammered a moment before shaking her head. 'No, Papa is well, although Hamish says that he will be unable to see him on his visit to London.'

'Why ever not?' Catherine asked.

'Because Mish has gone to war.' Imogen folded the letter and looked from the three women before her to the little boy in Catherine's arms. 'Do not become a soldier, Josiah,' she whispered. 'It is too much to bear for we who are left behind.'

Life at the lodge seemed to become overshadowed by news of the company's departure. Catherine vanished for hours at a time and all that could be heard of her was the occasional sound of metal striking the wall if she became careless or too impassioned, although the cause of her sullen disappointment was not the same as Imogen's own.

'It is not fair,' Catherine said, throwing a stone into the river as they walked along its bank. 'Why may they go to war and fight for their country when I may not? They have not stronger wills or greater ability.'

'They are men, Cat. You and I have no business in war, except to pray for their safe return.'

'Then what do we have business in?' Catherine looked at her sister, awaiting her reply.

Imogen sat down against one of the tree trunks and watched the rushing water with a slight smile. 'Would you truly wish to swap this for a battlefield red with blood? We are the fortunate sex, Cat. We have only to watch and wait for them to return.'

'But watching and waiting is so much harder than being out there and fighting.'

Imogen had no answer to Cat's argument. She was beginning to suspect that her younger sister was right, and that their situation was perhaps less desirable than having to fight. She looked across the river to the gypsy encampment and felt a void within her. Petrovia Lodge was all she had known save distant memories of their life before and occasional visits to some of the centres of socicty such as Perth and Edinburgh. Even the gypsies had a truer knowledge of the world beyond and it was knowledge that Imogen sought beyond all else.

'One day I will stand and fight,' Catherine said firmly. 'And I shall travel the globe in defence of my country.'

'I do not think your country will approve or appreciate such a gesture.'

'I can imagine nothing more glorious,' Catherine continued, ignoring Imogen's remark.

'I wonder what poor Arabella is doing, and how she is coping with the captain's departure.'

Catherine fell silent as she considered this, and together the two of them watched the water flowing down the little stream, imagining the great expanse of water that separated the girls from the soldiers who meant so much to them.

Like her sisters, Arabella's thoughts lay on the Prussian coast and, despite the company of Miss Pottinger and their trips into society, she thought of nothing but her husband. A week after Captain Pottinger had departed found an unexpected and unannounced guest at her door. She and Rose were sitting close to the window of the dining room, for it had superior light, stitching their embroidery, when Chloe walked in.

'What is it?' Arabella asked seeing the look of disapproval on her maid's face, for indeed Chloe was incapable of hiding her feelings.

'There is a visitor who is insistent upon seeing you and will not wait.'

Arabella rose to her feet and Rose followed her example as the visitor entered the room. 'Papa,' Arabella muttered. 'I did not expect you.'

'My dear daughter,' he began.

'Why are you here? You have shamed me, and Mama's memory. Have you not wrought me enough pain?'

'I fear I have wrought more than you know,' Major Tenterchilt replied softly. 'I did not mean the colonel to send his son to Prussia.'

'Prussia?' Rose asked. 'But the war is in France and Spain.'

'The war is across Europe,' the major replied.

'The colonel sent his only son away to war?' Arabella felt as confused as she looked and sounded. 'Why?'

'Spite for spite,' came the unwelcome reply. 'I am to leave tomorrow, my dearest Arabella, and I do not expect to be welcomed to London for some time.'

'What has happened, Papa?'

'I have made a terrible mistake, Arabella.'

'Sit down, Papa,' Arabella said softly, helping her father to a seat. Any anger or malice that she felt at his lack of defence in her mother's honour had melted away and she sat with him while Rose asked Chloe to make some tea for their guest.

'I am leaving, Arabella,' he said again. And he would say nothing else until he left in a dazed state after taking only a sip of tea and leaving the cake untouched. Arabella watched him limp down the street with the strangest of feelings, sensing that this second departure was almost as hard as the first.

'I have never seen him so,' she explained to Rose as they walked through the park the next day. 'He is always so certain of himself.'

'My parents are more than capable of sowing doubts in the most set of minds.' There was an acceptance in her voice that spoke of a bygone loss. 'But to send Roger off! If I had thought a little more about it, I should have worked it out.'

'How so?' Arabella asked sitting down by a tree before Rose helped her to her feet once more and led her to a seat.

'You are in London now,' she pointed out. 'It was very odd that the war continued in the same strength and pattern and yet within a fortnight of offending Father, Roger's company is sent out.'

'I swear I do not understand the minds of military men.'

'Do not swear,' Rose said absentmindedly. 'How far with this prolonged punishment must Father go before he sees it is too late to undo things?'

There was no answer to Rose's question, and indeed she expected none. She had only become close to her brother in the last few years when they had become adults, for their parents' expectations for both children were too great to have allowed them time to see one another. Her brother had been trained into the army from a painfully young age and was now doing the job that had been forced at his feet all his life.

Never had his hope of becoming a tailor seemed more remote and more appealing than now as the evening began on the Prussian coast. Three boats had been lowered to row the company to shore and now, as they landed on the pale sandy beach to the north of the tiny village of Putgarten, he was forced to watch as the boats returned to the ship.

He called together his two lieutenants, Keith and Portland, and began outlining his plan. 'There is a thin inlet we have to cross. There will be boats there waiting to secure our passage. We shall divide the company into three and meet there, we will attract far less attention that way.'

'How do we know that the boats will be there?' Portland asked quietly.

'We have to trust that our Swedish allies will have achieved their goal.'

'Yes, sir,' Keith said reluctantly. 'Perhaps the groups we came ashore in are the best ranks?'

'Indeed,' Captain Pottinger muttered. 'We should reach the crossing by midnight. As soon as you arrive you must take your men across. Wait there for the other two parts of the company.'

Hamish found himself in the third with the captain. They took the middle approach, following Lieutenant Portland's men, with Lieutenant Keith's men as a rearguard. This first step of their journey was a distance of twelve miles. To Hamish, the length of march and the hidden cover of darkness reminded him of his attempts to flee the bailiffs as a child, shunted from village to village, farm to farm in that horrendous exodus that became known as 'The Year of The Sheep'. His father had been taken and his mother, tired of running, died in the autumn of that year. Hamish had been forced to look after his younger brother and sisters. It had been a hard existence, finding food where they could, sleeping in the open. His brother and younger sister had both perished with such a lifestyle and he had found his other sister a position as a maid to a pastor's family. Hamish had continued in the peculiar drifting way of life until that moment when he had been caught by Major Tenterchilt for poaching deer on his land.

'Gordon,' Captain Pottinger's voice hissed. 'Sergeant Major, what are you doing?'

Hamish jumped out of his bleak thoughts and realised that all the men in the third were staring at him as he had wandered off in a different direction. 'Sorry, sir,' he muttered quickly and hurried back to the cluster of men. Captain Pottinger grabbed his sleeve as he walked past.

'God in heaven, Gordon. How can I protect you if you lose your mind?'

'Protect me, sir?' Hamish whispered, but the captain gave no reply and continued marching forward.

At a farm a short distance from the crossing, the third stopped and Captain Pottinger drew out a telescope that had hung from the belt at his waist.

'Lieutenant Portland's men are going across the inlet,' he said softly, offering the glass to Hamish who looked through. 'Sergeant Major Gordon,' he continued, 'you are second in command to this third. If we are attacked, see that the men are led back to the ship. There is no intelligence that you can bear to Rambin without me, for it is all locked in my head.'

Hamish nodded and peered back through the glass. 'Sir, Lieutenant Portland is returning.'

Captain Pottinger snatched the telescope back and looked through it.

'What in heaven's name for?'

Hamish did not know the answer to the question but, even if he had ventured one, he would not have been heard for the sky over the distant shore was suddenly lit up with the fire of artillery. Hamish did not wait to be told what to do but at once turned to the men behind him.

'Shoulder arms, we have to fight them, lads.'

'This should not be happening,' the captain muttered. 'Sergeant Major Gordon, take the men down to the shore and hide in the trees down there. We shall launch a counter attack if they should cross the inlet.'

'Yes, sir,' Hamish replied and rushed over to the men to pass on the orders. Captain Pottinger drew his sword and gestured for his men to follow him. The smell of gunpowder was carried over to them on the night breeze and there were faint cries of dying men audible, the agony in their voices frightening the captain's men. Hamish stood at the tree line and looked down at the shore.

'Why do they not have the mercy to kill them?' he asked, disgusted by the noise of the first third of their company.

'Look what it is doing to the men,' Captain Pottinger said plainly. 'That is why.'

Hamish turned back to the pale faces of the rest of the men behind them. Most were standing staring back at him through wide eyes, while two others were trying to calm a boy who looked scarcely old enough to carry the musket he held. Hamish walked over to him and the other two soldiers stood back.

'Private Goodbury,' he said clearly and the boy looked up at him.

'Sergeant Major Gordon,' he began, jumping to his feet. 'I was not scared, sir.'

'Just resting?'

'Yes, sir. I was just relieving my feet. They ache terribly, sir.'

'So you are not scared?'

'No, sir.'

'That is well,' Hamish replied tapping Private Goodbury's arm in a reassuring manner. 'For a scared soldier can make all manner of mistakes, and then he becomes a dead soldier.'

The boy swallowed hard. 'Sir, I will not let you down.'

'I know,' Hamish replied with great faith in his voice, but he could not feel anything but fear himself. He was not afraid of the French soldiers, indeed he could outmanoeuvre them but, in panic, one of his men might as easily shoot him as the French.

'We have lost the boat,' Captain Pottinger said as Hamish returned. 'There is someone down on the shore,' he continued quickly. 'Look! Is it a Frenchman?' He pulled out the telescope once more and gasped as he looked down. 'It is Lieutenant Portland!'

He lowered the glass and was about to step out from the trees but Hamish pulled him back. Before Captain Pottinger could make his angry response to such a gesture, Hamish rushed out from the copse and slid down the bank to the shore, running in zigzagged patterns to avoid the artillery fire that broke out from the far shore. He reached Lieutenant Portland after what had seemed like miles of beach.

'The second third is waiting in the trees, sir,' he explained as he helped the lieutenant to the far side of the beach.

'There was only one boat,' Lieutenant Portland began with a voice dazed and confused. His head had a long tear running down his left forehead and temple, and it was this injury that caused his speech to slur. 'I was returning to take the captain across. But I did not see the French until I was half the way across and the cannon fire upturned the boat.'

'Can you reach the trees if I help you, sir?' Hamish asked quietly.

'Keith?' came the reply. 'I cannot see any trees.'

'I am Sergeant Major Gordon, sir. Lieutenant Keith's men are not yet here.'

'You have to warn them, Sergeant Major. They have boats, and they will cross soon.'

Hamish glanced over to the other shore that had fallen silent. Even the noises of the English soldiers had ended. The tree line was not too far from him and as he looked down at the thin man before him he realised that their greatest hope of safety was for him to carry Lieutenant Portland there. He helped the man to his feet and, taking his arms, held them about his neck and began running back to the trees. There were occasional shots fired as they ran, but the southern shore had fallen frighteningly quiet and Hamish was able to crash through the trees with far more ease than when he had left them.

He lowered his burden down to the ground at the captain's feet. 'Sir,' he began as they both looked down at the unconscious lieutenant. 'It was an ambush. There was only one boat and they have many more. Lieutenant Portland seemed certain they would be crossing soon.'

'They will not manage a canon in a rowing boat, Sergeant Major. We will have our own ambush waiting.'

'Sir, they would be fools not to expect one.'

'They believe that we have fled. We must remain silent.'

'Then someone should be sent to warn the Lieutenant Keith's third.'

'You are right. And Portland should be helped back to Putgarten. He will not survive further conflict. Who should be sent?'

Hamish faltered under this new burden of responsibility for only a second before he jolted himself back to the task that the captain had presented him with.

'Goodbury,' Hamish hissed. 'Falkes.' The two men rushed over. 'You must retrace our course and return Lieutenant Portland safely to the ship.'

'Yes, sir,' Goodbury and Falkes said as one, before Goodbury added, 'but how shall we get to the ship?'

'That is not for you to think on. The marines will be there as soon as they see you.'

The two men hoisted the occasionally conscious Lieutenant Portland to his feet and Captain Pottinger added, 'When you pass Lieutenant Keith, inform him of the situation here and advise him to approach with care and stealth.'

'Yes, sir,' Falkes replied.

Hamish and the captain watched them struggle through the trees with the lieutenant between them.

'I hope they make it back to the ship,' Captain Pottinger said simply.

'They will, sir, for we will be their rearguard.'

Captain Pottinger, his thoughts absorbed with the wounding of his lieutenant and friend, recalled with Sergeant Major Gordon's words that his work was far from complete. He looked at Hamish thoughtfully before speaking.

'Round up the men, Sergeant Major, and tell them to wait for my order to fire.'

'What are they to fire at, sir?' Hamish asked flatly.

'The French, Sergeant Major Gordon. Who else would they fire at?'

'What Frenchmen, sir?'

'The Frenchmen that even as we stand here talking are pulling their boats up on the shore.'

Hamish turned back to the bank and realised that the captain was right. Two boats holding twelve men each were grating their keels onto the shale of the shore below. Captain Pottinger gave time for this realisation to dawn upon Hamish before he continued.

'I want absolute silence from the men and then a two tiered attack. They have to believe there are more than fifteen of us, or this ruse will not work. As in Spain, I want you to remain hidden within the tree line. They have not pulled any artillery onto the boats so we should be safe.'

Hamish nodded and, with great quiet and speed, went to impart the orders to the men. They assembled as required and each waited as the seconds went past, feeling them as heavy to endure as the passing of hours. Hamish loaded his own gun with trembling hands and forced himself to recall his reason for doing this. He had to protect the captain. He had to so that Arabella's life may remain happy and constant. He looked across at the man with a stab of jealousy before correcting his usually passive heart and leaning back against the trunk of the tree that hid him.

The plan was a simple one. When within the range of the muskets, the captain would order the first rank to fire. Sergeant Major Gordon was to order the second rank, and would thus give the impression of a far greater force rather than simply a third of a small company. Whatever misgivings such a plan instilled in Hamish, he was forced to abandon them, for the captain's plan worked beautifully in its naïve creation. Following the fall of sixteen French soldiers, the captain led them from the cover of the trees and out into the open. Some of the enemy tried to flee down to the shore but were shot by the English soldiers until at last the sound of gunfire ebbed and the smoke of shot drifted away.

'Make sure that they are all dead,' the captain ordered. 'I will not leave even a Frenchman to a slow death.'

Hamish nodded and the men went through the bodies ensuring all were corpses and lightening them of any money or costly items that they carried. Hamish knew it was the spoils of war, but to him it seemed no better than carrion picking the meat from a dead man's body. There was a peculiar feeling in the air, brought about no doubt by the gunfight. But Hamish could still smell burning.

'Sergeant Major,' the captain called to him, and he stepped once more onto the shale of the beach. 'These boats will serve us well, I see no reason why our mission need fail.'

'Yes, sir,' Hamish replied and turned back to address the remaining men, of whom they had lost only one. 'Fall in line, boys, we are crossing the inlet.'

'Sir!' came a frenzied shout from somewhere through the ranks. Hamish saw the men pointing behind him and he turned to see the advent of canon fire as it came hurtling across the water. It struck the beach with a force that caused the sergeant major to stumble backward.

'Get back,' he ordered and the red coated troops seemed more than willing to follow his command. Without heeding his own advice, he rushed down to the shore as a second explosion erupted. He crawled over to the captain where he lay on the ground and eased his head onto his lap. 'I am going to get you back to England, sir. I am going to get you back to

Arabella.'

'Hamish?' Captain Pottinger struggled. 'Get back.'

'What, sir?'

'I promised Arabella I would protect you.'

'And I you. I am not a man who wishes to abandon a comrade or disappoint a lady.'

'Be that as it may, I need you to do something more for me.'

Hamish nodded but rose to his feet and tried to assist the captain to his. He struggled to carry him a few paces before the force of another cannonball threw them both to the ground. Whether it was that Captain Pottinger was heavier than Lieutenant Portland or simply that the night had left Hamish too weary, he did not know, but he felt unable to carry the captain any further.

'Sir, there are more French crossing the river. I am afraid we have been ill advised. This mission should never have run.'

'Hamish?' Captain Pottinger lifted his trembling hand up to the young Scotsman's face. 'I am not a strong man. They know this was an intelligence mission.'

'Then there is all the more reason to flee. We are ill prepared to fight on this scale.'

'I am the only man who has such intelligence. I know I will not succeed in keeping it from them if I am taken, and I know,' he paused moving his hand down to his waist and shakily drawing out one of his pistols, 'I will not make the journey back to the ship.'

Hamish glanced nervously at the pistol that he held as it shuddered in his twitching hand. The French boats were almost on the shore now and Hamish felt the horribly compelling feeling of running out of choices and time.

'I love Arabella,' he confessed. 'I have to do what's best for her.' Hamish's hand trembled as he placed the pistol against his captain's head. The shot he fired was met by a stunned silence from Lieutenant Keith's third that arrived on the crest of the small hill.

'The men in the boats,' Keith shouted. 'Do not let them reach the shore.' He ran down the slope and over to where Hamish knelt, pulling him to his feet.

'You just killed him.'

'Yes, sir,' Hamish replied simply.

'How can you stand there and answer in such an uncaring manner? Speak up man!' Keith shouted. 'You will be shot for this.'

'I only did what I believed to be best.'

There was something in Lieutenant Keith's eyes that seemed to falter. Hamish's eyes shone brightly for they glistened with tears and streaks of moonlight showed where some had already been shed. The gunfire continued overhead and neither French nor British seemed concerned with the two people who stood on the beach.

'I am not so certain that the good captain would agree with you.'

'I know this may seem hard to hear, sir, and harder still to believe, but I followed his orders to the last.'

'I saw you shoot him,' Keith said, making each word detached and purposeful.

'Sir, this is not the place to stand and discuss such things. See, the enemy force is almost at the shore. I shall come as your prisoner, if that is what you wish, but I want a chance to declare my innocence before a court martial.'

'You are a damn fool, man. They are a hundred times more likely to condemn you than I.'

'Sir, I am innocent.'

'The men saw you shoot their captain, Sergeant Major. I am afraid they will not see it that way.'

The British troops from the remaining two thirds were gradually fought back from the shore over a distance of five miles by the superior French force. At last, they ceased to fire after the British had sustained significant casualties, including the deaths of nine, making the return march from the failed mission last painfully longer than the outgoing one. Hamish completed it all with his hands bound before him, now a prisoner to the cause that he had so violently sought to defend.

The boat journey back to England found him alone in one of the ship's cells, deep in the boat. He could hear the water striking and ebbing from the timbers of the walls and there was a pleasant calmness to it, but that was as far as his comforts extended. He received only one visitor save those who brought him rations. When they were close to the coast of England and soon to make anchor at Portsmouth, Lieutenant Portland appeared, flanked by two marines.

'He shall not escape by my hand,' the lieutenant announced and without a further word the two red coated men departed. For a time all the lieutenant did was stare down at Hamish, who returned the gesture with the fear of a cornered wild animal. 'What happened, Sergeant Major?'

'I shot Captain Pottinger in the head,' Hamish answered honestly.

'But, damn it man, why?'

'He asked me to.'

'What?' Portland looked down with confusion. 'A court martial will not accept such an answer.'

'Be that as it may, it is the only one they will receive, for it is the truth.'

'I do believe that you put me in an impossible position.' Portland sighed as Hamish stared back at him. There was such an openness to the sergeant major, an uncomplicated simplicity, that Portland muttered, more to himself than the prisoner before him, 'I can find myself believing you.'

'You owe me nothing, sir,' Hamish replied, realising what the lieutenant had meant by his earlier comment. 'I did my duty to you, I could not leave you to die.'

'And yet you killed the captain?'

'I promised Arabella that I would look after him.'

'Arabella? You address the wife of an officer in such a way?'

'Though it may seem strange to you, sir, Arabella Pottinger and I grew up as cousins, brother and sister almost. But I had to consider what was best for her as well as the company.'

'I do owe you my life, Hamish Gordon. If you are honest with me now, I shall speak for you at your trial. Though, in truth, I do not believe that your chance of clemency is great.'

'May you do something for me, sir?'

'What is it that you want?'

'I need to pen a letter, yet I am bound. Would you find me a scribe, sir?'

Lieutenant Portland felt torn. He wanted to believe in the soldier, for he had saved the lieutenant's life at great risk to his own, yet the man openly admitted his crime. Although Portland had given his word to speak favourably for Hamish at the trial, on their arrival back to England, the lieutenant was called away at once concerning the death of his uncle, as he was the sole surviving relative. Portland missed the trial that found Hamish Gordon guilty, stripped of his rank, and facing the punishment: death.

The trial, that took place on the third day of August, also saw the arrival of Major Tenterchilt at Petrovia Lodge. Imogen and Catherine, pleased as always to welcome their father home, were a little surprised to find that he arrived alone.

'Where is Alice, Papa?' Catherine asked openly. 'She is well, I hope.'

'She was when I left her,' their father answered. 'I must discuss some things with you, my dear Imogen.'

'What can you share with Imogen that you are unable to share with me, Papa? Imogen and I have no secrets from one another.'

Imogen, despite knowing this statement to be far removed from fact, did not correct her, for she also wished to know what had caused this premature and agitated visit from her father.

'I wish to speak to Imogen as she is the elder and will be running Petrovia Lodge when I am gone.'

'Gone, Papa?' Imogen asked, shocked by what she heard. 'You mean away, surely.'

'No, indeed. I am to travel to the Americas for a time.'

'Whatever for?' Catherine asked.

'A mission of peace. I shall not tire you with the business of politics, only to say that the heavy-handed navy may be starting a war where your cousin Mr Jenkyns and parliament wish for a war not to be started.'

'But Papa, you are a soldier, not a diplomat,' Imogen stated.

'It will bring in extra income, my dear, and Alice is so eager to see America.'

'She is going on this voyage with you?' Imogen asked at the same time as Catherine said,

'What about Beatrice and Josiah?'

'I would like you to oversee their development. Alice is afraid that they would be disturbed on the long voyage.'

'But they are her children,' Imogen protested, but the major held up his hands for silence.

'I know what you are trying to say. I understand it. Your dear Mama would never have left any one of you, but Alice is not like your mother. Imogen, my dear, you have longed to teach. I can imagine no finer pupils than your own brother and sister.'

Catherine shook her head and walked out of the room. Of late she had found much solace in her own company and Imogen was growing concerned for her sister.

'In the event of the voyage turning bad, or my mission being unfavourably received,' Major Tenterchilt continued, 'I have made young Josiah my heir. You shall be his guardian until he reaches the age of sixteen when I wish him to spend his money on a commission in the army. I will have one child who follows in my footsteps.'

'What of Cat and Beatrice? They will need dowries if they are to marry.'

'Five hundred pounds will be left to them each, and to you and dear Arabella, for I know it is no secret to you that your mama left you that much money.'

'How do you know?'

'Why, Mr Dermot told me,' he said openly and Imogen scowled at his words.

'What a vile man,' she hissed. She felt abused by the lawyer, who seemed to have viewed her as little more than a pawn in a game for sheer pleasure and entertainment. He had sown seeds of doubt in her mind concerning her father and his new wife, only to share with them everything she believed had been spoken in confidence.

'You do not believe such things, Imogen, and nor are such comments fitting of a lady. You would have drowned had it not been for Mr Dermot.'

'I should not have entered the river had it not been for Mr Dermot.'

'Do not think ill of him. He is a frighteningly shrewd man. Besides which,' he faltered and took his daughter's hands in his own. 'I do believe that there was an element within his words that was far more accurate than even I believed possible.'

'You did have another son, father,' she whispered. 'Hamish would have followed you anywhere you ordered him as closely as any blood born son.'

'Forget about the sergeant major, my dear Imogen. You must forget him. He has taken orders to the continent and I do not anticipate his return.'

'Did you send him?' she asked, her head becoming light and her eyes brimming with tears. 'Did you oversee this order?'

'I am not a monster, a demon or any such beast,' he said heavily. 'I bore a great quarrel with Sergeant Major Gordon, but I could not employ even an estranged and adopted son on such a foolhardy mission of such little worth. He who ordered it is the monster, for he sent his only son to complete the task, solely because he supported my daughters' honour when I did not. Then judge me, my dear Imogen. I am a weak man, but an ogre I am not.'

'Oh, Papa,' Imogen sobbed and sat down in one of the chairs feeling overcome with grief and worry. 'Poor Arabella and poor Mish.'

'I see now how great the wrong is that I have committed in my failure to do anything. I shall correct it with my post in America. I did not know you loved him.'

'Nor did I, Papa, until he left and I thought of him every day and I prayed morning and night that he should be protected from war, and that he might one day return and see how great a love I have for him.' She bowed her head, unable now to contain those tears that fell and uncaring that they did. Her father held her head to him and cursed himself repeatedly for his actions during the past two years.

Major Tenterchilt stayed only two nights in Petrovia Lodge before returning back to London to meet Mrs Tenterchilt and depart for America. The attack on the USS Chesapeake had left relations that were continuously tense between the two nations very much in tatters. It was both naïve and foolish to believe that any sort of envoy may appease the Americans, but the pride of the British fleet and army was too great to allow nothing to be done.

It was not until the fifth day of August, the day following Major Tenterchilt's departure from Petrovia Lodge that Catherine, on one of her long circular walks of the estate intercepted a messenger with a letter for Imogen. She assured the man that she would see it to its rightful recipient and hurried back to the lodge. She was wearing britches and a smart shirt with a heavy coat about her and looked so unlike a lady that there was little wonder that the messenger answered her with the words,

'Thank you, sir.'

Catherine felt indignant about this, tilting her chin in an obstinate and self important manner. But her indignation was second to her curiosity surrounding the letter for she had become accustomed to Hamish's hand and this elegant penmanship of beautifully manicured letters was certainly not Hamish's scrawl.

'Imogen,' she shouted upon entering the house. 'You have a letter, Imogen.'

Imogen appeared dressed in a sombre pale dress carrying little Josiah.

'Ladies do not shout, Cat.'

'I have just been addressed as 'sir' so I feel I am entirely able to shout. You have a letter. A letter from a gentleman I would guess.'

'Nonsense,' Imogen answered, reaching out her free hand to take the letter. 'It is probably from Papa saying that he has reached Perth and changed his mind.'

She looked down curiously at it and frowned. It was not the hand of anyone that she knew or recognised and she cracked it open with great awkwardness. Catherine took Josiah and waited for Imogen to tell her what the letter said but, with each word that she read, it became clear that Imogen was not fit to tell Catherine anything, for her face paled and she reached to the wall to steady herself.

'Imogen?' Catherine asked, stepping over to her, but her older sister waved her away and collapsed on the floor in a faint. 'Penny!' Catherine shouted and the housekeeper walked though muttering about Cat's shouting, although the moment her eyes fell upon Imogen's unconscious form she shouted for her sister in a voice that more than matched Catherine's. As Anne and Penny helped Imogen onto one of the chairs and rushed to fetch her some smelling salts, Catherine picked up the letter and read it slowly, hoping to discover what had caused such a moment of fear or concern in her sister who was as strong-willed as any man could be.

'To my dear Imogen,' Catherine read, feeling approval at the tone with which it began. 'This letter, by the hand of Lieutenant Portland, finds me with a message so grievous to me that I fear I must share it. I have killed Captain Pottinger. Tell Arabella it was for her. Look to hear from me no more. Always with love, Hamish Gordon.'

Catherine returned the letter to Imogen's lap and left the room carrying Josiah who seemed greatly intrigued by the events. She could not understand what had happened, could not fathom what may have led to such an action of hatred and evil within her brother, whom she loved and respected so much.

'There has been a misunderstanding,' she announced. Of course, Josiah could not understand the words that she spoke but she felt better for saying them. She paced the floor with the infant, tutting like a hen. 'He would not do that.'

This news stunned all the inhabitants of Petrovia Lodge and it took nearly a week for Imogen to take hold of her senses and begin straightening out such chaos as the letter had left them in. As she rose that morning, she knew that she had to do something to help preserve the family that were left to her, and so she marched through to the orangery where Catherine sat sharpening one of the kitchen knives in a rather threatening manner.

'I want you to go to London,' Imogen announced bluntly. 'If you are to find yourself a husband you will need to be amongst men. Of greater importance, I believe Arabella will have need of you. I cannot fathom why she has not written.'

'I would not know what to say,' Catherine confessed, reluctant to look at Imogen.

'On the first day you should say how sorry you are, and then you shall talk of things quite ordinary. The weather, perhaps, or how affairs have affected us in Petrovia Lodge. I will, of course, find you a chaperone to oversee your visit down to London, you could not attempt such a journey on your own.'

'Why ever not?' Catherine demanded.

'My dear Cat. It is not what a lady should do.'

'I can protect myself,' she replied, turning to Imogen with the knife still in her hand.

'I do not doubt that. But a lady, whether she can fight or not, should not need to.'

'I will not know what to do in London,' she muttered. 'I have no fashionable clothes, and society there may scorn a lady wearing britches.'

'That is true,' Imogen replied. 'You will have some money to spend and some to share with Arabella. I will not see my sisters destitute.'

Catherine nodded hesitantly. There seemed to be nothing that Imogen had failed to plan or account for and, indeed, Imogen had considered all the eventualities and outcomes she possibly could. Her plans were so often flawless that Catherine began to feel quite safe being a part of them. Imogen was aware that she would remain unmarried and furthermore her father had resigned her to Petrovia for years, employed in the education of her younger brother and sister. She had come to the strange realisation that she did not object to such a notion anymore, for she had loved Hamish so fiercely that she could imagine no man could fill the void left in her heart.

CHAPTER SEVEN
Wednesday 12th August 1807

Two days later, Imogen bade farewell to her sister and watched as the coach to Perth rattled down the dusty road. Summer was at its peak, a strange feeling, for some things remained so constant each year: the coming of the gypsies, the flowering and fruiting of the trees by the river, the long, stretched out days beyond the baking glass of the orangery. And yet, by the same token, things changed irreparably from year to year. Never again would the Tenterchilt family gather by the river to share one of their picnics, never would the major and Hamish work within the stables, sawing, building, and never would the three sisters hold their croquet games upon the hopelessly skewed lawn.

She stood now with Josiah and Beatrice in each of her arms and turned back to walk up the long path. It was one of the most lonely walks that she had ever made. It no longer felt that she was walking home but that the lodge was nothing more than a shell of former glories, of a cherished family that had cruelly and carelessly left her alone there.

Catherine, by contrast, met her journey as an adventure beyond measure. She revelled in the company on the coaches and both pleased and alarmed the other passengers with tales of the army and how much she yearned to fight. Upon her arrival in London, after three days of travel, she was exhausted beyond measure and now, for the first time since leaving the lodge, she began to realise the gravity of the occasion. She looked down at the address that she held in her hand and pondered on how to get there, wishing she had not dismissed her chaperone so soon after their arrival in the city. She tried asking people but they either hurried past, ignoring her, or did not know. She picked up the case she had brought with her and began walking. She had not been in London since she was a child and remembered nothing of it at all. The bustling of the crowd startled her and upon sighting an open park she rushed across to it and sat down. Nobody noticed her. Hundreds of people must have walked past her as she sat alone on the bench, but not one acknowledged her existence. The evening was drawing in now and Catherine's feelings of fear and pride began to confront one another. She knew that she had to ask for help, but pride forbade her to acknowledge any such form of weakness. She was still unprepared to admit to being uncertain regarding anything.

It was surprising how early it got dark here in the city compared with Petrovia and at last her fear began to get the better of her. She rose to her feet and looked around, but there was no one to be seen. At the edge of the park, lights were appearing and it was towards these that she began to walk, but they seemed so remote and distant that she felt she was making no progress at all. She dropped the case and sat down on it, feeling foolish and fearful.

She sat alone as the minutes ran by until, at last, she heard voices coming closer with every second. Grabbing her case, she backed away into the shadow of one of the trees and watched as two army officers walked into view. They were hissing at one another, talking in such quiet tones that they seemed afraid anyone might hear them.

'It is not that simple,' one said angrily.

'Sir, you must do this. Outside the army, there is no hope of being recognised.'

'Do not presume to tell me what I must or must not do!' snapped the first. 'I want to, truly I do, but captain is not a rank that holds any office in such matters.'

'It holds a greater office than lieutenant,' the other replied bitterly.

Catherine leaned forward to try and see their faces but it was to no avail. They continued to walk through the park and she emerged from the shadow. As they walked away and she watched their backs fading into the night, she realised that she needed their help and she rushed up to them.

'Sirs?' she asked and as one they faced her with pistols drawn.

'I am so sorry, madam,' one began and quickly holstered his pistol at his waist once more. Catherine trembled, waving away any effort that the officer made to ensure she was well. 'You made no sound, I thought - we thought,' he corrected himself, 'that you were a villain.'

'I was taught to track deer,' she whispered, dazed by the events and wishing suddenly that she had stayed hidden in the trees. 'I cannot help that I now move silently all the time.'

'Track deer?' the other asked lowering his gun but making no effort to return it. He had a Scottish accent and at once Catherine felt happier.

'You are Scottish,' she exclaimed. 'Praise God! I did not think to hear that accent in this place.'

'Are you lost?' the first asked.

'Yes,' she stammered, fighting back tears of relief. 'I am trying to reach this address,' she handed them the paper. 'But no one knows where it is and I have spent hours simply lost.'

'This address?' the Scottish man asked. 'Who are you?'

'What?' Catherine whispered, the tone of the man's voice making her feel that she had done something wrong. The other man held up his hands peaceably.

'What is your name, madam?' he asked softly.

'Catherine,' she whispered, taking a step back. Dark thoughts began to pass through her head, but she stumbled over her case and would have fallen had the Scottish officer not caught her arm.

'Come,' he said softly. 'We will take you there, for this address is known to us.'

'How, sir?' she whispered.

'We knew the gentleman who lived there. A captain.'

'Pottinger?' she asked eagerly.

'Indeed,' the other replied. 'Are you a friend of his? For I must advise against seeking him out.'

'I thought he was dead,' Catherine said flatly.

'You are a curious specimen, madam,' the Scot answered. They began to walk once more, back the way that they had come from. Catherine took the arm of the first officer whilst the second carried her case and continued to explain. 'He was killed in battle in Prussia.'

'Then Hamish did not kill him,' she exclaimed happily. Both men stopped and turned to face her. 'Pardon, sirs,' she said anxiously, 'I meant no offence. I simply could not believe that Hamish, that is Sergeant Major Gordon, was capable of such a thing.'

'You seem to know much of the regiment's news,' the younger man said. 'And openly talk of it.'

'Oh,' she whispered. 'I am sorry to have offended you, only my sister Imogen and I, we discuss these things quite freely.'

'Imogen?' he whispered. 'Good God, you are Miss Catherine Tenterchilt, the major's daughter?'

'Indeed,' she replied. 'I have come to be what service I may to Arabella, that is Mrs Pottinger, my eldest sister, but Imogen arranged a chaperone for me only as far as London and when we parted I did not think to ask him how to find my sister's house.'

'I am Lieutenant Portland,' the young officer said introducing himself. 'It was by my hand that such news reached you of the captain's death and your dear Hamish's guilt.'

'Hamish would not kill the captain. He would have followed wherever he led. Would that I were a man and could fight the foe with the gallantry of my adopted brother.'

'Hamish Gordon was condemned to death, more than a week since,' the other said firmly, glancing across at Portland. Catherine fell silent. She reached out her hand before her as though she wanted some support, but she did not want anything from these men. They were mistaken, she had to believe that they were.

'You are wrong,' she said firmly, snatching her case and walking purposefully from them. She did not know where she was going, only that she had to get away from these men. She began running, her dress tripping her with each step that she took until she reached the road, dropped her case, and collapsed on it in tears. Her outburst of sadness, so alien to one who always expressed anger, was only short lived before she remembered herself and rose to her feet. London was not all that she had been promised it would be. It was dirty and cold, and she saw no friendly faces as she passed along the streets.

'A lady like yourself should not be out at this time, alone.'

She turned at the sound of a man's voice behind her. A ragged man in clothes that might have been fashion a decade ago stood there with a boy barely ten years of age. She nodded to them but offered no reply and continued walking. They walked alongside her, one to her left and one to her right.

'He's right, miss,' the boy echoed. 'I ain't seen no one as fair as you ever in London all alone.'

'Let me help you with your case, miss,' the older man said, rubbing his bearded chin with the back of his hand before reaching down to the case.

'Thank you, but no,' she said firmly. 'My case stays with me.' She swung it to her other hand and at once the young boy snatched it and began running along the street. 'Wait! Stop!' she called but it was in vain for the boy continued running. She chased him a few steps but they both stopped and turned at the sound of another man's voice.

'Hold,' he shouted angrily and Catherine looked back to find Lieutenant Portland holding her second robber. 'Return that bag, boy, or you will face the inclement arm of the law, and you shall hang from it.'

'Get going, boy,' the other man called. 'Your brothers will be waiting.'

Catherine, so accustomed to dreaming and imagining such circumstances, but never having faced them, snatched the pistol from the lieutenant's belt and as the boy began running off she fired a shot at him. At the sound of gunfire, windows began to be lighted up but not a sound was made as Catherine walked over to where the boy sat on the cobbles, clutching at his ankle. She picked up her case and knelt down before him. The young boy stood up shakily, pushing her away before he looked down miserably at his ankle. The shot, which had continued its flight down onto the road, had cut only slightly into his leg causing only a little blood but considerable pain. He hobbled away from the street as Catherine turned and walked back to Lieutenant Portland who stood open mouthed, still clutching the older man.

'Turn him in,' she said angrily, handing the pistol back to the lieutenant. He did not answer. Indeed, he could find no words to express the shock he felt. She stood watching him, her eyes aglow in the burning lights from the windows. He nodded, feeling compelled to do as she ordered him through a sense of mutual awe and fear.

She remained in the street until the lieutenant returned by which time the hour was approaching midnight. He walked over to her and smiled slightly, shaking his head.

'I have never met a woman like you,' he whispered. 'Tracking deer? Shooting thieves? Is there no end to such attainments?'

'Indeed there is,' she replied sadly, all anger having left her in the time that she had stood waiting for him. 'For I may not use my skills as you may, solely because I was born a lady.'

'Let me escort you to your sister's house.'

'I do not think I wish to share the company of one who deems my brother guilty of so heinous a crime.'

'Then why did you wait here for me?' he asked simply, and his simplicity once again ignited a blaze of anger within her. He noticed her setting her chin in an obstinate manner and held his hands up quickly. 'I was not there.'

'When?' she snapped back. 'When he supposedly shot Captain Pottinger? When he was court-martialled? Or when he was executed?'

'I regret I was not there for any of them, though I swore I should speak for him at his trial.'

'Why did you not?' she shouted, throwing the case down on the ground.

'I beg you, show some decorum or you will find yourself in court before tomorrow is out.' He picked up her case and led her through the streets in silence for a time before he continued. 'I was called away on a family matter. I did not know that the trial would pass so quickly but it was concluded within a day and I could not make it back on time. Captain Keith, who you met in the park, saw Sergeant Major Gordon fire the shot. Not one of the men in the company can believe what happened, but it was seen.'

'Why did you not see it?' she asked softly.

'Sergeant Major Gordon had already risked his life to preserve mine. I was unconscious and halfway back to the ship when it happened. I believed him.'

'What?'

'The mission was a fool's errand, pointless and costly in coin and blood. Gordon swore he killed the captain on his own request, for he was terrified of torture at the hands of the French and knew he was unable return to the ship. I believed that he was just following orders, and Keith did too, but he could not speak at the trial as he was the man who was to replace Captain Pottinger and become promoted.'

'All these years, my father told me stories of the great feats of courage and camaraderie of army offices, but they were just that: stories. You have proved it so.'

Lieutenant Portland fell silent as they walked on until at last they reached the small house where Arabella lived. Catherine shook her head as she looked up at it.

'She will not long afford this on her own.'

'You have not been to London often, have you, Miss Tenterchilt?'

'No,' she replied, turning on the man when she knew all she should be doing was thanking him. 'What is it that you seek to imply by such a statement?'

'Ladies do not talk about money unless it is to say how much they have. It is not how society works.'

'Hang society,' she replied, and felt only greater anger as Lieutenant Portland folded his arms and laughed slightly. 'Why do you seek to anger me?'

'I do not seek to. Indeed, I do not mean to.'

'You do an efficient job of something to which you claim ignorance.'

'I believe in Gordon's innocence and of that you must believe me.' It was not the words that made Catherine trust him, nor the fervent look on his face but the tone of desperation and repentance that struck that chord closest to her heart.

'Mish was a brother to me, I knew him as well as any soul on the earth and I know that he could not kill a man in cold blood. Now you may know it, too. He does not deserve to be remembered in such a way.'

Catherine offered the lieutenant a sad and accepting smile before she walked up the steps to the front door, announcing who she was before she was admitted.

It was the hardest thing in Catherine's life to spend those first few weeks with her sister, for Arabella was hardly the same person that she had been only a month earlier. One comfort at least was that she did not apportion any blame to anybody. She had known when she married an officer that she had also married the army, and deaths happened with great frequency within it. She had become housebound by her own melancholy and for some time, Catherine was obliged to follow her example.

As September turned, however, Rose Pottinger arrived with an invitation that had never been more welcome in its reception. Major Charles Napier was hosting a ball, a masked ball, in celebration of the gentlemen returning from their country estates. September was spent in fervent preparation by all the young ladies of Town and Arabella Pottinger and Catherine Tenterchilt were no exception, so that, on the first day of October, they were fully prepared for this most exciting of events.

'We will know no one there,' Arabella said thoughtfully as she looked down at her black dress that Chloe was hastily lining with a silver hem.

'You might,' Catherine responded, looking with uncertainty at the low square cut neckline that showed considerably more of her bosom than the world had ever seen. 'Must you wear black, Arabella? It does not seem right to wear black to a ball.'

'Nonsense, Cat,' she said in reply. 'It is entirely fitting. Besides, I think it looks rather elegant.'

On this, Catherine could not dispute. Arabella looked more gracious than ever, the black was like midnight with the silver as stars. She was wearing a necklace that Catherine had never seen before that was silver inset with tiny pearls and it completed her outfit perfectly. Her black mask made her eyes shine only more brightly. Catherine, by contrast wore a simple white dress. In truth she did not wish to be going to the ball at all but, as it had been the first invitation to leave the house that they had received, she was grateful.

'Do you think it wrong that we do not have a man in our party?' Catherine mused, picking up the train of her dress and shaking it. Chloe coughed and glared up at her. 'Sorry,' she added.

'I have no doubt that the colonel and his wife shall be attending and that we shall be entering with them.'

Arabella's assumption was correct and, when the night of the ball finally arrived, it was to find Catherine crammed into the carriage with the four Pottingers. They arrived in silence at a large white fronted house before which was a huge driveway filled with coaches, some bore coats of arms and some seemed little suited to their grand surroundings. The colonel's own carriage was a perfect balance of the two.

They stepped out at some distance from the door and were forced to cross the wide drive, dodging the carriages as they went. The light had gone from the sky and the night had taken a full and complete hold, leaving them only the lamp light to see by, but when they walked through the double doors, they could only blink at the sudden change. There was a pristine glow of white and golden light that was the closest match to daylight that Arabella and Catherine had ever seen. A host of masked faces turned to them as they walked in, and the girls hurriedly lifted their masks to their faces. The house itself was formed of eight enormous rooms on the ground floor, all joining on to the neighbouring rooms with open doors, so that it took only a little time, if one was so inclined, to walk from one corner to the other. However, it bulged and brimmed with people, all so hideously alien in their masks that, after a time, Arabella became quite dizzy with it.

Colonel Pottinger and his wife disappeared almost at once to locate and discuss matters of war. There was great discussion concerning the victory over the Danish fleet, leaving it destroyed beyond repair, and the declaration of war that Russia had made against Britain.

'Damn it,' Major Bretwood announced. 'Have they forgotten what the French do to monarchs? The tsar had better watch his step or he may find his head guillotined.'

They all nodded in agreement, chuckling over the warmongering that they all shared. The Battle of Copenhagen had resulted from the late Captain Pottinger's failed mission. The Swedes believed that the British fleet sailed to assist them at Stralsund and, indeed, the British had thought to sail with that intention initially, until the senior officers had made the discovery that, following their initial attack on the Danish fleet, they had begun rebuilding the boats once more.

The three young women had no interest in such matters and wandered through the hall. Despite being relieved and grateful that Arabella's spirits seemed raised by such an outing, Catherine was increasingly aware of the impractical nature of her dress, and the manner in which Mrs and Miss Pottinger took all the attention from her. On one such dance, while Arabella danced with a gentleman from Norfolk and Rose with an officer of the navy, Catherine wandered off through the rooms until at last she found a free seat in the corner of the room and placed her mask down upon the floor to look at her white dress where it was trampled with footprints across the hem. She could not imagine Imogen's face when she imparted to her the news that her expensive dress had been entirely ruined on its debut. As she sat there, with her head lowered to better survey her dress, she saw from the corner of her eye a man pick up her mask.

'I think you should be wearing this, ma'am.'

She looked up to stare at the face of a grotesque gargoyle, whose only truthful features were the two eyes that stared from behind the mask.

'And look as ridiculous as you, sir?' she demanded, snatching it from him.

'Do you know, I was sure it was you.'

'I think you have mistaken me for somebody else,' she said quickly. 'I know no one here.'

'When a lady fires a gun she becomes a very memorable face.'

'Good God,' she whispered. 'You were there that night?'

The masked demon sighed heavily and shook its revolting head. 'Ladies do not use such statements, Miss Catherine,' he said desperately, pulling back his mask so that it sat atop his hair.

'Spare me your lecture, good lieutenant,' she said cuttingly and rose to her feet. 'For I may say back to you that a gentleman does not abandon an innocent man to execution.'

'And you would be right,' he said, so softly that Catherine, who had already begun to walk from him, scarcely heard. However, there was a tone to his voice that sounded so deeply repentant, that she turned back to him. 'Will you not find it in your heart, alien though it may be, to accept that my regret is a sufficient punishment for my neglectful crime?' All she could reply was to nod slightly, for there were no words that might convey the guilt that she suddenly felt. 'Allow me, please, to introduce you to my party.'

'If in return you shall do something for me,' she whispered, a playful smile reaching her lips. 'Return your mask, for I do believe I should rather walk forth with the devil at my side than the ever noble Lieutenant Portland.'

He smiled sharply and bowed his head with great mockery before putting his mask over his face once more and, snatching her wrist, he pulled her through the dainty crowd. After running through three rooms and bursting between dancing partners, one of whom was Rose Pottinger and her naval partner, they stopped by a small group of people. There were three men and several women who were gathered around to hear the stories of one of the gentlemen. Both Catherine and Portland stood for a time trying to regain their breath.

'Please allow me to introduce Captain Keith, who I believe you encountered on that first night. The Scotsman with a passion for blunt speaking.' Portland laughed as though he was drunk. 'And this young gentleman, at only nineteen years of age, is Keith's younger brother, Midshipman Keith.'

'Then who do I call Keith?' Catherine asked looking at the two men who still wore masks.

'Neither, Miss Tenterchilt,' Captain Keith replied. 'You call my brother Sir and myself Captain. Allow me to conclude the introductions. Midshipman Keith, this is Miss Catherine Tenterchilt.'

Each bowed to one another before the midshipman spoke. 'A European name, Miss Tenterchilt.'

'Indeed,' she replied, feeling that she should respond with the same seriousness as he showed.

'Tender Child, is it not?'

'Indeed, once again,' she said firmly. Portland sniggered into his shoulder whilst Captain Keith coughed to mask his own amusement.

'Never was a name less well suited,' Portland laughed. Catherine was about to snap back with some such witty remark, but she was unsure whether or not she should view it as a compliment. 'A final introduction,' Portland said, pulling back his mask, and tapping the shoulder of the man who was regaling the ladies before him with heroic tales. 'This is the man who does, quite truly, pick up the pieces of our jobs. Miss Tenterchilt, may I introduce-'

'Sleeping Tiger!' the man exclaimed as he turned around to face her, sliding back his mask. The three other men looked at him as though he had gone mad at this outburst and Catherine swallowed back the smile she felt at being remembered so. She pursed her lips and narrowed her eyes, looking every bit the tiger that had just awoken.

'Doctor Fotherby. The gentleman who dare not fight an opponent who has a sharpened sword.'

But, as a gentleman should, the doctor made no reply, instead just smiling sadly and nodding. The other men chattered amongst themselves trying to establish when these two may have met. Their ideas were ludicrous and were the only thing that stayed Catherine's tongue from apologising.

'Excuse me,' the doctor whispered and returned his mask, turning once more to the ladies behind him who flocked excitedly to hear his stories. Whatever the masks of the evening had been hoped to hide, it could surely not have been intended to be sorrow and hurt, although that was all that Catherine could think of as she lifted her own to her face.

'So, Miss Tenterchilt,' Captain Keith began. 'How do you come to know the esteemed doctor?'

'He is my father's physician, and was the man who managed to save Papa's leg from having to be amputated. We sparred and I struck him when his guard was lowered, only to discover that he had ensured my blade was blunt.'

'You sparred?' Midshipman Keith asked in dismay.

'Indeed,' she replied. 'Why must it be that men are horrified by such a notion? You may ask your friend, Portland, here. He will tell you that, had I not learnt to shoot as a man would, all my possessions would have been stolen from me.'

'It is true,' Portland concurred. He seemed to sober up instantly as he looked at the turned back of the doctor. 'Would you do me the honour of dancing with me, Miss Tenterchilt?'

Catherine froze and tried to invent a purpose for her refusal. She had never learnt to dance. Her time had been spent learning from her father rather than her mother. She considered in that split second what Imogen, the model of gentility, would have done and she smiled up at the lieutenant. 'I dare not dance, sir,' she whispered. 'I am quite warm as it is. I believe I shall go and take some fresh air.'

'Then allow me to accompany you,' Portland replied. She nodded a gracious approval and took his outstretched arm. They walked in sombre silence, wholly different to how they had done some minutes before. The terrace at the back of the house had been opened up to guests and they wandered outside. It was a clear night, bitterly cold, and it was little surprise that they were almost alone. 'You should be gentle with the doctor,' Portland said softly after a time. 'He is a truly sad man.'

'Indeed,' she replied harshly. 'Sad that he has so many admirers flocking to hear his story? That he left the army and now seeks a way back into it? Or that he is confined to a failing London practice?'

Portland turned to face her and looked down into her eyes. 'Whatever cruel twist left such a viper's tongue in this lady's mouth, you should beware of it. He left the army after failing to redeem a man on court-martial, not entirely dissimilar to why you were angered at the army in defence of your friend, Gordon. His 'failing London practice' still protects and ensures the safety of those wounded in battle rather like he saved your father. And as for your first point, you truly do not know the man.' Realising that he spoke the truth, Catherine could not bear to meet the gaze of the man before her.

'I am cold,' she whispered after a time.

'Come, then,' Portland said softly. 'Let us return to the party.' He offered her his arm once more and she took it, pulling him to face her.

'Forgive me, sir. I was not brought up for society. I cannot abide such strutting and prancing as courting here involves. I was raised to believe in a romance that sparked a love, not a fancy, and as such I find myself in very ill humour.' Portland opened his mouth to speak but she silenced him. 'Please, let me say this, for admissions have never come easy to me. I am not a mild person. I have a man's heart, a heart that longs to fight, and yet I am treated only as a woman, always. I did not know the doctor's past and my words were unforgivably cruel to a man who, strangely, finds himself in the same position as myself.'

'You are not so harsh as you hope, Miss Tenterchilt. And that is a great comfort to me.'

Neither of them spoke another word until they had rejoined their party in the hall. Doctor Fotherby was dancing with one of the ladies, as was Captain Keith, whilst his younger brother watched on with the envy that Catherine felt a share in. Perhaps she was unable to hide it, for Lieutenant Portland once more offered her his hand.

'Come, Miss Tenterchilt,' he laughed jovially. 'I shall have to ask Midshipman Keith if you refuse me.'

'In truth,' she began, uncertain that she should lower her shield of pride. 'I would love to dance, but I have never learnt.'

'Truthfully?' he asked. She felt her cheeks burn red as her temper rose at the embarrassment, but he ignored this and continued. 'Then we will be a fraction behind everyone else. I dare say you are a quick learner.'

The first dance that she took part in was amongst the most frightening experiences she had ever endured but, with each dance, following the steps of the other, more elegant ladies, she began to realise that it was a similar pattern of steps to that of fencing, only smaller. It required the same grace and timing. By the time Arabella walked over to her to announce that they intended to leave, Catherine had learnt to love dancing.

'Come, Cat,' Arabella said softly, tapping her sister on the shoulder. 'It is getting late and time that we left.'

'I have only just begun dancing,' Catherine protested. 'I do not wish to leave yet.'

'Mrs Pottinger,' Lieutenant Portland began, bowing his head. 'If it suits you both, I should be honoured to escort Miss Catherine home.'

Arabella looked from him to her sister, who had an uncharacteristically meek expression on her face. 'Very well, sir. Thank you.' She did not say another thing but turned from them both.

'Have you a sister or a brother, Lieutenant Portland?' Catherine asked, never taking her eyes from Arabella.

'Not anymore,' he replied.

'I do not think Arabella is the same woman that she was.'

'Miss Tenterchilt,' the lieutenant began in a cautioning tone. 'I do not think that such words are proper or fitting of this place.'

'I am sorry,' Catherine whispered and there was a tone of submission that spoke far greater than her words. 'I travelled to London to be a companion to Arabella, but her sister-in-law has already claimed that role, and I am left quite alone. I may have to find myself a companion.'

'You are a mystery, Miss Tenterchilt,' Portland said softly. 'A true enigma.'

The evening held much more dancing and laughter, and the hour was quite late when Lieutenant Portland's coach stopped outside Arabella's house. Catherine thanked him graciously and walked into the house. Chloe was there to welcome her but Arabella had already withdrawn. Catherine was in a daze, feeling both delighted and exhausted, but her only disappointment was that she had been unable to apologise to Doctor Fotherby for her behaviour for he, too, had excused himself early.

CHAPTER EIGHT
Saturday 22ⁿᵈ July 1809

Yet despite her complaints and loneliness, Catherine remained with Arabella, oversaw her accounts, for she had always enjoyed mathematics, and remained her companion while Rose Pottinger was not in the house. Miss Pottinger was charming and carried a simple quality that both irked and appealed to Catherine, but she could not forgive the woman for taking her place in Arabella's affections. When, some time later, Miss Pottinger married and became Mrs Bronstead it came as a great comfort to Catherine.

In order to escape neglect and to make herself useful, Catherine volunteered at the military hospital where she bandaged and dressed wounds. She had done it, also, as an apology to Doctor Fotherby, though she never had the opportunity to talk to him for his work occupied him constantly. Occasionally she would see him walking through the hallways, but whenever she tried to find him to talk, he had always moved to another wing or was tending another patient. She attended the hospital on Wednesdays and Thursdays, and believed that in this she was finally a part of the army. There were many men of the navy in the hospital, indeed it seemed at times that there could be no one left to man the ships for there were so many in the hospital. She maintained a close correspondence with Imogen, who loved receiving her letters detailing her friendships with Lieutenant Portland and Captain Keith with whom she would meet and walk out on most Sundays. If Imogen was alarmed by Catherine's silence regarding Arabella, she did not say so or even show it, but was simply grateful to hear from her sister, who she missed terribly.

Life in Petrovia Lodge had been hard and lonely for Imogen. She reached her twenty third birthday in quiet solitude. She enjoyed the challenge of raising young Josiah and Beatrice, hearing nothing from their parents save at each of their two Christmases when a lengthy letter in her father's hand arrived at the lodge in time for the end of the year. Penny continued to diligently tend to the job of housekeeper whilst poor Anne found herself in a position of disgrace, not only carrying a baby outside of wedlock, but carrying a gypsy baby to boot. Her acquaintance to Master Filman, one of the seasonal travellers, had borne forth fruit indeed and, although Penny would have cast her sister out for the disgrace that she brought upon Petrovia, Imogen could not send her away and ordered her confinement within the lodge until, in the following spring, she gave birth to a young boy who she called David, after her father.

Two summers after the major left for America, Imogen received a letter telling her that he would shortly be returning and intended to retire, as he had now reached his fiftieth year. There was little affection in it and Imogen felt stung by the cruelty of the tone that he used. Though she would never admit it to anyone, she felt robbed of her chance at having a different life, her circumstances restricting her. Nonetheless, she had tirelessly given the last two years raising the twins and little David when he arrived. When the letter arrived she at once wrote to Catherine to ask that she and Arabella might attend their father's return. She also wrote another letter, a letter of concern, to Mr Dermot for she was worried that, with her father's retirement, he may seek to access that money which the late Mrs Tenterchilt had left for her daughters.

It took two weeks for her sisters to return to the lodge and a further four days before her father and his wife returned. Imogen had worried that they would all be like strangers to her but, the moment they were reunited, the years seemed to fall away. The morning of their father's arrival found the three sisters walking along the river, remembering adventures of the past and reminiscing those daring days.

'It will never seem right here without Mish,' Imogen sighed. Arabella set her face hard and shook her head in a manner that might have meant anything.

'He did not-' Catherine began, but stopped as she saw Arabella setting her face. 'No, I must say it: he did not kill your husband.'

'I am certain that Arabella does not believe he did,' Imogen said quickly.

'But I do,' she whispered. 'It is the only way I can bear to think of him as dead.'

There was a crooked logic to this statement that both Imogen and Catherine had to respect, although both were equally horrified. Imogen was quietly impressed with Catherine's maturity since she had stayed in London. Her temper had ebbed and she seemed more willing and able to accept viewpoints other than her own.

They continued along the riverbank, each trying to consider words to say that would hark back to such carefree former times, but none could. Imogen realised sadly that they were not the same people they had been four years ago, and there was a burden that hung around the necks of all present.

'I wonder what Papa will think on his return,' Catherine mused. 'So much has altered.'

'Here nothing alters. Only time.' Imogen sat down at the river and tipped her head back to look up at the sky. 'And even then I sometimes wonder if it only seems that way.'

'I would forego anything to go back in time,' Catherine sighed. 'There are so many things that have happened that should never have been allowed to.'

'I do believe that we all feel that way,' Imogen whispered.

'Yes,' Arabella faltered, but there was a gleam to her eyes that belied her words. 'Though we should be grateful that we are alive and well. I cannot wait to tell you,' she added, feeling that she might burst with excitement. 'I was going to wait until Papa and Alice returned but-'

She stopped as they all turned at the sound of wooden cartwheels striking the driveway a short distance away. Each of them gathered their skirts and rushed to meet their father, though Imogen hung back, intrigued to know what Arabella had been on the point of saying for, by the colour it brought to her cheeks, it was something about which she was very eager. Penny and Anne were at the door instantly and Imogen knew that one of them had been standing at the window waiting for their return. Neither Josiah, Beatrice nor David made an appearance initially, though this did not seem to bother the two arrivals who stepped out of the carriage, clearly stiff from the journey. To Imogen the first thing that struck her was how much older her father looked and the expression that crossed her face was one of worry on his behalf and could not be fully hidden by her smile. The major did not seem to notice, or chose to ignore this as he rushed to embrace his three daughters. Alice hung back a little, only the faintest of smiles upon her features. Imogen walked over to her and kissed her cheek.

'Come indoors and see your children.' In spite of her misgivings concerning Alice, the true depth of which had only been shared through a series of letters with Mr Dermot, she could see something in her father's bride that she had not noticed the last time she had seen her. There was a vulnerability there, like a young child taking its first steps away from its mother. Alice graciously accepted Imogen's offer and walked after her.

One of the guest rooms had been turned into a nursery and the two children were both sitting there playing. Josiah had a set of wooden soldiers that had been sent to him last Christmas from a toy shop in London. The major was undoubtedly behind the purchase, but it had arrived with no message or note. Josiah loved them. He had two armies, British and Spanish that he pitted against each other. Beatrice was holding one of her rag dolls over David who tried to reach the plaits that hung down from its head. Both of the twins turned to face Imogen and Alice as they entered and they simply stared at the newcomer, understanding nothing of who she was or their connection to her. She knelt down to welcome them into her arms but Beatrice plodded slowly over to Imogen and Josiah simply stared at his mother before turning back to the soldiers.

Alice got to her feet and forced a smile. 'I see they have been well cared for.'

'This is your Mama,' Imogen said to Beatrice and Josiah. 'Come and meet Mama.'

'Anne?' asked Beatrice softly.

'No,' Imogen smiled. 'Anne is David's mama, this is your mama.'

Josiah crawled towards Alice and got unsteadily to his feet before stretching his hand out. Alice looked confused.

'He wants you to shake his hand,' Imogen explained. Whatever sympathy she had felt for the neglected mother disappeared quickly as Alice turned from her son and walked out. Josiah's lip began to tremble as she went and Imogen rushed over to him. 'There now,' she said, taking his hand. 'You can shake my hand instead.'

The disappointment that Imogen bore in her heart about Alice was confined to stay there. She did not speak of it to any of the others and indeed they were all so involved in one another's company that she had not the will to shatter such a thing. When at last the long day was drawing to a close, they sat down to a meal of beef and potatoes and, beaming with a radiance that Imogen had never thought to see in her again, Arabella made her announcement.

'I cannot undo the past,' she began. 'I loved Roger more than I ever thought to love another. But I must consider my poor position in London.'

'What are you saying?' Catherine whispered, horrified that Arabella could even consider their position in London as poor. Working in the hospital she had seen the standards of living that some of the sailors and soldiers had to return to and the selfishness of her sister seemed unbelievable.

'I have decided to be married once more.'

A chorus of questioning cries went round the table, except Alice who smiled across at Arabella.

'Congratulations,' she said softly. 'But be sure he is not a man to gamble.'

Imogen had not thought it possible to silence the room after Arabella's announcement, but nothing could have proved her more mistaken than Alice's words. The three girls looked from Alice to their father, but the major seemed too weary to argue.

'Well,' Arabella whispered, trying to turn the conversation once more. 'I do not believe that he is, though I know he is a great drinker. He is our cousin, Mr Jenkyns.'

'Why is it that Arabella can marry twice yet I cannot find one man to marry?' Catherine mused later as she spoke softly to Imogen.

'We are all of us different, Cat,' she sighed in reply. 'I do not care to think on what my future might contain only that I shall be here tending to the children a while longer, for I saw how ill prepared Alice is to raise her own children.'

'Poor Papa. She should not have said that about gambling.'

'No,' Imogen agreed. 'I foresee that their retirement might not be as idyllic as I had hoped.'

The following day, as a Sunday, found them eating dinner in the middle of the day. A large joint of meat had been collected from town and, after sitting through the church service, they returned home to one of Penny's exquisite Sunday meals. It was at the meal table then, when the food and dessert had been gratefully consumed and the sherry brought out, that the gathered family began their discussions once more.

'I was thinking of taking a ride later, Papa,' Catherine said enthusiastically. 'Can you join me?'

'I rather fear I shall have to disappoint you, my dear,' he replied. 'My leg only worsens with age, but I am certain that Alice would enjoy such an outing.'

'I am certain that she would not,' Alice remarked. 'It is far too muddy, Catherine. One outing in this weather is quite sufficient, and aside from our visit to church, I do believe I shall confine myself here for a time.'

'As you wish,' Catherine replied acidly. 'But mud and rain will not dampen my spirits.'

'Oh, Papa,' Imogen began, changing the subject as quickly as she could. 'Josiah loves his soldiers. He will be quite the commander when he is old enough.'

'That pleases me greatly,' the major responded. 'I had always hoped to have a son to enter the army.'

'Well, your gift to him has known barely a moment's rest.'

'I did not buy him soldiers, my dear girl,' the major laughed, and Imogen frowned. 'Imagine what my wife would say.'

'Then,' Imogen began and shook her head. 'Then where did the soldiers come from?'

'Certainly not us,' Alice responded. 'And I do not care for the fact that you are trying to raise a gypsy child as a brother to my children.'

'That is unfortunate, for I do not care for the fact you are unable to raise your own children.' The response had left Imogen's mouth before she had considered the damage that such words might cause. Alice's eyes flared and Imogen recalled all the words of caution that Mr Dermot had both spoken and written of to her. Alice reached forward and grabbed the hand bell that sat on the table, ringing it before any of the others could object. Penny entered the room and bobbed a curtsey.

'Tell your sister we wish to see her,' Alice said firmly, dismissing her with the wave of her hand.

'You cannot berate her so,' Arabella gasped. 'Papa, tell her that she cannot.'

'I know very well what I can and cannot do beneath the roof of my own house.'

'This is not only your house,' Catherine chimed and pushed herself to her feet. Anne entered the room, her eyes wide and her face as white as a sheet.

'Yes, ma'am?' she whispered, looking across at each one of the people that sat there.

'Look at my hand,' Alice said firmly, extending her left arm towards the maid. 'That ring means that I have a right to bear children. You have no ring, you have not even a man to support you, but look to be supported by us.'

'No, ma'am. Miss Imogen, that is Miss Tenterchilt, looks after David and I earn no money.'

'I daresay you can take your sentimental agreement with you out onto the street. I will not have the child of a gypsy and a common woman, little more than a worker in a workhouse, brought up alongside my own well-bred children.'

'But Ma'am,' Anne pleaded. 'Sir,' she added looking at the major. 'Surely you would not send me away as winter comes on. There will be no work and my poor David will starve and freeze.'

'Enough,' the major said firmly and Anne rubbed the tears from her face. 'I shall not send you away, Anne. You have been a good worker all these years. But likewise I will not tolerate the raising of an illegitimate child as my own. He must be sent away.'

'Papa,' Imogen began while the rest of the room remained in a stunned silence. 'You cannot do this, it would destroy the child and the mother.'

'Imogen, this is my wife's house and if she wishes that the child be sent away, then the child shall be sent away.'

'Do not worry,' Alice said softly. 'I shall not have him sent to the poorhouse. I know of a wonderful institution in America where they give children to couples who cannot bear their own. At least he will be given to someone who can raise him properly.'

'America?' Arabella whispered. 'I thought that you had no plan to return to America.'

'We have not,' Alice replied, as though the matter was simple. 'But I can entrust him to one of the boats that travel there. He need not go alone, for he may take all those soldiers with him. Josiah will not be needing them. Go,' she added, turning away. 'Make your farewells. There is a boat leaves Glasgow at the end of the month and I shall expect your son to be on it.'

'You do not know what it is to be a mother,' Imogen said flatly. 'Nor shall you ever know.'

'Oh, come,' Alice replied. 'I know better than you suppose, for I shall not send my son off to war and death, and I will not have him playing such games in his childhood. The illegitimate son of a servant is precisely the sort of person who should be taken as a soldier, so let him play with the toys.'

'Damn it,' the major shouted, crashing his hand down on the table. 'My son shall be a soldier! Do as you will with your daughter, but I shall have one child who joins Britain's forces abroad and does me proud.'

Imogen was unsure what to make of her father's words. They were both welcome for addressing Alice's unbearable dictation of their life and painful for describing her and her sisters as failing to make their father proud. She glanced at Arabella who seemed to be sharing her thoughts exactly, for her head was lowered with a sense of acceptance as much as pride. Catherine, who had not retaken her seat, walked out of the room but, before either Arabella or Imogen could excuse themselves, Alice and their father began once more.

'I saw how those soldiers were treated, and I shall not raise my son to join them, to lose limbs and life for ungrateful wretches.'

'Men have always fought,' the major snapped. 'He shall be a soldier, he will lead a battalion, a company, a regiment. He will guide his men out onto the fields of war and you shall be proud of him.'

'You forget that this is my house,' she replied. Imogen looked confused. It was their father's house and by right belonged to him, yet he seemed to ignore this fact. 'I shall raise the children within it to my own beliefs and standards.'

'Beliefs and standards?' he shouted back. 'Could you only hear yourself.

You are as pious and righteous as the parson. If that is your rule then rest assured that the moment he is old enough Josiah will leave your house and train in the art of warfare, far beyond your reach.'

Alice did not reply but rose to her feet and left the room. Arabella lifted her chin a little and surveyed the room. Her father's face was red with his clear rage, and it seemed to drain all of the colour out of the rest of the room. She rose to her feet slowly, knowing that she should go and find Anne and ensure that she was well after the eruption of anger and hate that Alice had directed at her. Imogen looked across at her and nodded quickly, a gesture that might have meant anything but that Arabella took to mean that she was right to leave the room.

Imogen waited until she had left before she walked over to the sherry that rested on a small table by one of the doors. She poured some into her father's glass and sat down again.

'Papa,' she whispered. 'What has happened to turn her into such a monster?'

He turned towards her, but his rage subsided as he looking into a face that truly loved him. 'Imogen, my dear, I have made such poor decisions.'

'Nonsense, Papa. You are a leader of men.'

'I failed Arabella. Her husband would still be alive today were it not for me. I lost our life in London, to come here.'

'I like it here, Papa.'

'But you do not belong here, and now shall be a spinster all your life because I have failed you. I lost the estate in London yet your mother still loved me. I gave Alice this house in exchange for fifty pounds of hers that I lost and she cannot bear the sight of me. Sweet Imogen, I cannot find my place in this world without your mother, though I have sought for almost four years.'

'Papa, your place is here, with me. What should I do without a gentleman in my life?' She paused before she added, 'Did you reconcile yourself with Hamish before you left for America?'

'No. I heard what happened to him, and that guilt, as the guilt of Captain Pottinger's demise, rests unbearably heavy upon me. He should never have been a soldier, and I should have respected him far more for the wisdom he showed.'

'It does not matter now,' Imogen said flatly.

'My dear, sweet Imogen,' he replied. 'I am glad that you were born a woman, for you would have made a poor soldier but a perfect wife.'

'I am rather afraid, Papa, that will never happen.'

'That, too, is of my doing.'

Imogen shook her head, but the gesture was not only to dispute her father's words but with a sense of despair. She would never be able to leave the lodge, never find a suitor and never marry, and perhaps that was in part her father's fault, but it was her own too. 'What shall you do about Alice?' she whispered after a time.

'I intend to change my will.'

'Are you sure?' Imogen asked, both shocked and yet relieved by her father's decision.

'Indeed. She disgraced me in America and caused my premature retirement. I shall be quite without funds for a time, and when at last I do receive money I have no wish that she should inherit it upon my death. I shall write to Mr Dermot at once.'

Major Tenterchilt rose and walked through to his study where he began, at once, to scribe a letter to the lawyer. Imogen remained in the dining room. She knew that what had happened between her father and Alice was not legally possible. The house, having been the only property left of their mother's, had passed into the hands of the three sisters. It was impossible for her father to have given it to Alice. Her only choice was to try and intercede with regard to the letter before it reached Mr Dermot. She rushed up to her room and began penning a letter to him.

'Mr Dermot, I find myself in the embarrassing situation of having been caught out. My father believes that he has given the lodge to his wife and wishes to rewrite his will. I am unable and unwilling to tell him of the intricate nature of my mother's will for I rather fear that he is sorely grieved and I wish to bring him no further pain or anxiety. I therefore beg you to attend Petrovia Lodge that the matter might be resolved with far more gentle diplomacy than can be hoped from a series of letters. I find myself in great need of your presence and skilled words to appease my father. Imogen Tenterchilt.'

She stopped as she finished reading it, cursing herself that she had ever become so embroiled in the realm of law and money. Her mother was a shrewd woman indeed to deal so successfully with these things.

The day was drawing to a close when at last Imogen walked down the stairs and rejoined her family. There was a hostile silence to the room that felt wrong somehow. She had never known a silence to be so tense and she looked about, trying to find something to divert it.

'Arabella,' she began as cheerfully as she could. 'Why do not you play the piano? It has not made a sound in far too long.'

Arabella jumped from the chair and cast aside the book that she had been endeavouring to read. Imogen felt pleased with herself as the gentle tones of the piano filled the room.

'Where is Cat?' she asked quickly and the music stopped. Her father looked up at her and even Alice lifted her eyes from the book that she held.

'She went out for a ride,' Major Tenterchilt replied with a tone that suggested he was attempting to hide his concern. 'I expect she retired to bed at once.'

'It has been dark for hours,' Arabella protested, leaving the piano. 'She would not stay out in the rain after dark.'

'I shall see if she is in her room,' Alice said, her voice and words softening her angry temperament.

'Thank you,' Imogen replied. 'I will go out to the stables and see if her horse is there.' She left the drawing room as calmly as she could. When the door was closed, however, she picked up the skirts of her pale dress and ran through the house, out into the rain and did not stop until she went into the stables.

It was dark and she had not thought to bring a lantern with her, for her haste had driven such things from her head. There was a warmth in the stable that caused her to shiver as she stepped in from the torrential rain. With the warmth came the overpowering smell of the beasts themselves and she heard them stirring in their stalls, looking to see who had come in, for the dark did not hinder them as it did her.

She walked past the curved divisions of each of the stalls checking the bolts were fastened until she reached that one where Arabella's stout brown horse should have been. The door was still open and it creaked as she walked in. Whatever her mind told her she would find there she was mistaken for the stall was empty with neither beast nor woman occupying it.

Imogen felt sick with worry and at once rushed to one of the other horses and threw a saddle over its back. She stopped as the stable suddenly flooded with light and Arabella entered carrying a lantern with far more forward thinking than Imogen's racing mind had allowed her.

'She is not here,' Imogen panted, stooping to try and tighten the saddle around the girth of the horse.

'Stop, Imogen,' Arabella said softly. 'There is nothing that can be gained by you riding out into the night. All that shall have happened is that both my sisters will have left me.'

'You are right,' Imogen sighed, pulling the saddle back from the horse. 'What is this dark cloud that has fallen over Petrovia? That last week we talked and laughed so happily, but now we are divided so cruelly.'

'I do believe you know as well as I what the cause is. We are not the family we once were, Imogen. No Mama, no Mish, even Papa seems absent from us despite sitting in the same room. We grew up, Imogen. Perhaps after almost four years, we should just accept this fact. Some day we sisters would always have to part.'

'But not like this,' Imogen sobbed. 'Why would she go like this? Why would she leave us without a word? She must have gone to London, she must have met someone there.'

'Indeed she must, and the moment the sun is over the horizon I shall embark to find her, for I cannot stay overly long. I have a fiancé to return to.'

'Yes, I am so happy for you, Arabella,' Imogen said hugging her sister tightly. 'I do remember that Mr Jenkyns vied for your eye and hand even at that ill-fated dinner party when you and Captain Pottinger formed your attachment.'

'He is as charming as Roger was loving,' Arabella smiled. 'But it does not mean that I shall cease to love Roger.'

'I did not expect it would. Come,' Imogen said, guiding her sister from the stable and recalling once more her role at the core of the family. 'I will be up with the dawn to see you depart.'

The following morning found Imogen and Major Tenterchilt waving farewell to Mrs Arabella Pottinger, soon to become Mrs Arabella Jenkyns. The wedding was arranged for the new year, allowing a further two months for each party to make ready their arrangements. The venue was fixed for Mr Jenkyns' small church on his estate close to Manchester, cutting out a great deal of travel for the Scottish family. Before any such grand arrangements could be made, however, Arabella had been entrusted to deliver the letters to Mr Dermot and she began trying to search for her sister.

Upon hearing that Captain Keith had returned from Spain following the horrendous butchering of the Spanish troops by Napoleon's forces just outside Madrid at a small town called Oscana, she at once wrote to him and sought an audience. She received a reply almost immediately and within the week there came a knock at the door and the captain stood there. He was but a shadow of that man she had known, the heavy woollen coat fell down around his thin figure, but as Chloe ushered him indoors and Arabella welcomed him into the sitting room she saw once again the hidden depths of soul that had made this man her late husband's closest friend.

'Captain Keith,' she said warmly. 'Come and sit by the fire. You look perished.'

'Thank you, Mrs Pottinger.'

'I heard of the terrible news concerning our Spanish allies. Were you there?'

'Not at all, ma'am, though I know many of my men had wished to be. Those French would not have ploughed through so many had the British stood side by side with their Spanish allies.'

'Of that I have no doubt,' Arabella said, feeling proud to be talked to so candidly.

'I am certain, too, that the reports might have made mention of Colonel Sir James Shorefield.'

'Yes, though not with a title. He is a sir?'

'As true a knight as any from King Arthur's time to this. His Majesty and Parliament saw fit to return the good work of Major Shorefield with a promotion to colonel and a knighthood to boot.' Captain Keith nodded sagely. 'None deserved it more.'

'Then he is in London to receive his knighthood?'

'He is an enigma, ma'am, for none know where he resides. He is a very private man and attends no public invitations.'

'A mystery indeed, Captain.'

'I do not think you brought me here to discuss the works of the army and their position in the peninsula.' He paused to thank Chloe who handed him a cup of tea. 'What is it that I can do for you, Mrs Pottinger?'

'You recall my sister, Miss Catherine?' Arabella asked.

'Indeed. A lively soul if ever one lived. Quite the light for our regiment.'

'She has gone missing, sir. I have sought her at the hospital and all those places that she loved to visit, but I have come to an end with no success. Can you think of any who might know of her whereabouts?'

'I am very sorry, Mrs Pottinger. I will ask Lieutenant Portland for, pardon my bluntness ma'am, I know he had hopes regarding her.'

'Have no fear, Captain Keith, I believe she had hopes of her own in a mutual capacity. In the meantime I am obliged to tell the authorities to search for her, though her face on every poster throughout town does not allow her the dignity she deserves.'

'Though it may help, Mrs Pottinger.'

The audience concluded some time later and the pair seemed greatly comforted in the company of one another. When the captain departed he might have been a different man to the one who had stood at the door over an hour before. Arabella was grateful to discuss trivial matters with a man who knew what she had suffered but did not know of the tension that haunted her family home.

Much of the conversation, as was the case for all of London, concerned Sir James Shorefield who, by all accounts, seemed to have led many of the skirmishes into Spain from Portugal to protect the interests of the Spanish allies. His men would do anything he ordered them and, though doubts were held by some in higher office, his results and ability were impeccable. Within the two months leading up to Arabella's marriage he was the fire in every woman's heart and the subject of every gentleman's toast, though no one truly knew who he was. For her own part, Arabella would have gladly shared in the common interest in such a man, but with the impending marriage and the worry over Catherine's disappearance she could find little time to do so.

Arabella appeared in public only once, at a Christmas ball hosted in a grand house at Chelsea. It was there that Colonel Sir James Shorefield broke his public abstinence and appeared. Cheers sounded from the gathered army officers and at once people, men and women alike, rushed to make themselves known to him. Arabella stood back and observed as the man tried to walk down the stairs yet could not for, with each step he took, twenty people blocked his way.

He was far from handsome, Arabella was disappointed to note, for in her mind she had pictured him as she had always dreamed a man should look. His hair was jet black, but caught the light in the most intriguing way so that at times it looked like a purplish blue. He wore a high collared shirt with a pleated front only just visible beneath his exquisitely knotted cravat, and a coat as black as his hair with shining brass buttons.

'He looks the height of society, does he not?' a man close to her asked.

'Perhaps,' she replied. 'But he certainly has not the intelligence to remove those people from his path.' She turned to see whom she was addressing and was surprised to find that Lieutenant Portland stood before her. 'Forgive me, sir, I know he is a great military leader.'

'Indeed he is,' Portland agreed. 'He removes only those who are his enemies, and I for one approve of that. You are alone tonight?'

'Indeed, it seems that way,' she sighed.

'This is the same house that held the ball where your sister did me the honour of dancing with me.'

'Yes, I recall it. Have you heard from her? For after two months I can only expect the worse to have happened.'

'You must not think that, Mrs Pottinger. I do not.' He sighed and offered his hand. 'Come, if you are not interested in meeting our esteemed colonel, perhaps you would do me the honour of dancing with me.'

'Of course,' she said, smiling up at him.

'Captain Keith tells me that you are soon to be married.'

'That is the truth, Lieutenant. My cousin, Mr Jenkyns, and I are going to marry in two weeks time.'

'Then I wish you much happiness, Mrs Pottinger. What of your other sister? Miss Tenterchilt?'

'Imogen?' Arabella asked. 'She remains the most vigilant of our family, carrying the burden of the house. Quite truthfully I do believe she will do that until she is an old maid.'

'You speak uncommonly candidly with me, ma'am,' he replied, shock in his voice.

'I have no mood to dance,' Arabella announced, leaving the lieutenant alone in the centre of the hall.

He watched her go and shook his head thoughtfully. Her behaviour reminded him of Miss Catherine Tenterchilt, with her cavalier manners and brash, bold actions. A concern had grown within him that these attributes might have led her to the reckless course she had embarked upon. Though he spoke to no one of his fears, they were proved well- founded when a letter addressed to Imogen arrived at Petrovia Lodge shortly after new year.

The Tenterchilt family were preparing to travel south to Manchester for Arabella's wedding, from where Imogen intended to travel on to London. The major and his young wife had shared barely a conversation since the day that Alice had forced the removal of David from the house. Anne was never to be seen and would conduct her work in the absence of any of the family, whilst Penny oversaw the meal table. Imogen might have given up believing that Anne was even there only that there were a few gentle touches to the preparations of meals and food. If the hatred that the household held for Alice was obvious, she did not seem to care. She filled her days with all the pastimes a lady should, and paid little or no regard to the two children who continued to grow believing Imogen to be their mother. Whereas to this point Imogen had corrected them, she no longer would or could, for Alice had turned into a beast with such malevolence and hatred that Imogen could not bear to tell the innocent children that they were in any part hers.

It was on that morning that Imogen found a letter on her dressing table in a hand that seemed unlike any writing she had seen before. She opened it with great curiosity but read on in horror.

'My dear Imogen, Please do not judge me on what I have done, for I have done it solely with the family interest at heart. I shall make Papa proud. I sail onboard an Indiaman and mean to fulfil Papa's dream of having a child raise a sword. Whatever love you can still bear for me through this news, please do not tell the others of the family. I wish my name to return home with honour, let them find out then. Ever yours.'

There was no name at the bottom but, although the handwriting was disguised, none was needed. Imogen read it so many times in those few minutes that she could have recited it by the time they left Petrovia Lodge. Josiah and Beatrice were to remain and Penny and Anne were informed how to look after them. Alice attended but surely only to anger and aggravate the family party. The major sat silently and clutched the walking cane that he carried as though he would lash out with it at any time. Imogen, for her part, gazed out of the windows and watched as the coach passed through snow covered scenery and towering mountains. She could not remember the last time that she had travelled and there should have been an unparalleled charm to it, but the letter she carried within her small case obscured that. The pain at her sister's disappearance far outweighed her shame, but she had no way of knowing how to send a message to Catherine to tell her.

They spent a night at the town of Newcastle before continuing on to Manchester. The silence of the second day would have matched that of the first except that this time they were joined by a Mr Coultard who, to her father's delight, had been a captain in the recent war before promotion had banished him from the frontline and placed him behind a desk. Imogen listened with only half an interest, yet she could not help but recognise the admiration that the man had for the soldier who had led them, a Colonel Sir James Shorefield. Indeed, it seemed that the whole of England was awash with tales of his successes and heroics, being awarded a knighthood by the king and an advanced rank by horse guards.

'Single-handedly fought back the French from the Portuguese border,' Major Coultard boasted on behalf of the absent man.

'No small feat,' Major Tenterchilt replied, only adding to the man's legend. 'For I hear tell that the French push strong against both Spanish Royalists and the Portuguese, too.'

'Indeed, sir, he succeeds where other men fail.'

Imogen sighed and shook her head but neither of the two men seemed to notice but continued their exciting tales. She had heard enough of the war and soldiers and found it dull and hard to listen to. They reached Manchester in the evening and, by the time they arrived at Mr Jenkyns' grand house at Horland Park, Imogen was so tired that she had to excuse herself at once.

Horland Park, as she was to discover the next morning, was to the south of Manchester where the hills began to climb to greater heights as they became the Pennines. They seemed tame to Imogen as she walked out into the fine covering of snow but, despite the apparent gentility of the area, she walked only a few steps before she felt chilled to the bone. She clutched continually to the letter that Catherine had sent and felt both sick with worry and cornered by her concern that she should not disrupt the wedding.

She breakfasted alone, as she always did. It gave her time to gather her thoughts for the coming day and steel herself against whatever hardships might face her. Subsequently she spent the morning staring out across the grounds of Horland Park and contemplating what she could do to help ease her burden. She turned at the sound of a knock on the door before walking over to answer it. Arabella stood there and Imogen embraced her before stepping back to let her in.

'Mrs Pottinger, soon I shall not know what to call you,' Imogen laughed and, remembering how greatly laughter helped her, she felt better at once.

'I hope I shall always be Arabella to you,' came the reply and Arabella walked over to the window and stared out. 'Do you think I am doing the wrong thing, Imogen?'

'Of course not. What do you mean?'

'In truth,' Arabella replied, sighing heavily, 'I am in love still with dear Roger. Am I wrong then to marry another?'

'You should not ask me, Arabella,' Imogen said softly. 'I who have never known love. How can I hope to advise or influence one with so much love in her?'

'Because you have never failed to know the best course of action. Dear Imogen, you must know that, since Mama's death, everyone in this family, and even those outside the bounds of family, regards you in the highest position for knowledge and information. Those two things upon which our world is based, and were you a man you should be more powerful than any living.'

Imogen felt shocked under the weight of such a compliment and her cheeks began to burn.

'Tell me please, dear Imogen, am I wrong?'

'Can you live a life in solitude?' Imogen asked. 'For that is the true question. There is no right or wrong, for you know you love our dear cousin, only not as dearly as you did the man who has gone. He can never come back, Arabella, so the true question is: can you live a life in solitude?'

'No,' she replied quietly. 'Yet I feel that I do wrong by Roger's memory.'

'Captain Pottinger would tell you himself that he would wish your happiness to come before his memory, Arabella. And you can be sure of it, for you would wish the same for him.'

'Whatever would I do without you, Imogen?' Arabella asked hugging tightly to her sister. 'And what of Catherine? Have you found any trace of her?'

Imogen stiffened and looked across at the desk where the crumpled letter lay. Arabella noticed and looked up into her younger sister's eyes.

'Was she so disappointed in my choice that she could not attend the wedding?'

'It is not that,' Imogen said warmly. 'She has chosen to travel, that is all. She found safe passage on board a boat and is travelling. Many ladies do it now.'

'Has she a companion?'

'Many,' Imogen answered with certainty and, in spite of the fact she had shared only a fraction of the truth, she felt happier for being able to reassure someone else concerning Catherine's safety.

'Have you been in love, Imogen?'

The blunt manner of Arabella's question left her stunned for a moment before at last she answered, 'I do not think so. You have enough love for us both and I fear Cat finds love rather more of a burden than a blessing.'

'It is a shame, for I know one young gentleman who I do believe would wish to change her mind.'

'I cannot foresee that she will marry soon.'

There were no more words spoken for a time and each sister tried to discern what the other was thinking and planning before at last Arabella said quickly,

'Meals are always so punctual here, we had better prepare and be ready on time. For a man who is not in the military, Mr Jenkyns is very strict with his routine and timing.'

'Then I shall make myself presentable and join you downstairs shortly.' Imogen watched as her sister left the room before she returned once more to the window. The snow was slowly melting from the ground, turning to slushy puddles with surfaces that trembled in the wind. The stunted spire of the church which would tomorrow play host to her sister's second wedding was visible to the south, poking over the curve of the hill. How unfair it was that Arabella should talk to her so much of love, and request advice on this topic that she agreed was alien to Imogen. She looked down at the letter once more and stifled the tears that formed in her eyes. Even Catherine, whose headstrong and unconventional approach to life was deplorable to the female race, had found a suitor knowingly or not, yet she was left to raise children that were not hers for a mother who neither cared nor expressed gratitude.

After a time she descended the stairs and walked through the halls trying to find the dining room. The estate house was very large with an abundance of halls and doors that led off. Imogen knocked on several of the doors to no reply and was relieved to at last hear voices behind one. She knocked and walked in. Two women were there, neither of them familiar to her and she quickly apologised. She began closing the door but paused as they both turned to face her. Their faces held a look of scorn and Imogen felt both riled and stung by the manner of their gaze.

'I said I was sorry,' she muttered. 'I am only looking for the dining room but this house is so large.'

'You are late for dinner, ma'am,' one said quietly. 'Cook hates to see the food go cold.'

'Imogen,' Arabella's voice said cheerily and she turned to see her sister. 'Come along, the dinner will be quite ruined.'

Feeling like a child who had been chided, Imogen walked after her sister and into the dining room a few doors down from where she had been. Her father and Alice were both there already, as was Mr Jenkyns and they all looked across at her as she entered.

'Sorry,' she whispered again. 'I became quite lost.' She kept silent through much of the meal, for the others did also, and stayed with her head down so that it was only at the end of dinner that she noticed a face looking directly at her. 'Mama?' she whispered although it was clear that no answer would come, for she addressed only paint on canvas.

'Yes, indeed,' Mr Jenkyns said with a smile. 'I like to have her here. My cousin, your mother, was a source of great inspiration to me and I like to have her in a room that I use often that she might be there when I need her.'

'She is so young,' Imogen said, smiling in a childish way as though the presence of even a picture of her mother enabled her once more to be a child again.

'Yes it was painted shortly before her marriage.'

'I remember,' the major said, surprisingly dreamy in the fond memory.

Alice stiffened and sighed.

'It is clear to see where your daughters gain their beauty,' she said, and Imogen felt almost regret for her. This was another part of her new life that she neither knew nor could understand.

'Tell me of this man who leads our army in Portugal,' Major Tenterchilt said looking across at Mr Jenkyns.

'Sir Arthur Wellesley?'

'No, man,' the major replied. 'I know of him. This Shorefield man.'

'Ah,' Mr Jenkyns replied with a laugh. 'He is quite the toast of the nation. A man so fearless in battle is easy to find, but one with luck is much trickier. I do believe he has a golden future ahead of him.'

'You believe in luck?' Alice asked quickly.

'I? No, but the men who fight for him do and that is all that matters. Until lately he never made a public appearance. Though, in the lull on the continent, he has been withdrawn to London and now walks the streets in disguise.'

'I understand why,' Arabella added. 'I saw him at a ball in London and he was quite suffocated by the surge of people wishing to accolade him. I should hate such a thing.'

'Indeed,' Imogen added. 'It makes me panic to think of it.'

'And is it true?' the major asked once more, returning to the original conversation. 'These things that he is reported as doing, did he do them?'

'I was not there, Major. I could not say for certain that he performed any such noble deeds, only that the king acknowledges a truth in them and that will have to suffice for me.'

'He does sound gallant,' Alice said in a dreamy way.

'He did not look so gallant with a look of terror upon his face,' Arabella laughed. 'What is the use of being fearless in battle if at home you must disguise yourself as a pauper? In truth, Alice, you are far better with Papa than any such charlatan.'

Imogen looked up at her mother once more and ignored the rest of the conversation. What would she have made of such a fuss over a hero? Undoubtedly she would have declared that the man was a hero because there was no one else to fill the position of a leader, and she and Major Tenterchilt would debate the importance of heroes to the common people. She could not imagine Alice sharing anything save an argument with her father. She looked across at Arabella and Mr Jenkyns and smiled slightly. In truth she felt that Arabella and her new choice of husband formed a much better couple than she had done with the captain, who had been far more gentle and soft than Arabella herself. Imogen was certain that the society wife of a parliamentarian was a better role for Arabella than the wife of an army captain.

If Arabella had any further nerves concerning the match she did not express them, but looked a radiant bride at the church in the morning. There were a handful of people there to wave them farewell as they embarked to Mr Jenkyn's second estate in Yorkshire. Imogen sighed as she stood behind the coach which disappeared beyond the hill.

'Are we to head home?' she asked her father, as they walked the short distance back to the house.

'Were you not to carry our affairs on to London, Imogen?'

Imogen nodded, wishing that her father had forgotten such things in light of the celebration, for she was loathe to visit London. She nodded slightly and walked through the porch, into the house. 'Of course, Papa. That is what I shall do.'

They spent a further night at Horland Park before readying to leave. Alice was ready early, waiting by the door for her husband to emerge. Imogen crept down once more to the dining room and opened the door. The furniture was covered in sheets but the picture of her mother still smiled down. She was sitting at a table, which seemed most unusual, and had her elbow on the desk and her right hand on the opposite shoulder. For the first time she noticed something peculiar about the picture, rather like it had been modified, as her left shoulder seemed raised and disproportionate. Imogen jumped as someone spoke.

'I thought I should find you here.' Her father stood there and smiled.

'I miss her terribly, Papa.'

'Yes, as do I.'

'There is something wrong with the portrait though. She looks taller on her left hand side.'

'It was amended I believe, to please the Jenkyns family. A man used to stand there, her hand rested on his, which was on her shoulder.'

'Why was he erased?' she asked. 'Who was he?'

'An army officer who threatened to dishonour her.'

'How?'

'Enough, Imogen,' he said firmly, but there was no malice in his voice, only resignation. 'I do not wish to remember anymore. Are you prepared for your trip?'

'I believe so.' She did not question her father anymore on the subject of her mother for it was evidently painful to him. Instead she collected her two bags of luggage and prepared for the journey down to the capital. She had not been to London since she was a child and yet she would not have had it any other way. Her life had been good to her and, though far from perfect, it had given her opportunities and chances that she had never thought able to take.

CHAPTER NINE
Tuesday 30th January 1810

She parted from her father in Manchester and at once felt very much alone as she stepped onto the stagecoach. There were three other passengers and all were men, but she had little cause for alarm for none of them spoke to, or even acknowledged, her. She was forced to stay the night at Peterborough for the journey to London was too great for one day, and the following morning she travelled south once more. She reached London late in the afternoon and stepped out as the chimes of Saint Paul's cathedral echoed four o'clock. There was a continuous flow of people who passed through the great square, coming and going in their efforts to return home before the night took hold. Imogen at once marched into the enormous building and looked around her. Candles were lit and there were a small number of people moving around the nave. She walked up to one of them.

'Pardon sir,' she began, biting back the shivers that the cold afternoon instilled in her. 'I am looking for a solicitor. A Mr Dermot.'

The man to whom she had spoken looked at her and shook his head. 'You are in London now, young lady. Solicitors are plentiful and individuals so rarely known.'

'Then how can I find him?' she asked softly.

'Where are you staying?'

'Staying?' she whispered, realising that she had nowhere to return to. 'I shall find somewhere.'

'Do not worry,' he said and, for a reason that she could not understand, she felt compelled to do as he said and almost at once she relaxed. 'Agnes,' he called and beckoned a woman over from where she stood further in the nave. 'Have you a bed for this poor child?'

'I should say I do,' Agnes replied warmly. She was an old woman with grey hair that still carried some streaks of brown. There was a warm expression on her sagging face and her eyes shone in the candlelight.

'I can pay you once I have met up with the solicitor.'

'Collecting riches untold, no doubt,' Agnes chuckled. She shook her head firmly. 'I will not hear of payment. What is a night's accommodation amongst two Christian maids?'

'That is most generous of you,' Imogen said warmly. 'I shall be no imposition, I assure you.' She picked up her bags and walked after Agnes and out into the darkening night.

Agnes Snirting owned a large house close to the river which she had opened to travellers, for she had no use for its enormous size. She explained to Imogen how it had been left to her by an uncle she had never known existed and subsequently she had been helping out poor lost souls since then. The building itself looked dank and miserable with boarded windows and Imogen began to feel afraid as they reached the door but inside she could hear the sound of music and, as the door was opened, warm firelight rushed to greet her. The sound she had heard was a fiddle, and a man sat with a peculiar drum that he held vertically and seemed to stroke with the heavy glancing blows of a beater in his other hand. There was a rustic feel to the environment and she felt at once both fascinated and sidelined by the surroundings. There was a rickety staircase that Agnes led her up, waving dismissively at the tenants who whooped and called happily at her as she entered.

'Here you are,' she said, pushing open a door that led off the landing at the top of the stairs. 'There will be food downstairs. I expect you will be starving after your journey.'

'I am not sure I am dressed for such a party,' Imogen replied which raised a warm laugh from Agnes' weather beaten face.

'Every night is like this here.'

'How do you sleep?'

'Only when we are very tired. Have you no music in your life?'

'Not since my two sisters left. I was never so good at playing the pianoforte.'

'Well, we have nothing so grand here. Fiddles and flutes for the main part, and the voices God blessed us all with.'

Agnes said goodnight and hobbled out of the room, telling Imogen to bolt the door after her.

'It is not that they would come in on purpose, but when they are merry they do not know what they are doing.'

Imogen followed her advice and bolted the door before preparing for bed. The room was cold and musty and unlike anything that she had ever known before. The window was boarded shut and yet somehow the wind whipped through tiny gaps too small to see through. The bed was like bricks and she eventually decided to lay out a dress over it before she curled up to sleep. The music continued to drift up from downstairs until at last the calls and songs gained the better of her and she walked over to the door, unbolted it and stood there listening.

The man who sang had a strange accent and it made his words peculiar and difficult to understand. Many of the songs that he sang were fun, boisterous ones that the other people joined in with during choruses in varying degrees of musicality but, as the evening wore on, the tone of the music altered and he sang softer, more haunting tunes and Imogen felt spellbound by it. Eventually the other inhabitants of the house began to disperse to their own rooms and she shut the door quickly not wishing to encounter any of the people. She leaned back against the bolted door and sighed thoughtfully. This was not the London she had heard about, neither as glamorous as Arabella had described nor as cruel as Catherine's letters implied. How strange it was that three sisters should find the same town so very different. She listened as she heard voices close to her.

'You are not sleeping in your own room, Agnes?' said the man with the peculiar accent.

'No, no. Now have no worries on my account. There is a young lady in there. Met her earlier. She has a better need of that room than I tonight.'

'I hope she is paying it at full rates.'

'Hush,' Agnes said with a laugh. 'I will not hear of money. Poor half starved lass looks like she has none anyway.'

'She did not come down for food,' the man pointed out.

'You Irish,' Agnes chuckled. 'You see the world so black and white.'

'Green and orange, Agnes,' he corrected her. They were moving further along the corridor as they spoke so that their words faded and only a mumbling was audible.

As the house fell silent, however, Imogen began to feel afraid. She rebuked herself for believing that she would be safe and lay on the bed awake, staring at the ceiling with both anger and fear. She did not believe that she should ever fall asleep although she must have done for she was awoken by a pounding on the door.

'No need to knock the whole house down,' she heard Agnes laughing. 'She was just so tired, bless her.'

'Who is it?' Imogen asked nervously.

'There is a gentleman here to see you, my dear,' Agnes said sweetly. 'He insists on shaking the timbers of my house so if you would be so kind as to assure him you are both alive and well then my home might remain standing a while longer.'

'Yes, of course,' Imogen laughed, and all the fear that she had felt in the darkened hours subsided. She rose from the bed and unbolted the door. She was not sure who she expected to see standing there, but it was a broad shouldered man who filled almost the entire doorway. He had a thin face despite his bulk and small eyes that shone when Imogen opened the door.

'Ma'am,' he said bowing his head. 'Mr Dermot asked me to come.'

'Mr Dermot?' she began. 'Oh, thank goodness, for I had no idea how to find him.'

'You need not have worried yourself, ma'am, for Mr Dermot would have found you.'

'Please wait while I collect my things.' She grabbed her bags but left the dress on the bed. 'Thank you, Agnes,' she said as she walked past the old woman. 'I know you will not hear of payment, but my conscience will not rest without it. You aided me in the hour I most needed it.'

'I did not do it for money,' Agnes said firmly, but it did not stop her from gratefully receiving the coins that Imogen gave her.

Imogen followed the man out of the house but stopped at the doorway.

'How do I know that you are who you claim to be?'

'Mr Dermot was certain that you would say something like this, I am only surprised that it took you so long to ask.' He produced a letter in Imogen's own hand and offered it to her.

'Mr Dermot does not miss anything, does he?' she said with a smile.

'No, indeed he does not. Some say it is the Scot in him, others the devil.'

Imogen shook her head and followed him out to the street. By daylight the city looked very different, though equally unwelcoming in its dirt and squalor. She began to understand what Catherine had spoken of in her letters, and she wished that her sister had remained in London, for she had found her place here. Imogen could not be free of her constant worry on behalf of her younger sister.

Around the corner of the street, a horse drawn coach waited and it was up to this that her guide led her. He opened the door and helped her into the enclosed carriage. Mr Dermot sat inside and Imogen began to feel that she had been made a game of in some way.

'How did you know where to find me, Mr Dermot?' she demanded, disregarding the usual pleasantries of meetings.

'I was at the square outside the cathedral, Miss Tenterchilt. There to meet you when your coach arrived. I confess I was intrigued to know where your proactive nature would find you. James,' here he indicated to the other man who, having helped Imogen into the coach had also entered, 'followed you last night. I could not have you disappearing into London with no care for your safety.'

'You might have approached me when I first arrived.'

'My dear Miss Tenterchilt, your haste was the only thing that matched my intrigue.'

Imogen sighed and shook her head. 'You know, of course, why I am in London.'

'Your father's will,' Mr Dermot replied, no emotion evident in his voice. Imogen looked out of the coach windows as houses and parkland vanished behind them.

'Was it wrong of me to ensure he did not gamble away the rest of Mama's estate?'

'The late Mrs Tenterchilt was the wisest woman I ever knew. She left the legal side of the estate to you in the hope that you would do exactly as you have done, although there are some matters that must be discussed relating to your father's affairs in America.'

'Must we discuss it now, in front of this man, who is a stranger to me.'

'I beg pardon,' James said quickly.

'You did not introduce yourself?' Mr Dermot laughed as he questioned the other man. 'No, I can see you would not. Allow me to introduce Mr James Hamilton.'

'Mr Hamilton,' Imogen said bowing her head slightly while he awkwardly did the same. 'Mr Dermot,' she continued. 'Knowing this gentleman's name does not mean I wish him to know my business.'

'Mr Hamilton has an interest in law and wishes to learn as an apprentice.'

'Are you not too old to be an apprentice, sir.'

'Miss Tenterchilt,' Mr Dermot began, but Mr Hamilton raised his hand slightly, stopping the words that the lawyer was about to say.

'I meant no offence, sir,' she protested.

'There is no offence taken and, should you wish me to no longer be a part of your affairs, I shall of course acquiesce.' Imogen raised her hand to her mouth, trying to stop the words that threatened to spill. 'Perhaps, following your disappointment at your venue last night you would, however, do me the honour of allowing me to walk you through some of the finer areas of the city tomorrow.'

'Thank you, sir. If my business is concluded, I should very much appreciate that.'

The coach stopped and Mr Hamilton stepped out. 'Then I shall call on you.' He took her hand and lowered his head before walking into a large building beyond a courtyard.

'Drive on,' Mr Dermot shouted and at once they rolled forward.

'What is that place?' she asked him.

'Horse Guards.'

'But I thought that Mr Hamilton was a lawyer?'

'A lawyer may work in many places, Miss Tenterchilt, and in many guises.' Mr Dermot smiled across at her as he watched her eyes narrow.

'How long must this incessant journey last?' she demanded.

'Not long.' Mr Dermot turned to look out the window and tightened the sleek black coat he wore. 'You were quick to accept Mr Hamilton's offer of a tour tomorrow.'

'What of it? As you have my interests so keenly guarded you would certainly have interjected had it been the improper thing to do.'

'You are not in your highland lodge any longer, Miss Tenterchilt. Please be wary, for even good men in the city have their own agendas and they may not be so Kantian in their beliefs as you are.'

'I do not like this place, Mr Dermot.'

'It is no place for someone so accustomed to freedom.'

'Why could you not have come to Petrovia Lodge?'

'Major Tenterchilt would certainly know of your amendments to the finances if I had done. And besides,' he paused and shook his head, 'I am still haunted by the harm I caused on my last visit.'

The coach stopped on a road of identical houses that reached, unending, in both directions. Mr Dermot stepped down and assisted Imogen out. She gratefully took her two bags from the footman and stepped back onto the pavement while Mr Dermot settled the bill. He turned and walked towards her, ushering her in to one of the buildings.

'And here,' he began theatrically, 'in the suffocated city, is my office. Perhaps the lodge would have been better.' He beckoned a young boy of scarcely twelve years of age to walk forward. 'Enough of your ogling, Thomas, take Miss Tenterchilt's bags. You must excuse us,' he continued, addressing Imogen once more. 'Law is so often the realm of men that we are quite unused to a lady's company.'

'Thank you, Thomas,' Imogen said as the boy hurried to take the cases into a back room only to appear moments later in the doorway, still staring at her. Mr Dermot led her up a flight of stairs into his own office where he found her a seat and stood at the window, looking down into the street. She began to feel uncomfortable as the silence stretched out before them.

'My father wishes to exclude the current Mrs Tenterchilt from his will.'

'That is not a problem, Miss Tenterchilt.'

'How so, Mr Dermot? Please speak plainly, for I was certain that his signature must appear on the document.'

'And indeed it shall, though we can draw it up together and you return with it to Petrovia. But your father has no money left to leave.'

'How so?' Imogen repeated, anxious suddenly.

'What do you know of your father's affairs in America?'

'He was sent as a diplomat, I believe.'

'Not *why* he was there,' Mr Dermot replied, turning to face her and leaning down on the chair behind the cluttered desk so that Imogen felt that she was being told off. '*While* he was there. Two years do not just pass idly for any of us.'

'I do not know,' she whispered in return. 'But what of his pension?'

'War brews in America even now. War your father was supposed to subside.' He pulled out his chair and sat down on it. 'It would appear that his rank and pension counted for little with his new wife.'

'Whatever do you mean?'

'That the current Mrs Tenterchilt was not only a sympathiser to the American cause, she spied upon your father and funded their enterprises with his money. Ignorance was a poor defence against the events that might have led him to trial, but it saved his life, though it cost him every penny he had and had hoped for.'

'Alice? Then why was she not tried?'

'That is information I do not have. Does my news shock you so, Miss Tenterchilt? You have gone terribly pale, come to the window and take some air.'

He helped her to her feet and guided her to the window that he opened wide. At once the chilled January wind rushed in and bit at her face, causing her to shiver. Mr Dermot snatched his great coat from the stand and placed it around her shoulders.

'Let me get you some food, Miss Tenterchilt.'

'Thank you,' she whispered.

'I will amend this wrong that was brought upon your family, Miss Tenterchilt. I shall not rest until I have apportioned blame to the guilty and justice to the innocent.'

'I know you will not,' she whispered. 'Nor shall I.'

She remained standing by the window as he departed to find her some food. Life in the London streets was hectic and tens of people passed through the streets, never once looking up at the window where she stood, a peculiar figure with a gentleman's coat wrapped over her delicate dress. She made a promise to herself that, whatever should happen in her life to come, she would never find herself once more in this city, for she loathed it so intensely.

The day passed by with much work and little talk, for Mr Dermot maintained the Scottish trait that, unless a word was necessary, it should not be spoken. For her own part, she appreciated this. Her father had shielded her from his downfall, and this revelation left her feeling confused and with much to think about. She could not imagine her mother ever doing any such thing and her thoughts turned once more to the peculiar and altered painting that had hung in Horland Park. When at last the evening fell and the day surrendered to shadows, Imogen raised the second query that she had.

'There is another matter I wish to discuss with you, sir.'

'Indeed, Miss Tenterchilt? Then let us discuss it quickly, for the streets of London are not safe for a lady after nightfall.'

'You spoke of knowing, and indeed admiring, our dear brother, Sergeant Major Gordon.'

'A-ha,' Mr Dermot said, almost victoriously. 'I knew when next we met you would mention him. Forget him, Miss Tenterchilt.'

'You praised him, Mr Dermot. You met him. You know he was not capable of such deeds they accused him of. He was not a killer.'

'Miss Tenterchilt, do not think that there is anything on this earth that a man would not defend so jealously as a woman. You must see that therein lies the factor you have forgotten from your logical mind. Hamish Gordon is dead, be content that we who knew him know that he died a martyr and not a criminal.'

'I cannot accept that. And I cannot believe that you would accept that either.'

'Then you hold me too high in your elevated esteem, Miss Tenterchilt, for that is exactly what I believe.'

'Where are my bags?' she asked, eager suddenly to leave the office, and indeed the city, behind her. 'You spoke truthfully that each person has agendas of their own. I was foolish enough to believe that yours was to assist and help my family and myself.'

'Thomas!' Mr Dermot snapped and the boy appeared almost at once. 'Miss Tenterchilt's bags. Have them ready.' The boy hurried off and Mr Dermot turned to Imogen. 'You are wise beyond your years, sex, and station, but those things will not be enough to protect you in the city if you show an interest in a topic the city does not wish you to. Hamish Gordon is dead, that is the end of it.'

'Thank you for your candidness.' She blinked away the tears that threatened to spill from her eyes but Mr Dermot did not comment on it. Instead his voice became soft and he continued in a gentler tone.

'I have arranged a room for you in a slightly more prosperous establishment than you enjoyed last night. And find yourself a shawl for tomorrow. Dear Mr Hamilton enjoys his outdoor walks even in the most inclement of weather.'

This change in the man left her confused, but she thanked him and took a coach to the address he provided. It was a house on the end of a street with steps going up to the front door, but before she had climbed them the door was opened and a woman bobbed a curtsey.

'I am Chloe, Ma'am.'

She spent the night in her sister's house feeling as though she were trespassing, and yet there was a part of her that so welcomed the homeliness that, for a time, she simply sat by the fire and cried. Chloe was a perfect maid, asking no questions but always on hand to comfort her. The night was in its deeper stages when at last Imogen withdrew to bed. She was awoken the next morning by Chloe knocking on the bedroom door.

'There is a Mr James Hamilton here, ma'am. He says he has an appointment with you.'

Imogen quickly rose from the bed and dressed. It was approaching midday before she was at last ready to go out with Mr Hamilton. She walked down the stairs and into the living room where he stood looking at the miniatures upon the mantelshelf. She regarded him, unnoticed for a time. It was clear by the manner in which his dark hair clung closely to his head that he was accustomed to wearing a hat. Indeed, she noticed as she watched him looking at the ornaments, he carried a wide brimmed hat under his arm. He had a withdrawn stance, almost apologetic, yet as she said his name, he stood at once to attention in a military fashion.

'Miss Tenterchilt,' he said warmly. 'You startled me, ma'am. This is you?' he asked picking up one of the pictures.

'It was. Some years ago. Are you to show me the beautiful parts of this city, or must I return to Scotland believing such places are a myth?'

'If you have seen nothing of London that inspires you before this day is out, then I shall accept such places to be no more than rumours.'

They departed and walked through the city streets, discussing such trivial matters as the weather and the difference between Scotland and England, and Imogen felt surprisingly comfortable with the man before her.

'What made you choose law, Mr Hamilton?' she asked at length.

'It is a short term fancy, Miss Tenterchilt. Wellesley prepares to launch another attack on the French shortly and I shall sail out once more. But a fighting man has only limited days before him in service. I will not always be able to fight with the vigour I have now.'

'Let us hope there is not always the need,' Imogen sighed. 'Then you are in the army, Mr Hamilton?'

'Indeed, for a time. I have joined ranks in France, Portugal and Spain, yet wish for nothing more than peace.'

'That is not spoken as a true soldier. My father would never entertain the thought of an officer becoming a lawyer.'

'He may be right. I seem ill suited to law.'

'No one ever learnt everything in one day, Mr Hamilton. I imagine you continue to develop as a soldier and the same must be said of law. You cannot train for a month, you must engage for years. Mr Dermot is a good man, despite his erratic nature and shifting manners. He will see to it that you successfully qualify.'

'You speak very highly of him, Miss Tenterchilt.'

'Indeed, I owe a great deal to him, my life included. He values those things that I, too, hold in high esteem. For the most part at least.'

'Then I have no fear in giving you this,' he drew from his pocket a leather-bound book. 'He assured me that you would see a significance in it.'

'Thank you, sir, but he warned me that each person in the city has an agenda private to themselves. I am almost too wary to take it.'

'He told you that?' Mr Hamilton laughed. 'Take it and see what significance you can find. I assure you my agenda is solely to abandon the boredom I find myself in.'

She looked puzzled and took the book from his outstretched hand, flicking to the front page and reading aloud 'Hours of Idleness'. She laughed. 'I cannot imagine what he means.'

'Perhaps a reading of it will help tease out the meaning. I am certain there is one.'

She paused in closing the book as she noticed an inscription on the front cover. '"Beauty shines forth from Scots in England, signed James Shorefield." You are not James Hamilton?'

'When not with the army I am James Hamilton,' he said, shame seeping into his voice for presuming to fool her. 'Is it so wrong to crave insignificance?'

'What a fool you must take me for,' she hissed, passing the book back to him. 'I have heard of you; your brave deeds and your heroic accolades: a promotion, a knighthood. Why would any man with so much wish to play a part in the cruel trickery of a woman who has nothing?'

'You misunderstand my intentions so severely,' he replied, and Imogen lowered her head. 'How you reacted to discover who I was, that is to always be my fate.'

'I would not have cared who you were so long as you were honest.'

'That is not true, Miss Tenterchilt, and I see from the look in your eyes that you know your own lies.'

'So is it true?'

'Is what true?' he asked, puzzled by the change in her tone and words.

'All those things that people say you did, all the feats of courage, are they all true?'

'I expect few women would understand, yet I know that you will. I have faced death too many times. It is as though when the end seems imminent there is a need to continue, to defend, to lead. That is all the men see, the bravery and heroic deeds belong to them, not me.'

'Well answered, sir,' she replied. 'How long have you been in the army?'

'A short time, only. I was called to service scarcely two years ago, but was fortunate to find such inspiring officers.'

'And your family? What of them?'

'I do not know for sure. I know that my father was a soldier, but my mother died when I was young.'

'I am sorry,' Imogen replied, feeling aggrieved by her own question. 'But I had not heard the name Shorefield before.'

'I do not come from the same class as yourself, Miss Tenterchilt, and relied greatly upon the kind generosity and encouragement of dear friends to obtain the position I have now.'

'I do not seem able to say anything right.' Imogen blushed.

'No, my dear Miss Tenterchilt, you must not think that. I am only open with you for I have been told that you are a woman with whom the truth might always so freely be shared.'

'Then, in token of my wish to show a mutual respect, please allow me a question of you.'

'Of course,' he replied and passed the book back to her before standing to attention awaiting her question.

'Do you know, or did you know, a Captain Roger Pottinger?'

Colonel Sir Shorefield's face faltered for a moment before he steeled himself and raised his chin obstinately. 'I know of him. I knew of him,' he corrected himself. 'And I know, too, that it was your older sister to whom he was married.' He sighed but Imogen was determined to draw out an explanation of events from the man before her. 'I cannot tell you what you want to hear, Miss Tenterchilt. I did not see what happened that night in

Prussia. I do not know. Though I have no such uncertainty that Captain Pottinger was sent on such a mission to fail.'

'What do you mean, sir?'

'Miss Tenterchilt,' he said, stopping to stand in front of her and he took her empty hand in his own two, his head bowed too low for her to properly see his face and expression. 'I care little for the wars that rage overseas but I will not condemn the men who fight them. Captain Pottinger lies in the dirt of a north Prussian village. Let this intrigue and obsession with his death lie there with him.'

'Forgive me,' she said coolly. She was lost in the city, yet she cared little for it as she walked away from him. He was right, of course, but there was a part of her that continued to question the truth of the story she had been told and the guilt that had been apportioned to her beloved Mish. Life at the lodge had changed beyond all that she had known the year he went away and, in her romantic soul, she could not accept that his fate had been in any way justifiable. She continued through the city alone now, for Sir James Shorefield had made no effort to follow her, and did not stop until she reached the river. For a time she stood rather like a beacon in her pale dress and fresh, clean shawl, for all those around her were drab dockworkers and they dutifully lowered their eyes as they trudged past her. She stood, overwhelmed by the stench of the water but fascinated by its sheer size and industry, for countless boats of varying sizes passed along its currents. How different it was to that river that she had left behind, where it rushed over rocks and raced onwards down the valley and out of sight. Here the river was slow and seemed to churn the very earth that it went through. It was brown and dirty and presently it filled her with a great disgust. She loathed London. How could her two sisters have found any place in such a godforsaken city?

'You would not believe the number I have fished out of this river,' a voice said close to her. 'Plenty of your type, too.'

She turned to face an old man, timeless in his haggard aging for, though his body seemed frail and weak, there was a light to his eye and a glow to his face that showed how alert he truly was.

'I was not going to throw myself in,' she said pointedly.

He just nodded and walked on his way, becoming lost in the crowd of other such persons. She continued to walk along the river bank. Sometimes it was easy to follow with the overcrowded houses overlooking it with their hollowed window gaze, at other times the road left the river at a wide berth falling into more illustrious surroundings before turning once more to the riverside slums. There were people everywhere yet no one talked, all seemed weary and eager to be heading home, or to whatever abode they had. As the afternoon wore on she remembered that she had not eaten since she left the house that morning. She resolved to approach the next store that she should find to ease her hunger, though when she reached for her purse it was to find that she no longer had it. She looked around her as though she expected the culprit to be close by, but in this city he might have been anywhere. She felt that she would weep but just continued walking until, at last, she found a park with a bench on which she sat down. Still more people walked past, but these people were of a higher class and resembled people that she knew and now, as the light was fading and the night closing in, she began to shiver.

Not one of the passers-by noticed her. For who could spare a smile for a poor frozen woman when so enwrapped in the comings and goings of society life? She did cry now. They were silent tears that were all but invisible for they froze to her face the instant they fell. She knew she should keep moving, continue through the dank and dirty streets if only to preserve her warmth, but she was exhausted beyond all measure. She took out the book that Colonel Sir James Shorefield had given her. He had mentioned a meaning to it, and for certain she could see none for the front page declared the quote 'He whistled when he went for want of thought' and she was sure she only thought too much. She ran her fingers along the text as though she could feel the words speaking through her hands though in truth her hands were numb with cold and could feel nothing.

Night was all around her now and, in her mind, those darker shadows beneath the trees or by a corner of a building became people, both those that she loved and those that she did not trust and now she felt too afraid to move. She imagined their voices, some friendly, others desperate and pleading, while further ones were harsh and cruel. All beckoned her so that she both wanted to leave and feared to stay, but could not bring her feet to carry her.

'Miss Tenterchilt,' someone addressed. 'Imogen,' another, and then Beatrice and Josiah calling her 'Mama' repeatedly and tugging at her shawl.

'Miss Tenterchilt,' said another voice, behind her this time and simultaneously to this she felt suddenly warm as someone placed a heavy coat around her. 'Come away from here. We shall get you home.'

'Home?' Imogen whispered. She shook her head, fearing that this voice was not a friend, and rose to her feet to move away.

'Miss Tenterchilt,' the voice said again. 'Come along, Imogen. We shall take you home.'

She was too tired to argue, too cold and too sad. She could not register the person before her except that he had small features in a stern face. She was not greatly aware of where they went, only that it was in a carriage, for she did not know the city and drifted in and out of consciousness. She was not alone with the man in the carriage, there was another woman there too and she fussed about Imogen as they travelled on.

CHAPTER TEN
Thursday 1ˢᵗ February 1810

As the war in Iberia intensified, so too did the list of casualties and Doctor Fotherby found that his work consumed all his time. Any hope he had maintained of freeing himself from the city that he loathed and returning to service had failed, for he now found himself approaching his fortieth year with neither the time nor will to abandon his position in the hospital. He had maintained a distance from Miss Catherine Tenterchilt when she had begun working there, for he wished to remember her as the woman she had been during his stay in Scotland. Despite this, he had been disappointed by her departure from assisting at the hospital and when his friend Portland, now promoted to captain, had told him of her disappearance he had been greatly vexed and anxious. There was a part of him, long buried, that wanted the same thing as Miss Catherine, and he knew that this part sought the freedom and heroism of the forces. She had proved she was skilled enough and, in disguise, she could quite comfortably have passed into the army. Captain Portland had been beside himself with worry concerning her, for he had become attached to Miss Catherine during her stay in London.

There had been a lull in the work of the hospital over the Christmas period and into the new year, for the British had retreated from Portugal towards the end of the year and were now preparing once more to go to war. Doctor Fotherby was walking through the large hall, his mind on each of the patients and haunted by those he had been unable to save.

'Doctor Fotherby?'

He turned to look down upon a man much shorter than himself with dark hair around a pale and pointed face. There was a stern expression there but a sense of urgency seemed to drive his words.

'I am Doctor Fotherby,' he replied. 'Who wishes to know?'

'It would be appreciated, sir, if you would come with me. I have no calling card. Indeed I had hoped that none would be required. Your services, Doctor, are required.'

'I cannot leave my post so readily.'

'But you are needed. Please make haste.'

Whether it was the words that compelled him to follow or the tone with which he spoke, Doctor Fotherby dutifully collected his case and followed the shorter gentleman submissively out in to a carriage which at once sped through the city at an alarming speed. He clutched the bottom of the padded seat, appearing rather like a spider curled in on itself in the corner of the coach.

'Might I know where we go and why it is of such urgency?' he asked at length.

'Indeed, we are almost there, and you were requested by name, sir. Your reputation is clearly well known.'

They both looked out of the carriage as it slowed to a standstill. 'Sir, I do not normally visit houses. My work turned a long time ago to a hospital and I have not looked back.'

'Yet you will for this one case,' the other man replied, climbing down and taking Doctor Fotherby's case. 'Come, she is inside.'

'She?' the stunned doctor replied, following his case of tools and medicines more than the man who carried them. His guide hammered on the door and was admitted by a serving maid who bobbed a curtsey to them both as they entered.

'How is she?' the first man asked.

'Poor, sir. She says such things that I cannot think she knows what she speaks.'

'This is Doctor Fotherby, take him to her room.'

She nodded and led the doctor up a flight of stairs and to a white painted door on a dark, pristine landing. The door opened silently and she stood back to allow him in. Doctor Fotherby stepped over the threshold, uncertain what he expected to find, whilst his guide walked a step behind, still carrying the leather case. It took a moment for his eyes to focus in the smoky room, for there was a fire that burned angrily and it smoked with an equal vigour. He walked over to the bed and looked down, faltering for a second.

'Eastern-, Miss,' he stammered. 'I know this woman.'

'And clearly she, you,' the man explained. 'For in her anguished delirium she spoke of you. Do for her what you can, Doctor.' He walked over and handed the case to him before turning from the room.

Doctor Fotherby felt uncertain, and stood for a time at her bedside looking from her to the door that had just been closed. There were heavy curtains drawn over the window and when he finally returned to his senses he walked over and pulled them back with one flourishing move. His patient made a whimpering sound and she turned her head from the light.

'I never imagined there could be anything to break your spirit, Eastern Sunrise,' he said slowly, turning back to her. 'Did you dislike the city so much?'

The front room of the house echoed with the sound of footfalls from the constant pacing of its inhabitant so that, when Doctor Fotherby entered, having to lower his head slightly to avoid the lintel, a dramatic silence fell upon the room as the man stood still. It was not the man who had fetched him. This man was younger and there was a curious expression on his face, a little like guilt. He had similar pointed features, but there the similarity ended for he was a wide gentleman with shoulders that spanned four times the width of his head.

'Is she well?' he asked and stepped over to Doctor Fotherby, having to look up.

'No,' he replied. 'Of course she is not well.'

'Do not jest, sir, for I feel so truly responsible for what has befallen her.'

Chloe entered, bearing a silver tray laid out with two china cups of tea. Doctor Fotherby took one and thanked her before turning back to the man before him. 'I should return to the hospital. There are people there who have a far greater need of my attention. Yet I must confess to having questions concerning this, and I have no notion where that abominable coach journey has stranded me.'

'Rest your mind, sir,' the other man said, looking and sounding calmer, as though he was content that Miss Tenterchilt's health was assured or the doctor would certainly not wish to leave. 'I am Colonel Shorefield, and I assure you I am as much a stranger in this house as you are yourself.'

'I have heard of you,' Doctor Fotherby said, his tone carried a neutrality that seemed to both confuse and gladden Shorefield. 'But how am I to take your words? Should they be a comfort or an explanation?'

'I had the honour of meeting Miss Tenterchilt less than a week ago. I presumed too much upon a brief acquaintance, and addressed her in a manner that aggrieved her so greatly she fled from me. No, sir, do not misunderstand me,' he continued hastily, seeing the look of disgust upon the doctor's face. 'I did nothing dishonourable, but refused to discuss a topic of her choosing. She fled from me into the city that she does not know.'

'Where is her family?' Doctor Fotherby continued, purposefully proceeding to talk of something else.

'Her father and his wife are in Scotland, I believe. Should I have them sent for?'

'No. She will be well, you have no need to concern her father.'

'Then you torment me, sir,' Colonel Shorefield replied. 'I see you, too, have fallen under the spell of the Tenterchilt family.'

'Alas, no,' the doctor replied with a slight laugh. 'The major enabled me to establish myself after withdrawing from the army. I owe him a great deal and would treat his family accordingly.'

'You are a man of few words, Doctor, though I would wager you have many stories to tell. For while I entangle myself with words, you offer no more than brief replies.'

'I regret, sir, that I have little to discuss that would make conversation with sophisticated company, much less an officer in His Majesty's Army.'

'May I ask you, sir, what you know of Captain Roger Pottinger?'

'You may ask, but I shall have to disappoint you, sir. For though I recall a colonel by that name, I do not know the captain of whom you speak.'

Shorefield nodded thoughtfully. 'This was his house. With his wife, the former Miss Tenterchilt. That is why we are here.'

'Pardon, sir, but I find myself confused by your brief and truthful statements. What I would wish to hear is where is this house and why was I brought here?'

Shorefield laughed. 'You shame me, sir. You are here because Miss Tenterchilt asked for you and here is in the heart of the City of London. You are, of course, free to leave and return to your work.' He rose to his feet. 'Do not think me rude, Doctor, but it is my hope that I should not meet you again, for it should certainly be in one of your wards.'

'Indeed? I heard that you were too lucky to fall.'

'I wish it were so,' Shorefield laughed and bowed his head before departing. Doctor Fotherby rose to his feet feeling more confusion than he had thought possible. He collected his case and left instruction for the maid concerning Miss Tenterchilt's care with the promise of returning the following day. He did not encounter Colonel Sir James Shorefield again and discovered from his friend Captain Portland that the regiment was to depart for Oporto almost at once.

'Indeed he is a confusing character,' Portland laughed, walking alongside the doctor as they crossed Westminster Bridge. 'But, my dear Fotherby, he is a soldier unparalleled in historical or modern times. How odd it should be that a family who reside so far from Town should unite such city dwellers as you, Colonel Shorefield and myself.'

'He spoke of being bewitched by them,' Fotherby confided.

'Were you not?' Portland laughed as he slapped the doctor's shoulder. 'You who call them Eastern Sunrise and Sleeping Tiger, I would deduce that you are further under their spell than you would care to admit. Mrs Allen no longer has a claim on you, Henry.'

Doctor Fotherby stopped and looked down onto the river below. 'I am their father's physician, and I shall not fail in that duty as I failed poor Kitty.'

'Deuce, man, listen to what you say. Kitty Simmons married a bookseller from Fleet. Nine years have passed since then and yet you would believe you failed her? My dear Fotherby, it is time you changed your climate and I do not believe that Scotland is far enough for you.'

'I have considered this often. But I have a place here where I can do what I am good at and aid others.'

'Be truthful. You do not wish to stray far from Kitty Allen. Or perhaps another.'

'What is it that you want me to say?' he asked as they walked along. 'That, like your hero, Sir James Shorefield, I believe in luck, fate and bewitchment? I believe in none of them, for all have failed me.'

'The shrewdest man perceives that all three may turn. Perhaps trusting to fate is the best way to cultivate luck and enchantment. There is no harm in choosing change, Fotherby. Just be sure that you make that choice and do not idly drift through life.'

'How is it that you fight when you should have been a diplomat?' Doctor Fotherby laughed, knowing that his friend spoke painfully candid and truthful remarks. They parted then, with wishes for each other's health as Portland prepared to return to the continent and Fotherby to his hospital, where those who survived the return voyage with injuries could be treated.

CHAPTER ELEVEN
Monday 5ᵗʰ February 1810

Imogen could hear someone talking, speaking words of comfort and home with such passion that it called her back from her fevered state. She opened her eyes and was surprised to find that there was near silence in the room. All the noises of hurried city life came through the slightly opened window, against which a figure was standing, undoubtedly a man by his size and stance. He had a hand on each of the vertical sides of the window so that he was a silhouette against the daylight outside. She felt uncomfortable and tried to pull the blanket up about her, but there was a leather case resting halfway on the bed that fell to the floor, so that the man jumped and spun around.

'Good morning, Eastern Sunrise,' he said and, as he stepped from the window and into the room, she saw him smile. Of course the moment that he called her by that name she had known who he was, but the doctor seemed weary with care and worry as though thirteen years had passed since she last saw him instead of just three. 'I see an element of pity in your eyes, Miss Tenterchilt. Do not waste it on me.'

'Doctor Fotherby,' she said weakly. 'Where am I? I heard someone talking of the mountains of home, yet this is not my room.'

'You were dreaming, Miss Tenterchilt, and have been these past four days.'

'I should be returning home then.'

'Wait until you are stronger. Winter is such an inclement season on the traveller. It is best to be in full health before any such journey is undertaken. Shall I have Chloe bring you a drink, Eastern Sunrise?'

'Thank you.'

Doctor Fotherby only smiled before excusing himself from the room, leaving Imogen alone. For the following three days the doctor called upon his patient who, much to her relief, was well enough to sit by the fire downstairs. They discussed trivial matters, laughed occasionally and reminisced often about the month that the doctor had spent in Petrovia Lodge.

'I have been reading Hours of Idleness, the book Sir James Shorefield bestowed upon me, a little at any rate. Do you read poetry, Doctor?'

'No, I have little rhythm within me so poetry only enhances my failings.'

'I find it odd, and should like to know more about Mr Byron. He writes with such structure, though at times I believe he wishes to shock his reader.'

'He is not a Mr, but a Lord,' Doctor Fotherby replied. 'Currently I believe he has travelled to the Mediterranean.'

'Does he fight?' she asked, startled that anyone who could write such beauty could kill another human being.

'No, though he has travelled through war torn countries they say. He is a Byron by title, but took his mother's name. He is a Gordon.'

'A Gordon?' she whispered.

'I believe so.'

'Thank you, Doctor Fotherby, for you have opened my eyes to a challenge laid before me.'

'I should leave you, Miss Tenterchilt, you look weary.' He rose and bowed his head. 'You should be able to return to Scotland soon, and I fear I shall be needed more urgently at the hospital in the days to come. Travel carefully, Eastern Sunrise.'

'Wait!' she said quickly and with such a sharp tone that the doctor looked surprised. 'Of course, you travelled to India.'

'Indeed, many, many years ago. Twelve, if my memory serves me correctly.'

'Were you in the East India Company?'

'No, Miss Tenterchilt, I was not. Though I travelled with them as part of an envoy.'

'I am concerned for Cat.'

'Miss Tenterchilt, your mind jumps. Take some rest.'

Chloe, who was always on hand, showed the doctor out. On the steps he bowed his head politely as he passed a lady approaching the house. Chloe bobbed a curtsey and admitted her at once.

'Miss Tenterchilt,' she said rushing into the living room. 'Mrs Jenkyns is here to see you.'

'Mrs..? Arabella?' Imogen rose unsteadily from the chair and embraced her sister.

'I came by the moment that I heard you were in Town. I did not know or I should have called upon you earlier.'

'Married life suits you, Arabella, you are glowing with life.'

'Indeed, I did not hope to be so happy. Nor so rich,' she added jovially. 'While Cat may travel with her companions, I can see no reason why anyone should long for anywhere but London.' Imogen forced a smile as she recalled the adapted truth she had shared with Arabella about their sister's disappearance. 'Do you not find it the most perfect place?'

'In truth, Arabella, I find it dank and dirty and I am eager to return home.' She realised as Arabella's face fell that she had said more than was necessary. 'Though I can see that it has its charms.'

'And who was it that I saw leaving as I arrived?'

'There is no scandal,' Imogen laughed, seeing Arabella's eyes light up. 'He is Doctor Fotherby, Papa's physician, and there is no plan I am party to that he should be anything else.'

It was pleasant to see Arabella again, but it could not compare to the relief she felt at returning home a few days later. The journey, as Doctor Fotherby predicted, lasted an unbearably long time and she was weary beyond all measure when at last she reached Petrovia Lodge. She was greeted by Penny and Anne who informed her that her father and Alice had been summoned to Edinburgh for a reason they did not know. Imogen realised with an anxious pain that it was almost certainly linked with those acts of treason committed in America. The cycle of the seasons continued to turn, and spring overtook winter with still no news from her father, although a letter did arrive addressed to her as April began. She looked at it for a moment, wondering at the peculiar writing and marks upon it before she opened it and read the contents.

'My dear Imogen, While I continue my search for glories and honours to make Papa proud I find that all there is here is unbearable heat and sickness. Of those I travelled with and learnt to trust I have but three comrades with me. Please bear my secret a while longer, they say that the summer brings the test of the European man, I may find my honour there. I think of you often and pray for you always. Ever yours.'

Imogen felt stunned. For a time she stood at the orangery door, staring out over the ill kept lawn and down to the little river. Why did Catherine seek such glories to please a man who had been removed and imprisoned for his innocent part in an affair? She stood there puzzling over the divided parts of the Tenterchilt family as the light faded behind the mountains and tears began to fall down her cheeks. She turned as Anne spoke behind her.

'Pardon, Miss Imogen, but Miss Beatrice and Master Josiah are abed now. Might I be allowed to retire for the night?'

'Yes, of course,' Imogen replied. She watched as Anne lowered her head and disappeared from sight. There was a streak of orange in the mountain pass to the southwest as she picked up one of the books from the orangery table. It was Hours of Idleness, a book she had not read since returning home. The pages were damp and cold, some so much that they had stuck together. She let it fall open on a page and raised the book to her face that she might read:

Round Loch Na Garr, while the stormy mist gathers,
Winter resides in his cold icy car,
Clouds, there encircle the forms of my Fathers,
They dwell in the tempests of dark Loch Na Garr

She placed her hand down on the book and closed her eyes. There was something, buried now, trying to resurface through the confinement of time. She could hear someone saying those words in a manner so sensitive and desperate with emotion that she struggled to contain herself. The sun had gone from the sky entirely now and she rubbed her eyes, which ached with the darkness. She thought she heard someone behind her and turned, but she was alone in the orangery. She felt close to her mother there. It had been her sole request of the lodge and she had spent much of most days there and, at night, Imogen had crept down to spend her time with Hamish. They were both gone from her now.

The days continued to roll by, but Imogen filled them with educating Beatrice and Josiah and, in the evenings, she began to maintain a strict routine of correspondence, addressing primarily Mr Dermot in relation to her father's situation, but also Arabella, Doctor Fotherby and even extending her generosity to Colonel Sir James Shorefield, to thank him for the book that she found a constant puzzle and inspiration.

It was May before any of her letters bore a reply and it was far from one she had hoped for. The lodge had undergone its annual transformation into the glories of spring. The trees were leafing and the ground around them was filled with the pale lavender blue of harebells. Imogen had taken Beatrice and Josiah down to pick bouquets full for different rooms of the house but still they swarmed the ground. The letter was waiting for her when she returned and she opened it quickly, reading the contents silently to herself.

'Dear Miss Tenterchilt, It is with regret and sadness that I am forced to enclose the following information to yourself. Alice Tenterchilt has been found guilty of treason and delivering intelligence to enemies of the United Kingdom. The punishment for this is death, a sentence that will have been carried out by the time you receive this letter. Though your father has been excused he has been formally stripped of his rank. I know you have the strength to guide your family through this dark time, Miss Tenterchilt, and I beseech you to forgive me for sending such dark tidings. Your father will be free to return home and may even arrive before this letter reaches you. Yours with sincere regret and sympathy, Cornelius Dermot.'

Imogen felt tears form in her eyes. 'Oh Papa,' she whispered again and again until she did not know what she was saying, only that there were words coming from her mouth. The army had been everything to her father and she could not imagine the hurt that this blow would deliver. Her father did not arrive home until two days later. He would not speak of where he had been and continued as closely as he could in the way of life that he had led before. Imogen felt sick with the pretence that he kept up and the manner in which he never mentioned his wife or the fate that she had endured. It was true that Imogen did not care for Alice in her manners and attitudes but she could not understand why her father did not wish even to consider the mother of his children.

Her next return of correspondence came from her sister and carried the welcome news that she was with child. Her father seemed elated by this and for some days Petrovia Lodge was filled with eager excitement, and plans were made concerning Arabella's inevitable confinement. And so spring turned to summer in the beautiful glen and once more the travellers arrived across the stream. Anne withdrew from them, unwilling to share the news of Filman's son's exile to America. Indeed, no one suffered more greatly than Anne, who thought day and night of the son who had been taken from her and handed to a stranger. She had seen it as justice that Alice Tenterchilt had been forcefully removed from her children, though she held a deep affection for the twins. There was little wonder that Anne had sought to remain hidden, for when Filman was finally told his anger surpassed Anne's sorrow and he swore such curses that even the former major was alarmed and shocked. Yet Filman dutifully tended the grounds in exchange for the travellers encamping on the Tenterchilts' land. But as summer drew to a close and the September harvest of apples ripened for picking it was to be the final departure of Filman from their land. He was tried for poaching and sentenced to deportation before the season had ended. Anne begged Imogen to raise a concern for him, but the daughter of a disgraced officer held little sway in the court's mind.

It was decided by Mr Tenterchilt that Anne should journey down to Horland Park to accompany Arabella in her confinement and so she left the house on the twenty-seventh day of September, the day before another letter arrived at Petrovia Lodge. The night Anne departed, Imogen put the two children to bed herself, insisting to Penny that she was more than capable. She returned to the orangery once more and stood staring out at the darkening sky. There was a peculiar feeling to the night air, stifling perhaps, and yet eager. She could almost taste the bittersweet anticipation. She turned quickly back to the house as she heard her father shouting and she rushed into the library, where she found Penny standing with her hands on her hips and regarding Mr Tenterchilt through angry eyes. She turned and curtseyed as Imogen entered.

'Pardon, Miss Tenterchilt. I had hoped you would not see your father like this.'

'What is wrong, Papa?' she asked anxiously, but jumped back as her father hammered his fist down on the table.

'That is what ails him,' Penny said, pointing to the empty glass decanter. 'I should not have filled it.'

'You were doing your job, Penny,' Imogen said softly, placing her hand on Penny's arm in what she hoped was a reassuring manner. 'You cannot be blamed for this.' She stepped forward but stopped as Penny cautioned.

'Careful, Miss, he does get violent.'

'He has been like this before?'

'Indeed, most nights for many months.'

'Thank you, Penny, you may leave us.'

The maid looked on the point of arguing but, recalling her station, only nodded and left the room, closing the door noiselessly. Imogen stepped forward and took her father's hand but he shook her off forcefully. 'That is enough, Papa. You will do yourself a damage.' She took the glass from his hand and walked over to the window, opening it and tipping out the contents. He pushed himself to his feet and flew at her in a burning rage. Imogen felt afraid for a moment before she caught his wrist and stared sternly into his face. 'Did you ever treat Mama like this?' she demanded, tears falling down her cheeks as her father struck her with his free hand. She pushed him backwards and rushed to the door. 'I have sought to protect you and our name with honour and instead you drink yourself to this intolerable stupor. Did you ever treat Mama like this?'

'Elizabeth?' he asked softly. A change came over him as he spoke her mother's name so that the tears of angry fear Imogen had wept became tears of sympathy and pity.

'You did not, did you, Papa?' She cautiously walked over to her father and sat down beside him on the library floor. 'I was thinking of that painting at Horland Park. It is good to know that Arabella will be giving life in the same house where Mama's picture hangs on the wall.'

'Scoundrels,' he said bitterly.

'Mama was no scoundrel,' Imogen said firmly.

'Those Jenkyns,' he replied, spitting the name with great venom. 'I was there!'

'Where, Papa?' she asked, confused by his words. 'Where were you?'

'At her shoulder,' he whimpered. 'As I always was. They painted me out.'

Imogen clung to her father as his anger subsided and he wept. All the tears that he had held back for almost five years fell from his eyes, as heavy and bitter as rain. Imogen lifted her chin, determined not to join him in such a display but struggling not to do so.

'Why had Fotherby not been there?' he demanded. 'He would have saved her.'

'Doctor Fotherby is a skilled man, Papa, but perhaps Mama was past even his hand to heal.'

'A fine suitor he would have made for you, Imogen, both so able and sure. You should never have had a moment's peace in your life.'

'I have great respect for Doctor Fotherby, Father, and enjoy his company and words, but I have no love for him so we shall never marry.'

'I have failed you, have I not, Imogen? I have banished you to this dark corner of the country, robbed you of suitors and forced you to be a carer and teacher to my two youngest children.'

'Papa, all I wanted in life was to share my knowledge with a new generation. I wanted to be a teacher. You have given me that.'

'A teacher?' He paused as she nodded and he laughed. 'What would the world be without you in it, my dear daughter? You have a talent for words and appeasement that I should not wonder whether you will not marry a politician yourself.'

'There is no honour there, Papa. I shall marry for love as you and Mama did, or I shall be content as a spinster. A lady of education.'

She helped her father up the stairs before returning to the library and tidying the mess he had left. She stood at the window and sighed out onto the night. 'It is not so bad,' she said firmly to herself. 'If it is good enough to inspire that rogue Lord Byron, it will certainly be good enough for me.' She withdrew to bed but could not sleep, as her thoughts rested with her father. He had been the one painted out of the portrait. He had been the one that had felt so alone in her mother's death that he had married another, while all she and her sisters had thought of was the effect Mrs Tenterchilt's passing had on each of themselves. He had been the one whose adherence to duty and family loyalty had seen him stripped of rank and robbed of pension. Yet all she had thought of was herself and those who had departed from her life. And the concern crossed her mind that perhaps when, on the eve of her wedding, Arabella had discussed her love for the late Captain

Roger Pottinger, she had been saying exactly how her father felt.

When at last the sun appeared in the sky, Imogen ensured that she was up before her father and instructed Penny to order no more alcohol and conceal that which was already in the house. She was determined to restore the Tenterchilt family to their rightful seat within society. Whatever had happened in the past was beyond changing, but she felt that the future lay within her scope. Penny seemed to approve of this new change in her, perhaps seeing something of her mother in her that she had never before noticed. For her own part, Imogen was pleased of this change and felt that she could conquer the world. She went out to feed her horse, which now stood alone in the large stable, but for the two small ponies that belonged to Josiah and Beatrice. Catherine's horse had been sold, for Imogen did not believe that her sister would return until she had riches enough to fund a horse of her own, and Arabella's had been taken by Catherine on that awful night. Her father's horse had been sold, too, for he was increasingly uncomfortable on horseback. She walked out of the stable and stopped as she saw a man riding towards her. He seemed driven by a great urgency and Imogen was both curious and anxious when he drew in the reins before her and announced, as out of breath as his horse,

'A letter to Miss Imogen Tenterchilt.'

'Thank you,' she replied, taking it from his outstretched hand. At once, having fulfilled his purpose he turned and allowed his horse a leisurely walk back down the drive. Imogen did not spare him a second thought but opened the letter and read the content.

'Dear Imogen. I am quite ruined and fear that where I sought glory and honour for our family I have brought only shame and humiliation. I have fallen under the hand of one of the so prevalent illnesses in Calcutta and, being referred to a hospital, could no longer hide my secret. I am afraid, Imogen, though when this letter reaches you I should have no cause to fear. Think kindly on me, my dear sister, I pray. Cat.'

Her hand trembled as she read once more the brief letter from her sister. She could not leave her there to whatever fate the illness may bring upon her, and yet neither could she leave her father at such a moment when she was so determined to help him. She could think of only one solution and rushed to the orangery, penning a letter in a hand that shook so greatly she could scarcely read her own words. Without waiting to greet Beatrice, Josiah or her father, she saddled her horse and rode to the nearby town with all the speed she and the beast could endure. After ensuring the delivery of the message with the greatest of urgency, and paying almost double that it should be so, she returned to the lodge and tried to continue her life as normal.

The letter she had sent in such a desperate haste, most uncharacteristic of her usual decorum, took almost two weeks to reach its recipient, though the moment it was in his grasp he responded immediately. The war in the peninsula was, for the most part, on a quiet lull, yet the sudden eruption of firing that broke out was to be the start of a new wave. The hopeless siege with which the French forces tried to contain the British and Portuguese had taken its toll and now a desperate attack was being launched upon the British who occupied the high ridge of Bussaco. Colonel Sir James Shorefield sat at a table with his officers, discussing the plans of Major General Leith who was leading the 5th Infantry Division in the battle. The weather was stifling and the opening of the tent flap was welcome as a young man rushed in.

'A letter, sir,' he said, saluting before ducking out of the tent flap once more.

If the other officers objected to this interruption they gave no sign of it, grateful only to enter the battle under such a distinguished leader. His approach may have seemed peculiar but it gained the results that they all hoped for. Now, as he read the letter, the officers watched him swallow hard and his face became stern yet pale.

'Return to your posts, gentlemen,' he ordered before adding, 'Portland. I must talk with you.'

'Yes, sir?' Captain Portland began, unsure why he had been called to remain.

'You are familiar with Catherine Tenterchilt of that family which we regard in mutual esteem?'

'Indeed, sir, a woman to surpass all others for courage and prowess.'

'You must return at once to England.' Shorefield left no room for any query but continued to explain. 'You have a friend there, a doctor?'

'Henry Fotherby, sir?'

'Yes, we met. And I believe he would not care to meet me again. Go to him and find him the fastest ship to India.'

'Pardon, sir,' Portland began. 'He may be unable or unwilling.'

'Miss Catherine Tenterchilt lies in an Indian hospital having concealed herself in the Company. She is sick, she may by now be dead, for this letter bears the date of almost two weeks since.'

'The Company? The East India Company?'

'Indeed, Captain Portland. Her sister writes that she joined almost a year ago.'

'Sir,' Portland whispered.

'You have no need to tell me, Portland. I know that you have affection for her.' Captain Portland could only nod in agreement. 'Then, with all haste return to England and employ the help of Doctor Fotherby. He is a man who has India in his heart, I believe. I am certain that his loyalty to the family and his love of the country will compel him to complete this task. Tell him that money is not an obstacle.' Shorefield rose to his feet as a persistent outbreak of gunfire issued from the valley. 'Go, man, the army will not miss you for this day.'

Captain Portland did not need a second invitation. He could not fathom why the man before him had employed him on such a task, but he was certain not to question the great Colonel Sir James Shorefield, to whom he owed his very life. A letter detailing and excusing his absence was handed to him and at once he began on his journey back to London. Despite his efforts to pursue a hasty course back it was five days before he at last burst into the hospital and rushed through the cramped wards until he made out the tall, slim figure of his friend, Doctor Fotherby. He could waste no time in pleasantries but gripped his arm, ignoring the look of confusion on Fotherby's face.

'Fotherby,' he gasped trying to steady his breathing. The doctor looked down at him with confusion. 'I have come with a commission that you are to execute at once.'

'Find yourself a seat, Portland,' Fotherby said gently. 'I shall talk with you soon.'

'Damn it, man!' Portland shouted and all the nurses and surgeons turned shocked faces to him. Doctor Fotherby only nodded. 'I have just travelled from the frontline in five days, the letter was sent twelve before that and I cannot imagine how long it took for her letter from India.'

'Captain Portland, you make no sense,' Fotherby stated, but it was with a gentle tone. 'Begin again.'

'You are commissioned to travel to India, sir,' Portland said, remembering himself.

'I am not in the army any longer. Who commissions me and to what end?'

'Colonel Sir James Shorefield,' Portland began and clutched Fotherby's sleeve pleadingly as the doctor shook his head and turned away. 'Please, Fotherby, please hear me out.'

'That man is insane, Portland. He believes he is invincible and commands and orders every living soul in Christendom.'

'I am sorry you do not like him, Fotherby. I even understand why you do not, but please take this commission. You love India, you speak of your exploits there so often and he has promised to pay for your voyage in full and on the fastest ship there is.'

'What is it for?'

'Miss Catherine Tenterchilt. She concealed herself in the Company and is now stranded there in disgrace and ill health.'

'What is this man's connection to that family that he is so intent to oversee their lives and health?' the doctor mused.

'In God's name, man,' Portland hissed. 'Not every man on this planet has an ulterior motive. Do you recall he spoke to you of bewitchment and said that he was held under their spell? Well, perhaps you are not, but I am, and I am begging you to leave the hospital to your qualified surgeons and doctors and go and help the one soul who can keep my heart whole.'

Doctor Fotherby simply stared at his friend, whose outburst of emotion was most uncharacteristic. Portland shook his head and began walking away, sharp, cruel retorts on the tip of his tongue though he would not speak them.

'Wait,' Fotherby said softly and Portland turned back, his eyes glistening with hope once more. 'If you will make the arrangements, I will be on the first boat leaving for India. Yet, Portland, it can take six months to get to India.'

'It will take you six weeks, my dear friend. I shall find you the fastest ship this side of the Americas.'

Portland vanished with a haste that was matched only by the way he had arrived. Fotherby shook his head and walked back to the hospital office to prepare to leave. He felt unable to contradict his friend, although he knew it was unlikely he would find passage on such a ship, and the best he could hope for would be a two month voyage. For some time Doctor Fotherby had sought a release from the stifled city life but to no avail. Now that he was able to, and indeed was needed to, he felt strangely nervous. There was something more. Kitty Allen, the woman he had loved for nigh on fifteen years, had become a widow during the last month. He had followed and supported her life for so long, hoping when the day came when they were both free to love they might once more be reunited. However, as he considered Captain Portland's proclamation of his love and heartache, he realised that he did not love Mrs Kitty Allen any more. Perhaps it was not the city that had suffocated him since he left the army and that he needed to escape from, surely it was the ghost of the past and the future that had eluded him all those years ago. It was this that gave way to a feeling of release as he walked out of the hospital that evening to find Portland standing there waiting.

'I have found you a ship to take you as far as Madeira. All the East Indiamen pass that way.'

'I have to settle matters at home, Portland, I must explain my disappearance.'

'Nonsense,' Portland protested. 'The Clementine sails before dawn, you must board her this evening.'

There was little use in arguing for, whether it was love or madness that caused it, Captain Portland would not be dissuaded. They sat silently in the coach that hurtled towards the docks, but when they arrived Doctor Fotherby sighed and shook Portland's hand.

'I will do my best to find her, Portland, though with this delay and tropical disease-'

'Just go, Henry,' Portland whispered. 'Go and find her. Look after her and bring her home. She should never have been left to go off like this.'

Doctor Fotherby nodded and Portland watched as the small rowing boat carried him out to the tall schooner that sat in the Thames. The captain had allowed a little too much of his soul to have been bared before the respected doctor but, without having done so, he did not believe that Fotherby would ever have gone. His duty now lay in Portugal once more and the compassion that Colonel Sir James Shorefield had shown in allowing him to leave would not permit his continued separation from his comrades of the 5th Infantry.

CHAPTER TWELVE
Tuesday 16th October 1810

And so, as the Clementine sailed in the blessing of a south blowing breeze and both Doctor Fotherby and Captain Portland sailed with different purposes towards the peninsula, Arabella Jenkyns sat in Horland Park holding her baby to her. She had been due to return south to London, but was left feeling too weary and so was waiting until Christmas to be reunited with her husband. Mr Jenkyns had travelled north to Horland Park to see his son but that was all she saw of him. His business was exalted and continuous so he could not long be torn from his London life. Anne was staying with her as a familiar face, always at hand if Arabella called for anything. She loved the baby and would regard him with a sorry expression, clearly remembering her own son, David, who had been so wickedly torn from her.

'Why would any woman be foolish enough to marry a man who cannot remain?' Arabella asked Anne as she stood looking out the window at the October rains that poured from the heavens. 'First I married an officer who had our cause to fight on the continent and now I have married an MP who has our cause to fight in London.'

'We cannot help where our heart lies,' Anne replied, rocking the baby in her arms.

'You sound like Imogen,' Arabella laughed. 'I miss them all so. And Penny, too.' She turned to Anne and frowned slightly. 'I confess, Anne, there is something odd about the staff here at Horland Park. I feel so often that they look down at me or that they are plotting something.'

'You need have no worries on that count, Mrs Jenkyns. They all seem very committed to your husband's service. I have not heard a word spoken against him. Even in his absence.'

'He is a good man,' Arabella agreed quickly. 'I belong in London, though, Anne. I always have done.'

'You can return there in the winter.'

The conversation died for a time and Arabella picked her son up out of Anne's arms and ran her finger along his cheek. Anne watched with great envy and sadness.

'I know Mr Jenkyns believes it is wrong, but I did so long to name him Roger.'

'It is perhaps well that you do not mention that to Mr Jenkyns.'

'Indeed,' Arabella sighed. 'But Timothy is a fine name too, and is a family name of Mama's, as Mr Jenkyns pointed out. It is wicked of me I know, but at times I find myself calling him Roger.'

'Foolish perhaps, but not wicked, Mrs Jenkyns.'

Anne's words were all too accurate and Arabella knew it was so. She had written to her father and asked that the maid should stay with her a while longer, and so November found Anne remaining in Horland Park, and Arabella was greatly pleased and relieved to have her company. Horland Park was not as warm or welcoming as it had been in the presence of Mr Jenkyns, and Arabella felt more of a nuisance than the lady of the house. Perhaps it was that she was forcing the staff to work additional hours or that she had brought in her own maid, but the servants were far from grateful and, as she passed through the halls carrying Timothy, she heard whispered conversations following her.

If Anne shared in this discomfort she never mentioned it. She was as diligent in Horland Park as she had been in Petrovia Lodge. However, she did not spend much time with the other servants, finding them unlike any other people she had ever met. The days here were not as short as they were in Scotland and Arabella tried to find time in each day to walk through the grounds, her favourite part being the extravagant pool to the west of the house where a stone fountain stood, spilling water into it in a continuous cycle. She loved the sound of the running water and, despite the onset of winter and the chill wind and rain, she would often stand for some time there. She did not bring Timothy for he was a sickly child and she was concerned that the cold air and wind would not benefit his ill health. Instead he was confined to a nursery that was as large as her own room at the hall.

It was on one of those walks that she stood staring out over the grounds, not caring for the glamour of the pool, simply content to hear the moving water, that she happened to overhear a conversation from the walled garden to the north of the house. It was a kitchen garden where some produce was still grown for the house, though most now came in carts from nearby Manchester. Two people were talking; a man and a woman. She had never before heard the servants openly discussing topics but perhaps it was the direction of the wind and their engrossing subject that allowed her to hear it so clearly.

'I only need another year,' the man said.

'I cannot wait a year, Peter,' came the frenzied reply. 'I must be out of this house before Christmas, else I will have no pride left.'

'Nothing could separate you from your pride,' Peter replied in an upbeat way. 'What did Mrs Barton say?'

'I have not told her. She will not stand for it, though. I will be out on the street and into the poorhouse before the day has set.'

Arabella was intrigued by this conversation. In the silence that followed the girl's remark, she walked closer to the voices. She did not mean to pry, but her intentions were of little consequence for the pair heard her and the girl jumped to her feet. She brushed aside the tears that she had been crying and bobbed a curtsey.

'I did not know you were there, ma'am.'

'That is quite alright,' Arabella replied. The maid said not another word but rushed back into the house. Peter scowled across at her, making no attempt to hide his dislike and mistrust. Arabella felt affronted but, before she could think of any words to speak, he walked away from her and out of the garden to the front of the house. She walked around the kitchen garden for a time before returning to the fountain. She did not pause to question what was being discussed with such hatred, only how hurt she felt by it. The sky grew dark and within seconds rain was pouring down, so that she was soaked before she could even reach the house. Anne immediately came and fussed around her, but Arabella was grateful of the rain for it hid her crying. She was in a daze that Anne mistook to be the onset of a fever and would have sent for the doctor at once but that Arabella was certain she did not want one. Even so, Anne remained faithfully by her side until, at length, Arabella began talking.

'Who is Mrs Barton?'

'She is the head of your kitchen staff, Mrs Jenkyns,' Anne replied gently.

'I met two young people today, Anne, who I think both work here. They both hated me with such intensity that I cannot understand it. I had never even seen them before.'

'Have no worry, ma'am, I am certain it was only that they were caught unaware. At times I have felt strongly opposed to anyone who caught me out.'

Arabella began to feel better as she continued talking but, despite the appeasement that Anne offered, that evening she penned a letter to Mr Jenkyns announcing that she would be leaving Horland Park earlier than Christmas and intended to be in London before December. She did not leave even the smallest room for argument for she felt that she had to leave Horland at once, a feeling that only intensified as the days wore on. Each room she entered felt chilling to her, and she began to feel afraid for the safety of her child and herself.

When at last she did leave Horland, she was sad to say farewell to Anne, who was to return to Petrovia. While Anne seemed equally upset by the parting, Arabella was certain that it was Timothy that the maid would miss the most, and indeed as Anne departed, the light to her eyes left also. Her husband was pleased to see her which came as a great comfort to Arabella, for she had felt that the whole Jenkyns estate was fighting against her. He spent much time away from the house during the day but in the evenings they sat together as a young family. Timothy was more than amply cared for and Mr Jenkyns showed a burning pride for his son when he had the chance to introduce him.

And so Christmas found the two sisters in very different ways. The Jenkyns' Christmas was rich and extravagant, filled with expensive meats and sweet pies, toys of the highest calibre for Timothy and hand woven lace and linen for Arabella. Petrovia Lodge observed a far smaller but equally appreciated feast. Josiah and Beatrice were old enough now to join Imogen and their father at the table, and each was dressed according to the celebration. Penny and Anne were invited to join them once the table had been laid and served. Although presents were not as plentiful as in the Jenkyns' household, there were nothing but smiles from those gathered at the table. Further soldiers were Josiah's present, once more from an anonymous benefactor, whilst Beatrice received a porcelain doll that she could clothe in one of several dresses that accompanied it. Mr Tenterchilt was delivered a sword of such beauty and balance that he declared at once that it could only have come from one of the skilled continental workers in London. Imogen had received a gift too, though she was far less certain of hers. It was a silver chain with a single pearl hanging from it. It caught the light in the most peculiar way, shining with rainbow colours and, though she loved it, she did not dare wear it without knowing who had sent it and with what purpose it had been sent.

How different Christmas was at the other side of the globe. Christmas Eve found the arrival of The Andrassa at Calcutta, and Doctor Fotherby beheld once more that land that he had known and loved. Little seemed to have changed in the city and the large British buildings looked as welcoming in their alien surroundings as ever they did in England. Richard Wellesley, the brother of Arthur Wellesley who led the British forces in the Iberian Peninsula, had left a great legacy for Calcutta. Buildings that he had overseen and commissioned to further the work of the Company filled most of the city so that, as Fotherby walked down from the ship and through the street, it was apparent that his first impression of constancy was incorrect.

For a time he stood close to the pier, simply looking about him.

Eventually he recalled his purpose and negotiated his way through the crowds at the docks towards Fort William, the large garrison that the British Army had built and that was now inhabited by those of the Company. Gaining admittance was surprisingly easy, for there could be little doubt to any of the guards that the tall, thin man before them was undoubtedly British and, furthermore, accustomed to the manners and etiquette of the army. However, on his admittance, he found that he was left for several hours outside a door.

Initially people came and went along the corridor though, little by little, the number of people ebbed as the light in the sky did too. Doctor Fotherby rose to his feet and began anxiously pacing, feeling that he had wasted his first day in his hunt for Miss Catherine Tenterchilt. Finally, as the bells from St John's Cathedral echoed through the still night, telling the hour as seven, Fotherby walked to the door and pounded on it. There was no answer so, in his annoyance and desperation, the doctor knocked once more, harder now so that the sound swirled down the corridor. It was opened almost at once by a footman, who looked as out of place in the fort as the doctor had begun to feel. Doctor Fotherby walked in and stopped before a large desk where a man sat. He looked weary, weighed down no doubt by the sheer grandeur of the room that was lined with hunting trophies, weapons of all degree, and some of the finest Indian tapestries that had ever been created.

'Pardon, sir,' Fotherby began. 'But I have been sitting outside your door for nigh on six hours, waiting for an audience.'

'Deuce, man,' came the reply in a mocking voice. 'Did you not think to knock earlier?'

'You were told of my arrival, sir. I know, for I sat outside and listened.'

'Then you are Doctor Henry Fotherby.' It was a statement of fact, but Fotherby found himself replying.

'Indeed, sir. My business in Calcutta is of a delicate nature.'

'I know why you are here,' the man interrupted. 'Though I confess it intrigues me to know why this particular person holds such great sway back in Britain.'

'Then you have not met her, sir.'

There was no intended malice or anger in the doctor's voice, yet clearly the man before him felt that both were evident for he rose to his feet and glared across at his visitor. He was a large, stocky man, clothed in the uniform of the Company, though the brass buttons of his coat failed to fit comfortably round his large girth.

'Be a little less impulsive, Doctor Fotherby,' he warned, though there was a look of approval in his features as the doctor remained calm-faced before him.

'Miss Catherine Tenterchilt has friends in the highest of places, some who even have the benefit of the King's ear.'

'The King is a madman, Doctor, and many miles away.'

'You forget that he still funds the Company and allows it to operate with a great freedom.'

'You are not a man who is easily scared or threatened, I think, Doctor Fotherby.'

'It is true, sir. I have seen such things that would instill fear into the strongest of men, and bravery I could never hope to match. Therefore your words do not alarm me as perhaps you desire.'

'You have wisdom, Doctor. That is good to see. And loyalty, too. Then forgive my crooked games. I am the Earl of Minto, Governor-General of this Presidency of Fort William. Come, I do not know where the woman you seek is, though I can tell you where you might find out.'

'My lord, she was sick when she last addressed a letter home. I must find her at once or,' he paused, realising with surprise that his voyage had taken on a personal and subjective manner. 'She may die,' he finished coolly.

'Who sent you?' the earl asked thoughtfully.

'Colonel Sir James Shorefield. A man for whom I understand many have great respect.'

'Yes, I have heard of him. A lucky soldier.' The older man nodded sagely before adding, 'there is no such thing, I am certain, in your understanding of the world.'

'I have seen too many when their luck has run out. Kindly point me in the direction of whoever may assist me in my search.'

Doctor Fotherby, a placid man, slow to anger and quick to forgive, felt his temper begin to rise at the man before him. The audience at this point had clearly ended and the Earl of Minto did not address him again, only handed him a piece of paper and waved his hand dismissively, showing the doctor that he wished him to leave. This he did without looking back, but he paused beneath one on the gaslights in the corridor to read what was on the piece of paper. It was a name and an address within the fort, for a gentleman called Peter FitzHammond.

The hour was late and he felt certain that he was expected to wait until the morning, but he had a new sense of urgency. Perhaps it was being back in this city, this country that he had loved and had seen gradually sink into the hands of rivaling opium traders and wearied by the continued building and advancement of the imperial forces. Or perhaps it was that the Earl of Minto had so angered him with his hasty words and foolish statements, or the driving sense of urgency for the health and safety of Miss Catherine Tenterchilt. Whatever the cause, he marched to the door, knocked once and pushed it open.

At once the sound of pistols being cocked filled the air, and there was little wonder, for the dark that deadened the sky behind him framed the doctor in an alarming and threatening way. The only light in the room came from a paraffin lamp on the centre of the round table where four men sat playing cards. Realising that his rash action could have been fatal, he raised his hands peacefully and took a step into the room.

'Stay, man,' one of the card players hissed. 'State your name and business or, with God as my witness, I will shoot you where you stand.'

'He may not speak English,' another man said, and pulled a second pistol from his coat, gripping it in his left hand that shook so much that the doctor was anxious he might fire without meaning to.

'I speak English,' he replied. 'My name is Fotherby and I seek a man by the name of FitzHammond. Is he here?'

'What is your business with him?' asked a third man.

'The Governor-General told me that he has information that I need.'

'Concerning what?' the man replied.

'Miss Catherine Tenterchilt. I have been sent from England to ensure her safe return.'

One by one the pistols were lowered and the third man beckoned that the doctor should come forward. Doctor Fotherby walked forward slowly blinking against the bright light and bowed his head slightly.

'I know the woman you speak of,' the man continued and rose to his feet. 'I am Peter FitzHammond.'

Doctor Fotherby bowed his head once more in a formal welcome but remained silent, allowing the gentleman before him to further the conversation. It was evident that no one in the room knew how to respond, for a silence lingered that was eventually shattered by Mr FitzHammond.

'Do you play cards, Doctor?'

'I am not a gambling man in general.'

'You sound to be quite the saint,' laughed one of the other men. 'Come, we play for little more than snuff and tobacco. I am certain even your tastes might extend to that.'

'Truthfully, I had hoped that you would take me to Miss Catherine Tenterchilt at once.'

'The moment that the sun is in the sky I shall take you to her,' promised FitzHammond. It was clear that none of the men were going to show him to Catherine Tenterchilt until dawn and so, with reluctance, Doctor Fotherby took a seat at the table.

Doctor Fotherby, a man of science for whom the sun and stars followed their patterns without the will of fate and luck, angered many of the men around the table, as he bowed out before he had the chance to lose greatly and remained betting only when there was a near certainty of winning. Clearly, however, it was not obvious to the rest of those gathered around the table who followed the lore of luck and chance in such games and each one cursed the doctor as they bowed out of the game a great deal poorer than they went in.

'Come, men,' a young man named Harrison began. 'We each of us have our days of luck and triumph. Today it is the turn of our new friend.'

'I would return to you all of your antes if you will take me to Miss Catherine Tenterchilt now.'

'This woman has quite a hold on you I believe, Doctor.'

'No, but I was commissioned to come here, find the sick lady and return her home. That is not a delegation I wish to abandon.'

'Who sent you?' FitzHammond asked thoughtfully. 'Who gave you this commission? For, in all the time that I have been in the Company, only peasants and disgraced women have tried to conceal themselves within it.'

'And yet she is neither,' Doctor Fotherby replied, rising to his feet.

'Will you take me to her?'

The other members of the carding table looked expectantly at FitzHammond, waiting like gannets to gather back the belongings that they had so recklessly tossed into the pot. Doctor Fotherby began collecting his winnings and each of the men sighed heavily and, one by one, began to gather their coats and leave the room.

'You are a strange man, I think, Doctor Fotherby,' FitzHammond said, pulling back the departing Fotherby's attention. 'You have an air of command and yet you allow yourself to live in servitude.'

'I serve only those who need my help,' came the placid reply.

'Who commissioned you?'

'Why should it make a difference whether it was her grieving father or the king himself? What have you done to her that makes you so desperate to find out from whom I have come?'

FitzHammond rose to his feet. 'It is a shame you never joined the Company, for I am certain you should have done well in it.' He walked over to the doctor, who stood a head taller than him. 'Who did send you?'

'Colonel Sir James Shorefield of the 5th Infantry.'

'You confuse me,' FitzHammond replied, uncertainty in his voice.

'Has this man a claim on her affections? And you to order so freely?'

'Indeed no, sir, to both your questions. But he speaks of a charm and bewitchment that the family places over him. Now, where is she?'

'Your sense of purpose is admirable,' FitzHammond replied and nodded reluctantly. 'I shall take you to where I know she was last, though that was some time ago.'

'I will pick up the trail from there, then. Come sir, tomorrow is Christmas and you and I are both well aware that the fort will be in a drunken stupor for the greater part. Kindly take me there now.'

FitzHammond looked torn before he nodded and walked from the room, beckoning the doctor to follow. Fotherby walked after his guide, who left the room, the building and indeed the fort itself. It was at the gate that the doctor stopped and looked back towards Fort William.

'Where are you leading?' he demanded. Whatever response he had expected or anticipated it was not what he heard.

'She may be a great many things to a great many people, Doctor Fotherby, but the one thing she is not is a Company man. She should never have been in the fort.'

'You sent her out into Calcutta?'

'I found her a home with people who would care for her, Doctor, so do not be so quick to rebuke me.' He continued walking and Fotherby followed, his long strides matching FitzHammond's pace easily. 'I did not know who she was and I did not know why she joined. Have you a sister, Doctor Fotherby?'

'No,' he replied briefly.

'I had. She visited me here some fifteen years ago and within fifteen days she had died. I do not understand what makes the fairer sex so ill suited to this climate. I was afraid when I met your charge that the same thing might happen. She is some man's sister, no?'

'No,' Fotherby replied, more gently now for he could hear the desperation in FitzHammond's voice. 'But she is sister to two more ladies, and daughter to a distinguished family.'

They walked on in silence, past the towering cathedral of St John's that was lit up internally on this most sacred of nights, and on through the wealth and riches of the British areas until the buildings began to change as they reached the edges of the city. Small huts began to appear with a thin tree line close to them. The heavy dust of the ill used road was cloying as it molded onto their boots. It was close to one of these, that to Fotherby's eyes all appeared the same, that FitzHammond stopped.

'There is disgrace on all women who enter under the Company's flag. Much as it is in the army. But I could not instigate that disgrace. I told them I had sent her home. I told them that, upon being discovered, she left with nothing save her soiled name. Yet I could not do it. Now the Governor-General shall certainly know and it will be my name that is disgraced.'

'You need only say that she was sent home and you sent me after her, sir. I shall not reappear at the fort to deny your story, for I see you as a man of compassion.'

'Thank you,' FitzHammond replied gratefully and stepped to the door of the shack before knocking and entering. 'Namaskar, Washima,' he began as an Indian woman stepped forward. He spoke to her in the language that was native to Calcutta, but that Fotherby did not understand. 'She says that the lady you seek is now with Mr Havishkar, their doctor.'

'Where?' Fotherby asked earnestly. More words were exchanged before at last FitzHammond turned back to him and smiled.

'Only a short way from here, within the tree line.'

'Can she take me there?'

'Yes,' FitzHammond replied.

If the woman was afraid to guide the doctor, a stranger to her, through the town at this hour she did not show it. Fotherby parted from FitzHammond outside the small house and hurriedly followed Washima, who padded barefoot before him. She had no lamp but continued walking in the dark as though it did not hinder her and Fotherby was continually amazed as she wove between the trees. They seemed to have been walking a great distance in the quiet night before, at last, a light became visible a short way ahead. His guide did not speak to him, indeed she knew no English and the doctor knew no Indian, but she ushered him into the house and called out to Havishkar. Fotherby paid no heed to the conversation that they shared, but stared around him at the rows of beds that lined this great room, each taken by a person so starved that they appeared wraithlike. Lamps were burning where they hung down from the ceiling at regular intervals, peculiar lights like burning grasses, and they gave off a smell that was both pleasing and sickly.

While he observed his surroundings with a mixture of awe, confusion and distaste, Washima departed, bowing slightly to him. Havishkar folded his arms before his chest and looked thoughtfully at the tall, thin figure that the doctor cut.

'You are a doctor?' he asked with an accent that recalled Fotherby to a period in his past.

'Yes, sir,' he replied. 'I am searching for-'

'I know.' Fotherby frowned slightly at the man before him. 'You come for the woman. Washima told me.'

'I have been sent to bring her safely home.'

'Come,' Havishkar said firmly, and moved further into the building. He continually mumbled under his breath so that Fotherby was uncertain whether he was being addressed or not, but followed meekly past a number of the beds. Some two thirds of the way through the room, Havishkar stopped. 'She lies here,' he said flatly, pointing to the bed on the right hand side.

How peculiar it felt to Doctor Fotherby. A journey that had begun two months before had finally reached its conclusion. He thanked Havishkar, but the man simply waved dismissively and walked back to where they had entered. It was impossible for Doctor Fotherby to be seated upon the bed for it was scarcely a foot from the ground and was more akin to a stretcher by his own standards. Perhaps it was because he towered over her so greatly, or because she had been his goal and had seemed so remote, or perhaps it was the illness that had ravaged her body, but she appeared small and childlike to his eyes. Her brown hair, cut so short to pass as a man in the Company, did not reach her shoulders but fell lifelessly onto the flat pillow. She was no exception to the other patients and was so thin that Fotherby could barely look at her. He leaned down to pull the thin blanket that lay at her side over her and sighed heavily.

'Sleeping Tiger, do not sleep forever.'

CHAPTER THIRTEEN
Tuesday 26th March 1811

With each day that passed by in silence concerning her younger sister, Imogen felt a great despondency grow within her. By the Christmas of that year, she had given up hope for the survival and return of the ill-fated Miss Catherine Tenterchilt. She did not allow her father to see this for he had suffered too greatly to burden him, and she had received no reply from Colonel Sir James Shorefield in response to her desperate letter. It had been a vain hope that her letter should ever reach him and an even deeper folly to believe that he should be able, and indeed willing, to help her. Her nightly weeping was known only to herself and she wished that it might remain that way. She heard nothing from the outside world, except for a message of Christmas well-wishes from Arabella and her small family. Nothing that is, until in the new year, when 1811 was into its third month, and an unannounced visitor arrived at Petrovia Lodge.

Rain was pounding on the windows as she looked out into the darkness that was setting in. There was nothing more than her own sad and lonely reflection visible in the glass, and no sound above the driving storm that battered the strong walls. Occasionally, the teeming river could be heard if the wind changed its direction for a second or there was a lull in the downpour.

'There is no joy to be had in this weather,' Penny said firmly. She walked over and pulled closed the heavy winter curtains.

'You are quite right, Penny. Spring seems such a long way off as the years turn.'

'Twenty five is no great age, Miss Tenterchilt,' Penny said softly.

'At times I could believe you, Penny. Then I am grateful of such a life as this.'

She rose to her feet, turning from the maid in the hope that she might disguise the fact that her statement was one of regret, but the attention of both women was pulled away as there came a beating upon the door. She exchanged a puzzled look with Penny before the older woman tutted and walked off to find out who it might be at this hour. Imogen was initially confused as the clock on the drawing room wall told her that it was approaching midnight. Her confusion turned to intrigue as she heard Penny show someone into the library and then hurry to find Mr Tenterchilt. Imogen crept down to the door, which was slightly ajar, and tried to listen for a sound. But the library was silent. Perhaps it was the unnatural quiet that made her agitated but, when she heard her father clatter down the stairs, she at once withdrew behind the door that opened onto one of the guest quarters. She left the door ajar and through it she could see her father in his nightclothes, with only a gown wrapped around him as he rushed as fast as his wounded leg and aged body would allow.

Whatever words were spoken in the library were hushed and behind a closed door so that all Imogen could hear was a constant murmuring. She walked away to find Penny so that she might find out who had come to the door on such a desolate and inhospitable night, but the maid was nowhere to be found, almost as though she were hiding. Eventually her feet led her out to the orangery and at once in the bitter cold she began to shiver and tears trickled from her eyes. The rain pounded upon the glass roof, at times so hard that she believed it would shatter down on her. Terrible scenarios passed through her mind concerning the man who had arrived in such great urgency that he could not wait until the morning to impart his information. Her first thought was for Catherine for, despite the sensible conclusion that she had perished in India, Imogen still needed an answer regarding her sister. Perhaps it was someone from the court who had come to arrest her father, or from the army to take him for Court Martial over his role in her step-mother's treason. The thought that anything could take her father from her once more seemed too much to bear. She pulled out one of the basket chairs and sat down, resting her head upon the table.

She remained like this for countless minutes before, at last, she heard the gentlemen leaving the study and her father bidding his visitor to stay the night before preparing for the long journey back. His guest did not audibly reply and Imogen felt once again intrigued by this silence that surrounded them. When the footfalls of both people faded away, Imogen left the orangery and walked noiselessly up to her room. All the evenings of creeping through the shadows to discuss the country with her beloved Hamish had stood her in good stead and her feet did not betray even the slightest sound.

She had a restless night, full of dreams that mixed reality with nightmares so that, when she awoke to find a grey, wet morning staring back at her, she could not tell with certainty what was real and what belonged to the realms of sleep. She rose quickly, recalling the guest whose urgency had doubtlessly been the cause of her broken night. She rushed down the stairs in bare feet, regretting her choice almost instantly for the flagstone floor was terribly cold. She did not stop until she opened the dining room door and looked across at her father who sat there, turning to face her as she rushed in.

'Imogen?' he gasped as he looked across at her. 'What is the hurry? And why are you in your nightclothes?'

Imogen suddenly felt unbearably foolish as she followed her father's quick glance across to their visitor, who politely turned away. She flushed crimson red as she realised that it was Mr Dermot who stood by the window, and she wrapped her shawl tighter about her.

'I was concerned, Papa,' she whispered. 'I heard the arrival of a guest late last night and I was worried that he may have brought bad news.'

Her father smiled slightly and nodded. 'Go and dress, Imogen, and then I am certain Mr Dermot shall tell you the news that he carried.'

Imogen walked out of the room and the lawyer turned from the window, his face a little ruddy but otherwise showing no emotion at Miss Tenterchilt's arrival. He walked over to the table and leant down on the back of one of the chairs.

'You would have me tell Miss Tenterchilt my purpose in coming here last night?'

'In part,' Mr Tenterchilt replied, rubbing his hands over his eyes and frowning. 'In truth she should be told all, but I do not wish to worry her. She bears so much silently. I fear she is desperately lonely in her soul.'

'I believe she may surprise you. She is the matriarch of the family now. It never did fall to Mrs Jenkyns.'

'I wish I had not confined her to this remote corner of the world.'

'You have not. It is her love and her loyalty that has done that. Allow her the freedom of that choice, to realise that she chose correctly.'

Imogen did not waste any time, for she was both desperate for and dreading the news that Mr Dermot might disclose. When she returned downstairs, she found that Mr Dermot stood alone in the dining room, staring once more out of the window. She concluded pinning her hair and cleared her throat slightly so that he would know she was there.

'I'm pleased to find you in better health than when we last met.' He never turned from the window as he spoke and Imogen felt indignant by this apparent snub, but her etiquette dictated how she should behave, and it was that code that she followed.

'Mr Dermot. I trust you are in good health.'

'Eternally,' he replied, turning to face her and Imogen felt her brow crease as she beheld the smile that rested upon his features, for it seemed so unnatural. 'Come, I know you wish to hear what urgency drove me here last night. Let us sit like gentlemen and discuss it.' He pulled out one of the chairs from the table and invited her to sit down.

'But I am not a gentleman, sir.'

'No,' he conceded, 'but you have a mind as open as one. And you shall need to have an open mind, Miss Tenterchilt, for indeed so much has happened of a nature that is inexplicable.'

'I confess to being intrigued, Mr Dermot,' she replied, sitting down upon the chair and waiting as he walked around the long table and sat directly opposite her. 'Though I am afraid also.'

'Wisely so. You wrote to Sir James Shorefield. Why?'

'I was of the understanding that a letter's content might remain personal between the sender and the recipient.'

'Do not misunderstand my meaning, Miss Tenterchilt. I have not come to enquire as to your personal secrets. Only, I am equally intrigued by you. You do not share your burden of knowledge with your father, and yet would beg assistance of a man with whom you have only a few hours acquaintance.'

'My father has enough concerns,' she whispered.

'My dear Miss Tenterchilt, do you suppose that he would not rather know the trouble and plight of his daughter. Your father might have had someone sent to India at once to protect her.'

'Is she dead?' Imogen whispered, caring nothing of this chastising but concerned solely for her sister's health. Mr Dermot smiled slightly and shook his head, realising the mistake he had made.

'She was not when last I heard.'

Imogen released a steadying breath and pushed away the tears of relief that threatened to spill. She felt determined to show no further weakness to the man before her. 'Then she is coming home?'

Mr Dermot, a man whose detached resolve was his shield and weapon against the world he lived in, faltered. He glanced out of the window, across at the door, anything to keep from looking at Imogen. Finally he met her gaze and forced a smile, so false that he could taste the lie upon his lips as he replied. 'She will come home.'

'Have you told Papa where she is and what has happened?'

'Yes,' Mr Dermot said simply. 'In part at least. I did not see fit in telling him that she joined the Company, for there is no reason to bring further shame upon your father. So I came to tell him, as I shall tell you, that Miss Catherine is alive and in the best of care.'

'You bring me such comfort, Mr Dermot,' Imogen said, smiling broadly.

'You went to great lengths to protect the integrity of your family, Miss

Tenterchilt. In my role as a lawyer, it is you who has brought comfort to me.'

'You must be sure to impart my thanks and admiration to the colonel when next you see him.'

'Colonel?' Mr Dermot faltered and his face held a look that suggested he had been caught out. 'Colonel Pottinger?'

'No,' Imogen laughed, too blinded by relief to notice the lawyer's hesitation. 'Colonel Sir James Shorefield. Only, such a name and title seems terribly long to use each time.'

'I shall indeed pass on your high regard. I am certain it shall be of significance to him. I hear the army are fighting still from the town of Bussaco.'

'Indeed.' Imogen paused as she tried to assess what reply she might receive to the question she was so desperate to ask. 'Mr Dermot, I do know that, as a woman, I have no place in the running of court and army, but I have to know sir, what happened in Prussia?'

'A sergeant major killed a captain. I can offer you no more, for I have no connection or association with the army. Consider that your sister is remarried, and has a child to raise. She would not wish for you to look back always to her dead husband.'

'What of Hamish Gordon? He was innocent, I know it.'

'It astounds me that from such a great distance you know something that contradicts those who were barely ten feet away.'

'You did not know him as I did,' Imogen protested. 'I know he would not do such a thing.'

'Indeed, I did not know him as you did. But have you learnt nothing of what it means to be a clansman? Do you think that each night you spoke to him - yes, indeed I know of your lessons of the Highland culture - he did anything other than what was loyal and right by you? That is the same loyalty that I have no doubt was present that night in the far north of Prussia.'

Imogen felt exposed by the man's words and she rose to her feet, uncertain of herself and everything around her. Mr Dermot rose, too, and reached across to her.

'Miss Tenterchilt, forgive me, I spoke sternly and out of turn. I did not mean to offend or upset you.'

'No,' she whispered. 'You clearly did know Mr Gordon far better than I.' She held up her hand, trying to block him from her sight, and walked out. Mr Dermot sat down at the table and dropped his head into his hands wearily. It was too great an effort to conceal one topic from one person and another topic from someone else. Indeed, he believed that the Tenterchilt family were now dominating his time and thoughts so that, with the poisoned affairs that encircled the unfortunate family, he could think of nothing else. But at the centre of it lay the terrible deeds that blinded all those involved, leaving lives torn apart and irreparably damaged.

Mr Dermot made no effort to speak to Miss Tenterchilt, and indeed made every effort to avoid her, until the following morning when the rain had stopped and Imogen was standing in the orangery. She was staring out over the sodden earth that divided the house from the river, so her back was turned as he approached. He knocked softly on the door and waited until Imogen turned to face him. She was surprised to find that he was wearing a long riding cloak and there was an urgency to his eyes that intrigued her.

'Are you leaving Petrovia Lodge, sir?'

'I am, Miss Tenterchilt. And taking your father with me.'

'Whatever for?' she whispered. 'He is not in trouble, is he?'

'Not at all,' Mr Dermot said, with such certainty that Imogen immediately felt at ease. 'I am afraid that I caused you anguish with my words yesterday and, though I am a man unaccustomed to correcting myself, I do wish, nay beg of you your forgiveness. Your continued friendship, Miss Tenterchilt, has kept me smiling in my toilsome work. I should not wish to lose that.'

'If I could change one thing,' she replied softly, 'it would be that I wish you could know the hardships of holding one's own council with such great periods of time to reflect upon it. I could never understand Cat's boyish tendencies, yet perhaps she only needed to occupy her mind in a way that we women are cursed never to do.'

'Do not wish it so, Miss Tenterchilt, for there are too many men whose ignorance stems from just that. Be pleased to have the time to stop and consider, but remember how dangerous it might be if we men did the same.'

Imogen found herself laughing without meaning to as she considered the flippant remark that the lawyer had made. In reply to this jovial sound Mr Dermot smiled and formally took his leave of her.

She watched them go with a heavy heart all the same, for she missed her father's company. Beatrice and Josiah took all of her time however, for they were growing into the most delightful of children, owing to the love of knowledge that Imogen had imparted to them. When at last the spring arrived and the trees came into leaf, it was a great relief to her. Even more welcome was a letter from Arabella detailing a planned event to which they were all invited at Horland Park. She wrote that she had spent some time with their father, although she did not know what his business in the capital was. Imogen, who could not trust Mr Dermot, was ever mindful of his cautioning words to her that all those in London worked for their own ends, and she was increasingly concerned for her father.

CHAPTER FOURTEEN
Tuesday 11th June 1811

June in the subcontinent of India was met with an equal portion of confused worry and concern. Since his arrival in Calcutta, Doctor Fotherby had worked tirelessly to better the care and sanitary situation of Havishkar's small hospital. He was of the opinion that the lack of cleanliness in the place was almost certainly what had resulted in the lingering disease that was so prevalent in the little forest hut. He helped Havishkar to build beds from the trees, eager to raise the patients from the ground, brought in cats from the nearby city to rid the house of vermin, and produced such western cures for ailments and injuries that the people of the small village now had superior care to those within the city walls.

Despite all of his industry, he did not lose sight of the reason he had returned to India and, from that night at the end of the year, he had spent six months trying to nurse Miss Catherine Tenterchilt back to health. It was a long and slow process that he initially despaired of, but the tiger he had observed in her soul was embodied in her will to live and, as the hot summer began to take hold, she was able once more to walk by herself through the tiny garden.

She could not recall waking from the sickness that had engulfed her, only that Doctor Fotherby had been there, a familiar face and voice that returned her to home. He seemed to have a greater urgency to him than she recalled but he was always calm and gentle with her. He never questioned her for her choice to leave, nor did he berate her, but maintained his own council until, in the blistering month of May, that last year had caused the illness she was still carrying, she confronted him.

He was working on a new door for one of the rooms, sawing one of the tall trees that Havishkar had helped him fell the evening before. He wanted to divide the house into wards, like his hospital in London, theorising that it might be possible to quarantine those with infectious diseases so that there would be a safer treatment for all patients. Catherine walked over to him and sat down opposite the long tree trunk.

'Did Imogen send you?' she whispered.

'You should be wearing something on your head,' Doctor Fotherby replied, panting from his labours as he looked up at her. He had discarded his own hat and Catherine picked it up and placed it on her head.

'Did Imogen send you?'

'No,' he replied, straightening to his immense height. His brow was beaded with perspiration and his open shirt clung to him. 'I was requested to find you by Captain Portland, and he was commissioned by Colonel Sir James Shorefield, I believe.'

'But I do not know a Colonel Shorefield,' she mused.

'Evidently he knows of you.' The doctor returned to sawing and Catherine lay back on the ground, staring up at the sky. There was a peace here that the Scottish skies, in all of their beauty, could never hold. They were too dramatic, always fuelling her need to seek adventure. But it had not been as glamorous as she had supposed.

'Dear Captain Portland,' she sighed. 'He is a special man, is he not?'

'I am not sure it is quite proper of you to say such things to me.'

'Indeed it would not be if I was in London, but we are not in England now.'

A silence fell upon them once more, broken only by the rhythmical movement of the saw blade. Fotherby, far from being a carpenter, was at least so keen and eager that, although all of his beds were crooked and his lengths for the door were not exact, it was without doubt an improvement to what was there already.

'I never managed to apologise,' Catherine whispered, sleep taking a claim on her. 'I wanted to say sorry, but you were so busy. Just like you are now.'

'Apologise?' he asked briefly, carrying the planks of wood back to the house. 'What for?'

'At the ball,' she murmured, her words slurring into one another. 'I was so cruel to you.'

Doctor Fotherby stopped and knelt down beside her. 'That was years ago.'

'A long time to carry guilt.'

He lifted the hat that covered her face but, as her voice had trailed, so too had her consciousness, and she lay asleep upon the ground. Awkwardly, he carried her once more to the high cot that had become her bed in the last few months. He considered the words that Catherine had shared with him as he sat in the evening and smoked his small clay pipe that he held. There was a mist moving through the trees as the water in the giant plants evaporated. It played games with his eyes so he was unsure what he was truly looking at and what was simply a willo-the- wisp doomed to vanish before it took form.

There was a pensiveness to him that was beyond anything that he had known, and he began to seek an escape from it as the days wore on and the year continued to turn. His labouring work and tending of the sick and wounded consumed all his time and he ensured that night usually found him too tired to think. He would sleep on the roof of the house, such was the custom of the area and falling asleep under a canopy of stars never lost its charm.

Miss Catherine Tenterchilt continued to receive the greater part of his attention. He would walk with her, coaxing her once more to enjoy the leisure that might be gained from such excursions, but ever mindful that she should be cautious of tiring herself in the scorching sun. As June wore on and the rains began, Doctor Fotherby confined Catherine to indoors. Having created a western house from the little hut, she was able to sit separately from the other patients, but the restriction did not seem to suit her temperament and too often she drifted into dreamy dazes, desperate for distractions yet finding none.

FitzHammond, the man from the Company who had helped to protect and assist Miss Catherine, had been of invaluable service to the doctor. Each Sunday Fotherby attended church and, each week, FitzHammond, a staunch Catholic, would leave food and provisions to be collected, for he would never set foot in a Protestant church. For Catherine, all the charity and donations grieved her but, when she discussed the topic with Doctor Fotherby, he corrected her sternly.

'Who needs charity more than the sick?' he asked bluntly. 'When you were drifting in unconsciousness, it was charity that saved your life.'

'I believed it was you who did that,' she had replied.

He shook his head and offered no words, in a way that puzzled Catherine so greatly that she had never made mention of it again. Now they sat on the earthen floor playing chess, for the monsoon rains prevented any hope of leaving the tiny hospital.

'It is so dreary in the rain,' Catherine sighed, adjusting the brightly coloured skirt that she wore. 'Can you imagine going to a Chelsea ball in something this vivid?' she laughed.

Fotherby smiled. 'I have not been to a ball since that October. A lady may wear what she wishes and be labelled as exotic or diverse. If a gentleman ventured a colour of any hue it would be deemed in ill taste and contrary to all laws of fashion.' Catherine looked at him in confusion before he added, 'you should be content to be a lady.'

Catherine's eyes flashed and her brow creased. 'I do not recall your objection to sparring with me. My mother never had a son. Nor did my father until he married the most ghastly woman I have known.'

'It was not my intention to berate you,' Fotherby said calmly. 'You broke many hearts when you fled. I wished only to show you that you are greatly cared for by so many.'

'I told Imogen where I was,' she muttered. 'She always knows what to do in every situation. I knew she would see to it that I might return safely.'

'Eastern Sunrise is without a doubt the wisest person I have ever known.'

Silence followed this remark and they continued to play until, at length, the doctor's gaze left the board and he realised that Miss Catherine Tenterchilt sat crying noiselessly. Fine streaks of tear marks daubed her face and she breathed raggedly, trying to hide it from the man before her. Fotherby did not know what to do. He reached his hand towards her before pulling away, recalling that etiquette did not permit him to comfort her in such a fashion. A horrible memory confronted him and, for a moment, it was Miss Kitty Simmons that he saw before him and he recoiled. It was this movement that gave Catherine cause to look up and at once she scrubbed her cheeks dry with the back of her hand.

'Is the sight of a woman weeping so deplorable to you?' she demanded angrily. 'Is it not the role of a lady to cry?' At once she knew she had spoken out of turn for the doctor, the very soul of patience, only shook his head. 'I know I have brought all this upon myself, that I am left reaping the harvest of my own downfall. Has it not been so since I was born? Since I was born a girl and my father wished for a boy?'

'It is not your fault, Miss Catherine.'

'But it is,' she sobbed, and now no amount of effort and control could stop the tears that flooded from her eyes. She moved away and awkwardly rose to her feet, walking to stand in the doorway and look out at the torrential rain. Doctor Fotherby rose too, and took a step towards her.

'You have done nothing that any other spirit so great would not have done. Come, you should sit down.'

'I do not wish to sit down,' she replied in a firm voice, but she reached out her hand to steady herself against the wall. At once Doctor Fotherby stood beside her, and she was grateful of his support as she leaned against him. 'I wasted it all. Mama died and I do not recall a fond conversation with her. Arabella was widowed and all I could think of was the bitterness of my feelings towards Rose Pottinger. Imogen always looks after me and I have robbed her of her own happiness through it and,' she stopped to take in a deep breath before she concluded. 'I ran away from them all, and the man I really thought to love.'

'Do you really think that these people care about those wrongs?

Compared to your safety and happiness, such things are trivial to them.' He looked down at her and shook his head. 'You shall return to them all, Miss Catherine.'

She made no response but continued to lean against him until she felt too weary even to stand, and the doctor assisted her back to her bed.

'Captain Portland told me why you left the army,' she said, looking up at him.

'That was many years ago,' the doctor replied and turned away from her.

'My brother was court martialed, too.'

'Your brother?' the doctor whispered. 'You told me your mother had no sons.'

But Catherine Tenterchilt did not answer and Fotherby was left confused to ponder on his own thoughts. Catherine regarded the doctor as the days turned, his sad, pensive expressions, the care and devotion with which he administered to the sick for, far from being alone in the hospital, there were many others. More came as word travelled, people from within the city walls would arrive, wishing for cures to all manner of ailments, and Havishkar and Fotherby diligently tended them.

It was on one occasion in the early days of July, when the clouds obscured the sun and rain beat down in droves, that she finally confided in him. She had taken on the role of nurse for whatever hours she could manage, against the doctor's distressed claims that a house of fever and sickness should be avoided by one who had suffered under the hand of typhoid. She dismissed him firmly and continued to follow the path she wished and, as a gentleman, he could do nothing to stop her.

'Do you suppose Captain Portland to be an honest man, Doctor?'

The bluntness of the question from the silence of the room startled him and he turned his face towards her. She handed him a roll of the colourful fabric that they were using for bandaging, and stared back neutrally as though no question could have been simpler to answer.

'He is the very best of men, Miss Catherine,' came the reply after a time, realising that one was not only expected but also awaited. 'He is honest and honourable.'

'I believed him to be,' she replied thoughtfully. 'Only, why should such a great man abandon an innocent soul to death? That is what I cannot fathom.'

'I cannot believe or accept that he would do such a thing,' Fotherby replied loyally, as he tied the patient's dressing in place before rising to his feet so that he towered over Catherine.

'Nor I, yet I have it from his own mouth.'

'Can you not excuse the past to the confines of history?' he said. 'He is a man in anguish and worry over you. There can be few who would not forgive a man a history that he could not escape.'

'You speak as someone who knows of this first hand,' she whispered, curious about the man before her. 'Yet you stood by the wronged man.'

'It is not only those that are found guilty who are condemned,' he replied.

'So I should forgive him for failing Hamish?'

'I know nothing of the affair of which you speak, Miss Catherine. Only that, sometimes, the best efforts by the truest of men are still not enough when rank and wealth are involved. You should not be so quick to condemn a man on what he has failed to do, but to look on what he has tried to do. Captain Portland is the best of men,' Fotherby repeated before adding, 'and the truest of friends.'

Catherine was quite content with this reply and once more dared to hope for a life with the young captain who awaited her in Europe. Before she could venture any further conversation, she turned as a strong voice sounded from behind her.

'Doctor, might I speak with you?'

The sound of an English speaker, albeit with a heavy Irish accent, caused her to turn and, at once, she faced a man who looked a little familiar. She could remember him in the red uniform of the East India Company, a man of note, she believed. Doctor Fotherby turned too and nodded, and Catherine watched as they left the room.

'I have found you passage back to England on a cargo ship,' FitzHammond explained. 'She is sailing as far as Aden and then you shall have to find passage north to the Mediterranean.'

'Thank you,' the doctor replied, shaking FitzHammond's hand. 'I confess that I had hoped to avoid the monsoon season.'

'She is called The Jewel of Madesh and sails in two day's time. You are expected by her captain, a man called Leon.'

'You must forgive me, sir, but I have a further favour to request.'

'That is dependent on your request.'

'I am a man out of place in English society, and have felt the pull of the orient since first I came here as a young man. When I have returned my charge safely to those who await her, I mean to return and properly establish this hospital of Havishkar's. Please help him continue this venture alone until I am at liberty to return.'

'You are a man of great sacrifice, Fotherby. How can I refuse such a favour when it is so selflessly asked?'

'Thank you,' he answered simply. FitzHammond took his leave of the small hospital and Doctor Fotherby returned to announce his news to Catherine. She received it most gladly, though she was sorry to part from Havishkar to whom she had tried to teach English in return for an understanding of Hindi. She felt certain that Imogen would have been proud of her for this, and she was eagerly looking forward to returning to her sister and indeed all her family. It would be untrue to suggest that she was not also looking forward to once more seeing Captain Portland. The young officer occupied many of her excitable thoughts.

Two days later found them standing on the enormous quay in the city of Calcutta. FitzHammond was there and offered them both provisions for the journey and, after introducing them to the captain, an Indian man whose real name he had shortened to Leon, he addressed the doctor.

'I will see to it that Havishkar is well provided for until your return, though I should advise you that I can do so only while I am here. If my removal of food and medication is noticed that may not be as long as we hope.'

'Your kindnesses are great beyond measure.'

They parted formally, bowing as gentlemen should, before Fotherby guided Catherine onto the cargo ship and she confronted him.

'You are returning?'

'What of it, Miss Catherine?' Fotherby replied, as calm as ever. 'I have no ties to our colder English shores, and there are people here, as you well know, who need my help far more than those in London.'

'But what of Captain Portland? He so relies upon your friendship.'

'And he shall have it, always, but if the intentions I have seen laid before me both in England and India are to be believed then he shall have a wife soon and shall want no more for such dull companionship as a doctor can offer.'

Catherine blushed and turned from him, collecting the packages that FitzHammond had gifted them and walking after Captain Leon, who seemed more than eager to escort her to her cabin. Fotherby remained on the deck and watched as the crew, an equal mix of Indian and Arab, readied the ship for sail. It was a small vessel compared to the towering Indiamen that lined the port, but it was large enough that both he and Miss Catherine might have their own cabins although, as he later discovered, his was little more than a cupboard in size.

As Calcutta drifted away from him once more, he felt a sense of longing: he belonged there.

CHAPTER FIFTEEN
Monday 24th June 1811

By contrast to the monsoon season of India, Britain enjoyed a dry June that was concluded by the journey down to Horland Park where Imogen was once again reunited with Arabella. Josiah and Beatrice travelled down also and were all given their first opportunity to meet Timothy Jenkyns, Arabella's pride and joy. Mr Tenterchilt also travelled north and joined the party some days later so that, in the presence of the late Mrs Tenterchilt's portrait, Imogen felt that only Catherine was missing from the gathering.

The event was a fair that was passing through the area, although in truth it was simply a device to unite the family once more. The gardens at Horland were in full bloom and each afternoon tea was taken on the large lawn. On the third day of their excursion, the day before their outing to the fair, Mr Jenkyns turned to their father and asked,

'What is the manner of your stay in Town, sir?'

Imogen looked equally as expectant as her brother-in-law, while Arabella turned away. 'Must we discuss these dull topics on such a bright day?' she sighed. 'Come Imogen, let us take a turn.'

Imogen was obliged to rise, and awkwardly straightened her skirts before stepping over to her sister. They walked a short way together before Imogen felt the silence ought to be shattered.

'Do you know why Papa has stayed so long in London, Arabella? For he has said nothing to me.'

'No,' Arabella replied, and Imogen was surprised to hear a tremble in her voice, perhaps fearful and certainly unsure. 'Do you know that feeling of anticipation, Imogen? That feeling that perhaps the world will fall at your feet or down around your head.'

'What is it, Arabella?' Imogen asked, taking her hand and turning to face her.

'The most peculiar feeling has been following me these last months. I overheard a conversation, one of despair and loathing, right here in my gardens and, since then, these eight months, I have borne it silently with the growing feeling of fear and regret.'

Imogen pulled her sister over to the small summerhouse and sat her down, hidden from view. 'Explain this to me simply, Arabella. I cannot understand your words.'

Arabella told Imogen of the conversation between the man named Peter and the young maid who she had not seen since that day. 'Since then I have jumped at everything, and have become fearful that I am being watched and followed at every moment. At times when I walk through London I take circles to try and lose my follower, but I cannot be rid of them. And now that I have returned to Horland I feel less welcome than anywhere I have ever been.'

'Then you must come home with us for the summer. You shall return to Petrovia, for none can follow there without being found.'

'I cannot. I would not leave Roger with his father.'

'Roger?' Imogen interrupted, confused.

'Timothy,' Arabella corrected herself and rushed to the door of the house, looking for someone as though she believed that they were not alone. 'I could not leave him and he would not enjoy the lodge so well as the house that he knows in Chelsea.'

'Then find yourself a companion,' Imogen urged. 'Someone with whom you feel great comfort and safety, that when you walk through the streets it does not matter if you are followed. What of Rose Bronstead? She was always so close to you in the past.'

'She has three children now, and seems to have little time beyond them. She and I have not spoken in so long. I know that a conversation I was not invited to hear has done this to me, but I cannot think what caused such hate and malice in the pair that they sneered at me. I am not a bad mistress, am I?'

'I cannot see how you could be, Arabella. Sit down a while.'

Arabella followed Imogen's advice and returned to her seat. Her hands were white as she clutched her own dress anxiously, and her face looked pallid and faint. 'I am afraid for Timothy,' she said at last.

'Afraid?' Imogen repeated, doubtful of both the word and the tone of her sister's voice. 'Why do you need to be afraid?'

'I have been driven to such fear,' she sobbed. 'Everywhere I take him there are such venomous looks and-'

'Stop.' Imogen interrupted, but not unkindly. 'You have nothing to fear in your own house.'

Arabella nodded slowly as Imogen knelt before her, taking her hand in a comforting gesture, and watching as colour began to return to Arabella's cheeks.

'You must never feel afraid,' she continued. 'For you can always return home to Petrovia Lodge where you will be safer than safe.'

'I don't know why I am driven like this. I cannot understand it.'

'Arabella, you have endured so much in these few years.'

'Come, we should rejoin the others.'

Imogen followed her sister back across the lawns to where the rest of the small family party was seated. After Arabella's moment of madness, Imogen began to notice how conspicuous they were on the lawn and, turning back to the house, noticed a figure at one of the windows. She reached for Arabella's arm but thought better of the gesture, unsure that she should worry her sister further. The rest of the day continued to run by with no further complaint from Arabella, although she jumped at everything and her wide eyes brimmed at times. If a servant placed something down without due care and attention Arabella would raise her hand anxiously to her chest as though her heart had ceased to beat. Imogen was greatly concerned by this, for her sister had always been so certain of herself that to see her in this manner seemed not only worrying, but wrong. She lay in her bed that night, trying to tease out the hidden strands of the puzzle.

When at last the dawn came, it found Imogen terribly weary, for she had failed to take any sleep save only passing moments when she had drifted off before trying once more to resolve Arabella's problem. She might not have worried, however, for her sister seemed far happier this morning. The promise of the summer fair and escaping from Horland Park seemed to cheer her, and Imogen took an anxious comfort from this.

The family journeyed together in Mr Jenkyns' spacious carriage. Dancers, musicians and craftsmen lined the streets and, as Arabella stepped from the carriage, she gave an amazed sigh at the spectacle before her. Imogen felt relieved by this expression of delight and found that she relaxed at once, enjoying each step that they took. They became lost in the spectacle that the fair formed but, ever conscious of her sister's fragility, Imogen followed Arabella closely and never let her slip from sight. This she maintained until she was startled to hear someone address her close at hand.

'Miss Tenterchilt,' a haggard voice announced, and Imogen turned around to see Madame Kerina, the old gypsy woman she had known from those years of summer encampment at Petrovia Lodge. 'I see much in you that has changed.'

'Please, Madame,' Imogen began. 'Do not tell me my future. I do not believe in it, and I do not wish to know what it holds.'

'Was I not correct the last time we spoke?' Imogen tried to recall the occasion but could not. It did not matter, for the gypsy woman continued. 'It is your sister, not you. She will learn a dark and troublesome truth. Guard her well.'

Imogen frowned down at the bent woman, who proceeded to hobble away from her, waving her hand dismissively as though she expected Imogen to be following but did not wish her to. Imogen just followed her with her eyes before turning back to Arabella. She felt an icy feeling grip her as she realised that, whilst she had stopped, Arabella had continued further into the crowd. Imogen rushed forward, having to recall that ladies should never run and sedating her pace, but looking all the harder around her. Fire throwers and spinning dancers whirled and circled before her, making her dizzy. She continued through them all until she caught a glimpse of the small train of Arabella's dress and she rushed towards her, but stopped as she noticed that she was with her husband. Surely nothing would happen with Mr Jenkyns there to protect her.

Despite the warnings of the gypsy woman, the family enjoyed their day in Manchester, though most were quietly relieved to be returning to Horland in the evening. The sun was setting when at last they reached the estate, laughing happily and sharing those amusements that had so lightened the day. They entered the hall jovially so that, at their arrival, many surprised servants peered from behind the doors or through the banisters. Indeed, their entrance was rowdy and better resembled a group of drunken peasants than ladies and gentlemen of high degree.

'Sir, there is a gentleman waiting for you in your study,' a servant said softly, addressing Mr Jenkyns.

'Find him a room for the night, and I shall see him in the morning.'

'He is rather insistent, sir.'

'Very well,' Mr Jenkyns said. 'Excuse me ladies. Sir,' he added, bowing slightly to Mr Tenterchilt. He walked away from them and at once the merriment in their eyes died. Arabella once more seemed agitated and Imogen, mindful of Madame Kerina's words, placed her hand upon her older sister's arm.

'I am sure it is something quite unimportant,' she began, trying to soothe Arabella. 'No doubt it is someone from London, come on business.'

'Of course, you are right.' Arabella's anxious face made it clear that she did not believe her words. 'Come, we shall have some supper.'

Arabella loved being a gracious host. She was the best of the three Tenterchilt sisters at being a society lady and nothing pleased her more than sharing her possessions with those she cared for. The table was set and they sat down together to eat but, as the clock chimed nine o'clock in the main hall, Arabella rose.

'I am sorry, but I must see what it is that so detains my husband. He should be here.'

Imogen tried to stop her but no amount of words could prevent Arabella from walking out of the room and towards the study. She knocked gently before pushing open the door. Mr Jenkyns was standing behind his desk, leaning down on the tabletop, his face crimson and each muscle throbbing with rage. Arabella paused, fearful, but this anger was not aimed at her but at the man who stood opposite her husband. Beside him, on a chair sat a woman holding a child and Arabella gasped as she realised that it was the girl she had seen in the gardens not a year before. Her eyes penetrated Arabella's heart with their pity and determination.

'Arabella, wait outside,' Mr Jenkyns said firmly.

'What is this?' she asked, fearful that she might already know the answer. 'Why did you not come to supper?'

'Wait outside.'

Arabella nodded and pulled the door closed behind her. She could not bear to remain still. She paced the floor incessantly as she listened to the sound of murmured voices and at times her husband's angry shouting. She recoiled from the opening door and watched as the gentleman folded bank notes into his pocket as he walked out, guiding the young girl, who still clung to the tiny babe. She watched as they walked away and she remained rooted to the spot. Finally she walked to the study door and stood looking across at her husband.

'Tell me, I beg you, that I have misread this situation,' she said softly. Mr Jenkyns was sitting now, drinking whisky from a crystal glass. 'Tell me that child had no connection to you.'

'Of course it did not,' he said angrily. 'Leave me, Arabella. I need time to think.'

'Then why did you give them money?'

'What do you want me to tell you?' he shouted across at her.

'The truth,' she pleaded. 'That is your child, is it not?'

'Too fine to be a serving maid,' he spat angrily. 'Had I only known.'

'Known what?' Arabella whispered, unsure that she wished to hear the words that he was going to speak.

'Who her father was,' he said simply. 'That rogue! Did he not think that perhaps she was as willing as I? And yet I do not see him drawing out banknotes to protect my name.'

'But you are married. To me. Do you not remember?' Arabella felt tears come to her eyes but her sorrow turned to fear as he walked over to her and seized her wrist.

'And you are a perfect wife, are you not? Calling my son by your first husband's name. Spending my money on your society, for whom I care nothing.'

'I did not know,' she begged, cowering away from him and squeezing her hand free from his grasp. She did not remain in the room but ran to her own, bolting the door so that when Imogen tried to enter to console her, she could not.

Arabella did not rise in the morning to see Imogen, Josiah and Beatrice leave, but the evening of the same day she announced her plan to travel south to the capital once more under the protection of her father. Her husband did not refuse her request, indeed he seemed indifferent to his wife and did not even look at her during the meal that they shared. For his part, Mr Tenterchilt saw it all but spoke not a word, he was relieved only to be leaving this place and the haunting picture of his wife that watched down on him in solitude.

CHAPTER SIXTEEN
Thursday 22ⁿᵈ August 1811

As the months passed Arabella watched as London became elated in the late summer, basking in the sunshine and, when the sun was not forthcoming, basking in the heroic stories of campaigns won overseas. If there had been a time when Britain seemed set to lose its independence to the Emperor Napoleon, that now seemed to have passed. Respect for those who wore the military uniforms of the army or navy had replaced fear, and paths would clear before them as though before the king himself. Two of these men, both in officer's dress, walked purposefully through such a parted crowd until they came to the door of a tall, thin terraced building that, upon inspection, revealed itself as a lawyer's chambers.

They walked up the few steps and, without first knocking as the evening hour might suggest they should, they walked in. The moment they entered they were confronted by the owner of the establishment, Mr Dermot. He looked at the two of them for a moment, and this silent inspection was reciprocated.

'Colonel Shorefield,' Mr Dermot said at last. 'Major Keith. To what purpose do I owe such distinguished guests?'

'To the loss of a friend,' Shorefield replied, a peculiar accent holding onto his words as though his time in Portugal had only added to his bohemian mixture of dialects. 'Come, we have been friends long enough to dispense with such civil but meaningless words. We are seeking Captain Portland.'

Mr Dermot chewed his lip thoughtfully while Keith explained. 'He returned to England on a commission, but he never rejoined the company.'

'That was nigh on a year ago,' Mr Dermot replied.

'We only just returned to London not a week since. We have sought for any news of him but to no avail. Though Doctor Fotherby who, as you know, he was sent to meet, has not been seen since that time.'

'Miss Catherine Tenterchilt,' Keith said firmly, as Mr Dermot's face remained firm and emotionless. 'She was the reason for his departure.'

'Indeed, I know,' came the calm reply. 'Colonel Shorefield wrote to inform me. You must surely understand, Major, that there is nothing that happens to that family that I do not seek to know of.'

'Then you should perhaps widen your knowledge to include Captain Portland, sir, for I foresee a time when he shall become a part of that once respected family.'

'Indeed, Major Keith, I believe that you are right. Furthermore, it would be unfair of me not to inform you that I have already accommodated for such an eventuality. That is why I am obliged to tell you with anxiety that, since landing safely in Lagos, I have heard nothing more of him.'

'Perhaps if you should learn something of him, Dermot, you would seek us out and inform us.'

'Of course, James,' Mr Dermot replied, and the two officers turned to leave. 'Mrs Jenkyns is back in Town with her father,' he ventured. 'She and her husband are now together at the Chelsea house. She might be grateful of a visit.'

'Not from me, Dermot, I assure you. There is nothing I could say to her. Perhaps Major Keith might find some time to share with her.'

'Indeed, nothing would give me greater pleasure,' the major replied with a warm tone despite the military clip to his voice. 'Captain Pottinger deserves nothing less.'

'As well I know,' muttered Shorefield, thoughtful suddenly. 'What of Miss Catherine? It was Miss Tenterchilt's request that she be found, helped and brought safely home.'

'Once again, Colonel, I can offer you no intelligence beyond that which you already know. Doctor Fotherby embarked ten months ago and I have neither seen nor heard reports of either of them since.' Mr Dermot turned as he heard a door opening on creaking hinges further in the house and an anxious expression flashed across his face for a moment before composure returned and he said quickly and softly, 'You should both leave, quickly. All that we had hoped to come to fruition is so close to being sealed, but if Major Tenterchilt were to see you here I fear that he may not be so willing to help.'

Shorefield and Keith nodded as one and all three bowed before the two military gentlemen took their leave. The disgraced major entered from behind Mr Dermot and raised an eyebrow quizzically, demanding an answer without speaking any words.

'I have other business to attend to than simply ours,' Mr Dermot replied curtly. 'Those gentlemen were seeking news of a friend. In fact,' he continued, a calculating smile crossing his face, 'you may know them. The taller of the two was Major Keith and the other Colonel Sir James Shorefield.'

'Indeed, I have heard of them both. Why did they hurry off? It would have been an honour to have made their acquaintance, especially having heard so many great stories of the colonel.'

'Their business here was concluded and they had meetings elsewhere to attend to. They came in fact, for I am certain that they would not disapprove of you knowing this information, in the search of a captain; Portland, who I believe shares a reciprocated admiration with Miss Catherine.'

A dark cloud passed over Mr Tenterchilt's face at the name of his daughter. 'I do not even know what has become of my own daughter, how can I hope to understand what might have become of one who seeks her hand? Who is to say that they have not engaged in such riotous ill games as that Gordon, Lord Byron, so notoriously partakes in across the continent?'

'Sir,' Mr Dermot said firmly. 'You speak of honourable persons as though they are guilty of such abominable deeds. Hold your tongue, I beg you, for I shall hear no such slander against innocent souls.'

'Then you know where my daughter is?'

'No,' Mr Dermot replied truthfully, for he was unsure what had become of her. 'Only that she travelled for the best purpose and with the most honourable wish.'

There was a moment, then, when Mr Tenterchilt looked firmly at the lawyer. If Mr Dermot was lying to him or concealing any known truth it was impossible to tell, for years of experience had trained him well. Not a muscle of his thin face moved and, for his part, Mr Dermot returned the gaze, entirely unfazed by the gentleman before him.

At last Mr Tenterchilt excused himself from the office of the lawyer and vanished into the London evening. There was a brilliant glow from the setting sun that painted the streets in a rich gold. Mr Dermot took only a second to admire it before he walked through to another room and began writing a letter, glancing across repeatedly at a book whilst he did so.

The letter that he wrote took a week to reach its recipient, who was to be found in this early autumn sitting at a table in the orangery of Petrovia Lodge, assisting the young twins in their handwriting. Penny brought the letter through on a plate, a courtesy that had never dimmed in spite of the desperate times that the family had endured over the years. Imogen took it and looked at it for a moment before she prised it open and read on in interest.

'Miss Tenterchilt,' it began, in Mr Dermot's unmistakable hand. 'It is with disappointment and sadness that I am unable to give you the answers that you seek. Accept please that I would never lightly cause anguish to yourself and, were it not necessary for your father to remain in London a time longer, I should at once return him to you. He is safe and shall be whilst I have a breath left in my body. Do not be anxious, and continue in your endeavours, as your father shall his. Counsel like mine is as a brother's. I remain your faithful servant always, Mr Dermot.'

In a moment of anger, most uncharacteristic, Imogen gripped the letter tightly and felt it crumple in her hand before she remembered herself and at once turned to Josiah and Beatrice, who watched her in a confused manner. Imogen had taken on the role of educating her young charges and it would be a poor example of a lady if she showed such anger to them. She smiled down at them and sighed.

'Papa may be gone a while longer,' she said softly. 'It seems that London will keep him for a time.'

The day passed in glorious sunshine that seemed only to mock Imogen. She became weary of the sun and longed that the evening might arrive quicker, so she might be free. Josiah and Beatrice were in their beds, each with their own room now. Giving Arabella's room to Josiah had been difficult for Imogen, but it did not compare to the painful stab to her heart as Beatrice moved from the nursery to the room that had belonged to Catherine. As she closed the door on the room, she felt that she was turning her back on Catherine and tears pulled at her eyes as she wished desperately for her sister's safe return.

Disappointed by her own self-pity, Imogen returned to the orangery and looked up at the stars through the glass ceiling, trying to dispel such melancholy thoughts. The sky was as clear now as it had been during the day, with only thin clouds limiting the radiance. But she could not escape her bleak thoughts and imagined for a time that the five years of turmoil rolled back, that she was there once again with Hamish, that she had crept down to speak with him as she once did, anxious in case her father might find out. She began to believe in her imagination so much that at once Hamish was there, young, unaffected and indeed unaged by time.

She knew it was not possible, that she was only dreaming with her sleepy consciousness playing the most cruel of tricks upon her. But she could not remain silent before him and she looked across and asked softly,

'Do you not miss our conversations here, Mish?'

'I sought not my home, til the day's dying glory gave place to the rays of the bright polar star.'

Imogen heard the words, knew the words and accepted even that Hamish had spoken them. But they were not his words, nor his voice that spoke them. This riddle caused her to start and she awoke to find that she sat at the table in the orangery. Her head was resting upon the book that Colonel Sir James Shorefield had gifted to her, and it lay open upon that most enchanting of all the poems, Loch Na Garr. She shook her head as she read aloud the line that Hamish had spoken in her dream.

It was a peculiar feeling, that she knew these words so well, that someone with an overwhelming yearning had spoken Byron's words to her in that voice she could not place. The desperation of the homesickness to its tone haunted her as much as the pleading words that the poet had so skillfully penned. She walked out of the door and looked to the mountains of the north. Somewhere there sat Loch Na Garr, but she did not know which one it was or even if it was visible from the lodge. Despite the heartbreaking past this place held for her, she felt the curious pull and majesty that Hamish had taught her.

She pulled her shawl tightly about her, feeling for the first time the chill that was in the air. A slight breeze whipped through the strath and she recalled those haunting words of Byron's verse. She rushed back to the orangery, afraid to hear the voices of the dead, and bolted the door before snatching the book and rushing up the stairs. She had never forgotten the path that could take her noiselessly to her room. She still used it although, as mistress of the house, she had no need now to worry about being caught. She sat upon her bed in the dark with her hand resting upon the open book and became lost in her thoughts until, at last, sleep claimed her.

CHAPTER SEVENTEEN
Friday 13th September 1811

September overcame August in a quiet fashion in Petrovia Lodge, but how different was the change in London. Society turned to the gentlemen who returned from their estates across the countryside of England, preferring to winter in the city. There had been an increased rainfall in the West Country and this had driven them prematurely east to the capital. Arabella stood at the window of her Chelsea house and looked out onto the street as the gentlemen walked, some discussing engaging topics with men of similar status, whilst others walked out with ladies on their arms. Arabella was racked with envy at these ladies, and she sighed despondently as she saw each one of them.

Mr Jenkyns never escorted her out of the house anymore and, in the absence of her husband or any friends, she was confined to the indoors to gaze out over those more fortunate in affairs of the heart than she would ever be. The fear of loneliness and the desperate anguish at spending an impoverished life alone had driven her to marry her cousin, to be blind to such faults that she wished he did not have. She was trapped in a prison laid down by social allowances and emotional uncertainty.

She had tears in her eyes before she had given thought to stop them and she choked them back, determined not to show them to the world beyond her window. How long she stood like that she did not know until, at last, amongst the passers-by she saw a face that she knew. A man of a military stance was walking purposefully down the street, his sword tapping his leg as he paced forward. She almost knocked upon the glass to gain his attention but she recalled herself in time and only watched silently as he walked past. She tried to tell herself that she had done the right thing and that a lady should not seek the attention of a gentleman in such a vulgar way. She knew that he belonged to a part of her past that bore no relevance to her current position, but she felt downcast and sorrowful that she had allowed the opportunity to pass her by.

She turned as there was a knock upon the door and she looked across with wide eyes as a servant walked in and bowed.

'Major Keith, madam,' he announced formally and stepped back to allow entrance to the man Arabella had watched walking down the street only moments before. She stepped forward to him and stood before him, feeling that she wanted more than anything to embrace him, but maintaining her decorum long enough to greet him formally.

'Major Keith, it is such a pleasure to see you,' she said, with perhaps more open honesty than was proper. Her recipient seemed to think nothing of it but became seated on the chair that she guided him to. 'You must tell me, how do the affairs on the continent go? I hear we are quite safe now from the emperor.'

'That is true, Mrs Jenkyns,' he replied.

'And once more your friend, the colonel, has distinguished himself,' she stated and the major nodded in return.

'It is true. There is not a man in the British army that more troops wish to fight beside. Even Lord Wellington.' Major Keith smiled across at her for a moment before he continued. 'I hear you have a son now, Mrs Jenkyns.'

'Yes,' Arabella replied with a slight smile. 'At times I forget myself.'

The shadow that seemed to pass before Arabella's face caused the major to start before he quickly changed the subject. 'You must excuse my neglect. I found out that you were in Town almost four weeks ago, and can only apologise for the delay in presenting myself.'

'I am simply pleased that you have paid me a visit at all, Major. I confess, I have been distracted by loneliness and, at times, have been quite beside myself. I rather fear I have had too much time to think. Mr Jenkyns is so often occupied with business that takes him from my side.'

'It is a man's curse to be bound by work,' Keith replied gently.

'I fear it is rather more than that which drags Mr Jenkyns away. Forgive me,' she said at once, and raised her hand to her mouth, knowing that she had said too much.

'There is nothing to forgive, Mrs Jenkyns. I came unannounced, I should be asking forgiveness from you.'

'No, sir, you have come as a champion to me. Might we not take a turn for a time? Around a park, perhaps. I am anxious for fresh air.'

'Of course,' the major replied, berating himself for failing to offer this.

'Then come along, Major.' Arabella smiled across with such infectious relief that the tension that had clung to the two of them dissolved and, after snatching a shawl from its place on the back of a chair, she walked out of the house for the first time in many days. They continued in silence for a time, Arabella simply happy to be free of the oppressive house, and Keith content to serve the widow of his late friend and leader.

'How did you become a major?' Arabella asked at length.

'Battlefield commissions are plentiful in Portugal, and Colonel Shorefield is eager that his men should take those that are offered.'

'And what of the brave colonel?' Arabella laughed, something she had long forgotten how to do. 'I am amazed that he is not a general by now. All the reports seem more than favourable.'

'I do not believe he wishes to raise himself further in the army, but rather seeks a way out. He is anxious at this time, as I am, to find our friend, Captain Portland.'

'Portland?' Arabella whispered, turning ashen suddenly.

'Indeed,' Keith said with interest as he regarded the change in her countenance at the sound of his name. 'Do you have news of him, Mrs Jenkyns? For we have neither seen nor had word from him for a year.'

'No,' she whispered. 'Poor Cat.'

'Miss Catherine?' Keith asked.

'She had quite set her heart on him,' Arabella replied. 'Should she return to England I feel most certain that it would be to find him.'

'In return for your openness, Mrs Jenkyns, I can tell you that I know her feelings to be requited.'

Arabella stopped outside the high iron gates of a town house and a curious expression crossed her face. She moved from Major Keith and rested her hand on the black leaded iron and smiled slightly.

'Are you well, Mrs Jenkyns?'

'Well?' she asked, almost surprised that she was not alone with the house before her. 'Yes. This was our house. This was our home before Petrovia. It is so sad to find it now unlived in. And yet it seems fitting somehow.'

The house was indeed unoccupied. Many of the windows had their shutters closed and, through those that did not, there was no sign of light. Arabella became overcome by the sight of it, for she had actively sought against visiting it in all her years in London. Major Keith seemed to notice, and he took her hand gently.

'Mrs Jenkyns, I had no wish to hurt you by walking here. I did not know this was your property. Though,' he paused and a flash of recognition passed his features. 'Come, be comforted that when its lineage is known it shall be returned to its glory.'

These words that were aimed solely to comfort Arabella seemed to pacify her sorrow, and they began walking towards Mr Jenkyns' house. When they reached the steps, Arabella took the major's hand and smiled across at him.

'Will you come and meet Roger?'

'Roger?' Keith asked, and immediately Arabella's eyes widened with fear. 'You named your son after Roger?'

'No,' she whispered quickly. 'He is called Timothy.'

'Yes, of course,' he replied gently and silently followed her into the house.

'Where have you been?' demanded a voice as they entered, although the tone of Mr Jenkyns altered as he looked across at the major. 'Major Keith, is it not?' He bowed formally while Keith did the same, though perhaps not as deeply.

'I am sorry,' Arabella whispered. 'I did not know the time. We only walked a short way.' Her eyes became dark and subdued and she stood submissively before him. 'I wanted to introduce the major to our son. That is all.'

Mr Jenkyns lifted his hand to his mouth thoughtfully and Arabella recoiled from the movement in such a panicked state that Keith's eyes narrowed.

'Then I shall have him brought downstairs at once,' Mr Jenkyns replied, before asking one of the attending servants to have his son brought to him. 'Come and sit in the drawing room.'

The three of them walked through. Mr Jenkyns had taken his wife's arm and together they led Major Keith through to the panelled room that was filled with comfortable seating and the host at once walked to a small circular table and poured his guest a drink.

'They say that our army has distinguished itself,' the MP began.

'That is true, sir, and we proudly serve for the king and our country.'

'And what makes you a soldier, Major Keith?' he said jovially, while Arabella turned wide eyes to the major.

'I fight for my king, my country and my officer.'

'That is loyalty to Wellington indeed, that you should name him in the same breath as King George and England.'

'Britain, sir. I am certain my name and accent must have revealed to you that I am not an Englishman.'

'Well spoken,' Mr Jenkyns said, laughing slightly. 'My sister, Imogen, lives there still.'

'Indeed. I have the pleasure to know of Miss Tenterchilt. Though I must further inform you that the gentleman to whom I paid such honour was not Wellington, but Colonel Sir James Shorefield.'

'Indeed,' Mr Jenkyns replied, 'I have heard much of him.'

They turned, all three, as there was a knock upon the door and a nursery maid entered, carrying a young boy. Arabella smiled then, the first genuine smile she had given since returning home, and her husband flashed a proud smile as she rose to take the young boy from the maid's arms.

'This is Timothy,' Arabella beamed as she held her son close to her.

'Timothy, this is Major Keith, a dear, loyal friend to your mother.'

The child did not understand. At a year in age there are few things that any child can comprehend, but the major felt privileged to carry the burden that such words invoked. Arabella seemed to notice this and now a sad smile came to her face. This silent exchange was lost upon Mr Jenkyns, who was a man incapable of listening beyond the sounds he could hear.

Their conversation continued for a short time before Major Keith rose to take his leave from the small family. Mr Jenkyns bowed whilst Arabella said quickly, 'Allow me to show you out, Major Keith.'

They walked from the room together under the stern eye of Mr Jenkyns, but neither spoke until the major stood outside the door and placed his hat upon his auburn hair.

'You are blessed to have your son, Mrs Jenkyns.'

'I know,' she replied, tears forming in her eyes. 'And yet I wish it had been different, that he had a different father.'

'Do not torture yourself by accepting blame for what happened to Captain Pottinger. He died an honourable death, protecting the one thing he loved beyond all others. That was you.'

Arabella clutched Timothy to her with her left hand and raised her right to her face as she lowered her head so she might not be seen with tears in her eyes. Major Keith looked uncomfortable for a moment before he bowed his head and turned from her. He descended the steps so quickly that he was already at the bottom as she called out to him.

'Please, come and visit me again. I had forgotten what it was to hold such conversations and to recall memories with fondness instead of sorrow.'

Major Keith nodded and bowed before he turned and walked through the streets towards his lodgings. He was true to his word and visited Arabella every day that his duties permitted. Upon being asked about his work and what curious events might have caused any absence, he would answer her by saying that 'the army has few rules that would be understood by a woman and there are but fewer women who could understand those rules.' Arabella loved to talk with him of such nonsense and in a manner so carefree that she once more began to find her smile and even, on one occasion, returned to her love of music and sat down upon the seat at the piano and entertained herself.

It was on this day that Major Keith, having missed two days of visiting through the mysterious business that he would never speak of, arrived at the house. He was shown in by a servant who guided him to the room that

Arabella occupied. The servant was about to announce the guest, but Major Keith raised his hand and shook his head. He silently opened the door and stepped, unnoticed, into the room. Arabella, despite years of silence, had not lost her beautiful voice and the major stood, spellbound, until she finished her melancholy song and slouched forward upon her stool. Her shoulders trembled and he realised that she was weeping, believing herself to be alone in the room. Awkwardness overcame him and, without considering his next move, he coughed slightly to let her know that he was there. At once Arabella spun round and jumped up so that she collided with the pianoforte, fear evident in her wide eyes. He frowned slightly as she gave a relieved sigh.

'You must excuse me, Major. I did not hear you come in.'

'Nor did I wish you to, but it was a selfish gesture for I wished to hear you continue singing.' He lowered his head. 'I did not wish to alarm you.'

'I lost track of time, sir,' she said, and now there was no sign of tears in her eyes, only where they had streaked her pale face. 'I thought you were my husband returning.'

'Does he not enjoy listening to you sing?'

'No, indeed,' she said with a smile. 'He tells me I have the finest voice in the land. But he should not find me crying.'

'I do not believe I know the song that you sang,' Major Keith said softly. 'What piece is it?'

'A song of homesickness. A folksong, can you believe?' She laughed slightly. 'Far from fitting for a parliamentarian's wife.'

'I am certain it would enchant any mind, Mrs Jenkyns.'

'Roger used to like it,' she said with a slight smile. 'Though we had no pianoforte for accompaniment.'

'Indeed, Mrs Jenkyns. You could have sung on any topic and Captain Pottinger would have been enticed.'

'Did Hamish truly kill him, Major?' she asked quickly. 'With each day that passes and with each time I wish that life could have been different, I find it harder and harder to bear.'

'You should not ask me such things, Mrs Jenkyns. I was there, and that is what I saw.'

'Through all my hardships I cling to the hope that he may return. I cannot ever be convinced by the truth that they have told me.' Major Keith watched as she rushed over to him and took his hand in her own. 'I wonder always how he would have treated us, my son and myself. How different it would be to what we endure now.'

'I cannot give you any answer, Mrs Jenkyns. It is not right that I should do so.'

Arabella seemed to realise what she had done, how she had so grossly revealed her thoughts, and she stepped quickly away from him, her eyes welling with fear as she muttered repeatedly, 'you must not tell him. Please do not tell him.'

'What is it that I should not tell?'

'That I live in hopeful fear that Roger might come back, that he might protect me.'

Whatever conversation Major Keith might have hoped for, whatever enchantment had lured him, unannounced, into the room, he was ill prepared for the words that Arabella spoke and the panicked tone with which she referred to her husband. The woman before him continued to pale until, at last, she sat down upon the stool at the piano and swayed as though she might faint. Major Keith recalled himself to his senses and stepped over, kneeling down before her and holding her arms.

'Arabella,' he said firmly and she started, as though she was just awakening.

'You say my name just as Mish did,' she whispered.

'Come, Mrs Jenkyns,' he replied. 'I shall take my leave, and you should take some rest.'

She nodded quickly. 'I am so sorry to burden you, Major. Please excuse these words I have spoken, for you found me flustered and confused.'

'I am the one who should seek forgiveness, for it was I who intruded upon your thoughts.'

When he was satisfied that Arabella was well enough to support herself, he took leave of her and, though they continued to see one another as often as time would permit, neither of them spoke of that singular conversation. It was on one day, barely a week since that peculiar change of words that Major Keith confided his deep concerns to his friend, Shorefield, uncertain where else he might take his thoughts. The two gentlemen were sitting across a small table from one another in the officers' lounge when Keith gave a heavy sigh and set down the crystal glass from which he was drinking.

'I am concerned for Mrs Jenkyns,' he said simply. 'She is not happy.'

'Major Keith,' came the bemused reply, 'we are officers in His Majesty's army. We are not in the business of handing on tales of gossip.'

'We all made a promise to Captain Pottinger on the event of his marriage that we should protect his wife. Now she is in need of that protection.'

'Mrs Jenkyns needs protection?' Shorefield mused, anger in his eyes.

'Did I not just say so?' Keith replied.

'That is quite a different matter to her being unhappy. From whom does she seek protection?'

Major Keith paused before he answered. He was uncertain that he had correctly understood that confused conversation of a week ago. His words might slander an innocent man, might disrupt a family's happiness, for he knew well the hold that the Tenterchilt ladies had upon Shorefield.

'I hardly dare say, sir,' he responded, chewing his lip thoughtfully. Shorefield's eyes seemed to burn into his skull before at last Keith whispered, 'but I think it is her husband.'

Shorefield laughed harshly. 'You torment me, sir. You know that Mrs Jenkyns holds me under an enchantment and you seek to tease me. Never has a match been more acceptable than that of the two cousins. They have known each other from birth. Shame on you, Major Keith. You seek to tease me.'

'No one wishes so more than I,' the major responded. 'She wept before me, pleading that I should not tell him that she yearned to be protected from him.'

'My God,' Shorefield hissed, shaking his head as he looked across at Keith. 'You speak the truth.'

'Indeed. She was left in such a panicked state that only when I addressed her with her baptismal name did I awake any sense in her. And then she spoke of a man named Mish.'

'Truly?' Shorefield whispered. 'And who should this man be?'

'I do not know,' Major Keith answered truthfully. 'What is to be done?'

'I feel it is time that we once more seek advice from her lawyer. He is a good man and sees to it that all of the Tenterchilt daughters are protected.'

Colonel Sir James Shorefield had barely spoken these words than a young boy rushed up to the doorway of the mess lounge, shouting the colonel's name frantically. He was being removed by some of the soldiers but kept calling out Shorefield's name repeatedly. The colonel stepped forward and looked severely down at the boy.

'What is it?'

'Colonel Sir James Shorefield?' the young boy asked and snatched the cap from his head respectfully. 'I was sent to tell you that Mr Dermot, a lawyer, sir, has a message for you.'

'Then why did he not send this message through you, boy?'

'He told me that you might ask that. He said that it was not a conversation for an officers' hall, but of a delicate nature.'

'And do you know what this message is?'

'No, sir, he did not entrust it to me. But pardon, sir, I ran all the way here.'

'Then here is a penny for your pains.' Shorefield handed a coin to the runner and at once he and Major Keith walked from the hall and made their way as quickly as possible to Mr Dermot's chambers.

The weather was changing now, and a misty rain heralded the greyest of autumns for the city. Neither one of them spoke, each concerned with what the lawyer might say and their own ill news they wished to impart. They cared little for the puddles that splashed and stained their fine clothes but persevered on until they reached the steps that rose up to the lawyer's office. Neither knocked but they walked in and at once stepped through the rooms until they found the lawyer.

Mr Dermot's face did not betray a word of the message he wished to relate to them. Instead he simply watched them enter and then said softly. 'There is something you want to tell me.'

'Yes,' Shorefield began. 'Though we are here primarily on the instruction of yourself. A matter of great pressing urgency, we were led to understand.'

'Yes,' Mr Dermot replied briefly. 'Upon your request for news on Captain Portland I sent out letters and messengers to seek word of the gentleman. Today I heard back from one of them. I am certain that you are both aware of the town in Spain called Badajoz. On its outskirts, beyond the city walls and across the river, lies an area called Gebora.'

'I know it,' Shorefield replied. 'The remnants of the Spanish army from that battle were forced back towards where we were camped in Portugal.'

'Indeed,' Mr Dermot replied. 'It was with that Spanish company that Captain Portland sought his return to the 5th Infantry.'

'Wait,' Shorefield said quickly whilst Keith, seeing what the lawyer was implying, lifted his chin a little in a determined manner. 'Why did he not land at Oporto or Lisbon?'

'I believe events at Cadiz required a detour,' Mr Dermot responded. 'I am sorry to bear the news that I know you do not wish to hear, but Captain David Portland died at Gebora at the hands of the French cavalry.'

'They were not even his men,' muttered Shorefield, whilst Keith stood firm and watched silently. 'How vain was his trip and how foolish was I to commission it.'

'He was a soldier, sir,' Keith replied in a firm tone, though it was clear that this news had unsettled him. 'He died as a soldier.'

'I should have protected him,' Shorefield sighed. 'I owed it to him.'

Mr Dermot stood silent at the opposite side of the desk and watched the two officers with a thoughtful expression, whilst Major Keith remained staring ahead of him as though he was on patrol. The room fell silent for a time before, at length, Mr Dermot said softly,

'James? Would you care for a drink?'

'Thank you,' Shorefield replied, taking the glass from the lawyer's outstretched hand. 'Major Keith and I have business to discuss with you that seemed imperative.'

'Sir, it is still of great importance for, despite the sorrow of the news that Mr Dermot has given us, Captain Portland is at rest while Mrs Jenkyns is still in danger.'

'In danger?' Mr Dermot hissed. 'How so?'

Shorefield, who was overcome by grief at the loss of a friend who he felt he had sent to his death, gestured to Major Keith to take up the telling of the story. Mr Dermot's eyes narrowed as the major began his tale and he remained silent, taking in all of his words. Keith omitted nothing and, when at last he had finished telling it, it was Shorefield who spoke.

'Is there anything we can do to protect her, Mr Dermot? Is there no law that can shield her from this man?'

'I rather fear that, unless she admits this offence, she can do nothing and we certainly cannot.'

'She is afraid for her son,' Major Keith interjected. 'If she knew that he would be safe I am certain that she would comply.'

'Mr Dermot,' Shorefield began, leaning forward in his chair. 'I have sought at every turn to help these sisters. At every stage I have felt overcome and enchanted by them and, at every step, I repeatedly seem to fail. Help me to succeed in protecting Mrs Jenkyns, please. I know of the diligent loyalty you showed to their mother. I know of the continued work you do for their father. Allow me to help support Arabella.'

'Where would she go?' Mr Dermot asked thoughtfully. 'You are a man well known around the city and some of the country also, you cannot protect her.'

'I still own that house where she began her married life. Let her go there.'

'Are you certain that she will be safe?' Mr Dermot asked. 'Moving her from him will only protect her as long as she remains hidden. If she does not it may only serve to put her in more danger.'

'She will be safe,' Shorefield whispered. 'I shall oversee it.'

'Then you must talk with her,' Mr Dermot replied. 'You must tell her this news.'

'No,' Shorefield said firmly, shaking his head. 'Major Keith shall go. It is not important that she knows whose house she has, but that her friends care for her still.'

'There is one further matter,' Mr Dermot said, turning to look out of the window at the London sky. 'Captain Portland left a will, and you are both named in it. It would seem that a cycle is about to turn and inevitably a new beginning will rise from the ashes.'

'You speak riddles, man,' Keith said firmly. 'Talk like the Scot you are that we might all understand one another.'

Mr Dermot turned back to them. 'It would appear that Chanter's House is to be left to you, James. An inherited property of Captain Portland's. You shall come to understand its significance. Major Keith, I believe you are left the late captain's Cornwall estate.'

'Chanter's House?' Keith muttered in surprise. 'James, he is right.'

Shorefield looked one to the other as though he thought that they were both mad before he shook his head. 'Does he name anyone else?'

'It is well that you never entered law, James,' Mr Dermot laughed slightly. 'You ask of Miss Catherine, surely, for your face betrays it from you. No, she is not mentioned, and it would be unfitting that she should be. A lady of standing cannot be implicated in this way, but I am certain that he would wish her to be provided for from what he leaves behind.' Mr Dermot shook his head before he said softly, 'they seem ill fated, the Tenterchilt daughters, though no family could deserve it less. There shall be a reading of the will, of course, but I shall need to find everyone named in it first.'

'And how goes our other affair?' Shorefield asked.

'Well. Although, as you must surely know, the army does not take kindly to being made to abide by the laws of we mere civilians.'

'None more than the colonel,' muttered Shorefield. 'And what of Major Tenterchilt?'

'He fares well, also. Though he pines each day for the company of his late wife and his children. Miss Imogen remains alone in Petrovia Lodge, Miss Catherine is lost to the orient, and he is unable to visit Mrs Jenkyns for there is a mutual loathing between him and Mr Jenkyns that is only set aside at certain events. But he is pleased to have a role in such a case as ours.'

CHAPTER EIGHTEEN
Sunday 29ᵗʰ September 1811

The dark events that Mr Dermot had described at Gebora were to haunt Shorefield. He lay awake that night, and indeed for several nights afterwards, questioning whether he had done the right thing to send Captain Portland away at the arrival of Miss Tenterchilt's letter. He might have managed to protect him, to shield him and keep him for Miss Catherine, that they might have had a life before them. When at last he would succumb to sleep, he was plagued by the most fearful dreams that combined reality with fiction and, on many nights, he awoke himself calling out in fear and sorrow. He could not escape from his thoughts in waking or sleeping. He shed tears in the solace of his own room and company, but remained a strong figurehead to the men who, upon hearing of their captain's death, observed a respectful silence. Being a Scotsman, Major Keith bore his own sadness at the death but occupied himself in visiting Mrs Jenkyns until, as September came to a close, he finally dared to mention the subject that the two officers had discussed with the lawyer.

'What audacity!' Arabella exclaimed, stepping away from the major. 'You make plans based on assumptions.'

'You are not as alone as you feel, Mrs Jenkyns. You have friends and there are a host of men who would risk everything for you, for they loved your late husband, and each officer of that company vowed to Captain Pottinger that we should protect you.'

'Assume, then,' she muttered, feeling the weight of his words pour down upon her. 'Assume that the words you speak are accurate, that I do indeed suffer at the hands of my husband. How can you protect me?'

'Colonel Sir James Shorefield has your best interests at heart and he will protect your location. Indeed, he now owns that house which was once your home with Captain Pottinger and he wishes to give it to you. Mr Jenkyns shall not search for you there.'

'But he may not grant me a divorce and I shall be quite ruined, and little Roger, too.'

Major Keith had become accustomed to the confusion of the young boy's name and no longer wondered at it. 'You shall never be destitute, Mrs Jenkyns. You have people who care for you. Far more than you can imagine.'

'And you will protect my son?'

'With my life, Mrs Jenkyns.'

'God help me, Major Keith, for I believe I am beginning to trust you. Please do not fail me.'

'My dear Mrs Jenkyns, I shall not live or die without your permission.'

Arabella nodded sadly. 'Roger truly valued your support. He said you taught him what loyalty was, far more than his father ever could.'

'Colonel Pottinger shall know nothing of this, Mrs Jenkyns, I give you my word. You shall see only those you wish to, and go only to the places you wish to visit.'

Arabella's heart began to believe once more in that freedom she had not felt for more than two years and, as the sun rose the next day, she was greeted by a carriage that was standing by the door to the house. From it stepped Mr Dermot, the family lawyer, who she had not spoken with since he had saved Imogen from the river. He bowed respectfully and helped her into the carriage before handing Timothy back to her, and she clung tightly to the child. Finally he climbed into the carriage and closed the door. They travelled in silence before at last Arabella spoke.

'Thank you, Mr Dermot.'

He only smiled across at her.

'Do you hear still from Imogen?'

'Indeed,' Mr Dermot said softly. 'Miss Tenterchilt does me the honour of maintaining a correspondence.'

'She is so very far away from us all, now.'

'My dear Mrs Jenkyns, you are all so very far from one another.'

'Yes,' Arabella responded. 'But Catherine has hopes to marry on her return, and I have a close friendship in my late husband's friends. I fear Imogen is quite alone.'

Mr Dermot opened his mouth to speak before he realised that Arabella surely did not know of Captain Portland's death, and indeed there was a chance that she did not know of Miss Catherine's situation. Arabella did not notice this hesitation but took his silence to assume that Mr Dermot was considering Imogen through her words. She smiled slightly as she looked down at Timothy.

'I cannot simply vanish, Mr Dermot.'

'Nor shall you.' He was grateful of the change of topic and continued to explain his plan. 'I shall draw up a letter, which you shall countersign, stating that I shall represent you in all negotiations. Are you willing to sign such a document?'

'Mr Dermot,' she replied with a wondering expression. 'Your tireless work for my family is overwhelming. I would trust you with all my heart, for you ask nothing in return.'

Mr Dermot forced himself to smile for he felt unable to openly contradict the woman before him. In truth he did seek remuneration for the obsessive nature with which he handled the Tenterchilt affairs, but Shorefield tirelessly paid him every farthing he needed, having also fallen under the spell of these most enchanting sisters.

The carriage continued on until they arrived at the house Arabella had sought so hard to forget but that still claimed her most sacred of memories. Tears fell from her eyes as Chloe opened the door and curtseyed to her mistress as though not a day had passed since she left. There was no sign that the house had ever been empty. It smelt fresh and clean as always, the polished wood shone and already the table was set as she walked through to the dining room. The drawing room remained as it always had save that four new leather chairs had been brought in. But Captain Pottinger's worn chair remained before the fireplace, where a healthy fire was already burning.

Arabella was overcome with it all and she clutched Chloe in an embrace, sobbing onto her shoulder. Chloe, a true servant, waited until Arabella was calm before she began settling her and her son into the home that Arabella wished she had never left. Mr Dermot, who during this display of such heartrending emotion had remained motionless at the door, now turned to leave, content that things were as they should be. He stopped however as Arabella spoke.

'This house belongs to Colonel Sir James Shorefield, does it not?'

'Indeed, Mrs Jenkyns, it does.'

'Did he own it when Cat and I lived here?'

'Yes, he has owned it almost since your husband's death.'

'That is why the rent became easier. Cat could never explain it. Why has he done this for me?'

Mr Dermot took a deep breath to steady his thoughts before he walked into the room and was about to take the seat opposite Arabella before he recalled with how much tenderness she had viewed it and, realising it had been her husband's chair, he instead remained standing.

'He heard of your circumstances. He was greatly moved by the devotion that your husband received from all his men, and he saw in you all the reasons that both the captain and his men so cared for you. He could not let an officer's widow fall into ruin for loving a soldier.'

'When can I thank him?'

'He will meet you when he is ready. I believe he carries a heavy heart at this time.'

'Thank you, Mr Dermot.'

'I do only what your friends have asked me. Should I tell your father that you are here?'

'Oh, Papa,' Arabella sobbed. 'Yes, I do so want to see him.'

'I shall tell him, then.' Mr Dermot bowed formally as Chloe returned and he took his leave from the house.

Arabella's days might have passed by pensively, had it not been for the frequent visits of Major Keith and her own dear father. On these occasions Arabella and Mr Tenterchilt would laugh, reminisce and weep. She had arranged the room so that Captain Pottinger's chair would remain beside the hearth, untouched but greatly loved and cherished. Mr Dermot was true to his word and maintained the strictest confidence regarding Arabella's location and continued to handle her affairs with her estranged husband.

Initially, Mr Jenkyns had denied any hope of accepting the terms of a divorce but, as Mr Dermot continued to delve further into the MP's affairs, it began to become clear that he should be ruined if he refused. By the end of October, Mr Jenkyns had chosen to protect himself by remaining hidden from the lawyer and refusing to correspond with him. For a time, this suited Arabella well but, as the hours of sunlight dwindled, she longed to be outdoors so that she might fully appreciate them.

CHAPTER NINETEEN
Thursday 31ˢᵗ October 1811

If it was a change to her in the confines of her house, how much more so was it to her younger sister, Miss Catherine Tenterchilt, as she beheld the white cliffs that supported the town of Dover. After four months of travel, she was weary for home. She gazed out across the channel to the war stricken continent and felt relieved to be leaving it behind. Her companion, Doctor Fotherby, looked at England with very different eyes. He was not returning home but to a land of hateful memories, and it was with a heavy heart that he watched on silently. But Catherine was beside herself and, as the ship continued up the Thames until London came into sight, she talked incessantly to the man beside her. He responded patiently but could not share her enthusiasm. As the anchor was lowered, a small river boat appeared to take them to the shore. Doctor Fotherby carried down the small collection that was their luggage whilst Catherine, without sparing a thought for how a lady should behave, rushed down the lowered ladder.

There was a light in her eye that could not be extinguished and, as the sun began to fall from its low height in the sky, and she set foot once more upon British soil, she felt a broad smile cross her lips, reaching her eyes.

'Where shall we go?' Catherine asked the doctor.

'There is a house which is under the ownership of Captain Portland's friend. You will be safe there, Miss Catherine. I shall escort you.'

'Miss Catherine?' she replied playfully, as though nothing could dampen her spirits, even the heavy clouds that were drifting down from the north. 'I thought I was Sleeping Tiger?'

'To me you always shall be, but to Britain you are Miss Catherine Tenterchilt. You have a duty to a noble family to be that person.'

Catherine looked puzzled, but the smile never faded. Instead they walked together, on through the streets that had scarcely changed in their absence. There were more men in military uniform than she had remembered, but Doctor Fotherby did not seem to even notice them. He led the way, and Catherine allowed him to guide her, leaning proudly on the arm of her dear friend. She felt, at last, that she had righted the wrong her cruel words had caused him, and she knew even Imogen would be proud of her. At last they stopped outside the house that she had occupied with Arabella after her husband's death. She frowned for a moment.

'This was Arabella's house, but I do not think she lives here any longer.'

'No. It is Colonel Shorefield's property. And look,' he continued, 'there are lights burning within. I will take you to the door but once I know you will be safe, I must leave you.'

They both ascended the steps and Catherine beat three times upon the door and waited.

'Chloe?' Surprise was clear in Catherine's voice as the maid opened the door. She kissed the maid upon the cheek in a manner that alarmed both Chloe and the doctor.

'Miss Catherine, we all feared you dead.'

'And so I would be, had it not been for my good friend, Doctor Fotherby.' She now turned to the doctor and smiled. 'Now you know I am safe, you may go as you wish. But, Doctor,' she called as Fotherby handed her the luggage that was hers and began to descend the steps once more. He turned back as she addressed him. 'I shall not forget all you have done for me. Shall you come and visit me?'

'Without fail,' he promised, before he walked away and vanished into the labyrinth of the city streets. Catherine watched him go with a proud smile before she turned and entered the house.

Without waiting to be announced she rushed into the drawing room and a smile lit her face as she saw her sister, but it could not compare to the loving recognition that passed over Arabella's features as she threw herself upon Catherine in an embrace so strong that Catherine could barely breathe.

'I thought you were dead,' Arabella sobbed. 'Oh Cat, I thought you were dead.'

'It shall take more than my foolishness to kill me, I fear, for I have the most loving friends to protect me even in the furthest reaches of the world.'

Arabella released her sister and asked quickly, 'Where have you been?'

'Did you not know?' Catherine whispered, confused, before she recalled that she had asked Imogen for her silence concerning the exact details of her disappearance. 'I was in Calcutta, in India. That is why I am no longer the pale girl I was. The sun is almost unbearable there.'

'But surely you did not travel alone?'

'No, I was escorted back by Doctor Fotherby.' Catherine stopped as she realised for the first time that they were not alone in the room. Major Keith stood watching the two sisters with a curious expression upon his face. It seemed to her that he was unbearably sorrowful despite his happiness at seeing such a reunion. Arabella followed her sister's gaze and said quickly,

'You remember Major Keith, Cat.'

'Yes. Though not as a major. Congratulations, sir.' She bowed her head and noticed the child that sat by his feet and she looked quickly back at

Arabella. 'Are you Mrs Keith?'

Arabella laughed nervously whilst the major blushed, uncertain how to deal with such a mistake.

'No, sister, I am Mrs Jenkyns.'

'Then why are you still living here? You should be in Chelsea.'

'And so I was,' Arabella said softly. 'But it did not agree with me.'

'Then this is your son?'

'Yes. I call him Roger.'

Catherine wanted to ask so many questions but there was an expression upon her sister's face that made her hold her tongue. Instead she simply stated, 'I have so much to find out, I see that now. Where is Imogen?'

'She is in Petrovia, still.'

'With Papa and that awful woman?'

'No, Papa is in Town, and Alice was convicted of treason and spying. I do not know what became of her, but Papa was left quite ruined.'

'May I see him?' Catherine asked numbly.

'Indeed. Though it would be best that you did not mention Alice's name. It grieves him still that she betrayed him.'

'And there is someone else that I must ask after, though I hardly dare to for fear that in years of absence my memory was not enough.' Catherine turned a pleading eye to Major Keith who inhaled sharply and at once his face became firm and set. 'You do not need to explain to me, Major, I fear your expression already has.' She felt tears stab her eyes.

'Miss Catherine,' he began, stepping forward to her and taking her hands in his own. Arabella stood back and clutched her hand to her face, not wishing to see the exchange that was about to happen. 'Come and sit,' the major said, guiding her to a chair and kneeling down before her, never releasing her hands.

'Speak, Major, that I might know the truth I believe I have identified.'

'Miss Catherine, I wish it were not this news that I carried, or that some other unfortunate soul might have borne it to you. Captain David Portland died in Spain, in February last. Though I have to tell you, that he did so believing in your safe return.'

'He is dead?' she spluttered. 'Why could he not have loved another? I would have had time then. How did he die?'

'On his return to the peninsula he became involved in a battle at Gebora.'

'Were you there?' Catherine asked feeling a desperate, sorrowful anger seize her.

'No, I was fighting in Portugal. He was forced to detour as a result of the events of war, and could not return to the 5th Infantry directly.'

'I came home for him,' she whispered. Major Keith lowered his head and Arabella stepped over to her sister who, only moments earlier, had been elated by her return and the promise of what it carried. But Catherine did not wish to be comforted. She rose from her seat and walked from the room. She would have walked from the house, but she had nowhere to go. She felt frighteningly alone, as if with Captain Portland's death she had not a friend left in the world. Instead she simply rushed up the stairs, where she sat on the floor outside the room that, in better days, she had occupied.

And then she wept, desperate and violent tears. How long she sat there she did not know. There were voices and movements to be heard from downstairs but she ignored them all. All she could think of was the captain whom she had loved, though the world had stood between them, and whom she had lost. It was certainly her fault, she could not understand why, but she felt that it was.

She was surprised to find that the next face she saw was her father's. He awkwardly knelt down beside her, struggling with his wounded leg, and took her hand before he pulled her to him and held her as close as Arabella had done. This display of such emotion, from a man who never exhibited it, startled her, and she gripped him to her just as tightly.

'Oh, Papa,' she sobbed. 'I came back.'

'And I thank God for it, Cat. My dear, dear daughter. I am just sorry that it could not be to the welcome you deserved.'

'That is not so, Papa, for I disgraced you and our family.'

'I believe I did that by myself.'

'What is to become of me?' Catherine whispered. 'What can I do now?'

'You can live the life you should always have done,' he replied, stroking back the loose strands of hair from her face. 'You shall go out and embrace society. Take up hobbies. You have seen the bitterness of war, my dear Cat, you should never see it again.'

'But, Papa, you wanted me to marry a military man, and I found the best of them.'

Her father did not answer, but struggled to his feet before helping her up. He took her shoulders and looked levelly across at her. 'Do not blame yourself, Cat. It gnaws at your soul.'

'I know,' Catherine said, nodding slightly. 'I have seen what such guilt can do. I shall just retire for the night. Has Arabella this room spare, still?'

'I would think so. She is downstairs with Major Keith, and Mr Dermot who brought me here. Why do you not go and ask her?'

'I shall just lie down for a time. I feel so weary and I confess that the thought of sleeping on a stationery bed is quite exciting after so much sea travel.'

She kissed her father and turned from him to go into the room. Mr Tenterchilt watched as she closed the door before he began walking down the stairs to join the gathered anxious faces. Mr Dermot betrayed nothing as he looked levelly across at Mr Tenterchilt whilst Arabella clung to Baby Roger, shaking with tears that had yet to fall. Major Keith stood as a soldier awaiting a command. He would have left earlier but that Arabella had begged him to remain.

'Is Miss Catherine well?' he asked softly.

'She has taken to her bed,' her father explained. 'I believe she is weary from her travel and the bitter news she has received.'

'I shall take my leave,' Mr Dermot began but stopped at the sound of a bitter, piercing cry from upstairs. At once all three gentlemen rushed out, whilst Arabella tried to calm and soothe Roger, who began crying at such an alien noise. Chloe joined the gentlemen and pushed past them all to get to Catherine, who sat on the bed pointing to the window and gasping for air. Perhaps because he was a military man and used to action, or perhaps because he berated himself for bearing such grim news to Miss Catherine, it was Major Keith who first reached the room behind Chloe. Following Catherine's outstretched hand he ran to the window, placing his hand upon the hilt of his sword as though he expected an assailant.

'I have seen a dead man,' Catherine gasped. 'Papa, I saw him.'

'There is no one here,' Major Keith said softly lifting his hand from his sword.

'It is quite normal for this to happen in grief,' Mr Dermot said. He himself had not crossed over the threshold of the room, but stood in the doorway.

'No, Papa, it was not Portland,' Catherine whispered, her voice failing with each word. Major Keith looked across anxiously at Mr Dermot, whose face remained entirely calm. Catherine had fainted in her father's arms whilst Chloe forcefully pulled a heavy curtain across the window and silently drove the other two men from the room.

CHAPTER TWENTY
Friday 1ˢᵗ November 1811

The following morning passed Catherine by without her rising from her bed until there was a knock at the door. She lay awake but ignored the sound until it was repeated and Arabella's voice accompanied it softly.

'Cat, are you awake?'

'Yes,' she replied in a tone that made it clear that she wished she was not. The door opened a little and Arabella entered, carrying a small bunch of flowers.

'I thought you might like these to brighten up the room a little.'

'You did not need to trouble yourself.'

'I did not,' Arabella said, sitting down on the edge of the bed. 'They were on the doorstep this morning.'

Catherine sat up and looked intently at them. 'How strange,' she muttered. 'Why did Papa want us to marry military men when both our loves died at the hands of the military?'

'But what made us love them at first, Cat? The fact that they were gallant, that they were brave. Would you have exchanged who they were that they might have lived but as lesser men?'

Catherine shook her head as she considered this. 'I need to do something, Arabella, I cannot live like a lady, sewing or painting. It is tiresome. I shall have too much time to think, too much time to reflect.'

'What will you do?' Arabella asked softly, never trying to dissuade her sister from the path she had chosen.

'I do not know.' Catherine sighed. She swung her legs from the bed and sat next to her sister. 'I shall start by rising from this bed. And there is a certain gentleman who I must seek out.'

'Indeed?' Arabella whispered.

'I must ensure that Doctor Fotherby has heard my tragic news,' Catherine explained. 'Captain Portland was his very dear friend.'

'Then indeed you must seek him.'

Catherine was forced to wear one of Arabella's dresses, for she had nothing save the clothes she had travelled in, which Chloe had taken to wash. She walked into the streets of the city of London trying not to recall how she had imagined this would feel, but recalling instead that there was a reason why she was wearing black. She made her way to the hospital. It was the only place she could think to find Doctor Fotherby but, upon arriving, she was told that he had been called away on another matter that no one could be sure what it was. She chose to stay and wait for him but, as she sat, she found her thoughts ever strayed and the sight of these men so wounded in battle caused her such grief that, without considering anything else, she discarded her bonnet and cloak and began tending those who lay upon the hospital beds.

When Doctor Fotherby returned in the evening it was to find Miss Catherine Tenterchilt stepping from bed to bed, checking on each of the patients, talking to those who sought comfort, placing her hand upon each one of them to let them know that they were not alone. He watched through his gentle eyes for a moment before he stepped forward.

'You do not need to be here, Miss Catherine.'

'You are wrong,' she said, turning to face him and feeling at once tears spring to her eyes as she recalled why she had come. 'I do need to be here. I need to be where people need me. I cannot have time to think.'

'I am so sorry, Miss Catherine,' he whispered as she stepped over to him. 'I can think of no words to speak to you.'

'Then do not speak any,' she said with a slight smile, that was the saddest gesture he had ever seen. 'I only came to ensure that you had heard this sad news.'

'I have heard it,' he said softly. 'Though thank you for thinking of me.'

She nodded briefly before she walked from him, collecting her hat and cloak on the way out.

Through her desperation to occupy her mind, she continued to work at the hospital, caring for those that she could. Little by little, as time passed, she began to clear her thoughts and a life started to appear before her. She maintained a friendship with Doctor Fotherby, although she could rarely find words to address her friend and, in return, he was so often occupied about the hospital. November saw Major Keith and Colonel Sir James Shorefield forced to embark once more to the continent. Catherine was sorry to see the major depart, although she still had never met the colonel and found him noticeable through his absence.

It was one day in December that she was working in the hospital, as she so often did, when she witnessed a peculiar exchange. She was preparing to leave in the evening for, as the nights drew in, she was reluctant to travel through London. She was once more going from bed to bed checking on her patients when she noticed a woman standing in the doorway. She had gentle golden hair and eyes that were wide with fear as she stood and gazed into the ward. It was true that she did not look like a nurse at all, indeed she looked most uncomfortable to even be in the hospital. Catherine was about to approach her when the woman called out.

'Henry!'

Doctor Fotherby, who had just entered from another room, looked across at her and Catherine watched as he drew in a ragged breath. Miss Catherine Tenterchilt, being born a lady but raised a man, saw no harm in listening to the conversation, but had at least the elegance and decorum to pretend that she was not doing.

'Henry, how long have I sought you?' the woman began softly for, although the doctor had not noticed Catherine listening, his companion certainly had. 'Where have you been?'

'India. In Calcutta.' His reply was brief. 'What is it that you want? You are not ill, are you?'

'No,' she said gently, shaking her head, and Catherine realised that the woman was smiling. Eager to avoid being caught listening, she continued to move from bed to bed, halving her attention between the patients and the conversation. 'I have been alone these past fourteen months. I have sought you, but you were not to be found.'

'I watched silently over you those nine years of your marriage, and you returned me nothing, Kitty. Not even a smile upon the street.'

Catherine turned sharply at the familiarity that the doctor used and she walked into the adjacent room, pressing her ear to the door.

'I did not see you,' she replied.

'Then you did not love me, and what a fool I should be to believe that you do now.'

'I have sought you, Henry. For over a year my thoughts have all been of you.'

'I do believe you, Mrs Allen, but I sail for India and the life I have begun on those shores. They are not so fickle in their choice of doctors as a woman may be in her choice of love.'

'India?' she whispered. 'Good God, Henry, you cannot be serious.'

'It would seem that your love is not so strong as you suppose, Mrs Allen, for I would marry no one less devoted to me than their devotion to a country that had served her so ill.'

'Then I shall go to India with you,' she said, so faintly that Catherine had to open the door a little to hear.

'And I would welcome your company, Mrs Allen, but you made your choice once before and turned from me. I cannot trust that you would not do the same again.'

'Do not go to India, Henry. You are needed too greatly here.'

'No,' he replied shaking his head, and Catherine watched through the crack in the door, believing that he would concede to her. 'I have a life waiting for me in India. You have so many physicians here, I must go where I can do good.'

'Always a martyr,' she replied cruelly. 'Just as you were eleven years ago.'

Catherine was torn. She wished to storm into the room and explain to Mrs Kitty Allen that the doctor was a good man who wished only to do good for those around him, but she felt overwhelmingly curious to discover how this conversation might conclude.

'You are right, Mrs Allen. But recall for whom I was martyred eleven years ago.'

Catherine shrank away from the door, hoping that she might remain unseen, as she saw the woman turn towards her.

'As you wish, Doctor Fotherby. A lady cannot rely on a man who might abandon her so easily. I am only sorry that this is how our friendship must end.'

'I am sorry, too,' he said, lowering his head as though he was ashamed by his words. 'But it was you who ended our friendship all those years ago.' He paused, thinking about the words that he would say next. 'I loved you, Kitty, but you did not love me. Is it so surprising that, after more than a decade, I may have changed my mind?'

'Goodbye, Henry,' she said briefly and turned from him. Doctor Fotherby did not raise his head for some time, and Catherine watched as the seconds ticked past and still he did not move. Catherine began to feel uncomfortable, for she wished to leave but did not wish to be found having spied on their conversation. She turned around as she heard one of the patients make a groaning sound and she rushed to the side of the bed. He did not hear her as she spoke to him, but continued making such a sickening sound that Catherine felt afraid and called out for the doctor.

Whatever Fotherby's conversation with Mrs Allen had meant to him did not seem to have affected him in the least. He was his usual calm self as he walked over to the bedside.

'Take his hand,' he said automatically, and Catherine took the man's burning hand in her own.

'What are you going to do?' she asked, her eyes widening with fear.

'There is nothing I can do,' he said sadly.

'There must be. You must be able to do something. You can always do something.'

'I'm sorry, Miss Catherine, the infection has spread to his organs. I cannot help him.'

Catherine looked down at the man before her and felt her lip tremble as she released his hand. Fotherby looked across at her for a moment before he said softly, 'Go and fetch my bag, we may at least ease his pain.'

She ran to complete his orders and returned with the leather satchel that the doctor carried with him on his rounds of the hospital. He took from the satchel a glass bottle and, instructing her once more to take the patient's hand, he administered the liquid to the wounded man.

'That will ease his pain,' the doctor said, while Catherine continued to grip the dying man's hand tightly. Fotherby stood on the opposite side of the bed and remained with his hand on the patient's head before Catherine whispered,

'He has stopped breathing.'

There was a curious tone to her voice that caused Doctor Fotherby to turn and face her. She remained gripping the man's hand, though her face suggested that it was she who had died. All colour had drained from her cheeks and her lips were a cold blue.

'Miss Catherine,' he said, walking round to prise her hands from those of the dead man. 'Are you well? You can let go of his hand now, Miss Catherine.'

She stood as she felt him help her to her feet, but she could not take her gaze from the body before her.

'He is dead,' she whispered.

'Yes, but there was nothing we could do for him. Do not blame yourself.'

'And Captain Portland is dead. Do you suppose he had someone by him when he died?'

'I am certain of it,' Fotherby replied gently, guiding her away. 'You must not think about such things. He died doing what he believed in for those that he believed in.'

'Martyred?'

'Yes,' whispered Fotherby, frowning down at her use of the word.

'I am sorry,' she whispered. 'I did not mean any harm, but I heard your conversation.'

'Do not apologise, Miss Catherine. I do not apologise for anything that I said to Mrs Allen.'

'I should return home. Arabella will be expecting me. She has taken such good care of me. She knows what it is.'

'I came to see you that night,' Fotherby said softly. 'I wanted to make sure that you were well, following the news of Portland's death.'

'You left the flowers,' Catherine whispered.

'Do not ever feel alone, Miss Catherine.' He smiled slightly before escorting her to the door and ensuring she had a coach to take her safely home, for the night was deep now and, following from his bitter conversation, he had no wish to be in company for any length of time. He returned to the hospital and walked purposefully to the small room that was his office. Here he poured, with an unfailingly steady hand, a glass of claret and sat down at the desk, looking at the small painted miniature of Miss Kitty Simmons that rested there. He took it up in his hand, still gazing at it for a time before he turned to the fire that burnt in the hearth and cast it into the flames, lowering his head in the desperate loneliness that a man of duty is forced to endure.

CHAPTER TWENTY-ONE
Monday 6th January 1812

The conversation that Catherine had witnessed appeared never to sway the solid doctor, his resolve to help people was steadfast and Mrs Kitty Allen did not make another appearance at the hospital. Catherine maintained a distance from him, however, feeling guilt at overhearing the conversation, especially as she had intentionally done so. The Christmas period came and went with many festivities, although they felt a little bitter in the mouths of all present as they mourned for those with whom they had shared happiness. Imogen, however, was able to rejoin the family in the small house, whilst Josiah and Beatrice remained in Petrovia with Anne and Penny. It almost mimicked those happy years when their mother was alive and nothing could ever have separated them.

It was not until the new year, the eve of the day that Imogen was to return to Scotland, that she and Catherine were able to talk alone. Their father was attending whatever secret business so occupied him and Mr Dermot, and Arabella was with her son, so Imogen and Catherine sat alone in the drawing room.

'I have never thanked you, Imogen,' Catherine began at length. 'You risked your happiness to see I was safe.'

'Colonel Sir James Shorefield was the man who oversaw it. I only brought it to his attention.'

'I have yet to meet him, this noble warrior and chivalrous hero.'

'He is peculiar,' Imogen laughed. 'At times he reminded me so much of an emotion I had forsaken, and he does not like to be studied. He seems most uncomfortable under a gaze.'

'Have you hopes of him?'

'No,' Imogen said, smiling sadly. 'I have hopes to continue teaching Josiah and Beatrice.'

'I was remembering,' Catherine began, a teasing light in her eyes. 'As I was watching Mr Dermot this evening, I was remembering seeing him carry you from the river.'

'Cat, do not be foolish,' Imogen said firmly. 'I do not trust Mr Dermot. He told me himself that each man in London works to fulfil his own ends and I cannot understand what these ends are that so involve Papa.'

'Think like a lady, Imogen, not a man.'

Imogen gaped at her sister's words, for she had so often used them to direct Catherine. Catherine seemed to follow her thoughts and she sighed. 'I have realised that I am no soldier, Imogen. I took too long to realise it and Captain Portland died before I had chance to behave like the lady he deserved. If only I had listened to you and Mama before, I might have been saved this. I might have had a son, as Arabella does, that I could teach to be the soldier I should never have believed myself.' She sighed. 'Doctor Fotherby warned me. He told me I should be grateful of who I was, instead of wishing I was someone else. Everyone could see it but me.'

'Oh, Cat,' Imogen said, smiling proudly. 'You are so brave, and I am so proud of all that you have done. You shall make a fine wife for a lucky gentleman.'

Catherine only laughed at this comment. 'But, truly, Imogen, my very being here is reliant upon your good sense and love, and I shall not forget it. There have been so many kindnesses shown to me, but they all began with you.'

'I would not let my sisters down,' Imogen vowed. 'You are dearer to me than anyone. You must never forget that.'

Their conversation was ended as Arabella entered and the three of them laughed and talked before the roaring fire until the night became deep. As the morning dawned, Imogen prepared once more to return to Petrovia and her two charges that awaited her there. She was making her farewells to her sisters when there came a pounding upon the door that Catherine, being closer than any of the others, pulled open. Mr Dermot stood there and at once her face lit up with a broad smile, believing his purpose for being there was to see Imogen on her journey. Both Imogen and Arabella curtseyed slightly before Mr Dermot removed his hat and addressed each one of them.

'Misses Tenterchilt, Mrs Jenkyns, I have come with news that I wished you might all receive at once and together before the world knows and, indeed, before you return to the dear hills of the Gordons, Miss Tenterchilt.'

'Is it Papa?' Imogen asked. 'Is he in any trouble?'

'It is your father, Miss Tenterchilt. But to the contrary, he is free from trouble.'

'You speak in riddles, Mr Dermot,' Arabella began. 'Speak plainly, for Imogen's coach leaves imminently.'

'Then I shall say bluntly that your father has returned to his post as a major in the army of His Majesty King George. I believe he is to commence a position at Horse Guards at once.'

'You do not jest, Mr Dermot, do you?' Catherine asked. 'For this is all Papa could ever have wished for.'

'May we go to him?' Imogen pleaded.

'But you have a journey to make,' Mr Dermot replied.

'One day will make little difference,' Imogen continued.

'It may,' he whispered thoughtfully, but he felt unable to deny the three sisters who at once rushed to the coach that Mr Dermot had arrived in and, accompanied by the lawyer, made their way through the city of London. They talked with happiness of all this could mean to their father and to themselves. At length Catherine, with an irrepressible smile of mischief upon her face, turned to Mr Dermot and spoke coyly.

'Do you recall that summer when you stayed at Petrovia, Mr Dermot?'

'Very clearly, Miss Catherine,' he answered, his features never failing to break from calm. Imogen, by contrast, openly stared at her and shook her head, but Catherine was never one to listen.

'I recall it clearly, too. How foolish of you, Imogen, to have fallen into the river.'

'I do not think it was the foolishness of your sister, Miss Catherine,' Mr Dermot replied. 'I believe I startled her and that is why she fell.'

He smiled at Imogen, whose cheeks burnt, yet still no embarrassment or shame crossed his calm features. Catherine held a look of concentration, as though she was trying to decide what angle she might come from next. Arabella hid her mouth behind her hand but it was clear that she, too, was smiling. Imogen looked through the window of the carriage and remained silent as Catherine began talking once more, this time on a different topic, for which Imogen was very grateful.

When at last they reached their destination, Mr Dermot descended from the carriage and helped the ladies down one by one. Major Keith, returned from the continent for a short time, approached and took Arabella's arm, whilst Catherine rushed forward, leaving Imogen alone with Mr Dermot. He offered her his arm as though he saw nothing in it but a gesture of politeness. Still, as she took it, Imogen frowned slightly, feeling exposed by her sister's words.

'I cannot begin to express how grateful I am to you for all you have done for Papa, Mr Dermot.'

'I am not the one to thank. Indeed, it has been you who has inspired all this.'

'Do not jest, Mr Dermot,' Imogen said, feeling unbearably uncomfortable.

'I do not jest, Miss Tenterchilt. Your mother commanded the very best from my father, and myself when I took over. In you I have seen that her strong spirit lives on. You are a strong woman and an inspiring lady. You inspired Colonel Sir James Shorefield to compel me to assess your father's case, so indeed it is you who is responsible.'

They walked into the hall that was filled with gentlemen congratulating their father, but Imogen was beside herself, wrapped in memories that this hall brought flooding back to her. From the tiled floors to the gold gilt of the ceiling, she knew this place.

'It is Chanter's House,' she spluttered. 'This is where I grew up.'

'Indeed,' Mr Dermot said calmly. 'And there is your father.' He motioned to Major Tenterchilt before releasing Imogen's arm and stepping back.

'Oh, Papa,' Imogen laughed, throwing her arms about her father's neck. 'Is this not the most wonderful thing? I shall return to Scotland so much happier now.'

'You are returning to Scotland?' he asked. 'We are wealthy once more, Imogen.'

'I am pleased beyond words, but I wish to return to Petrovia.'

Her father nodded thoughtfully and kissed her forehead before walking off to be amongst the guests who had gathered in his honour. The celebrations continued for many hours but eventually Catherine rushed over to Imogen and seized her sleeve.

'Please take me from this place. There are ghosts here.'

'Ghosts?' Imogen laughed.

'Do not laugh at me, I beseech you, Imogen. The night I returned to England I saw him standing outside the window. And now I have seen him here.'

'Very well,' Imogen replied thoughtfully, for there was true fear upon her sister's face. 'We shall return to the house.'

Catherine did not speak on the journey, nor did she mention it the following morning when Imogen prepared to leave. There was a very different atmosphere this morning as Imogen bade farewell to her sisters and they promised a close correspondence through letters. No one stopped her departure today, though her father stood there to wave goodbye, dressed in the military uniform that he prized above all other possessions. The world felt strange to her as she left. It was truly as if all the bad luck, the ill fortune that the years had piled on her, was drifting away. As she travelled onwards, she drew from her pocket that book given to her by Colonel Sir James Shorefield and read once more the haunting words of Lord Byron's Loch Na Garr, hearing that homesick voice with each line. She truly did belong to Scotland as much as Arabella did to London.

CHAPTER TWENTY-TWO
Wednesday 8ᵗʰ January 1812

Arabella did not waste a moment after Imogen's departure, but rushed across the city until she stepped down from the coach outside the venue of yesterday's celebration. There might have been another one happening now for, as she walked forward, she heard music. A beautiful but sad song was being played by a violinist. There was a part of her that called back to the past. It was a song that she knew, a song she had heard so long ago and never since, but it had been a turning point in her life. The violin stopped. She stepped forward to the open door and looked in to see Colonel Sir James Shorefield placing the instrument down on a table before he rose to his feet and walked away from her, seemingly failing to see her. Yet Arabella could see his face in one of the mirrors and she gasped. He heard her then, but still did not turn to her.

Instead Shorefield said, as he had so many years before, hidden by a different name and appearance, 'there are words.'

Arabella placed her hand upon the doorpost and gasped once more. 'All this while, I could not understand why a man would wish to help us so.'

'Because he felt like a brother to you,' Shorefield replied, turning to face her. 'I have done everything that I have achieved for each one of you.'

'You killed Roger,' Arabella whispered, as they stared at one another.

'It was his father who did that. We were all left to die.'

'They saw you shoot him.'

'Captain Pottinger asked me to. He would have been taken. He wanted to defend your honour.'

Arabella paused as she looked at him. 'I did not recognise you. When you were Colonel Sir James Shorefield, I did not know you.'

'It is just as well, for it has protected us both. But now events are resolved, so you may know who I am, you and Imogen. For no amount of dye or expensive clothes could mask who I was from Cat both times she saw me.'

'You were the ghost?' Arabella asked and accompanied her words with a laugh. 'Oh, Mish. I thought never to forgive you, but then I thought never to see you. Why did everyone believe you were dead?'

'Let us not talk of such things, Arabella, for we have plenty of time. You came to see the house, did you not? I want to give it back to you.'

'What?' she laughed. 'Do not play games, Mish, this is not your house.'

'Unfortunately it is,' he said softly. 'Your father lost it to Mr Bryn-

Portland, whose only heir was his nephew, Captain David Portland, whose death left it to me. I want to return it to you, for all that you did for me, and because I know it is what Mrs Tenterchilt would have wanted. And I have never forgotten the debt that I owed to you both in helping protect me from deportation so many years ago.'

'I do not know whether to laugh or cry!' Arabella exclaimed.

'Then do both,' he said, smiling, and at once she could not understand how she had not recognised him before. For with all his blackened hair and tanned features, that smile was unique in all the world.

She embraced him so warmly and with such relief that she could not help the tears that streamed from her eyes. 'Promise me you will protect me, Mish. Promise me.'

'Arabella, that is all I live to do.'

Such a realisation needed to be shared so, at once, Arabella rushed to Catherine to share the news, and a letter was immediately penned to Imogen. To Arabella, to know that Hamish had protected her husband's honour was a bittersweet pill. But she felt overwhelmingly pleased to have her beloved brother back with her. Catherine, also, felt pleased beyond measure to have him back and brimmed with sorrowful pride to hear of the bravery of her lost Captain Portland.

'And what of the good doctor?' Hamish asked jovially as they sat around the fire in the drawing room of Chanter's House. 'For he seemed quite under your spell, Miss Catherine.'

'Indeed he is not, Colonel Shorefield,' came the teasing reply. 'He is a friend only.'

Catherine ignored such questioning but, upon returning to the house that she had shared with Arabella, Chloe met her with a curious expression.

'A gentleman left this for you,' she said, guiding her into the drawing room and pointing to a sword that sat upon the table.

'Chloe,' Catherine laughed. 'This is a sword. Who left it?'

'He did leave a note.' Here she tucked her hand into the pocket of her apron. Arabella walked in and looked shocked.

'Chloe? What is this?'

The maid gave no answer but bobbed a curtsey before walking out of the room.

'What is this, Cat?' Arabella persevered.

'It is a sword,' came the numb reply. 'It is a sword that accompanies this letter.' She held up the paper, which Arabella felt reluctant to take. 'Nurse Tenterchilt,' Catherine began reading. 'As you know, I have commitments in Calcutta to which I must return. This gift is not what it should be, but it was a gift to me from our late mutual friend, Captain Portland. I know you will see it comes to good use.' She turned to Arabella. 'Then it is signed with a postscript saying: 'I have ensured it is sharpened to atone for my past mistakes.' And that is all. He has gone to India.'

'It is honourable that he has gone to do such sterling work there.'

'But he has gone without me.'

'For he sees that you have a life here.'

'Oh, Arabella, I don't want a life here. Not where he is not. This is madness. I did not love him. Why do I feel like this?'

'Cat,' her eldest sister replied softly. 'You might have loved him from the first day that you knew him but not seen it yourself. The words you have just spoken are what love is. To be unable to see a life without someone, to value their views over anything else. If you cannot bear the thought that you might never hear him say your name, or see his smile, then you do love him.'

'But he is gone. Without me. I knew he was going, but I thought I might go with him.'

'Then you must get down to the docks,' Arabella laughed, driven by a giddy excitement. 'He may not yet have left.'

'I do not know where he is sailing from.'

'Someone must know,' Arabella said softly, but Catherine could only lean upon her sister's shoulder in tears. Had she truly not known how she felt? Could Hamish have been right? After all the months Fotherby had spent with her and all that he had risked for her? And how she felt each time he called her by name, each time he smiled across at her? That evening at the hospital, the flowers by the door, it could all have meant that.

She pushed herself from her sister and smiled assuredly. 'I believe he did love me.'

'And I believe he still does,' Arabella said wonderingly.

'But he left me.'

Arabella stumbled over the words that she was about to speak. 'He was doing what he believes will best serve you. You are the daughter of a major once more. He is preserving your honour.'

'As Mish did yours.'

'Yes,' Arabella whispered with a sudden realisation. 'Might I marry him now he is a colonel?'

'You are a blind fool, Arabella,' Catherine laughed. 'He has loved you since first he saw you. What a pair we make!'

'Come,' Arabella said with a smile. 'I know exactly what to do.'

CHAPTER TWENTY-THREE
Thursday 13ᵗʰ February 1812

Doctor Fotherby had not lightly made the decision to return to India, but he felt a yearning for the orient and now had no obligation to remain in England. He had purged himself of his faded love for Miss Kitty Simmons and had hoped that he might ignite a flame within the heart of Miss Catherine Tenterchilt. Whatever duty and loyalty he owed his dear friend, Captain Portland, had stopped him from admitting the feelings he had for her, whom he had come to know before ever Captain Portland had rested his gaze upon her. But when he had been confronted by Mrs Allen he had realised that his belied love for her had only been a mask to hide his true feelings for Catherine.

It had taken him five weeks to reach Madeira, for the vessel had anchored at Oporto and Lisbon for some days to take on fresh hands and supplies. Indeed, the captain seemed in no hurry to take to the waters again. Now, the town of Funchal was becoming clear. All the East Indiamen stopped here before sailing round the southern tip of Africa. He had been here a number of times and it always felt like a peculiar mix of England and India, though by rights it was Portuguese.

He climbed down the ladder into a small rowing boat that was to carry him to the shore, for he had supplies of his own he wished to collect. The bay was filled with tall-masted ships as well as flat, squat, cargo vessels. Funchal was a marine crossroads and subsequently its bay was always full of all countries' ships. He climbed up by the ladder that was fastened to the legs of the jetty and stood straight upon the land, relieved once more to have ground beneath his feet. He walked towards the town but stopped as someone called his name.

'Doctor Fotherby? Sir, is that you?'

He turned to face a young man, who walked up to him and bowed formally.

'Midshipman Keith?' Fotherby muttered, confused and surprised.

'Indeed, but a lieutenant now.'

'Congratulations,' Fotherby said warmly. 'And how is your brother?'

'He was very well when last I saw him. He was preparing once more to travel to war on the continent. I believe his colonel has become entwined with Mrs Jenkyns, the lady whose sister you knew.'

'Colonel Shorefield? I knew he would wed one of them.' Doctor Fotherby sighed sadly. 'I am happy for them both. But, tell me, you cannot be on duty here. What has brought you to Madeira?'

'Indeed, I am on leave. What a poor soul I must be to carry out such missions when I should be in Southampton drinking myself senseless. But here I am all the same. Why, my dear Doctor Fotherby, you are a gentleman without a sword.'

'Yes,' the doctor replied softly. 'I bestowed it as a keepsake in place of my heart.'

'Then let us find you another,' Lieutenant Keith said merrily. He walked away, still talking, so the doctor felt obliged to follow. 'You cannot be a gentleman, even in India, without a sword.'

'I am a doctor, Lieutenant.'

'That is true, but even a man such as yourself should possess a sword. No lady would marry a gentleman without one.'

'That is not a concern for me.'

'That is a shame,' Keith continued, walking into a hotel lobby and finally turning to face the doctor.

'We shall not find a sword here,' Fotherby said, confused. Lieutenant Keith only smiled and shook his head. 'Are you drunk, sir?'

'Not at all. Look,' he walked over to one of the tables in the dining room of the open hotel. 'Here is a fine sword to wear to a wedding.'

Doctor Fotherby began turning away, feeling that he had been played for a fool, but stopped as he looked down at the weapon. 'This is my sword.'

'Indeed,' Keith replied calmly, suddenly serious. 'And I do believe, Doctor, that the beauty who sits at the table in the far corner is your lady, should you go to her.'

Fotherby turned to look across at the corner table and felt the breath catch in his throat as he beheld Miss Catherine Tenterchilt. For a second, maybe a time longer, they just stared disbelievingly at one another before Catherine rose to her feet and at once Doctor Fotherby rushed over to her. There were few people in the hotel dining room and those that saw might have remarked upon the nonsense or impropriety of such an amorous outpouring, but they were strangers to the pair who so lovingly embraced one another. No one could have known the illogical relationship the two had shared, from sparring in the Petrovia stable, the suffering and willing to life in the forests of India, and the despondent desolation that the death of their dear friend had caused them. Certainly, Catherine did not care and nor did Fotherby, who wept freely into her hair and clung to her, fearful that he should ever be parted from her again.

CHAPTER TWENTY-FOUR
Saturday 29ᵗʰ February 1812

News of Colonel Sir James Shorefield's true identity, and of Catherine's decision to travel to India to be with the man that she loved, reached Imogen some time later. Snow had restricted the messages and it was February before she was able to share in the joy that her sisters had felt at the new year. It was bittersweet that, after having Catherine returned to her, she would lose her once more to the orient. She could not express her mystified joy that Hamish had lived, and had a host of questions that she longed to have answered. But she was alone in Petrovia Lodge, but for Josiah and Beatrice. Penny and Anne were pleased to share in her joy but they knew less of the affair than she did herself.

It was on one night at the end of February that she stood in the frozen orangery and gazed once more up at the sky. No stars were visible, for snow was falling down in gentle swathes that cushioned themselves against the roof and walls of the orangery, and indeed the rest of the house. She no longer had to imagine Hamish was in the room with her, for he was alive. There had been a curious feeling to the discovery that had both troubled and surprised her for, while she thanked God for his safety and longed to see him once more, there was no longer the hope of love. She could ask for no more than to have this man, more dear to her than a brother, alive and well.

There was a peculiar feeling in the air, as though this great revelation somehow freed her from care and worry. What did it matter that she was alone at Petrovia if the worlds of those she loved were finally in harmony? It was all that she had asked for. She walked back to her room, no longer caring if the floorboards creaked or the stairs groaned. She was at liberty from such anxiety. She lay awake for a time until, at length, a knock sounded upon the door and, as she called out permission to enter, Anne walked into the room.

'Would you like another peat for the fire, Miss Tenterchilt? I thought I heard you walking through the house.'

'And so you did, Anne. I was burying a ghost. Or freeing a spirit.'

'And the peat?' Anne asked gently. 'Are you cold?'

'No,' Imogen said, smiling. 'I have a burning well of happiness that warms me through.'

'That might not be enough to see off the snow,' Anne answered, as practically minded as her sister. She walked to the basket of peats and carefully threw another on the flames so that it smoked heavily. 'That should last you a while.'

'Do you ever feel that there is something missing, Anne?' Imogen asked as the maid reached the door. 'Do you ever feel that however happy you are, you might never be so happy again?'

'You will be, Miss Tenterchilt, when you see your brother once more.' It felt nice to hear Anne talk of Hamish in such a way, and Imogen wished that she could just accept it as freely as the maid. But she had too many questions that burnt within her soul and, to that end, she had written to Mr Dermot in the hope that she might hear from him regarding the mysterious circumstances of Hamish's survival. She had received no reply.

When at last she fell asleep it was to a deep sleep from which she was startled by a man's voice. She hurriedly pulled on some clothes and rushed down the stairs into the library where the voice now came from. She pushed open the door and beheld the soaked figure that was barely recognisable as Mr Dermot. He did not seem at all bothered by the state of his appearance, although he graciously refused the offer of a seat as a result of it.

'I can see you have questions, and plenty of them,' he said, his face never altering. 'So ask your question and, now that our business is complete, I shall answer you with entire honesty.'

'I do not know where to begin,' she laughed, overwhelmed by the events of the past six years. 'How did Hamish survive?'

'By his honour. And the protection of his friends.'

'But did he kill Captain Pottinger?'

'Yes, but if the captain had been taken, for he lay dying, the French would certainly have taken the intelligence he bore and robbed him of his honour. And that, therefore, of your sister. He explained this to Portland and Keith, who had seen him act and fight so bravely that they were compelled to believe him. I was happy to help when I was asked, for I knew what he meant to your family. And moreover, he was a Gordon, my family.'

'Hamish is your family?' Imogen asked, puzzled by what she heard.

'Indeed. My mother was a Gordon.'

'But Hamish was sentenced to death by a court martial.'

'Indeed he was, but it is not hard to find a man sentenced to death in the gaol at Newgate, and those who condemn are not those who execute. Major Keith presented a different man for execution, whilst Portland, who was called to preside over the reading of his uncle's will, offered Hamish a safe place to hide in his Cornwall estate. It had to be a man who resembled your brother, but that was a deed easily done.'

'But I met Colonel Sir James Shorefield. He could not have been

Hamish, I would have known.'

'Care was taken to ensure you would not, again by his friends. He was taught to speak with an English accent and, for a time, was employed under my care that he might have practise at using his new language. And so he became James Hamilton, before he finally took his ancestral name of Shorefield.'

'But I thought he was a Gordon.'

'And so he is, of the clan Gordon, but his father's name was Shorefield.'

'But it was not just his voice I knew,' Imogen protested. 'Why did I not recognise him?'

'Did you expect to see him? Was not the dying of his hair, the changing of his stance, and the perpetual frown he adorned enough to trick your unsuspecting eye?' Mr Dermot shook his head and stood by the fireplace, where Anne had just lit the laid fire. She stood at the door listening eagerly to the telling of such a tale. Penny walked past frowning but, in a moment, she joined her sister.

'You told me every man in London had his own agenda. I took it to mean in a negative sense, but you were warning me.'

'Yes, I am guilty of deception, Miss Tenterchilt. But it was necessary. The matter of Shorefield's true identity had to be kept a secret, and indeed it still should be. How close we came to losing it when Miss Catherine recognised him on her return. It was a wise decision he made to maintain his distance from her.'

Imogen tried to work out the meaning of all that she had heard, but it was too much for her. Whatever she had expected when she had discovered that her dear brother was living, it had not been such devotion from his friends to protect him and give him a new life. She recalled at once how the conversation had begun and she lifted her head before whispering, 'What is the business you speak of? What is it that had to be complete before we might know of Mish's life?'

Mr Dermot smiled slightly. 'That, my dear Miss Tenterchilt, was the clearing of your family. There was talk, even at the time of your father's marriage, that your family might be shamed by it. That notion deepened ever more when Captain Pottinger was killed in such a way. Although in truth the manner of his death was to protect your sister, Arabella. I talked often with Hamish regarding that voyage, the nonsense that drove it, for there could be no sense to the mission. When Major Keith discovered, quite by accident, that the company had travelled out on one man's request and without the backing of Horse Guards, it fitted into place.'

'Colonel Pottinger truly sent his son to his death?' Imogen whispered disbelievingly.

'Truly, Miss Tenterchilt. For Roger had publicly scorned his father for the colonel's prejudice against his choice of wife. And his choice of sergeant major. It was, furthermore, Colonel Pottinger who encouraged your father to marry Alice, and had them sent overseas. He planned the downfall of your family, Miss Tenterchilt, and was so blinded by it that he succeeded only in causing his own, for all he has achieved is a date for his own court martial.'

'How could a man do such a thing?'

'I fear the poisoned friendship between him and your father has a long history and I am certain that, even now, I do not know the full extent of it.'

'It was his wife's words that caused Mama's death,' Imogen muttered, swallowing back tears.

'Indeed,' Mr Dermot said softly, seeing the need for a gentle voice. 'And yet, in spite of the sorrow, that day is one that I am grateful for.'

'Of course. For you met Hamish and knew that he was a man worth saving.'

'Yes,' he said quickly. He turned as a giggling sound came from the hall. Feeling that he had been exposed by these listeners, he walked over and pulled open the door, looking sternly down at Penny and Anne. 'I am certain that Miss Tenterchilt will share with you whatever news she wishes you to know.'

They curtseyed quickly and left, still discussing in excited tones what they had heard. Mr Dermot closed the door and leaned forward upon it for a moment so that Imogen became anxious.

'I am certain they meant no harm,' she said, defending her maids.

'As am I,' he said, turning to face her once more. 'So, Miss Tenterchilt, have you any further questions? For I have business in London to attend to.'

'Only one,' she whispered. 'Why have you risked so much for us?'

'That is easy to answer,' he said, walking over to the window and staring out. 'Your mother's family have always been clients, and respected ones. I confess that I did not wish to let go of such a partnership, for I saw a strength there that I had never known in a woman. And she passed that to you.'

'I am not strong, sir,' Imogen laughed. 'Catherine is the strength in us.'

'You are quite mistaken, for you have the strength of mind, the burning desire for knowledge and, beyond all else, you want to use it.' Mr Dermot sighed. 'If your father had only two daughters and you were not here, I do not believe I would have achieved this ending. You were, as I said to you in London, my inspiration. You have inspired a great many people, Miss Tenterchilt. I am the least of them.'

Imogen did not know what to say. She shook her head and laughed slightly before she rose to her feet. 'What of my sisters? And Papa? Were they well when you left London?'

'Indeed, yes. Miss Catherine has followed her heart once more to India. Safely this time. Mrs Jenkyns, I believe has been taken into the care of James Shorefield who has granted her Chanter's House, which should always have been hers. And your father is the toast of Horse Guards, as I hope it will remain. I wonder that you did not remain in London with them.'

'No,' Imogen said simply. 'I have no love of the city. I wish only to be here. It is where I feel I belong. When I stepped into Chanter's House it no longer felt I had a place there. Here I always feel safe and protected. I believe it is the mountains. They guard me as Hamish told me they protected his ancestors. It is a great bond the Scots have with the land, and I hope to share a little in it. Lord Byron's poems burn my heart each time I read them.'

She blushed as he turned to her, realising that she had spoken in an improper way.

'Then you like the book?'

'Yes, thank you. Shorefield, Mish, told me that you had recommended it. Though in places I find it quite improper.'

'Have you a favourite?'

'Indeed, yes. A poem that haunts me, for I hear someone say it each time I read the words. It is called Loch Na Garr.'

'Indeed. Did you know that you can see its summit from here on a clear day?'

'No,' she whispered, and looked up at him. 'Will you show me?'

'Another time, perhaps, Miss Tenterchilt, for it is far from clear today. Lord Byron knew well how we should find it, did he not?

> *Round Loch Na Garr, while the stormy mist gathers,*
> *Winter resides in his cold icy car,*
> *Clouds, there encircle the forms of my Fathers,*
> *They dwell in the tempests of dark Loch Na Garr*

He captures it well. And hauntingly, as you say.'

Imogen did not say anything but only stared at the man before her. He had spoken it as she had heard it. It was his voice that fitted so beautifully, so desperately to the words. He offered her the quickest of smiles before turning to the door and walking towards it.

'Forgive me, Miss Tenterchilt. I have business in London.'

She watched as he, so sure and composed at all times, struggled to find the words he wanted, and he fumbled with the handle of the door. Before Imogen had come to her senses, he had already rushed through the hall, gathered his hat and coat, and was walking purposefully to the stables. She ran after him, shivering against the cold, or perhaps the burning giddiness of her heart. She called after him, causing him to stop as he reached the stable door.

'Wait,' she cried, stumbling through the snow. 'You cannot leave at once, Mr Dermot. Will you not stay a while?'

'Miss Tenterchilt, you will catch cold. Go back indoors, I beg you.'

'You knew the poem?'

'Yes, I believe Lord Byron captured the soul of each exiled Gordon with that poem. I read it to you. When you were ill, in London, I sat by you. It was folly, Miss Tenterchilt, and I beg you forgive me for it. I shall return once more to London and I swear I shall not trouble you any further with correspondence.'

'But why?' Imogen spluttered. 'What have I done?'

'My dear Miss Tenterchilt, you are not to blame.'

'Will you not stay? Not even for a time?'

Mr Dermot's calm face faltered before he came to his senses, pulling the coat from his shoulders and wrapping it about Imogen. He stood behind her, pointing over her shoulder. 'There it is: the peak. Topped by cloud, just as Lord Byron wrote it.'

'All this time it watched over me, and I never knew.'

'I am pleased it did. It kept you safe.'

She turned, and found her face next to his own. 'I believe it was you who did that, Mr Dermot. You who protected those I loved. You who preserved my honour. And you who talked to my heart in words that my head could not understand. I know you have business in London, sir, but can I not tempt you to stay a time longer in Petrovia? You cannot go in the snow.'

The corners of his pale mouth turned up in a smile. 'My dear Miss Tenterchilt, if you asked it of me, I should remain forever.'

She looked shocked for a moment and he feared he had offended her. Before he could find words to beg pardon from her, however, she placed her hand over his frozen lips.

'Then, Mr Dermot, will you remain forever?'

He did not answer her and nor did he need to. Instead he kissed her hand gently before he lifted her in his arms and carried her back to the house under the watchful, weeping eyes of Anne, who rushed to help Imogen out of her sodden clothes.

Acknowledgements

This book has been in the making for a number of years and, as such, I have a host of supporters and encouragers who I would like to take a page or two to acknowledge for their support.

Firstly, my enormous thanks go to Barbara White for being the first person outside my own family to have read and given me feedback on this book. Her help, editorial notes and encouragement inspired the speedy release of this novel and gave me the belief in my book to publish it for you all.

To those of you who, without having read my book, put your faith in it and supported the Crowdfunder project. Most particularly to Marian Long to whom I promised this space in the acknowledgements. I really hope the book has lived up to your expectations.

And here's to those great Duckeggs, most especially Haley and Jonah who have put up with my nagging and suggestions throughout the lead-up to the book launch. Their encouragement and their time turned the launch into an amazing performance. When this book is made into a blockbuster movie(!) I will not forget the hard work you put in, drawing up the first script, bringing the text from the page and turning it into life.

To Kerry Speirs at *Tartan at Heart* who has created an amazing Day's Dying Glory range of products. For enabling me to follow the creative process and for the amazing products that resulted.

To my Grandma for giving us a place to stay for the book launch. To *The Ropewalk* in Barton-upon-Humber, *The Library of Innerpeffray* and *The Saint Magnus Centre* in Kirkwall for hosting the book launches. To Colin Stewart at *Caithness Print Solutions* for printing our banner, and for always being interested in the book each time we called by the shop.

And finally, but by no means the least, to a very special bunch of people. It seems customary to write a long spiel about your family in the acknowledgements of any author's book. But my family have given hours of their lives to this book, clocking up to days, weeks, months and years of their time. So, here's to Daddy, from whom I feel I have claimed a great victory, in that he has read the book at all. Thank you for being the first person to read the novel in book format. Thank you Mimsy for all the inspiration and encouragement you've given over so many years. For allowing me to steal your poetry books and igniting my love of the Romantic Poets whose works are the undercurrent of this novel. Thanks to Lydia who wept at the book, and yes, I do view that as praise. To Judith for editing, re-editing, re-re-editing. For giving so much of her time to preparing for the book launch, creating the website; calling around people; for designing and creating the front cover and making sure I lost thousands of 'worthless' words. But, most of all, for falling in love with the major! And thanks to Clemency for her illustrations; her planning and riding shotgun on the book launch; for contacting people and getting the ball rolling on the launch, but most especially for being a very willing guinea pig in the early days of this novel. In all honesty, this book was only finished because you kept asking for the next installment.

So, while it's my name that appears on the cover, without each of you there wouldn't be a cover on which it could appear. The text is mine, but the inspiration was yours.

Virginia